With One Look

Jade slid her hands forward, over his flat muscled abdomen and slightly curved chest, lingering where she felt the race of his pulse. Victor didn't know how much he could take, and he caught her hands in his.

"Please," Jade whispered. "I don't know what you're feeling."

"Pleasure," Victor said simply. "Intense pleasure. Love, here, let me show you . . ."

She flushed as his huge wet frame came on top of her. His lips met hers and she, too, abandoned herself to a passion too great to resist. "And when I kiss you," he whispered, keeping his mouth close, so very close, "I feel the force of my will slip from my grasp—"

A sweet tingling awakening raced through her. "A surrender . . ."

"Aye." He kissed her again. "I surrender . . ."

WITH ONE LOOK

JENNIFER HORSMAN

An Avon Romantic Treasure

AVON BOOKS ◆ NEW YORK

WITH ONE LOOK is an original publication of Avon Books. This work has never before appeared in book form. This work is a novel. Any similarity to actual persons or events is purely coincidental.

AVON BOOKS
A division of
The Hearst Corporation
1350 Avenue of the Americas
New York, New York 10019

Copyright © 1994 by Jennifer Horsman
Inside cover author photo by Phoebe Horsman
Published by arrangement with the author
Library of Congress Catalog Card Number: 93-91011
ISBN: 0-380-77596-4

First Avon Books Printing: July 1994

AVON TRADEMARK REG. U.S. PAT. OFF. AND IN OTHER COUNTRIES, MARCA REGISTRADA, HECHO EN U.S.A.

Printed in the U.S.A.

RA 10 9 8 7 6 5 4 3 2 1

This book is dedicated to Zig, the number one BF, who is always there during a firestorm, as well as closed pool days and whose musical gift has been invaluable to me . . .

A Vision of Horror

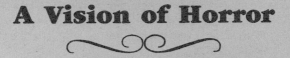

New Orleans, 1818

White women were so ridiculous!

Abe rolled his eyes with a sorry shake of head as his mistress, Madame Pearl Williams, stepped down from the carriage in front of the inauspicious brick town house in the fashionable district, Vieux Carré. "Oh, I do hope I look well enough," the plump woman said nervously as she patted her neatly chignoned red hair, the hand staying in front of her face to fan it. Gracious! The sun had set and 'twas still so hot. Her face powder was bound to cake if she perspired. "Abraham, I'll just be an hour. You may wait right here."

"Yes'm," Abe said, but with a contemptuous look. Wait right here, she says, as if he was gonna hightail it away and start chasin' the north star to freedom. Visitin' a voodoo queen! Wastin' hard-made monies on a colored woman's flattery and fortune-tellin'.

White women were so ridiculous. . . .

A pretty serving girl led Madame Williams through the flower-filled sitting room to the back, where Marie Saint greeted her warmly. The tall, exotic woman sat regally upon her throne—an ornately carved wooden bench beneath the opened window of her parlor.

Marie Saint's beauty was exceptional, the kind of loveliness that had made New Orleans's quadroons famous. She had a voluptuous figure, always meticulously outfitted in the finest silks and latest fashions. Today she wore yellow silk, trimmed in creamy lace, the pale colors complimenting her flawless café au lait skin. She had the perfect diminutive nose and provocative mouth, a stunning smile that lifted easily and often. Her beauty was given a considerable depth by her soft, liquid brown eyes. These eyes were almond shaped and deep-set, emphasized by unusual straight brows, and in her presence, one always felt their benevolent scrutiny.

A servant indicated the cushioned seat opposite, and as Madame Williams settled her voluminous weight and silk skirts into the seat, a beautiful Negro girl approached with a giant peacock feather fan. Slowly, rhythmically, she began fanning the air. Another servant stepped forward with a tall cool glass of spiced tea. Madame Pearl smiled widely, and as soon as pleasantries were dispensed, she launched into an explanation of her most current trouble.

Of course, Marie knew everything about Madame Williams, the wife of Monsieur Sam Williams, a landed American gentleman. Madame Pearl's concerns centered on the constant flux and ebb of her social standing, less frequently her family's health. Tonight Madame Williams's question concerned whether or not to attend the soiree at the neighboring Triche plantation. The problem, it seemed, lay in that it had been less than a year since the youngest of the Triches' daughters had scandalized the parish by running off to Kentucky with a young riverboat man.

A riverboat man! Filthy, uncivilized barbarians! Madame Williams still felt tremors every time she thought about it. She could not imagine a worse fate!

Madame's hand went to her heart as she conveyed this dilemma of potentially devastating social consequences, consequences which depended entirely upon who would accept the invitation and who would not. Like many, she was particularly concerned with Madame Lucretia Josset, the wife of Mayor Etienne de Bore.

"You understand if Lucretia doesn't go, well! 'Twould look very bad on all those who did. . . ."

As the clairvoyant listened intently to the many nuances of the Madame's difficulties, she projected an aura of absolute stillness and calm, much like the smooth glass surface of the sea on a summer's dawn. A surface that concealed a boundless depth. Few could escape the sensation of intense, and yet somehow charitable, attention. Madame Williams found the sensation similar to what she felt in the confession booth, and though she would not want to admit it, she found her monthly visits to Marie Saint's far more beneficial.

Madame Williams was the third woman to consult Marie on this question of the Triche gala. Marie told all of them the same thing: the soiree would be a success; to miss it, an injurious social faux pas, as the entire parish was finally willing to show support for the Triche family and their well-known trials.

The matter had been decided some time ago. Madame Triche, the mother of the riverboat man's wife, had wisely solicited Marie Saint's help before a single invitation had been issued. She had presented the dilemma to the famous seer first, asking if Marie saw the soiree as a success or no—this after mentioning a sizable contribution to the Negroes' charity hospital to one of Marie Saint's most trusted servants. Pleased with Madame Triche's generosity, Marie Saint had assured the Madame her gala would be an enormous success, that she foresaw her neighbors and friends hastening to her side in a demonstration of their love and sympathy.

Once settled, Madame Williams proceeded to solicit a directive on the important question posed by the new tailor in town—Marie's fashion advice always proved as invaluable as her health amulets and charms. The beautiful mulatto seemed to direct half of all traffic heading to the tailors, hairdressers, shoemakers and hatters, and always with explicit directions religiously adhered to: "Marie Saint said only Spanish lace would do . . ." "Marie Saint swore bodices will be falling and hems will be rising—I want to be the first . . ." and so on.

The superficial banality of her patronesses' concerns never elicited a comment from New Orleans's most famous prophet, at least not directly. Such was not Marie

Saint's way. Rather, Marie might remind Madame Williams—and the numerous women owning similar sensibilities—of someone who might benefit from the Madame's well-known kindness. She might mention her knowledge of a cruel overseer, or an aging field hand who needed easier work, or the benefits of Sunday passes for their whole slave population. Last month she mentioned that the young Negress Monsieur Williams meant to sell at the market the next Saturday was meant to be the Madame's favorite house servant, who would: "Yes! Mercy but, Madame, I see her one day saving the life of a cherished grandchild . . ."

"Oh, my heavens!" the Madame had declared, and before the sun had set, her husband was listening to a lengthy and barely sensible explanation of why his wife must have the young girl in the house. . . .

Marie knew well that every soul forged its own path home. And hers was a difficult road. Especially at times like now, when she saw the tragedy waiting for the good woman before her. Madame Pearl's second and favorite son, Jared, would die in an outbreak of yellow fever. Marie saw Madame's tear-washed face as the dirt fell over the coffin placed forevermore into earth; she felt the woman's grief and its lesson. Madame Pearl would never again worry over an invitation. Her grief would drive her to serious reflection; it would sharpen her understanding, soften her heart as it led her to the true comfort of the Church.

Presently the more benign dilemma was between Lacroix, the four-year dictator of New Orleans fashions, and Dumas, the newer, more innovative tailor in town. Marie decided the matter with a pleased smile. "Dear Madame Williams, I have been made aware that Monsieur Dumas has just received four new fashion plates from Paris—"

Marie stopped mid-sentence and froze as suddenly the third eye opened to the future. Of all the myriad ways her sight worked—the elaborate network of friends and servants who constantly brought information and news to her attention, or the feeling of the emotional content of an event, the dreams and trances, the numerous spirits who spoke to her—the third eye always proved the most significant, powerful, the rarest. A circle of vision opened on her forehead with a startling clarity.

Alarm changed the handsome features of Marie's face; she looked a hairbreadth from screaming. She saw the famous young lady, Jade Terese, a look of heart-wrenching terror as a hand reached from behind her, a cloth came over her mouth. Who was it? Who was doing this? The young lady desperately struggled for breath as she frantically sank her nails into the hand and fought with all her strength. Yet Jade was sinking, falling into a blackness.

Flames rose in the blackness and through them Marie saw the gris-gris. Death. The voodoo sorcerer's amulet of death.

Fear had changed Marie's beautiful face and her hands had risen to her cheeks with a silent scream. Then the vision was gone, vanished, and she looked about her familiar surroundings, bewildered. Two servants stepped forward in alarm. Ignoring her patron, Marie whispered: "I must warn Mother Francesca immediately! Jade Terese is in danger!"

Chapter 1

New Orleans, May 1818

A t thirty-one years old, and perhaps four lifetimes more of experiences, Victor Nolte had long ago passed the age or temperament where beauty alone might attract him to a woman. Yet, as he sat with his lady and friends in the governor's box at the Theater d'Orleans scanning the tiers below, he spotted the young lady in a semicircle of light that shined from an usher's gold lantern.

She looked beautiful and young, too young, he saw; somewhere between the ages of seventeen and twenty-one. A blue ribbon tied her thick, waist-length dark hair in back. She wore a modest and plain gown of white muslin. A pretty blue-flowered silk shawl hung loosely at her elbows. A matching blue ribbon circled beneath the generous lift of her breasts, demurely covered in an unfashionable high neckline. Short puffy sleeves revealed slender arms. She had unusually pale skin and delicate and fair features. A rosy flush spread across her high cheeks. She held the program, a pair of gloves, some kind of rope and a small blue reticule in her hands.

The spring night air still felt hot, if not oppressive and the young lady fanned her face with the program. Her manners seemed slightly exaggerated, though hardly practiced. Rather strikingly innocent, he thought abstractly, smiling slightly as he studied her.

The play had just begun, and already Nolte was bored. His fluency in French was as good as any American's, which was to say the French production of the *Opera Co-*

mique was largely incomprehensible. While he could read French fairly well, and despite having taken up residence in the French-speaking city, he rarely spoke the language.

So he studied the young lady below, a fixed point in the neat rows of dark bodies. As he watched her, the peculiarities of her circumstances began to multiply. The gentleman at her side reached over and, laughing with the audience, he squeezed her hand. Victor drew a sharp breath. He knew the gentleman, a wealthy gens de couleur, one of New Orleans's more successful real estate brokers. The man was an articulate spokesperson for his people; he recalled the man's brief speech before the Louisiana legislature on the ill-conceived proposal to withdraw the free Negroes' property rights. What was the man's name?

She and her gentleman sat in the second tier, the portion of theater relegated to the gens de couleur, libres or free Negroes. Yet the girl's skin appeared as white as the sunlit petals of a daisy. With a slight, disparaging shake of head, Victor sighed and settled back in his seat.

The strictness and rigidity of New Orleans class lines seemed to reach absurd proportions. The rules were meticulously adhered to among whites, colored and the multitudes of Negroes beneath. Just the Negroes, freed and slave, were classified according to the darkness of their skin, and these distinctions took on the intense scrutiny and study of a science: the griffe looked down at the pure-blooded Negro; the mulatto regarded the griffe with scorn and was in turn spurned by the quadroon; while the octaroon refused to have anything to do with the others. The young lady definitely belonged in the class of *passe blanc,* those who could pass for white.

He had traveled over a good portion of the world, and of all the world only India herself could claim a more tangled or incomprehensible web of caste and class than New Orleans. Like most all the Americans in this new state, he found it all quite ridiculous, if not downright barbaric. That beautiful young lady sitting in that section had to be a free person of color, but the entire course of her young life—what she could and could not do, whom she could and could not marry—would be determined by an imprecise consensus that had been leveled on the shade of her parents' skin.

He leaned forward again. A quick scan of the aisles on either side of her confirmed that the gentleman had escorted her. She was no doubt his mistress. Probably selected from one of the quadroon balls, the weekly parade of beautiful colored girls and their ever-watchful, careful mothers, whose sole purpose was to establish their daughter as mistress to the highest bidder. This tradition seemed at once archaic and disgraceful, a practice he had no doubt would end with the Americanization of this city. . . .

Madame Marguerite Chappell noticed Victor's fleeting attention and she sighed, reaching a gloved hand to his thigh. He turned to his lady, smiling as if caught by surprise. He took hold of her hand and absently, distractedly, he gently massaged her fingers as his gaze returned below.

Maggie accepted his caress, but saw that she had lost his attention. That was the problem. In the semidarkness of the theater the handsome features of Victor's face took on an ominous air, like the ghostly lover of her imagination. He stood half a foot taller than most men, and a lifetime spent working the docks, the lumber mills and ships had made him that much stronger as well. She reached her free hand to caress a lick of Victor's copper-colored hair curling about his ear. His profile appeared striking and handsome; his face was long, his skin sunwashed. He had a prominent nose, one speaking of strength and character—two things he had in abundance—while his formidable intelligence showed in his widely spaced, dark blue eyes. He possessed an air of authority and confidence, a bold, undaunted straightforward character, qualities that attracted legions of women. Add to that his wealth—he owned the largest shipbuilding company south of Boston. The only things more plentiful than the ships his company built were the privateers buying them. The result was, as Doc

Murray said, "The women practically line up outside his bedroom door."

With a sad and wistful look in her eyes, Maggie turned away, trying to concentrate on the performance, but soon gave up the pretense. Despite Victor's explicit warnings to the contrary, she had so hoped that following him down here from Philadelphia would result in a marriage proposal. She knew now it would not.

So she would be leaving at week's end to return to her fair city. A good life waited for her: she had her late husband's fortune to spend, after all; her beauty still; and an established place in the upper echelon of society, a place that she loved and enjoyed. She didn't regret a moment of her liaison with Victor; her only worry was that all future lovers would compare unfavorably.

A new usher moved swiftly down the aisle. He approached the standing usher. Words were exchanged. A finger pointed to the very young lady Victor had been staring at. The usher hurried to her side. Leaning over her gentleman friend, he imparted an apparently urgent message.

Alarm lifted on the pretty features of her face. She passed quick words with the man at her side, apparently urging him to remain seated. The usher took her elbow as she rose and escorted her down the aisle. A friend's hand reached out from one of the boxes as she passed. There came a brief exchange before she and the usher continued out the door.

Victor abruptly decided he could use some fresh air as well—what little one could find of this precious commodity in New Orleans due to the damnable lack of modern sewers. Disengaging Maggie's hand, he rose, and leaned over to whisper to his friend Sebastian that he would be back shortly.

Sebastian hardly stirred, enthralled as he was by the performance. His fine blue eyes, framed by locks of thick blond curls, danced merrily as he watched the stage below. The handsome Austrian-born lord spoke French as easily as he did English and German, and was devoted to opera. Victor sighed as he left, wondering how Sebastian could be one of the best and most vicious swordsmen on the Continent and yet have a passion for the soft sentiments of a small city's opera and the lastest foppish clothes. . . .

A gentle breeze blew from the river and the air felt mercifully cooler as Victor opened the doors and stepped outside. Only to confront the amusing scene. Speaking in rapid French, the young usher pointed to a place several safe yards away where two dogs were copulating.

Suppressing the sound of his amusement, Victor stood, feet apart, hands on hips, watching the young lady's distress increase as the young man explained it would be dangerous, if not impossible, to separate the creatures now.

Hands flew to her cheeks in dismay. "Ham! Oh, Hamlet! Oh, please!" Her pleas received no attention from the dog, and with dejection and a string of impressive French curses, the young lady sank down on the garden settee in a perfect circle of crumpling white muslin.

Victor withdrew a half dollar and handed it to the usher, his request obvious. The young man looked at the shiny coin, then at Monsieur Nolte. He, like many New Orleans residents, had been made familiar with many of the rumors surrounding the new American.

Monsieur Nolte was said to be a war hero. Those stories were surely exaggerated, though his fighting ability was heralded from Kentucky down to the mouth of the Mississippi. Rumor claimed Nolte had lost only two of his cargo boats to the river pirates, but that was enough. It was said that Nolte and a group of well-chosen men—including the unlikely personage of an Austrian lord, a man reputed to be the best swordsman on the Continent—had cleared a two-hundred-mile area of troublesome water thieves, so that now word had it that all saboteurs gave free passage not just to Nolte's own ships but to any ship built by his company. This naturally brought considerable business his way, while winning the appreciation and favor of everyone from the governor to the merchants and longshoremen.

Someone had told him Monsieur Nolte was the blood son of Father Nolte, the American priest. They had said that Father Nolte had been married, a theologian at the College of William and Mary, and that after his wife died Father Nolte had taken the vows of priesthood. True, the two men looked very similar, he saw . . .

Victor's brow rose as he noticed the young man's scrutiny. The boy abruptly straightened, and thinking Mademoiselle Devon could not be safer with a constable, he nodded and left.

"So which is yours, the bitch or the male?" The question was asked as one booted foot lifted onto the bench and he leaned over.

With surprise, Jade Terese turned to the voice above her. In the moment he met her eyes, a tingling alarm raced down his spine. They were quite simply the most beautiful eyes he had ever seen: finely shaped, large and translucent, thickly fringed with coal-black lashes and colored the most extraordinary dark green. Perhaps he only imagined the mysterious depth there, for it disappeared as she turned back to the dogs and gestured. "I am afraid 'tis the male, Monsieur. Hamlet." She sighed prettily. "I suppose you can grasp my sorry predicament."

With a sympathetic smile, Victor confessed, "I have seen worse, Madame.'"

"Mademoiselle Devon," she supplied, utterly unselfconsciously. "Of course you are right. Though I have been through this before. A mating takes so long," she informed him in the event he was ignorant of the actual mechanics. "I shall be missing my creature's companionship for at least an hour."

Amusement sparkled in his eyes as he listened to the musical lilt of her voice, the clear French and English inflections, and so perfectly fitting, as beautiful as she was. The elegance and pronunciation of her speech came as a surprise, for she was obviously well educated. The suggestive hint of her words seemed incongruent with the innocence of her manner. As he stared he caught the faintest trace of her perfume. Lilac water.

"The worst of it," she told him, her tone going cross, "is that new policy Mayor Etienne de Bore has recently adopted to rid the streets of stray dogs and cats. Have you heard of this hateful practice?"

"I can't say that I have."

"The constable's men set poison out for the helpless animals. Poison! Once every two months. So if puppies result from Hamlet's reproductive, ah, enthusiasm, I'm afraid they will live only to face the most pitiful end."

She recalled just this very morning as she and Maydrian, her servant, had been shopping at the market, she had chanced to meet Monsieur de Bore's beautiful wife, Lucretia Josset, the grand and sensational director of New Orleans's most prominent Creole social circle and a woman reputed to have tremendous influence in shaping her husband's career and policies. Like so many of New Orleans's residents who knew about the Devon family tragedy and the extraordinary circumstances surrounding the young woman's life, Madame had always condescended to show an interest in Jade Terese. After they had exchanged initial greetings, Jade had politely asked if Madame might attempt to reverse her husband's heartless decision. Lucretia assured Jade that she had shared the very same sympathies and that she had already attempted to do so. Sadly the mayor appeared quite resolute on the matter. Stray dogs were a growing menace. . . .

Jade shook her head again. "Just last month Maydrian, my servant, and I managed to catch four of the poor creatures before the night of the poisoning. It cost me three dollars in bribes to convince a raucous group of flatbedmen to take the dogs upstream to safety! Three dollars!"

He chuckled. "An outrageous sum!"

Jade Terese quite agreed. She still could not get over the iniquity. "Of course,"—her eyes narrowed contemptuously—"I told them it would be wrong to spend such a sum on creatures when so many people suffered wants. I even offered to donate the money to the Negro infirmary in their names—"

His voice was rich with suppressed laughter as he said, "I wager that received a quick response."

"Indeed!" The girl's brows went cross again. "The man laughed at the idea! He said, 'Miz, you might be an eyeball of delight but even you ain't pretty 'nough to make me pass coins on to a passel of dyin' colored folks. Ah'm afeared my charity begins and ends in this here pocket.' "

Victor laughed out loud at this imitation of a Kentuckian's speech, watching as she reached a hand up, delicately brushing back a loose strand of hair, a gesture somehow so feminine as to make him want to do it for her.

Wondering at his response, he looked past the small grove of trees and spotted the two men watching them from across the road. No doubt someone's drivers waiting for the theater patrons to appear after the opera. A howl drew his attention. He glanced at the dogs behind the three sprawling oaks and commented wryly, "I'm afraid, Mademoiselle, it appears as if you are in for a long wait now."

She looked for a moment confused, then she seemed to make a study of her hands and reticule.

"Perhaps you should return to the theater to enjoy the play while your creature is so engaged?"

Jade considered the measure but she shook her head. "This is the third time I've seen the opera this week—" She laughed. "I believe I could sing it myself!" She tilted her head; her gaze swept the surrounding area. "The breeze feels wonderful here."

"Shall I send the usher to fetch your gentlemen?"

"No, please. I'd rather sit alone. Besides, Monsieur Deubler has not yet seen this opera." She paused, abruptly realizing she might be keeping the gentleman. "Please, Monsieur, do not let me keep you from the theater—"

"Quite the contrary." He smiled. "You have provided me with the perfect excuse to escape that place."

"Oh? You did not like it?"

"I'm afraid my French is inadequate to the task."

She turned to him again. "You are an American?"

He stared openly. Those eyes, those beautiful eyes. There was something about them, some inexplicable depth or enigma there. "Yes,"he answered in the moment. "Now don't tell me you hold that unfounded prejudice against Americans?"

Jade Terese laughed at this. "Oh, no," she assured him. "I rather admire you Americans, all your industriousness and smart business methods. Why, I have expected to wake one morning and find proper sewers, lanterns, street signs, new ferries and faster postings." She did not see his smile at this prediction of the American character's effect on her French city. "Did you take one of the land grants?"

"Yes." He nodded. "Though that was three years ago. I've been away and have only recently returned."

"The war?"

"Yes."

The audience's applause sounded in the distance, stopping for a moment the pleasant hum of crickets. The deep rich timbre of his voice sounded so gentle and kind and somehow wise. She felt a heightened interest and curious self-consciousness. "So?" she pursued casually, fanning her face. "Shall you now build a plantation on your property and make your fortune?"

"I think not," he said with a wry grin, the idea amusing, for he was not the kind of man who could leave his fate, or his wealth, in the capricious hands of nature. "I'm afraid I would make a very poor farmer."

The truth was, his presence in New Orleans owed itself to the persistence of Governor Claighborne and his very own father. Since Louisiana had just been brought into the union of states, his father, an American priest, had been appointed vicar general of New Orleans in an effort to assure the Catholic populace of Louisiana, and New Orleans in particular, that one of the most sacred tenets of the United States Constitution was freedom of religion and separation of church and state. Catholics would not be prosecuted, nor their religious practices in any way hindered by the predominantly Protestant government.

The next step in their ambitious program involved implementing American law and order in the city. This meant eliminating the well-entrenched thievery of so-called freebooters or pirates. Pirates like Jean and Pierre Laffite and Don Bernardo had a hand in every piece of merchandise sold in New Orleans. Three years ago, Claighborne, working with his father, held the lucrative land grant out to him as a lure, soon convincing him he would not be affected by the labor shortage in this region, that there would be enough white working men or free men of color to fill his requirements without forcing him to resort to slave labor. They had lied, of course, labor problems had become the bane of his existence, but they had done so in desperation. And desperate they were. They needed all the help they could get to rid New Orleans of its savage criminal element.

Victor hoped tonight would be a success. . . .

She was waiting for him to say more. She felt his gaze upon her, his scrutiny intense. Her intuition was keen, her sensitivity more so; she could always decipher the complex language of people's feelings—this one's hurt and anger, that one's anxiety—the silent meaning that underlined verbal exchanges. Yet his interest and her response confused her. She felt a shiver of both danger and excitement.

His gaze rested on a small jade cross hanging from a thin gold chain around her neck, and in an apparent shift of subject he suddenly asked, "Tell me how you came to name your dog after Shakespeare's most famous tragic character?"

A faint smile played on her lips as she remembered finding Hamlet and choosing his name. "My mother was English, you see, and she did so love Shakespeare that she had me memorize all the major speeches long before I even knew a single psalm." She sensed rather than saw his smile. "Anyway, when Hamlet was first presented to me and I agonized over whether or not to keep him, the words of that famous speech flew to my mind: To be or not to be. I think it quite determined my decision."

The brief sketch held a curious piece of information. "Your mother was English?"

"Oh, yes." She nodded. "Born and raised in London."

He looked at her curiously. "Do you mind me asking why you were seated in the second tier?"

The question appeared to surprise her. "Why, I am escorted by Monsieur Deubler. The senior Deubler often invites me to join him and his family, knowing how very much I love operas. And those are his season billing seats."

More confused, Victor waited for her to clarify the point. The brief explanation gave no indication of her relationship to Monsieur Deubler except that she often joined him with his family. Was the man married or widowed? As liberal a society as New Orleans was, especially concerning a man's unmarried liaisons, surely if she was his mistress she would not be joining the family at the opera? The man must be widowed then. . . .

Those eyes were green, her skin whiter than fresh-fallen snow. She could not be a person of color. Then how did she manage to sit there? How could she be the man's mistress if she was white?

She offered nothing more. A thoughtful yet troubled expression came to her face and he asked: "Is it a very difficult decision?"

The stranger's sensitivity startled her. "Yes, as a matter of fact," she answered. "Perhaps the most difficult decision I will ever make." Determination had entered her voice. "And I believe I have finally reached it."

She would not take the holy vows. God forgive her but she couldn't. Not in good faith, which was the whole of the problem. Somehow she couldn't escape the doubts, the myriad of doubts and unanswerable questions. She believed in God absolutely, and yet the older she became and the more she understood, not only about herself and the world, but also about the diversity of other religions and dogmas, the more she had come to realize 'twould be an irredeemable mistake to speak the holy vows, that she could not do so with honesty.

Father Nolte had said while hers was the most philosophically oriented mind he had ever had the pleasure of knowing in a woman, the question of the vows was a matter of heart. She must follow her heart. Somehow, in the deepest part of her soul, she felt, she hoped, there was another purpose for her. . . .

From his position above her, Victor found himself contemplating a far more earthly matter. The girl's obliqueness, the intrigue she presented, proved almost as maddening as the innocent lure of her beauty.

He chuckled, pinching the bridge of his nose. If her age weren't warning enough, clearly she was already committed. The last thing he wanted was to end up in one of these ridiculous challenges or duels the men of New Orleans seemed ever anxious to initiate. He should return inside.

Still, just in case she was about to end a liaison, he could hardly resist the next question: "Tell me, Miss Devon, will you be breaking someone's heart?"

To his utter surprise she laughed at the question. "I certainly hope not!"

He gave up. Victor glanced at the dogs and saw that they had separated. "Call Hamlet now, Miss Devon. I believe he might come."

Jade straightened, appearing to look off in the general direction. "Ham," she called enthusiastically. "Here, boy! Come, Ham!"

The dog looked over, then back at his playmate, who had laid down, panting from her exertions. The sweet sound of his mistress's voice won. He bounded excitedly over to Jade Terese. Loving hands came over his head as she scolded him gently, slipping her hand around an unusually short lead tied to his neck. The dog sat nobly then, gazing longingly at his female friend. Victor knew the feeling, and he came around, bending over to pet the handsome dog.

"So, there you are!" Sebastian appeared with a servant in tow. One of Victor's servants had interrupted the performance with a message—and it was good news—but the words stopped on Sebastian's lips as he beheld the girl. His hands clasped over his heart and he almost dropped to his knees in appreciation. "I might have known you'd somehow single out the most beautiful young lady in the theater for your attention. Oh, I do see! A thousand pardons, Madame. My judgment was rash. I should have said the most beautiful lady in all of Orleans. Who are you?"

Jade Terese suffered a moment's confusion. He could not be addressing her? She turned around as if to spot another lady, which made the two gentlemen laugh.

"Oh, yes." Sebastian motioned toward the waiting servant, though his gaze remained fixed on the young lady, "Vic, I believe our ship has returned. Our good captain is waiting."

Victor chuckled at the news. "Send Carl with the carriage to take the ladies home after the opera," he told the waiting man. "And bring our horses 'round at once."

"Yes sir," the man said, and he departed.

Sebastian still stared at the young lady.

"Mademoiselle Devon," Victor said, returning his attention to Jade Terese, "allow me to introduce my friend, Lord Sebastian Van de Auxere."

A gentle hand came over hers, and the Austrian bowed as he lifted the delicate hand for a kiss. "No fairer maid has thy eyes ever beheld," Sebastian said, quoting Shakespeare.

Jade consulted her intuition, a considerable gift, and decided his flattery was a tease, his title a pretense but one she would humor. The sweet girlish sound of her laughter sang like musical wind chimes as she stroked Hamlet's head.

"Lord Sebastian, is it?" she questioned. "I'm afraid Louisiana does not often get to host titled nobility— indeed, much of any kind of nobility! You must tell me what brings a nobleman all the way to Orleans?"

"Ah, Mademoiselle, I ask myself that at least once a day. I can only say I came escaping an even worse fate than this swamp-infested town and its relentless heat."

"What he means," Victor supplied, "is that being the fourth and last son of the Van de Auxerre title, and with no fortune to recommend him, his parents had arranged a marriage to rectify these troubling circumstances." He leaned over, grinning as he confided, "This worse fate refers to the lady he left at the altar."

The lovely green eyes sparkled with mirth but she pretended to be properly shocked. "You didn't leave a lady at the altar?"

"A lady?" Sebastian questioned. "No, not a lady. As I recall she resembled more of a cow and my own sweet grandmother looked like a bonny spring maid in comparison." The young lady's amusement encouraged him. "So I departed to take refuge in the lovely ladies of the English court, and it was there in just such a lady's bedchambers that I met Victor and what seems to have become my fate."

"Pardon? A lady's bedchambers? What can you mean?"

Victor chuckled, but sighed. "The incident hardly bears repeating but I see you are imagining the worst. You see, that night I had been at some or another social function and after being introduced to my lovely hostess—some duke's daughter—" He stopped and looked to Sebastian. "What was her name again?"

"I believe it was Melissa," he supplied.

"Yes. Anyway, Melissa and I discovered a shared interest in great work of art. She invited me up to her rooms to examine her collection. No sooner did we arrive there than Sebastian, who I'd yet to meet, jumped out from nowhere and demanded to know what I was doing there. I merely explained that I had come to examine the lady's paintings—"

"He neglects to mention," Sebastian interjected, "that there were no paintings in the room."

"Well!" Victor exclaimed. "The lady deliberately misled

me to believe otherwise, to what purpose ... well, one might only imagine." Jade's laughter told him she was perfectly capable of imagining. "Then the lady was at a loss to explain Sebastian's presence there," he continued. "Sebastian reminded her of an earlier arrangement. Since she seemed unable to recall it, I suggested he ought to take his leave. It was about then that Sebastian challenged me and demanded that I name my weapons."

"Oh, my goodness! And did you fight?"

"Victor told me he had no desire to kill or be killed over such a ridiculous situation." Sebastian grinned at his youthful idiocy. "I thought him a coward and told him so."

"Yes," Victor resumed, irritated as he remembered it. "And his insults grew louder and more passionate by the minute. Before I could back out, his shouts roused the house. The next thing I knew, the duke and two other gentlemen, along with a whole handful of footmen, broke through the door.

"And then for some reason, the lady suddenly thought Sebastian and I were a danger to her person. As soon as she saw her father, she started screaming, accusing us of ... ah, intentions better left unmentioned. Naturally the duke became rather upset, demanding justice for the thwarted attack on his daughter's virtue. Only to hear Sebastian tell him he was far too late, that his daughter had lost her virtue years before—"

"You didn't really say that?"

"I did have it on the best of authorities!"

"And so that's it," Victor finished. "We were thrown together in an effort to escape with our lives. I have been unable to shake him ever since. . . ."

Through her laughter, Jade Terese wondered out loud if she should believe such an outrageous tale, only to hear Sebastian, with characteristic drama, claim his veracity was a matter of honor, that he would be gravely wounded if she doubted a word said.

Listening to the benign banter, Victor twirled a straw in his mouth as he watched her. He was thinking he'd make inquiries about the lovely creature on the morrow when Sebastian, peering closer, waved a hand in front of her face.

A hand she did not see.

He looked to Victor for his reaction.

Victor glanced down at the dog, his short lead, and then back to the beautiful eyes and the mystery there. Could it be? She seemed so graceful and attuned to everything that went on around her. Victor was shocked he had not noticed, but as he grasped the nature of the game she played—concealing her blindness with carefully practiced manners—he felt a curious lurch of heart. A less sensitive man might assign simple pity to the feeling but he knew better. It was as if he were a patron of the arts, presented with a beautiful painting and lured into appreciation and admiration, only to abruptly discover the ruinous flaw and a poor attempt to conceal it.

Then inexplicably he felt a prick of anger. She might have carried a blind stick or mentioned that she could not see where her dog was, indeed see anything at all. To pretend she was normal all the time he talked to her seemed perverse, a folly only the youngest and most vain women might commit.

Jade Terese was trying to make sense of the sudden silence that had come over their happy party when Sebastian said, "Ah, our horses. We must leave you, Mademoiselle Devon. My gracious lady." And with a click of his boots, he bowed. "I do hope we meet again."

"Miss Devon, it has been a pleasure," Victor said next as he took her hand in his. With a last lingering look into the beautiful green eyes, he brought her hand to his lips for a kiss.

Jade felt a curious tingling lift through her midsection. She forgot to breathe. The brief press of his lips brought a sensual warmth flooding her, revealing itself in color to her cheeks. "Au revoir, Monsieur."

He turned and walked away.

Jade Terese listened to his boots move swiftly to the

theater doors before turning toward the street. He called quick orders to the servants; she heard him ride off with young Lord Sebastian. Victor . . . Who was he? Why, oh why, had she not asked his surname? And how did he affect her like that?

She smiled, hoping she encountered the new American again. If he had settled a land grant, he would be in town often, no doubt. She reached to pet Ham's furry head. "Was he handsome, Ham? Was he?" She sighed at the absurdity, realizing of course such a detail could hardly matter to a blind person.

Across the road, the two men who'd observed the entire episode exchanged relieved glances. They were glad to see Nolte and Sebastian depart. M. Deubler wouldn't pose much of a challenge, but those two young adventurers would have been another matter.

The last thing they wanted was a run-in with Nolte.

The woman watched from behind these men in a carriage, her gaze filled with intense emotions and her heart pounding with anticipation. She might have left Jade Terese Devon to go through her miserable life blind, except for the repeated nightmares plaguing her sleep. These nightmares revealed the young lady miraculously had her sight restored. She would take no chances.

The young lady, she suspected, would make a fine whore anyway—the thought kept making her smile. Charmane, an old friend, had strict instructions for Jade Terese. Charmane could use the girl's dead servant to force obedience and perhaps employ the potion to start. Don Bernardo himself would be her first patron. It would be many years before Jade Terese felt the sun on her face, and by then it would be too late.

Jade Terse Devon, New Orleans's finest whore . . .

She felt a heady rush of sensation, a heightened sense of her powers. She had waited such a long time for this. The voices of the dead whispered to her, rushing to where the circle had been drawn, gathering in the spot.

Perhaps she should do something for Mother Francesca as well. Something that would tease her fears and form her nightmares. She deserved it! A hanging present . . .

The old maid might be just the thing.

Monsieur Deubler and Jade Terese strolled through Vieux Carré, passing the old Spanish Barracks, recently converted into a well-frequented cabaret that served both white and colored. The crowd was thick along the bar, then broken into clusters around wooden tables where cards shuffled back and forth among players. Gay piano and violin music sounded in the din of laughter, shouts and conversation. The sounds poured out from the open doors, where men gathered too, squatting on their haunches, playing games of dice. The air was filled with the scents of tobacco smoke, spirits and fried shrimp. From these telling signs Jade Terese knew the exact number of steps to her front door behind the convent on Basin Street.

Their voices rose as Monsieur Deubler and Jade sang favorite arias from the opera as they strolled home. Jade's hand rested lightly on his arm, while the other hand held tight to Hamlet's lead. Her laughter rang sweetly in the moist night air. She occasionally interrupted her friend's song to supply the correct words, though her thoughts kept returning to the earlier encounter with an American named Victor.

He had ben so engaging and charming and . . . well . . . something! Her inexperience prevented her from the immediate understanding most women had when meeting Victor. She settled for the descriptive words: intriguing, somehow exciting and interesting, but these words felt entirely inadequate.

Still counting her steps, she stopped. "Shhh." She motioned. "We must be quiet now. The convent is just ahead and I know the good sisters will be sleeping. Let's go the back way around. I fear the mud's too thick to pass in front anyway."

Monsieur Deubler made no response at first. He stared

at the oddity in their path. A dead fish surrounded by a circle made of some kind of white powder and—Mon Dieu! What was that? It looked like some kind of heart.

Jade sensed something amiss. She went very still and asked, "Is something wrong?"

"No, nothing," he assured her, relieved that she could not see the grotesque configuration. He shook his head. These voodoo practitioners! Imbeciles! Something must be done. He would bring it to Father Nolte's attention Sunday next. "Just step to the right, cherie . . ."

Jade Terese did not understand what had happened, but Monsieur Deubler seemed suddenly subdued, his gaiety and high spirits disappearing. She tried to press him again for an explanation but he politely changed subjects. Silence came between them as they at last turned onto Basin Street.

Jade Terese maintained a modest cottage conveniently close to the convent, where she acted as an instructress in the Negro girls' school. Her position as the music instructress at the school had been an accident of her family's tragedy. Jade's mother, Elizabeth Devon, had been a Catholic by marriage, but not by faith. However, long ago Elizabeth had solicited Mother Francesca's help with a situation she had found troubling and quite foreign to an Englishwoman's sensibilities, and she had found the Reverend Mother's advice not only intelligent but also helpful. And over the years, their friendship had grown, deepening and blossoming, surprising them both as they each trespassed the conventions of society and the disparities of their stations and backgrounds to find a comfort in their shared beliefs and intelligence. Elizabeth's death had been a devastating blow to Mother Francesca, until Jade began to fill the missing place in her heart.

So of course Mother Francesca had known all about Jade Terese and her uncommon gifts long before the fateful day that she had stepped into Jade's life. First of all, Terese was graced with a perfect memory. In addition to a wealth of poems and verses, including much of Shakespeare's works, Jade knew half of the Bible, verse by verse. She could play chess in her mind or complete a ten-row sum of numbers without benefit of pen and paper, and much faster than anyone else. She spoke four languages fluently. And after the accident and her resulting blindness, she used her considerable resources to painstakingly live as normal a life as possible for a blind person.

This often caused trouble for those who knew her well. Presently Monsieur Deubler and Jade had almost reached her doorstep, but the good man had completely forgotten he escorted a blind person. She slipped right into the oozing muck between the wooden boards. Monsieur Deubler quickly caught her fall, cursing himself for his carelessness. "Jade Terese, just look at your hem! Your boots," he said, not realizing the ridiculousness of the suggestion, too horrified at what he had done. "It will be ruined—"

Hamlet stiffened, sniffed the air. The smells were wrong. He smelled man, the faint air of spilt blood, death. Danger! He barked, reared back, jumped forward and barked again. The hairs lifted on his coat, he barked warning. "Oh, Hamlet!" Jade said, alarmed. "Hush! You shall wake the entire neighborhood."

The dog quieted obediently but maintained a low menacing growl, his body stiff as he stared off at the house. Watching the dog, Monsieur Deubler felt a sharp premonition of doom and, for no reason he knew, his hands went clammy. He studied the darkened windows of her house. No lights shone inside but then there was no reason for Maydrian to leave a light on after she retired. Still ...

"Let me escort you inside Jade Terese," he said at the bottom of the stairs.

"'Oh, 'tis not necessary," Jade tried to assure him as Hamlet's growl lifted to a bark again. She laughed at her dog and bent over to remove his leash. Maydrian had taken to feeding an old tomcat, and the cat had taken to teasing Hamlet unmercifully. She imagined the cat sat on the sill or roof and as she set Hamlet free, she warned,

"That cat will make mincemeat out of you yet!" To her friend she said, " 'Tis no doubt this cat Maydrian has taken to feeding. Do you see him somewhere about?"

"No, no," Monsieur Deubler said. "He's looking at the house, Jade Terese. There is something wrong. Let me go inside and make sure all is well first—"

"I'm sure it is nothing—"

"But of course." He smiled as he reached for the door-knob. "Let me just make certain, Jade Terese."

Standing on the porch now, Jade acquiesced. Hamlet growled menacingly still and she knelt at his side, trying to comfort him. His body felt as stiff as a board and his fear became hers. She listened intently as the door opened and Monsieur Deubler stepped inside.

Darkness permeated the front sitting room. He could see nothing. "The sitting room is so dark . . ."

Above her dog's growl she heard Monsieur Deubler's boots move away from the door. A sudden unnatural thump sounded, a sucking of breath, another thump. Jade leaped up with alarm. "Monsieur Deubler!"

With arms extended, she started toward the door, imagining her friend had stumbled over a table or chair in the darkness. Hamlet barked a warning, racing ahead into the house. Jade stumbled after him, feeling her way through the darkness, calling for Maydrian and Monsieur Deubler.

She screamed as Hamlet's vicious growls sounded.

A painful howl died as a whimper. Jade froze, terrified. A hand came over her mouth. Her muffled scream sounded as she was jerked backwards into the house. The door slammed shut. The man held her tight, forcing breath from her, and during the first few seconds she felt too shocked to struggle. A pure animalistic terror claimed her and like a drowning person, her body convulsed in an effort to draw breath. The hand stayed over her mouth but loosened somewhat and she caught breath in gulps, fighting the dizziness that threatened to overwhelm her.

Then he grabbed a handful of hair, forced her head

back, and she screamed again as he pressed a wet cloth to her face. A sickly taste saturated her mouth, nostrils and lungs, choking her. She squirmed desperately but then darkness—a darkness from within—spun around her and she felt herself sinking, sinking . . .

Chapter 2

Darkness spread across the river and the forests beyond as Victor Nolte, Sebastian and Murray, Victor's former ship surgeon, made their way back to Shady Faith, Victor's new manor house some five miles north of New Orleans. The night air felt mercifully cooler. A thousand stars laced a night sky, dimly illuminating the well-traveled road that followed the Mississippi up through New Orleans all the way to Baton Rouge and beyond. Huge gangly oaks lined the road. Thick moss draped the boughs and looked eerily like the black mourning crepe abandoned after a funeral. They occasionally passed a fishing hut or house, that was all. Above the soothing sound of rushing water and the steady trot of the horses, their laughter and loud exclamations disturbed the sanctity of the quiet night.

A happy mood it was. The *Fair Winds* had met with astonishing success. Victor's ship had captured Don Bernardo's *Black Crest* just after the pirate ship had raided two American clippers and left over half of the crew dead. It had been a vicious fight but, slowed by the weight of its bulging holds, the *Black Crest* had been unable to outrun the *Fair Winds*. In the exchange of cannon fire, the *Fair Winds* suffered only minor damage, while the *Black Crest* would be dry-docked for months. Then Don Bernardo's remaining crew, outnumbered almost two to one, had been forced to endure the humiliation of transferring the ship's riches to the *Fair Winds*, a procedure they were used to watching, not enduring.

With the *Black Crest* rendered defenseless and motionless, Don Bernardo's crew watched the *Fair Winds* sail out of view, sinking mysteriously into the horizon. Afterward, the *Fair Winds* met with another of Victor's ships, the *Minerva,* and the cargo was transferred again. The pirate would have no revenge. For no one knew who stood behind the *Fair Winds* or which port the graceful ship called home.

The *Black Crest* was the fourth victim of the mysterious pirate's pirate, and within days everyone in New Orleans would be asking the same question: Who *is* the pirate's pirate? Victor, his ships and crews were never suspect. In addition to his shipbuilding business, Victor sailed three ships from New Orleans, each engaged in legitimate trade. No one besides his father and the governor knew of Victor's fourth ship, the *Fair Winds,* docked sixty safe miles away in the Gulf of Mexico.

With his sword in hand, Sebastian began vigorously attacking overhanging branches as they rode along. With branches left in neatly sliced pieces behind them, Sebastian turned his attention to invisible enemies as a quiet dawn began stretching across the landscape and they neared the Mississippi's levee. For several miles along the riverbank, ships and boats of all kinds rocked at moorage. When Victor's ships were in port, they occupied the far southern end with the other proud oceangoing vessels. Next, in a perfect rank order according to size—and therefore importance—came smaller vessels, sloops and schooners. The boats continued to become smaller the closer one came to the city until, stretching for miles upstream sat row upon row of the dirty and uncouth backwoods flatboats, archaic vessels that Victor hoped to soon replace with new river steamers he had started to build.

The night lanterns of New Orleans—another thankless innovation of Claighborne's—still burned as they reached the marketplace. Bordered by darkened shade trees, the long, earthen dike stretched before them, marking the focal point of the marketplace. Even at this hour longshoremen had begun gathering, and would soon start the endless loading and unloading of the mounds of coal, the bales of cotton, the barrels of tobacco and sugar, the case after case of merchandise that filled the levee as far as one could see. One by one sleepy-eyed merchants and their servants began arriving to direct the day's traffic. Seated beside huge baskets of goods, Negro women assembled in their own small groups, gossiping as they sipped coffee before a long day of selling. Behind the levee sat the actual marketplace, row upon row of canvas-shaded stands spilling out in every direction from the long brick structure in front of the Place d'Arms. Servants had already begun the morning stacking of goods at the fruit and vegetable stands.

The three riders reined in their horses and turned them around a stack of boxes piled across their path, and as they did so, Victor caught sight of a half dozen Ursuline Sisters up ahead. Their curious costumes—the long black robes topped with starched white wimples whose tips looked like birds in flight—made them stand out. They talked in whispers at the river's edge, anxiously looking upriver as if they were waiting for someone. He wondered if they could be waiting for his father, whom he heard had left to deliver last rites to a dying priest in Baton Rouge. Then he noticed the man with the good women.

A nod of his head indicated the direction. "Look who's standing with the Sisters."

"Girod?" Sebastian appeared surprised. "I don't believe I've ever seen the good constable outside of Crescent Hall Saloon. I know I've never seen him standing sober at dawn."

"No doubt some imminent disaster awaiting your father's return," Murray guessed. "Should we stop and find out?"

Victor watched as two other constables rode quickly up to the group, appearing to report some news. "No." He shook his head. "I'd rather let my father handle his own catastrophes." He sighed with a telling grin. "Somehow I have no doubt if he needs me, I'll hear about it soon enough anyway." He quickened his mount into a trot. His friends followed suit. "It's been a long enough night . . ."

"But she must be somewhere! She must!" Sister Catherine cried, dabbing her reddened eyes with a handkerchief. She could not imagine a worse tragedy. She could hardly believe this was happening. "And Maydrian? Where is that old woman?"

There was no answer. Last evening, Marie Saint's servant had arrived with the mysterious warning of some mishap waiting for Jade Terese. Mother Francesca and Father Nolte were away giving last rites to old Father Lopez in Baton Rouge; Mother Francesca was not expected back until midday at the earliest, Father Nolte not until the evening on the morrow. So, just in case, three of the good Sisters had set out to find the young lady and bring her into the protective walls of the convent for the evening.

They soon discovered Jade Terese had gone out with Monsieur Deubler, who often escorted her and his family to the opera or the theater. It took a number of trips to find where that man lived. Finally they had made their way through the streets to his residence. Only to be told he had not yet returned from the opera, even though the opera should have been over sometime before. So they had rushed back to Jade's house.

Hamlet lay in a pool of blood; Monsieur Deubler lay unconscious, hit on the head with a heavy object. Maydrian was nowhere to be found. And Jade Terese had vanished.

Constable Girod looked away from the sorrowful and frightened faces of the good Sisters. He withdrew a silver tin from his back pocket. " 'Tis a most regrettable situation. Very bad." He shook his head and sighed before raising the silver cask.

The constable swallowed the whole of his cask, returned the cap and placed it back in his trouser pocket. He surveyed Place d'Arms, wondering if he should stay with them as they waited for the Reverend Mother or if he could quit their company.

He supposed 'twould look bad if he left them alone. . . .

"There must be something more you can do?"

"I am doing everything possible, I assure you."

He offered them a patronizing smile, but the four good Sisters met the smile with something akin to horror before they looked away. The corpulent constable was not known for his energies or his sobriety. The sorry effects of drunkenness showed plainly in his large puffy nose, its hideous mauve color and visible capillaries, all of it squashy in texture. Sister Mary shuddered in disdain as she stared, unable to hide her disapproval.

The constable threw his hands up in a gesture of helplessness. Madonna! What did they expect him to do anyway? 'Twas close to midnight when they had summoned him to the young lady's house. Once they had revived Monsieur Deubler, he could not provide any clues or descriptions of the culprits. The man remembered nothing. The dog had been killed—a knife through his belly. The blind young lady and her aging servant were gone, missing, kidnapped or more likely dead. Murder was hardly a rare event. Just last Saturday night there had been three murders, all sadly unresolved.

There were dozens of murders in the swamp every month, and while these were usually drunken riverboat men, or aging prostitutes, it was occasionally a more respectable personage who had inadvertently met misfortune. Still, assuming it was possible she might be alive, he had sent all his men on the impossible task of trying to find this one young lady in a city of thousands.

Girod sighed, wishing he had another cask. The nuns were so naive and he didn't have the cruelty necessary to dash their hopes. But the sad story was hopeless, he knew. If the young lady weren't already dead, she would no doubt be placed in the white slave market that catered to the multitudes of brothels.

Which was odd, actually. He scratched his head, thinking on this. The slavers rarely took white women and then only if the poor creatures were destitute, with neither connections nor relations, the kind of woman who would sooner or later end up in a brothel anyway. "Are you certain no one had an argument or vendetta against the young lady?"

The question drew instant attention.

"Of course not," Sister Margaret cried. "Jade Terese was an innocent angel! An instructress at our school—" She stopped suddenly, and met Sister Catherine's horrified glance as her pale hand covered her mouth. Why had she said "was"? As if Terese was already dead . . .

Girod failed to notice the slip, for he had thought of the young lady in the past tense from the start. " 'Tis just that it is unusual, this whole business." He nodded with the thought. "All the rumors about the Devon family . . ."

Sister Mary took affront at the oblique reference to the Devon family tragedy. "That was years ago, you know, and an accident. Nothing was ever proven."

"Yes, yes," Girod said, dismissing this, ignoring the anger on the Sisters' faces. Ah well, in any case 'twas nothing he could do about it. If she were alive and brought to a brothel, papers were already drawn up that proved the young woman was indentured. The young lady would be doomed to the fate, not always a bad fate either, he could have pointed out to anyone other than Sisters of the Church. Besides, how could he possibly search each and every brothel in the city? 'Twould take years! Mercy, but there were over a hundred. New Orleans was famous for them, everything from twenty-dollar parlor houses to the fifteen-cent Negro "crib," as they called the lowest kind of whorehouse and of course all of them paid quite well for protection.

Doomed, the young lady was doomed. Ah well.

He wished he had gotten another cask. . . .

The sun rose toward the meridian, beating down on the wooden planks of the curved bow of the flatboat where Mother Francesca stood, waiting for the city's levee to come into view. She had slept surprisingly well; she had found the apartment assigned to her quite adequate for her modest needs, despite the constant scuffle and noise of the hog pen to the rear at the stern. Over seventy feet long and twenty feet wide, the flatboat housed five passengers, including Sister Benedict and herself, domestic implements, a crew of eight, a hog pen and a number of crates to be delivered to the market. They had hit only one sandbar along the way, which, as the good captain had informed her, was "A bit o' luck, no doubt delivered straight from above on account of the *Cheery Queen*'s most important passenger. . . ."

Mother Francesca had not believed in the direct intervention of God since she was five and lost her mother and sister to influenza, but nonetheless, she had acknowledged the thought with a warm smile.

Standing at the front of the barge and dressed in traditional costume, the good woman looked like a black-and-white bulwark ornament decorating the bow. Her unnatural height was accentuated by the habit. No lines marked her advancing years, past sixty now and closer to seventy. The smooth strong lines of her face were softened by her religious life and many hours of meditation. A meditation that, as now, she often felt more intensely as she exercised her deep sensitivity and appreciation of the natural beauty of God's world.

She drew the fresh air deeply into her lungs. How she loved riverboat travel! God forgive her but she had barely been able to conceal her joy upon learning she was to accompany Father Nolte to Baton Rouge for the last rites of dearly departed Father Lopez.

The air felt fresh and moist, while the running water sounded like a soothing caress. She stared at the lone fisherman in sight. He sat in his boat in such perfect stillness on the water that he looked like a painting. A surprised smile lifted on her face when he waved to her. She waved back just as she heard the familiar shrill voice of her traveling companion, Sister Benedict. "Mother Francesca, you would do well to draw into the shade before you catch a burn. . . ."

Mother Francesca turned to see her fellow Sister standing in the narrow shade of the cabin, hands neatly concealed in her habit. Actually, she could only see the black-and-white outline of the Sister's dress up close. The sun made her eyes worse. Ah well. Sister Benedict's directive was right, she supposed.

"Heavens, but I had a terrible night's sleep," Sister Benedict complained as her superior drew close. She cast a disparaging glance at the hogs nearby. "I could hardly sleep with the incessant racket of those uncouth creatures." Sister Benedict's high-boned face took on a grayish tinge against the starched whiteness of her habit.

"I'm sorry to hear that," Mother Francesca replied. She turned back to the lure of green water, striving for, as always, an attitude of tranquil acceptance.

Sister Benedict considered her superior for a moment. "You look so pensive. I wouldn't wonder if you were contemplating the girl's decision just now?"

"Quite the contrary. I was enjoying the morning's warmth and air. I believe I am ready to face Jade Terese's decision, Sister Benedict." Whether or not Terese should take the vows was one of the many subjects she had discussed with Father Nolte. They both guessed she would not; indeed, Terese had hinted of it all week until they had realized she was trying to spare their feelings. "Father Nolte has convinced me it's for the best."

"The best? The best would be that she take the vows!" She shook her head, clacking her tongue in disapproval. "Perhaps if there was an alternative path. Despite her gifts, the unpleasant fact remains."

Mother Francesca sighed, searching for and finding a measure of patience for Sister Benedict's opinion. They had always disagreed on the subject of Jade Terese. "If by that you mean to imply she is ill suited to any other course in life, I would ask you to view it from the reverse position: does blindness or health problems necessitate or determine one's eligibility to say the vows?"

"Of course not." Sister Benedict's thin lips pressed to a

hard line. "But what else can she do? The idea of spinster-hood and Jade Terese seem as likely as the Second Coming. The curse of her beauty attracts many scoundrels." She added with feeling, "Already! And yet what man would have a blind wife, even if she did not suffer from the seizures?"

"She has not had one for two years now."

Sister Benedict ignored the point as she shook her head, as if settling the matter. "Her countenance brings her trouble, and a good deal of it."

A frown sat on Sister Benedict's face as she thought of all the turmoil caused by the young lady—all her liberal ideas, for one thing, political ideas that were so brazen, modern, and sometimes, she felt certain, blasphemous. Jade Terese had ideas that would be most unbecoming from a man but that seemed positively indecent when expressed by a woman. And she was always up to something. Just two weeks before the girl had the presumption to correct Visiting Bishop Romanus's Latin! It was so irritating and embarrassing—no matter that she was right. And during this last week of blistering heat she had found Jade Terese's entire class adjourned to the shade of the oak grove and missing their boots. Every last one of those girls had been barefoot.

The young woman was wild. She was sure Jade Terese snuck off with her servant and swam in the lake—her mass of hair was always wet in the midafternoon heat. She still remembered the youngster soon after she had joined them at the convent: the girl refused to bathe in her chemise to protect her modesty. Lord, she knew then the girl was trouble. "Sister Benedict, I am blind. What good is modesty if there is no witness?" Horrified, she told Jade God was the witness. Jade Terese only laughed. "I am quite certain God has little interest in my bathing habits. . . ."

"That young lady is in desperate need of a guiding authority, and since marriage is out of the question, it should, it seems to me, be God."

The harsh point held some measure of truth, and Mother Francesca shifted uncomfortably. It was a moot point after all. The day Mother Francesca had learned of the terrible accident that resulted in Monsieur and Madame Devon's death, she had gone to retrieve the thirteen-year-old girl from the neighboring plantation. Jade Terese had lain in a semiconscious state of shock. There had been no family to send the young girl to. It had been her own tender and gentle care that gradually brought Jade Terese up from the darkened abyss back to life, only to discover that part of the darkness remained. The girl had lost her sight in the accident.

Oh, the terror of that time . . .

Mother Francesca thought of Elizabeth and she knew Elizabeth would not have wanted her daughter to take the vows. "I can but hope Jade Terese's options in life are not as narrow as you suppose, Sister Benedict. In any case, we cannot force her to take the vows, can we now?"

The crew guided the boat to the eastern shore, preparing to dock.

"Reverend Mother," the captain called. "Look there! A number of good Sisters are waving from the market. By the shade trees!" He paused as he took in the anxious faces. "Well, Lord a-mighty, looks as if somethin's wrong. And the constable is hastening toward us!"

Alarming words. The two women rushed quickly to the side, searching the crowded marketplace. The mid-morning sun shone bright and hard, and their hands shielded their faces as they surveyed the long rows of stands spilling out from the Place d'Arms. Mother Francesca's gaze passed over the stands of housing wares in the far corner and the many fruit, vegetable and bread stands, all the restaurants closer to the levee. Sister Benedict pointed to where Sisters Margaret, Catherine and Mary ran toward the boat, black streaks made by their habits as they maneuvered around the multitudes of peasants, beggars, Negroes, common folk and grand dames strolling with their gentlemen. They saw Sister Catherine almost topple over a Negro boy obediently fanning flies from a fruit stand, then righting herself before catching up with the others, now following the riverboat.

"Goodness!" Sister Benedict gasped. "It *is* Constable Girod!"

The crew tossed long ropes to the waiting longshoremen. The Sisters frantically waved their arms. Constable Girod tried to straighten his shirt and coat as he followed. The plank lowered.

Nearby a young Negro boy ran from the fishmonger's stand to the river, where he dumped a bucket of rotting fish. Mother Francesca caught sight of the omen made by the half-eaten skeletons floating between the boat and the levee, their torn and silvery backs catching and reflecting a spectrum of sunlight. A shiver raced up her spine. She withdrew a small wooden statuette of Mary from the folds of her habit and clasped it tightly, bracing for terrible news.

"What? Merciful heavens!"

The whole awful story poured out before Mother Francesca's black boots had even touched land. For a long moment she only stared as the horror of the details mounted: Monsieur Deubler being found unconscious, apparently recovering from the ordeal but unable to tell anything more than the barest facts. The disappearance of Maydrian and Hamlet found in a pool of blood.

Sisters Benedict and Catherine grabbed Mother Francesca's arms to steady her as her mind absorbed the shock and, with effort, she suppressed a cry of utter anguish. Constable Girod was offering some placating words but Mother Francesca hardly heard. She felt her heart swing out over a black void, and bewildered, she waited for it to tremble back to safety.

Her thoughts raced in a frantic circle made of images she kept in the farthest recess of her mind: the rope twisting and pulling, Satan's own hate in Juliet's eyes as she died. She did die, she did! There would be another explanation for this. . . .

Mother Francesca's hands went clammy; the world spun viciously. As if from far far away she heard Sister Benedict's alarm pulling her back. "Easy, Reverend Mother, easy. We need you now. . . ."

A person of tremendous inner resources, Mother Francesca at last steadied herself. For Jade Terese. For the girl, whom she loved. Abruptly her sharp eyes focused on Constable Girod, as if seeing him for the first time. The intensity of her scrutiny could pierce all but the most obtuse. The constable was not only rumored to be a drunkard but also was not known for his professional exertions. "How many men are out looking for her?"

"Ah well, my good men are doing their best—"

"How many?"

"Well, I have eight men at my disposal—"

"That's not enough," the Reverend Mother interrupted. "Sister Catherine, leave at once to alert Governor Claighborne to the situation and request his services in securing more men for the search. We need at least fifty. We need a headquarters to coordinate the effort. His office will do nicely. . . ."

Within minutes she had directed everyone to tasks: arranging for posters of Jade Terese to be hung about the city, sending someone upriver to hasten Father Nolte's return and so on. "Now"—she turned her attention back to Constable Girod—"from you, sir, I want to know in frank terms exactly what you believe has befallen the young lady."

"I cannot say," he said, spreading his arms and shrugging. "In truth, it could be anything. She could be anywhere! She might have been taken into slavery, perhaps a . . . a house in the swamp."

This, the Reverend Mother knew, referred to an area of town aptly named "the swamp." It was a hellish place made up of bawdy houses, taverns and gaming halls, a place frequented only by criminals, lowlifes, riverboatmen and the saddest of the fallen women.

"I'm sad to say," Girod added, "the young lady could be halfway downriver as we speak!"

This brought a stifled wail from Sister Benedict.

Mother Francesca's face reddened beneath her habit. She would not let this happen; if she had a breath left in her body, she would find Jade Terese. So help her God. . . .

They called Mercedes's room the sunshine corner. Customers were often surprised, at least those who noticed, for the room looked like any proper young lady's room. It was similar to their wives' or daughters' bedchambers, perhaps a bit more femininely ornate and kept as clean as a treasured crystal glass. At a glance, one would never think it belonged to a young lady who made her way in a brothel.

Mercedes took pains to keep it that way. Madame Charmane never voiced objections and allowed for Mercedes's peculiarities, for the girl was her most popular and, therefore, her most expensive. Everything in the room was a shade of sunshine: not pale but bright lemon yellows. The room had hardwood floors and white wicker furnishings, though the dressing and sitting tables, and the bedclothes, were covered in ruffled layers of pretty yellow cloth. Even the mosquito net and the damask curtains matched the curious color scheme. The room faced the east too, though it was a rare morning that Mercedes rose early enough to see her small haven flood with sunshine. Sunshine that brought a momentary illusion of light to this house; sunshine that, like books, reached through the burgeoning obsession of her thoughts and allowed her to escape, however briefly.

Mercedes sat in a wicker chair near the bedside, trying to read. Reading was not normally an effort. Books allowed her temporary relief from the oppression of the house, a dark and heavy thing that always threatened to crash down upon her, worse lately as her thoughts kept returning insistently to an idea of murder. Reading, she suspected, had kept her sanity.

The young woman's growing book collection started

with Monsieur Matthew Duim, one of her favorite customers. He was only a shopkeeper but once every month he managed to find money to afford Madame's outrageous prices. Monsieur Duim had taken a fancy to Mercedes, and despite his large family and poor means, he always tried to leave a gratuity. She finally gathered enough courage to stop such thoughtfulness, confiding secretly that Madame Charmane collected all gratuities. While she preferred that he keep the coins for his family, the kind man insisted he bring her something to show his affection. Books were the only thing she wanted and might be permitted to keep. It worked so well with Matthew, she had asked the same favor from her other regular customers. The last book, the one she presently tried to read, was the first volume of a fascinating history of a man named Tom Jones. Unfortunately, the engaging story was written in English, and reading English was difficult for her.

Mercedes's beauty found its way into the hearts of many regular customers. Strawberry blonde curls, thick and rebellious, cascaded around her shoulders, framing a lovely pixie face. A rosy pink complexion spoke of glowing health and vitality, despite her confinement indoors. She wasn't large, and while slender, her figure leaned toward the voluptuous. Few men managed to resist the promise in her soft, hazel eyes.

Presently, Mercedes's face was troubled, and every few moments she interrupted her reading to study the young lady behind the mosquito net. Jade Terese reminded her of Sleeping Beauty. Mercedes wished for a magic wand to banish such beauty, to replace it with a plain face and a figure to be ignored.

"Your beauty is a curse, Jade Terese," Mercedes whispered into the quiet room. "Only magic or a miracle will save you. Oh, if only I were a sorceress able to wave that wand! I'd not hesitate to transform you from the fairy-tale princess into an ugly and scarred woman, a gross object of pity. I'm so afraid for you, Jade Terese. It is too late for me, but you have yet to see the beginning. . . ."

Mercedes closed her eyes, released her emotions in a sad sigh. Madame had said the young lady's name would be changed from the lovely Jade Terese to just plain Mary. Madame changed almost everyone's name, as if changing a name had the awesome power to alter an identity, as if she could erase memories and histories with this small stroke of her will. It was amazingly successful. She herself had been one of the few to escape such name banishment. Mercedes was a very common French name and, she supposed, she had needed no encouragement to forget her past. . . .

Mercedes moved to the dressing water, where she scrubbed her hands, dried them and carefully folded the yellow towel she had used before sitting down with a jar of rose oil to soften them. Madame said Jade Terese had been brought here as a gift from a friend, that previously she had been associated with the convent. "Mon Dieu! Not a holy Sister?" she had asked, horrified by the idea.

"I saved her from that now, didn't I?" Madame had laughed, adding the shocking piece: "She is said to be blind. I don't imagine the sport will be hindered by that pitiful fact. She's too beautiful now, but later I'll use her for those customers who might benefit from her sightlessness."

Mercedes did not want to think of those customers who might benefit from a woman's sightlessness. Seven months ago Angel had been found hanging in her room after Madame had forced her to be with one of those hideous creatures. Angel, like her name, so sweet and gentle and—

She banished the memory. She could not fathom the evil seed that grew and thrived in Madame's heart. Greed motivated Madame, but to what end? She had no love, no one to share her riches with, and as far as Mercedes could tell, she had no wants. So why make others suffer so?

To feed the evil thirst that consumed her. . . .

The Madame's sadism demanded the suffering of others, and while the women of the house were usually spared the worst abuse—trips to the cellar—the poor servants were not. Burn and whip scars marked all of them, even the youngest.

A throng of menaces wove clouds about Mercedes's thoughts. She needed a pistol. If only she could get hold of one! The very night of Angel's suicide she had asked one of her men—Frank Callahan, an American—to secure a pistol for her. Pistols were strictly forbidden upstairs and she could think of no other means of obtaining one.

She had thought to end the suffering, the torment and the misery of *all* who lived here. But Frank had thought mistakenly she wanted the pistol to kill herself and he'd warned Madame, generously leaving a small fortune in Madame's hands to help start his favorite girl on a new life. The Madame had been so amused. Mercifully, the Madame too, had assumed she had wanted the pistol for suicide. "I'll be more than happy to do you the favor when your terms are up, Mercedes. You won't have to ask twice," she'd cackled.

The noon bell rang. Mercedes carefully returned the oil to its place on her dresser and moved to the bed. Madame promised to be up at the noon sounding. She pulled away the netting. Lifting a stray lock from the sleeping face, she wondered what color Jade's eyes were, wondered, too, if they showed her blindness. Surely, there must be a flaw to such beauty.

"Wake up," she called softly, gently shaking the bare shoulders. "Wake up."

The voice beckoned from the depth of her sleep. Jade turned into the pillow, trying to ignore it. Mercedes shook her more firmly. "Please, wake up."

Jade stirred, opened her eyes but remained still as she took stock of her circumstances. She was in an overstuffed bed, covered with layers of quilts, and she was completely naked. A pleasant fragrance gathered in the air. Heaven? Did God take her to heaven?

"Green eyes!" Mercedes declared with delight. "You have beautiful green eyes!"

Jade reached a timid hand to the face, touching something too real to be an angel. Her wits returned all at once, and though still dazed from a long induced sleep, she became immediately aware of many things. She needed water, had to relieve herself, and she needed to know where she was, who sat with her and what happened to poor Monsieur Deubler!

Jade sat up, careful to bring the covers up with her.

"I'm Mercedes," the voice said.

Jade imagined the voice smiled at her.

"This is Madame Charmane's house. How do you feel?"

It sounded all very well with Jade. "I feel thirsty and I must relieve myself."

Mercedes smiled as she held out a long orange silk robe, but remembering that Jade could not see, she placed it around Jade's shoulders and helped her from the bed to the chamber pot. She guided her back to a wicker chair, poured a tall glass of water and pressed it into her hand.

As soon as Jade drained the contents of the glass, the sleepy fog lifted and her thoughts traveled with abrupt panic. Color drained from her face as she remembered Monsieur Deubler's alarm, his caution as he went ahead to make sure the house was safe. Then Ham, poor Ham, and the brief fight, and the cloth coming over her mouth! Then . . . then nothing. She must have passed out. A man brought her to this house. "Monsieur Deubler?" she asked excitedly. "Did he bring him here, too?"

"I don't know about that—"

"We must alert the authorities!" Jade interrupted hastily, imagining Monsieur Deubler and perhaps even Maydrian were still lying unconscious in her house. "Something horrible has happened! A man abducted me! Kidnapped me! Oh, goodness, we must send for help!"

Mercedes did not know what to say, but when Jade rose to her feet and demanded her clothes, she knew something must be said. It would be worse than she had imagined, and God knew she did not want to be the one to tell her.

"Please, calm yourself," Mercedes begged, gently sitting

her back in the chair. "You will fall faint getting so excited after sleeping so long."

"Oh, but you don't understand! I realize my circumstances must seem odd to you but my servant—"

She stopped at the sound of the door opening. It seemed three people entered and approached the sitting table.

Madame Charmane first greeted Mercedes, and then introduced herself to Jade as the mistress of the house. Two huge Negro menservants accompanied the tall, angular woman. Short blond hair curled about her face, and the idea that she was attractive, even beautiful, always surprised Mercedes, as if her deeds would at any minute appear in heavy lines etched deeply into her pale complexion. Her manner and dress were elegant too, and tastefully so. Nothing indicated the beast that lurked beneath her skin.

Seeing only darkness, Jade remained ignorant of the calculated appraisal there or the blank, emotionless faces of the two Negro men, beaten into unnatural subservience. But oddly, she felt Mercedes's apprehension. Mercedes stood alongside the bed, squeezing Jade's hand in hers in a silent warning. Mercedes's tension caused confusion, for Jade assumed the mistress would extend assistance.

Madame Charmane hardly listened to Jade's hasty and excited explanation, concluding with, "I know it is all very hard to believe. I, myself"—she pointed for emphasis— "Have difficulty believing it! But we must hurry to alert the authorities!"

The woman stared at the lovely green pools, mirrors with no reflection. "I see Mercedes hasn't had a chance to explain your situation," she said, casting an irritated glance at Mercedes. "We have no reason to call the authorities—"

"You have already done so! Are they on their way?"

"No authorities have been called or will be called," she stated flatly. "Let me explain. You now belong to me. I am your mistress."

"You . . . you what?" Jade questioned, confused. The very choice of words made no sense. She was not a person of color, nor was she a servant. "There is a mistake here. You see, last night I was at the opera, and true, I was seated in the second tier but because of my blindness and my association with the convent, you see, no one comments—"

An amused smile lifted the Madame's face. "I assure you, I don't care a whit about your circumstances. You are in the finest brothel in New Orleans. The whole of your pitiful life will now be dedicated to pleasing my customers."

Relaxed and at ease, the woman assumed the other wicker chair. Mercedes's obvious concern annoyed her but she always tried to forgive Mercedes everything: the ludicrous sunshine room and the money lost on books; her raw, reddened hands. She would do the same for this one, for "Mary" had just as promising a future.

Unfortunately, enlightenment, or rather reality, eluded Jade, for the word *brothel* was not one she often encountered. Of course she knew what it meant, but it made no sense when applied to her. "A brothel?" Jade first repeated stupidly. It occurred to her just what had happened. The man had brought her to a madhouse, one of the insane asylums where they kept people who lost their wits. Yet wouldn't she have heard if there was such a place in New Orleans? She hadn't known of any, but perhaps she had been carried to another town? Where? Where was she?

The delusions of the insane often took on bizarre, perverted natures, she knew. She must not panic; these people could be violent. "Is there someone in charge, a surgeon or a housekeeper, or someone I might speak to?"

"Whatever for?"

Jade bit her lip with vexation, wishing she could see these people. It was all so confusing. "I cannot see," she thought to explain. "I'm very confused and I need to speak to someone, someone who can explain what has happened to . . . to me."

"I am explaining to you." The Madame's voice lifted

angrily. "You are in a brothel, a bordello, a whorehouse—does any of that sound familiar?"

"No." Jade shook her head, becoming more confused, frightened. "This cannot be. . . . Please," Jade insisted, "I should like to see someone in charge."

Mercedes's heart broke as she witnessed Jade's inability to accept the situation. Before the Madame lost all patience, she tried to intervene. "Mary—"

"Mary? My name is Jade Terese—"

"Not anymore," Madame Charmane interrupted. "From now on you are Mary. I like it much better. And. . . ." She came off the chair and leaned over the girl. Her hand reached up to the jade cross hanging from Jade's neck. A hard yank and the chain broke with the young lady's gasp. "I can't have you reminding my customers of their religious obligations, can I?"

Jade Terese looked confused as she reached a hand to her bare neck. She didn't believe this. How could it be true? A brothel? This woman bought her from those men and thought she would work in a brothel, bedding men!

"No!" She shook her head, looking suddenly fierce. "No, never! I would die. . . . I would die! What makes you think you can do this to me? I am not alone in the world. The Reverend—" She stopped, her panic rising. "I have to get out of this place."

Someone, one of the men, gently pushed her back to the chair and she heard a simple statement through her mounting terror. "I see a little persuasion will be necessary. Especially if you are to stand the block."

"Oh, no, Madame! Please don't do that to her, I beg you! She is too new, too frightened!"

"Exactly why I will have it." Madame Charmane moved to the door, the silent shells of her men followed. "Welcome to my house, Mary. Let's see to the first lesson. Obedience, absolute obedience . . ."

Chapter 3

Later, the Madame opened the door to Mercedes's room. She found Mercedes kneeling at the bedside apparently deep in prayer. Mild amusement entered her voice as she asked, "Think your God listens to a harlot's prayers?"

Startled hazel eyes came opened, and Mercedes stood quickly to her feet. She took in the signs, the terrible signs: the relaxed features of the Madame's face, a detached and calm air that surrounded her, like a lazy and well-fed cat who watched the world from indifferent eyes.

The vicious lust had been satisfied.

Now would be the time to ask for a favor, Mercedes knew: the rare outing, a new gown or perfume, a mailing posted. For horribly, the Madame found this generosity only after a violent episode.

It had been very bad for Jade Therese.

"We should have a full house tonight. You are to prepare Mary for the block."

Mercedes searched the woman's face and knew it would be futile to protest the cruel measure. "Madame, please. She should have the concoction then, to ease the horror of it."

The concoction was a powerful potion made in part of opium cubes and strange-smelling herbs and secret medicines, a potion bought from the voodoo queen—whoever she was. It would send Jade Terese to a heavenly plane of intoxication, a place where it would be impossible to feel pain or fear, a place where all women welcome a man's desire. Even a virgin, if she was a virgin. It did not last very long, a couple of hours, but it would be enough. It was very expensive, and the Madame used it sparingly. Once in a situation similar to Jade Terese's. For Angel on the eve of her death.

Mercedes held her breath as the Madame looked for a moment irritated. "My friend had mentioned that the potion might be best. Perhaps she does need a little help acting the part. Very well—"

The two menservants appeared, holding Jade's arms, half dragging her, half holding her up. Mercedes quickly assessed the damage, searching for signs of physical injury, though it was not likely the Madame would damage the physical beauty she meant to sell. Jade wore only the thin orange silk robe, her hair falling over that in chaotic disarray. Tears streaked her pale face. The two men brought her to the bed and pushed her down.

"Don't disappoint me, Mercedes."

"Yes, Madame," Mercedes said, nodding curtly as the Madame and her servants shut the door.

Mercedes went quickly to Jade's side. Jade stiffened with alarm until Mercedes whispered, "Jade Terese. It's me—Mercedes."

"Mercedes . . ." A trembling hand reached to touch the voice before she fell into Mercedes's arms. "Did you hear her scream?"

"Who?"

"My servant, Maydrian!" With a trembling voice Jade told of the nightmare she had just survived. "Maydrian, poor old Maydrian, is tied and bound in the basement. She was being tortured . . . somehow. I couldn't see, and the stench, the terrible stench, and I couldn't see! Maydrian was screaming." Jade squeezed her eyes shut as if to escape the memory. "A horrible muffled sound . . . The Madame made me fall to my knees to save her. I told her she would be hung for this, tarred and feathered, pillared and then hung, that she was too horrid to be believed. She slapped me! She says she will let me tell my sorry story to the constable tonight, that he is one of her most loyal customers. Is that true? Can that be true?"

"I am afraid that the constable often visits this house. The Madame pays him very well for his protection."

Jade stiffened, her thoughts tumbling with confusion and incredulity over this world gone mad. "She said she will be happy to kill the old woman if I do not prostitute myself tonight, doing exactly as she commands. So! I said do you think I can believe this? That you will not kill Maydrian? For how can you ever let her go now? She would go straight to the convent.

"Then, dear Lord, Maydrian started screaming again and the Madame laughed when I started screaming to stop it. She says she will never let Maydrian go, that she would let her continue serving me in my new position and whether or not the dear old woman had a good day or a difficult one would depend entirely on my obedience." Panicked breaths came fast and hard. "She can't do this to me, she can't. I've got to save Maydrian! I've got to get out of here. I must escape—"

Mercedes pulled back, her hands holding Jade's shoulders for support. "Jade Terese, there is no escape. The house is full of her servants, posted at every door every hour of the day. There are women who have been here for years and have not found a way to escape."

"How can that be? I don't believe you!"

"You must. I beg you." In an impassioned whisper she said, "The Madame is a dangerous woman; a beast lives inside her. She would make you beg for death over and over before she'd ever grant you the mercy. I have seen this. Many, many times."

"She murders people?"

Mercedes paused, unwilling to discuss details. She had been here three years, and in that time she knew of four slaves who had disappeared, and two of the women. And only once was attention called to the hideousness of the Madame's evil: when one poor little girl leaped from the rooftop to escape the Madame's punishment.

Mercedes did not want this to happen to Jade.

Something alerted Jade to the magnitude of this implausible and yet all too horrifying reality. She reached a hand to Mercedes's face. Slowly her fingers found the tense lines of fear etched in Mercedes's forehead, the slight tremble of her lips. She felt Mercedes's pain, bought by her unnatural existence here. She felt the young woman's terrible longing to escape.

Unanswered desire. Mother Francesca said the unanswered desire is Satan's torment, the worst fate, and until she'd felt the magnitude of Mercedes's longing, she had not fully grasped what this had meant.

"What about you? How long have you been here?"

"Three years now. And one month, five days."

The words hung heavily in the silence. "Were you brought here by force as well?"

"Yes." Mercedes stood up suddenly. .

Jade heard her trembling sigh. She had turned away, putting her back to where Jade sat as if to hide her emotions, while mentally debating what to say. "I was born on Saint Dominique," she began in a changed voice, one curiously devoid of emotion. For to court the emotions behind her words felt more dangerous than a descent to Madame's basement. "My family was wealthy. I grew up in a beautiful plantation house. We called it Belle Saint Bleu. It was, I'm afraid, the last place I knew happiness. . . .

" 'Twas a large airy house that sat on a high cliff overlooking the sea. Sometimes if I close my eyes and remember, I can feel the salt breeze blowing through my bedroom windows, and I see a stretch of the crystal-blue sea and white sand beach, edged by row after row of sugarcane and the lush green jungle beyond.

"I was ten when my papa sent me to a convent in faraway Montparnasse in Paris. I had rarely been off our land, never once off the island, and after the long voyage, I found Paris so large and strange, noisy and filthy. I was not happy there. I was used to a lush green island, the beautiful sea, to going barefoot and riding my pony on the white sand beaches beneath a tropical sun. The other girls singled me out for my accent, and difference. I was so lonely there! I was allowed one letter home each month. Every faithful letter I sent begged my father to let me come home. He always promised he would send for me the next year. Then the next year and the next.

"I was thirteen when he died."

"Oh, I'm sorry."

Mercedes shrugged unseen, her finger tracing a smooth line at the scrupulously clean windowsill where she stood. "I barely remember him now. I received a letter from my brother, who of course had inherited Belle Saint Bleu, and he too, promised to send for me soon. But within two years he had lost everything at the gaming tables, everything: our land, over a hundred slaves and the house, all the servants, even the house servants. I have not heard from him since. I sometimes wonder if he is dead or if he has just deserted me.

"Anyway, the Sisters had little choice but to put me to labor, and I was given a matter of months to choose between the holy vows or a position as a servant in a nearby house. I was ill suited to the vows; I am too sensitive to doubts, and I do not like the confines of such a cloistered and quite existence."

On the heels of a thoughtful pause she explained: "I know that I was too in love with my dreams. Sometimes I wonder if God is . . ." She felt the hot sting of tears and for a moment it shocked her.

Mercedes stood very still, confused, quite unable to continue, when Jade did it for her. "Punishing you now?" she asked quietly. "Punishing a young girl for enchanting dreams made of beautiful seas and white sand beaches, of a place where she could be loved and love again? Not the God of mercy and compassion."

Mercedes swung around to stare at Jade, struck by the poetry of her words. But what could she know? The young lady too, had been cloistered in a convent, and God knows, 'twas a world apart from a harlot's sinful existence.

Mercedes stepped to the fresh dressing water, where she bathed her hands to rid them of the dust from the sill. She thought of little Missy, her favorite, of the day she leaped from the rooftop to her death. A merciful God? A compassionate God?

"Well, I made my choice." Her smile disappeared as she dried her hands and folded the yellow towel neatly on the table. "It was a mistake. I was dismissed after less than a month of my new life."

"What happened?"

A pause followed a bitter sigh. "I was apparently not vigilant enough in warding off the Madame's husband's advances. She dismissed me and dispatched a letter of dismissal to the convent, and this prevented me from ever returning. So, foolishly, I decided to set off for the Mediterranean. It was my hope that I would find work until I could afford passage back to Saint Dominique. I planned to swallow my pride and beg the mercy of our good neighbors. I don't know what I was thinking, it seems so foolish and naive now: a young woman with no means or family to protect her. I was accosted in the seaside town of Biarritz and forced aboard a ship heading here to Orleans."

The voyage to New Orleans appeared regularly in Mercedes's nightmares. Those few times she referred to it in the light of day, she found that the years had mercifully reduced it to vague glimpses and pictures of a young girl's worst nightmare. She had awaked from a daze in this very room with a man's weight on top of her. She had screamed. The first descent to the Madame's basement had been her last. Life as she now knew it began the next day.

"What happened? How did you end up here?"

"The captain of the ship had false papers that claimed I was a tried and convicted criminal of France, sentenced to seven years of indentureship. The Madame bought my papers."

Mercedes never let herself reflect on all that had happened to her. She shared her history to make Jade see that it was impossible to escape and that the sooner she accepted this the easier it would be. Yet the weight and oppression of her story broke through her protective walls. She tried to recover, quickly wiping a lone tear sliding down her cheek.

Jade did not need sight to perceive the emotions gathering in the room, and guided only by the quiet sound of Mercedes's breaths, she rose and with an outstretched arm, she made her way to Mercedes's side at the window.

Mercedes turned to find Jade there.

The extreme wealth of Jade's compassion would not have been a surprise to anyone who knew her: it stretched to include all of humanity, from the uncouth drunkard lying in the mud to Mad King George himself and everyone between. Indeed, the Ursuline Sisters often watched Jade work miracles with it. . . .

Mercedes was unfamiliar with the largeness of Jade's sympathies, but the very love and compassion she spoke of marked her face. One look into the sweetness there broke something deep inside her.

Jade held Mercedes in her slender arms, gently stroking her soft curly hair as she wept. Her thoughts turned this terrifying situation over a dozen times.

It was impossible to escape. For now. For however long that beastly woman held Maydrian hostage. She would have to play this part until Maydrian was released or—

Jade closed her eyes tight. Dear Lord, please save Maydrian! Do not let her suffer more or be killed!

She thought of Maydrian's three daughters and that good woman's grandchildren, how much they loved the old woman. How much she herself loved old Maydrian. She would not shorten her life. No matter what. . . .

So she'd have to do this tonight, perhaps tomorrow and until Maydrian was safe. Or until somehow she could get a message out to alert Mother Francesca and Father Nolte of this hellhole and its suffering without endangering Maydrian.

Tonight. She could do it. Many women had done it. Women bedded men all the time. She knew the bare facts

of the physical act. She would just pretend she was somewhere else. For one night . . .

For she knew her fate had been tied to this poor suffering soul for the greater purpose. She had been sent here by
a greater design to rescue Mercedes.

It was all meant to happen. . . .

Mon Amour,

*You must visit Madame Charmane's house tonight—
the night of the full moon.*
Important.

Marie Saint

Victor took the note from the tray, read it and passed it
to Sebastian. He had hired a new cook, an old woman
named Chachie, on his father's recommendation. Tonight's
dinner of fried oysters, red beans and rice, spicy corn
bread and stuffed artichoke hearts was worth a month's
pay. At least. "That lady is getting a raise," Victor said as
he motioned his servant Reed to clear the plates. The men
at the table: Murray, Sebastian, John and Steffan, two of
their foremen, all growled agreement. "Reed, ask Chachie
if she's married yet, if she wouldn't mind an older man
who appreciates a woman's talents?"

Reed cleared the table with a chuckle. "Will do, sir."

Sebastian read the short note twice. Victor had never
said what had been between him and Marie Saint, the
beautiful quadroon woman and one of the city's most re-
vered and eccentric citizens. Marie reserved the affection-
ate title "amour" for Victor, while the mere mention of
Marie's name always brought a glimmer of fondness,
mixed inexplicably with some secret regret or sorrow.

Victor had known Marie Saint since he was a boy of
twelve and Marie was a young lady of fifteen. Apparently
as Victor's mother, Claire, had become more ill, his father
heard of Marie's mother's talents and, desperate to save
his wife, they had journeyed here to New Orleans to seek

out the woman. Marie's mother could not save Claire, but her potions had given Claire six months of freedom from her pain, months Victor had said he would "remember always."

Marie's mother had something to do with Victor's father's joining the priesthood too. Father Nolte had been a theologian teaching at Virginia's College of William and Mary when his wife had first become ill. All Victor would say about it was that Marie's mother had offered his father unusual counsel after his mother's death, counsel that led him by a roundabout path to a faraway retreat for priests in Scotland. Sebastian only knew part of the story. Apparently Father Nolte had left his son in a boarding school in Boston, a school fatefully close to the shipping yard. Victor had lasted less than a month in this conventional setting before he signed up as deck hand on a clipper sailing to the Orient. After a few years, his gifts had landed him a spot in a London shipbuilding firm where he began amassing the knowledge and skill of ship design and building—and eventually enough of a fortune to start his own company back in America. Then some years later, at his father's and Governor Claigbourne's request, he had returned to New Orleans, where he renewed his liaison with Marie.

Presently Sebastian asked, "Is this not that ghastly overpriced brothel? The one frequented by some of our most favored adversaries?"

Victor nodded as the coffee was poured. "The very one."

"Why," Sebastian remembered, "I believe we went there once, about three years ago, just before you left for the war. A pretty little redheaded girl was being auctioned like chattel." His tone changed, his voice outraged as if it were Victor's fault, "You Americans are so barbaric! Anything can happen here. The worst things do!" He shook his head with disdain. "Which, I suppose, is just what one would predict in a country governed by a flimsy piece of paper."

Murray looked up to point out, "Better a constitution of laws than some mad king's psychotic whims, or a despot's mad quest for power." This of course referred to Napoleon. "Flimsy piece of paper indeed," he mumbled. Sebastian's aristocratic ideology always irritated his Irish utilitarian sensibilities. "And I don't think whorehouse auctions are discussed in the United States Constitution."

Yet Sebastian was hardly listening as he remembered the pretty redheaded girl and her terrible fear, his own outrage. He had been about to kill the eager bidders when Victor had stopped him, then taught him how to handle one of this city's more uncivilized practices.

"Aye," Victor said, wrapping a large hand around a cup of steaming coffee as he dumped a good deal too much sugar into the cup. "Marie's been after the lady of the house for over two years now. Charlemagne or something. A little girl, a servant, apparently flung herself from the rooftop back then."

Murray looked up from his plate of pecan pie and muttered a curse.

"I remember that," Steffan said. "Didn't you tell the men to stay away from there?"

"Aye." Victor nodded. "For Marie. The lady claimed it was an accident, but Marie said she saw the girl's terror in a dream, that the little girl was trying to escape a torment of some kind."

"What about Girod?" Murray asked.

"Hell," Victor swore. "He probably collects a clean ten percent off the top."

"Well!" Sebastian stood up and grinned, seeing a bit of excitement for the evening. "What say you?"

"Not tonight." Victor shook his head. "I need to go down to the shipyard tonight and check those rafters they were putting up. Then later I'm meeting with Claighborne. Ride over to Marie's and ask her if you can take my place. And Sebastian"—Victor's eyes narrowed but a lift of grin gave him away—"do try to exercise a little restraint with that sword of yours, will you? If Don Bernardo is there tonight, you just might discover if his dull wits have generated a suspicion of the town's new player."

"You always ask too much, Vic," Sebastian said as he motioned for their mounts to be brought up.

John, Steffan and Sebastian turned their horses from the quiet streets of the garden district and headed straight for the heart of town. New Orleans was an exercise in contrasts, and Canal Street revealed them all, neatly separating the Creole east side from the new American west, and so, offering something for everyone. Taverns, gaming houses, restaurants and brothels flourished alongside honest shops and businesses, modest residences, two churches and a hospital.

The day had started bright and beautiful, but like an angry mistress, the sky darkened and now threatened rain. A smooth canopy of menacing clouds hung motionless in the evening sky and covered the light of a full moon. The air felt oppressive, hot, humid and like potent wine, stirring souls to restlessness. Outside Marie's house, Steffen parted from the rest and headed back to Victor's town mansion with her message. She insisted Victor go to Charmane's. The clairvoyant had dreamt of Victor at the house and Marie Saint did not ignore any warning given in a dream. . . .

Madame Charmane's house was in full swing when John and Sebastian arrived. Sebastian spent several minutes flirting with two pretty hostesses before John finally managed to pull him away. The gaming room appeared relatively deserted. Everyone seemed to be in the barroom; something was happening there.

Men packed the large black-and-white marble squares of the space, crowding every table as well as the stools lining the mirrored bar. Comely women, scantily clad, served drinks. Thick smoke and fumes of hard liquor filled the air, already heavy with a near-deafening sound of drunken talk and laughter. Sebastian's gaze flew about the large room, seeking Don Bernardo.

Just as Victor had suspected. Don Bernardo and his

crew were there, occupying the far corner of the room.
Sebastian smiled as his gaze settled on the large, corpulent
Spaniard. He sat partially turned around, so Sebastian
viewed his profile. His long wiry dark hair made a plait
down his back. Sebastian's dancing eyes greeted this oddity. It would make such a fine trophy! He would decorate
it with red ribbons and hang it on his saddle. The huge
man's face, made grotesquely larger by a full beard,
showed numerous signs of one too many fights. What
bothered Sebastian the most were the man's eyes; they
were eyes that flashed with the same emotion whether killing or wenching. As usual, the pirate laughed loudly and
boisterously.

"Madonna," Sebastian whispered to John, "look who's
with the bastard."

None other than one of the two Laffite brothers, perhaps
the only men Victor disliked more than Don Bernardo. Pi-
rating normally kept the brothers busy and away on their
little island; this was a rare appearance. Leaning back and
appearing disinterested, even bored, the tall red-haired
man's pretense of respectability disgusted Sebastian. The
Laffites alone were responsible for more rapes, murders
and other bloodthirsty cutthroating than most of the other
so-called privateers combined.

"Can you tell which weasel it is?" Sebastian asked,
never able to tell the brothers apart.

John, himself a huge, quiet man, known for his good
humor and able fighting, shrugged. "I have trouble with
weasels but I believe it's the lesser of evils. Pierre."

They made their way across the room, greeting friends
as they passed. The sumptuous chamber smacked of the
ostentatious. Elegant chandeliers strategically lit the thirty
or so tables. A huge marble fireplace dominated the side
of the room opposite the bar. Outrageous tapestries depict-
ing naked nymphs in frantic orgy scenes hung on the
walls. Sebastian swallowed his good taste as they assumed
two seats at the bar, positions that offered a complete view
of the room. Drinks were ordered.

"There's about twelve of them. How many do you think you could handle, John? Just in case."

"Ah, well, I feel lucky tonight. Three or four. Just in case."

Sebastian liked the odds. He then turned to the bartender, an elderly Negro man, and asked what was happening, in hopes of discovering why Marie Saint had insisted that Victor be there.

"Madame is offering a young lady on the block," he replied, scrutinizing the young man. Mercedes had told him of Madame's cruelty upstairs, and while he had worked in the house too long to be surprised, the trick she'd pulled on the new girl seemed particularly wicked. The least he could do was what Mercedes asked, encourage the nicer-looking men to bid. "She is more beautiful than can be believed. You will bid, no?"

"I'm afraid not, old man. Buying a woman's favors takes half the pleasure out of having them."

The old man liked that answer and he smiled back. Sebastian saw nothing in the situation to warrant calling Victor, but he turned to John. "Have you ever witnessed one of these auctions?"

"A few. They never really set right with me. I look at the girl up there and then at all the bastards watching her, and well, it makes me think of my little sister. And then my blood heats up and my knuckles need cracking."

Sebastian nodded understanding. "It's not so bad if the lady's enjoying the attention, playing up the part. But I'll never forget the first time I witnessed one. I had just arrived in New Orleans with Vic about three years ago. We were right here, too, in this house. This pretty little redhead was put up there, and to this day I've never seen a girl looked as frightened. Vic held me back from killing the bidders and all he said that wasn't the way you do it. He was right, too. Vic waited for the last bid, he doubled it, paid the money, and without saying so much as a word to the girl, he left."

"That's Vic, all right."

The young lady was escorted out. Ripples of murmured awe first swept over the crowd, quickly breaking into lusty exclamations. Sebastian turned, beheld Mademoiselle Devon, and lapsed in a state of shock.

She appeared as every man's most fanciful dream. The long dark hair, pulled to one side, cascaded over a bare shoulder before falling to her waist. She held her head high, her cheeks flushed hot. She wore only a maroon velvet corset, the dark color accenting the whiteness of her skin while revealing every curve of her slender figure for the pleasure of the crowd: the full thrust of her uplifted breasts that tapered to a waist as narrow and slim as a child's before the gentle flair of her hips and her unbelievably long shapely legs.

No one saw the rope holding her elbows behind her back or the strand of hair tied into a knot to force her head up, but only the most insensitive failed to notice that her eyes were closed in abject shame.

John let out his breath in a whistle, and like every man there, suddenly swallowed his drink whole.

"Mademoiselle Devon," Sebastian whispered, finding his voice. The reason Marie wanted Victor here. "My God, it's Mademoiselle Devon!"

Watching from the bar, Madame Charmane overheard Sebastian's recognition and, quickly hiding her panic, she approached the two men. "You know my Mary?"

"Mary?" The name did not suit her, he thought. "Apparently not," he said, more than surprised the young lady was one who made her way in a brothel. He turned to the woman suspiciously and demanded, "Where did you get her?"

Madame Charmane smiled brightly as lies came effortlessly to her lips. "She has been with me for over a year now."

"A year? I can't believe it!" Sebastian shook his head. He then explained how he had briefly met her at the opera just the other evening. "She gave the impression of an innocent and rather charming maiden, and her blindness. . . .

Why, I believe Victor saw her escorted by ... well ..."
He paused, momentarily searching for words. "We had
thought she was someone's mistress."

The Madame's laughter held her relief. "I assure you,
Mary's days of innocence are long gone. She fools many
men about that; it is her repertoire; it is also why she is the
house favorite, the reason the bidding will go high. Men
love to destroy what only they can—a woman's innocence.
Few even care that it's only a clever illusion. It's even better that way," she finished, turning away. "Enjoy."

The bidding began. Within minutes most men were
priced out. All too soon only three bidders remained: two
wealthy landowners and, to Sebastian's consternation, Don
Bernardo himself. The price rose. Sebastian kept looking
from Don Bernardo to Mary and back again. He shuddered
and felt ill; the thought of that blackguard's foul hands on
the sweet, beautiful lady sent the unpleasant taste of bile to
his throat. Even if he didn't have to win Mary for Victor,
he'd certainly not be able to stand by and let such a treasure go to Don Bernardo.

One of the landowners reluctantly opted out, his friends
hissing with disappointment. Don Bernardo raised the
other man's bid, accepting the help of Laffite, who no
doubt would share in the spoils. The other man raised his
cup to the pirate's last bid. A last call sounded. Sebastian
waited for the final sound and just as he was about to double Don Bernardo's last bid, a voice from behind did it for
him.

Chapter 4

All eyes turned to confront the tall man standing at the entrance. He needed no introduction. Dressed in black—black boots, black breeches and an open gray riding vest over a white shirt—his towering presence radiated a quiet, threatening air as his fine cold blue eyes focused sharply on the girl.

Jade jolted at the sound of the last bid. The American? Dear Lord, was it him? Of all the people in the world to see her like this—not him! Anyone but him!

The silence broke with a hearty bellow from Don Bernardo, and unhesitating, he bid again. Murmurs rose in the crowd. Silence descended as everyone turned back to Victor, waiting.

Victor doubled the bid again.

The men turned to Don Bernardo once more. Followed by two of his men, Victor moved to Sebastian, who quickly explained. Victor stared at the Mademoiselle Devon whose Christian name Sebastian said was a plain Mary. "And she's worked here for over a year," Sebastian added.

"Has she now?"

Victor tried unsuccessfully to believe what he saw. A wicked amusement rose in his eyes as he tried to reconcile the startlingly beautiful and seductive woman with the charming and lovely young lady he had met at the opera. It was impossible! She had seemed so beguilingly ... innocent. The extreme gentleness of her character so pronounced that it had become manifest in an amusing concern for the city's stray dogs, a riverboat man's impoverished morals. "Sebastian," he said under his breath, "it would have been easier to believe she was a convent girl."

"Easier perhaps, but not nearly as entertaining." Sebastian grinned, motioning to the bartender to pour another drink.

Victor chuckled as he raised his glass. "To Marie, who somehow always knows the secrets of my desire. . . ."

Don Bernardo raised the bid again.

The price didn't matter; Victor would have Mary at any cost, but he wasn't going to waste any more time. Followed by his men, he approached the pirates' table. He offered Pierre the briefest nod as he leveled his gaze on the Spaniard and said simply: "I will ask you once: withdraw your last bid."

Laftite slammed down his cup. The explicit threat, its enormous arrogance, stunned him. This was too much. "You go too far! Do you know who you're speaking to?"

"Rest assured," Sebastian said, "your reputation follows you like maggots to manure."

Two of Laftite's men jumped up, but only to find Sebastian's rapier and sword pointed at their throats. Laftite motioned them down. The men slowly lowered back into their chairs.

"Look around you, Nolte," Don Bernardo said, unconcerned, rubbing his beard thoughtfully as he leaned casually back in his chair. "Even you must admit, the odds are not even."

What Victor did next shocked everyone in the room. He looked around the room, assessed the numbers, and he ordered Steffan and his other man out of the room. "There, now." He turned back to Don Bernardo. "I evened the odds for you."

Sebastian burst out laughing and Don Bernardo was just about to tell Victor to go to hell when Victor—who never fought fairly and never took the first blow—made his move. He kicked the underside of the pirate's chair, sent Don Bernardo falling to the floor in a most undignified manner, and before anyone jumped up, he turned the table into Laftite.

Victor bent over, swung around and up, and slammed a hand into one man's stomach while kicking another. Two men jumped him, but never came close as Victor merely anticipated, blocked and struck without mercy. Swords, sabers and an occasional fist or two slammed at him from all directions but only to find him ducking, jumping, escaping each blow and moving with lightning speed to disarm before his arms and more often his feet struck back.

At Victor's first move, John had sprung on Laftite, hoping to save Victor the added trouble of a particularly menacing opponent.

In perfect harmony with his first laugh, Sebastian struck the three men on his side, with a straight line of blood drawn neatly across their chests. He sliced off their shirts, rapier and sword flying simultaneously, and before a groan was uttered, Sebastian cut bright red X's into their chests. A mark more humiliating than painful, the cuts would scar, and so they'd be worn to the grave. Two other men never managed to withdraw their swords before they fell victim to his speed and skill. He faced three long swords and a saber and the result was a furious clanging of metal. . . .

The room had cleared to one side, allowing the men ample room to fight, and in typical New Orleans fashion, bets were placed on the outcome. Madame Charmane had, of course, called her bodyguards to the scene, but hardly knew which side to send them in on. Don Bernardo had always been a good customer but on the other hand she had always wanted Monsieur Nolte and his men's business. After watching for a few minutes, she shrugged and decided to let the men decide themselves. She left to see to Mary.

Victor finished off five men before he managed to turn back to Don Bernardo. The chair was empty, the pirate gone. He swore softly as, to the crowd's astonishment, he sat down at a table and passively watched Sebastian and John finish the group off.

Laftite lay moaning on the floor, his face bruised and bloody, and another man in a similar state lay next to him. John, with only a bloody nose and a bruised eye to show for his trouble, smiled triumphantly as he, too, took a seat at the table.

Sebastian's victims sprawled out in an almost perfect half circle around him. Blood covered everyone and everything nearby. While the motionless men looked headed for hell, the vast majority of the wounds were superficial. Each wore Sebastian's red X. The last man, being no fool, tossed in his saber and ran from the room.

"I do hate cowards," Sebastian said breathlessly as he assumed a chair at the table.

John shook his head as he surveyed the scene with obvious disapproval. "You make such a bloody mess of them, Sebastian. It's archaic, cutting people up like that. Look at Vic's side, the bastards crumpled into neat piles, no blood ... hell, hardly a bruise."

Victor grinned in apparent agreement.

"It's the only way I know." Sebastian still sounded breathless and excited. Servants and bodyguards alike began clearing away the wounded and unconscious. Madame Charmane approached the three men. A servant followed behind her, carrying a tray with three glasses and the finest house brandy.

"That's her, the Madame," Sebastian said.

"Yes. I recall."

"Congratulations." She smiled as though the fight were nothing more than a card game. "Brandy, gentlemen?"

"Where is the lady?" Victor asked in a demand.

"She is upstairs, waiting for you in our best room."

Victor studied the woman for a brief moment, knew he did not like her, and not just in honor of Marie's sentiments. He did not hide the fact. "I'll have her at my house."

"As you wish," she replied, knowing Monsieur Nolte

was not a man to be dissuaded. It didn't matter. She owned Mary's obedience now, and she had taken the concoction. "The pleasure will cost more, Monsieur."

Removing a money clip, Victor tossed three bills on the table. Madame motioned to the servant, who quickly swept up the bills. Then she left again, to give Mary new instructions before she lost all sense and coherency.

John shook his head as he splashed the brandy into a glass. "I suppose I've known my share of the working wenches, but I've never seen a treasure quite as beautiful."

" 'Tis a flawed treasure after all," Sebastian said. "She's blind, you know."

"Blind?" Like so many others, John reacted with surprise. "I knew there had to be a flaw," he said, repeating a common thought. "Nature does not create such perfection."

"Aye," Sebastian said, still somewhat breathless from his exertions. "Still, there is something more than a little odd about her being up there, do you not think so? Her beauty alone would open the wealthiest men's pocketbooks, add to that her charm, intelligence, her humor. Victor," he said, his voice lowering with suspicion, "that very same lady who just auctioned her flesh to the highest bidder was blushing like a schoolgirl at our rather tame story, as I recall. That Madame claimed her innocent was a well-acted farce but—"

"Well-acted farce?" Victor questioned, and then laughed. "One could not find a better performance in a London theater—she could make a fortune as an actress. And didn't I mention that I inquired into Monsieur Deubler's mistresses, only to be told he kept none. "This"—he motioned toward the room—"certainly explains their relationship."

"I don't know." Sebastian shook his head. "Just think of what she was wearing that night. Remember? Now, granted her beauty makes advertising particularly unnecessary, but I've seen more seductive gowns on house-keepers—"

John shook his head, recalling many youthful mistakes he had made in the judgment of a woman's experience, expensive mistakes. "Lots of women play the innocent with absolutely no flaw or sign of the sham," he said, and laughed at the thought. "Why, one time I'll never forgot this pretty little lady . . ."

Jade waited in a small room, her emotions raging and turbulent. Mercedes had given her a laced glass of wine to calm her down, but this was impossible. The afternoon's terror fueled the fires of fear and consumed all thoughts. The Madame had entered Mercedes's room and found them wrapped in an intimate, tender embrace, Mercedes crying in her arms. As if the Madame had suddenly realized her threats and Maydrian's screams were not enough to receive her obedience, she had taken her back to the basement and . . .

Do not think of it.

Could it really have been he who had walked through those doors and called the last outrageous bid? Was it really him? Or was it some cruel trick played on her by her desperate mind? How could it be he, of all men in the entire world, to know her as a whore, a woman who bedded men and took money for her love?

Her thoughts felt fragmented. She struggled for a clear head, desperate to reason her way out, but somehow she tumbled into panic as she tried. She didn't know what she could risk, that she could risk anything. Dear God, she was mutilating poor old Maydrian! "I will kill that old bag before anyone you might alert could find her. Remember it!"

Remember it, remember it, remember it. . . .

Madame Charmane had instructed her to accompany the American to his house, to dissuade any suspicions he might have and to act in accordance with his pleasure. His pleasure. He would take off her clothes and—

Her hands went clammy, her legs felt shaky. How could

she do that? Mercedes swore it was usually very quick, a matter of minutes. A couple of minutes for Maydrian's life, but what if . . . what if Maydrian was already dead? She was so old, almost sixty and there would be so much blood loss. Remember it, remember it, remember it. . . .

At the second sounding the Madame would send an escort to take her back. She struggled to think of how to save Maydrian. Fate was dealing her a card, she reasoned shakily. He had wanted to take her away from here to his house. This was the time to act. If she just pretended to be this, this woman who bedded men for money until she was safely away from here? Then if she alerted Mother Francesca and Father Nolte . . . But weren't they far away in Baton Rouge? Or had they come back?

With alarm she realized she didn't even know what day it was. A distressed hand went to her forehead, only to realize she moved too slowly.

Think! It they were still gone and she could not appeal to the constable either, then who would save Maydrian? Would the poor woman be dead by then?

Think, think, think. . . .

Thinking felt so taxing all of a sudden, like climbing a steep hill weighted with heavy packages. Her legs felt heavy, her heated blood seemed to slow and warm by degrees. She tried to imagine frail old Sister Mary and Sister Catherine marching into Madame Charmane's house of ill repute demanding Maydrian's safety, yet falling faint at the first sight of a woman's undergarments.

No, no, 'twould never do.

Who else, who else? She knew the mayor. She seized the thought. It was followed by the realization that she knew many, many people and by the time she told any one of them, Maydrian would be dead.

Dear Lord, she might already be dead from blood loss alone. She had begged to be taken to her but the Madame only laughed. "In due time, Mary. . . ."

The words sounded in a curious slow echo through her mind. She wondered if she might faint. What was wrong with her? She felt hot and flushed, as if sitting next to a raging fire.

Just pretend until she was taken from this house. She'd tell the American . . . She'd tell him . . .

She felt a servant's hand on her arm to escort her out. She started forward slowly, with great difficulty. Another hand came to her for support. They stopped. She found herself concentrating so hard on appearing normal that she didn't realize men were rising out of their chairs until she heard the American's greeting followed by introductions. She felt Victor's hand guide her to a chair. She closed her eyes, bit her lip and forced herself still as he studied her.

Don't cry. Dear God, just don't cry—

Victor drank in the sight of her, unable to believe it was really her, unable to believe any woman could be that beautiful. Obviously, she was afraid. She lowered her head and closed her eyes while her arms crossed her bosom, each hand rested on a shoulder, hiding what other women in the house flaunted. There seemed two possible explanations for her fear: she was afraid of that woman or she was afraid of him.

"I'm sure you understand my surprise at finding you here, Mary? That is your name, is it not?"

The question caused a slight visible jerk. 'Twas his same voice. The American she had met. Mary. Yes. She nodded, feeling her warm blood pounding in a curious slow thud.

"Mary." He said her name with a curious chuckle. "The name ill suits you." There was masculine amusement in his voice as he reached to brush a stray wisp of hair from her face, the intimate gesture causing a startling rush of shivers. She felt suddenly warm. "Rather like calling the Black Prince's ruby a piece of rock. Is it true that you've worked here for over a year?"

She nodded again. "Yes, Monsieur."

On the heels of a long pause that filled with his scrutiny, he said: "Why do I think you're lying, sweetheart?"

Why? Dear lord, what could she say? She struggled for

a coherent thought but she felt so strangely dizzy. The silence grew as they waited her response and her silent panic mounted. How many? How many men stared at her now?

"You are lying—"

"No, no, Monsieur." She shook her head, sending a river of dark hair sliding over her shoulder. "Please, you cannot expect me to answer why you think that, why you think anything. I do not know. Many men are surprised."

Laughter erupted from the men around her. The man Sebastian was saying something about a line forming that reached to the Gulf of Mexico. More laughter followed the remark. Someone got up from the gaming table, the man named John. She wondered if she should smile but by the time she finished wondering, it seemed like time had stretched and slowed. She reached a distressed hand to her forehead. Victor was speaking to her but she could hardly grasp his words. . . .

"I had thought you might be Monsieur Deubler's mistress; I even made inquiries but was told that Monsieur Deubler does not keep a mistress and never has."

Victor waited her response, watching closely. He had started to make another inquiry concerning the lovely lady Monsieur Deubler had escorted that night, only to sense this would be a mistake. He could not even say why, past the fleeting understanding—considering the circumstances now, an obviously mistaken understanding—that she would not be a casual affair and perhaps selfishly, but certainly rationally, he knew he could never offer anything more to a young lady who suffered from sightlessness.

"So was this Monsieur Deubler a patron?"

The Madame watched from across the room with increasing anxiety, an anxiety she rarely had cause to feel. She felt a tremor of alarm. Perhaps she should return his money and withdraw the girl—

No, he would be more suspicious. . . .

She motioned to Mercedes to intervene.

Jade tried to focus on the words of his questions long

enough to generate an appropriate reply but somehow her mind seized only the dear name. What had happened to Monsieur Deubler? What he injured or, dear God, was he dead? She tried desperately to reason if this inquiry had concluded or if perhaps he had discovered her true identity, and as she struggled, his hand reached gently under her chin, turning her face to him.

A sea of beautiful colors swam through her mind, startlingly vivid, drawn from the long-ago time when she could see. They were so pretty! For a long moment they held her spellbound. . . .

Victor watched her closely. Oh no, he thought, she was too beautiful for this house. Indeed, seeing her here was like finding a royal gem in a pawnshop. She kept her lashes closed over those jeweled unseeing eyes; the thick black lashes brushing the high flushed cheeks. Lips the color of dark red wine and set on the palest of complexions, skin—his finger brushed her cheek—as soft as a kitten's underside. There was something wrong here. . . .

"Is it drink or opium, sweetheart?"

A slight gasp escaped her lips. He was so clever! She struggled to find an answer, the right one, hardly knowing whether she should confess or deny when suddenly Mercedes did it for her.

"It is a potion," Mercedes said as she came to the table, still reeling from the heady relief of seeing the man who had made the last bid. "The Madame permits this only on nights of an auction. Just enough to enhance rather than inhibit desire."

Victor still stared, hardly taking his eyes from her. He had spent enough time in the Orient to know she was not an addict, at least not yet. Her beauty would have been lost after a month of opium addiction. Though that certainly would have explained everything.

He held her in his gaze, even as he sipped his brandy, his eyes revealing brash desire and suspicions that bordered on confusion. He looked across the room to where that woman stood watching. He suddenly just wanted his prize out of here, whether or not she was what she said she was.

He motioned to a waiting servant. "Have my horse brought 'round and fetch a cloak for the lady."

Sebastian thought it was love at first sight, and if it wasn't, the pleasure of merely watching the gorgeous creature walk to the table abruptly changed his attitude regarding the purchase of a woman's favor. She had an angel's face, a breathtaking feminine shape revealed in a pink striped gown and a smile that was at once seductive and demure. Like all men, he instantly recognized the promise in her soft hazel eyes.

Mercedes curtsied and introduced herself. Victor watched Mercedes's arm slip around Mary's shoulder. Mary reached for her friend's hand: their fingers locked quickly and tightly.

"Monsieur Nolte, I have waited many years for this opportunity to thank you for a kindness you once showed me."

Victor looked up but found nothing familiar, though he was immediately taken by her manner. Something about her spoke of a gentleness of person, uncommon in women who worked in these houses.

"You don't remember me?"

"No, I'm sorry—"

"You should, Victor." Sebastian smiled. "You once paid a fortune for her."

"I believe I'd remember such a thing."

" 'Twas years ago, Monsieur," Mercedes explained. "As tonight, you doubled the last bid, but then left without seeing me." Her eyes lowered, her sincerity obvious. "It meant a lot to me and . . . and I have thought often of your kindness since then."

"While Victor might have forgotten," Sebastian said, "I could never forget such a beautiful young lady."

Mercedes laughed lightly, met the blue eyes and felt an unexplainable flutter at Sebastian's open admiration. He was so handsome! With his blond curls and fine blue eyes, he looked like a perfect image of Adonis. "I'm flattered, Monsieur. Madame Charmane has asked me to extend the house hospitality to Monsieur Nolte's friend, to show her appreciation of his generosity tonight."

Nolte, Nolte, Nolte, the name echoed through Jade's mind. Yes. She needed to find Father Nolte but he was away. . . .

"Ah," Sebastian inquired with a lift of brow, "just what does this hospitality include?"

"Perhaps you would care to visit the sunshine corner?"

"The sunshine corner?" Sebastian repeated. His tone caused Victor to chuckle, roll his eyes. "That depends," Sebastian said. "Just who is the mistress of such a place?"

"Yours truly." Mercedes curtsied, confused by her excitement. "It would be my pleasure to show you, Monsieur."

"I will make certain of that!"

Victor chuckled again, standing up as a man finally returned with Mary's cloak. "Sebastian, I do believe you have just met your match." Turning to Mercedes, he said, "Mercedes, you are a delight. No doubt Sebastian will enjoy his visit to your 'sunshine corner.' "

Mercedes thanked Victor again before she leaned over, whispering something in Jade's ear. Jade had spend the last minutes floating on a not unpleasant sea of warm sensations; she felt as if she could actually feel the blood moving lethargically through her limbs. The whispered words pulled her back. She nodded at Mercedes as she felt Victor's arm come around her. She did not want to move, or be changed, but she grasped that he was waiting for her to stand. She stood up, and only vaguely realized she had no sense of direction.

Normally she spent many hours exploring a room's contours, her mathematical gift allowing her to remember the exact number of steps to the door or the dresser or a writing table, so as not to constantly depend on others. She had never been in this room. Her keen sense of direction was inhibited.

Her legs felt unsteady. . . .

Then for some reason her disorientation brought a prick of amusement. She was so ridiculous! "Monsieur," she said, almost laughing, "I fear I—"

Victor felt her falling weight and quickly bent over to catch her up in his arms. The long hair slid over his arm, falling in a thick mass halfway to the floor. He met the glassy, amused green eyes, only to realize the trick of it. Somehow she made a man imagine she was looking at him. "Just how bad off are we, Mary?"

The question was asked as he carried her outside.

The night air felt cool on her feverish skin but she hardly noticed, taken by the compelling timbre of his voice. "I love your voice," she told him. "It is so rich and deep and kind. . . ."

She suddenly tried to think of the terrible things that had happened to her, the reasons she should be afraid, but it seemed so long ago, as if time itself had eroded its intensity. Like a distant memory. She could only think of him, the tall American, the man named Victor. . . .

Victor was smiling down at the lovely intoxicated creature. Seeing that his horse had yet to be brought up, he set her to her feet on the wide porch, careful to keep her close and hold her steady. He noticed the oddity of velvet slippers on her feet that matched the corset. She still seemed to stare up at him. She reached a hand up to touch the textured surface of his chin. "You are so tall," she said. "How tall?"

"About six feet four."

Tall like Father Nolte. She had a crush on Father Nolte. She couldn't help it. She knew many Catholic girls had crushes on priests and she felt so foolish about it sometimes, trying to banish the thoughts, but he was just so . . . so interesting, magnetic, wonderful, like the American. . . .

He felt her hand gently trace the contours of his face— the first and only time she had dropped the pretense of sight. He held still for her, though he realized too late the innocent touch had the unnerving effect of a lightning bolt.

Jade didn't understand the warm pleasure brought by touching him. As if the nerves on the pads of her fingertips leaped up to greet this fun. "I can read physiognomy."

"I might have guessed," he replied, teased by her fingers moving feather light over his face. He had as much faith in the so-called science of physiognomy as he did in fortune-telling—which is to say none—but he was nonetheless interested in her perceptions, if indeed she even had any.

"You have a most distinguished face, Monsieur." Her fingers returned to his broad, dominating forehead to begin a closer, more specific inspection. Her nerves tingled queerly. She tried to concentrate on what his face told her about him. "You possess a formidable intelligence, one guided by logic and rationality. And these lines here are like . . ." Father Nolte's, she thought.

The name echoed in her mind like a warning, resonating softer with each beat of her heart. Suddenly her consciousness focused only on the unnaturally loud thud of her heart.

"Like who?" he asked.

She returned but forgot the question. She laughed lightly, for no reason she knew, but enough to throw her head back too far. A warm wave of dizziness washed over her in force.

"Easy, sweetheart," Victor said.

Her clumsiness made her laugh again but her curiosity was pricked. A shiver of a queer excitement raced up her spine. She breathed in his clean masculine scent, wanting to brush her hot cheek against him as she returned her hands to his face.

"What color are your eyes?"

"Blue."

"What color is your hair?"

"Dark brown."

"How old are you?"

"Thirty-one."

Jade continued and felt the lean, strong lines of his face,

the finely shaped nose. "I have never read such a strong character in a face," she said, feeling wondrously expansive suddenly. "You have enlightened views, governed by very liberal attitudes." The idea came to her that Sister Benedict would not like him, and as she imagined Sister Benedict's shock, she felt a bubble of mirth in her throat.

Yet her fingertips were gently sliding over his mouth, discovering a smile of patient amusement. "You are generous too, exceedingly generous. But here"—she traced a line and smiled—"the lines of benevolence cross with this line marking a fine temper."

Victor chuckled at last; it was only too true. He returned his gaze to the lovely upturned face. His smile disappeared. She looked suddenly feverish, her cheeks were flushed crimson, her eyes held an unnatural shine. He watched her lips tremble slightly as if she were suddenly holding back tears. "I am not afraid of you," she whispered. "I know you will not hurt me. . . ."

The words struck him somewhere deep inside, stirring a place he had never felt before, as if . . . as if the moment were misplaced in time. It was not just the lure of her startling beauty or the bright shine of her intelligence but rather the extreme fragility brought by her sightlessness, followed by the unpleasant idea of what she must have endured to reach this place. "Never," he whispered as his thumb slid under her chin. "Never."

He held her face and his lips lowered to hers. They hovered there for a long time as if measuring her response. She struggled with confusion, sensing how very close he was but not understanding why. For she had been kissed many times in her imagination but never in fact.

Black lashes fluttered over her eyes. He tenderly pressed his mouth to hers, pulling back to assess her reaction before gently kneading her bottom lip until she gasped, her lips parting slightly. One taste of unknown spices and delicious sunshine of her mouth and he wanted more. She tensed ever so lightly but as his tongue swept into her mouth with compelling eroticism, she went limp, melting into a sea of thick honeyed sensations.

The waiting groom coughed, pulling Victor up from his brief sojourn into the beckoning lure of her sensuality. He broke the kiss reluctantly. He had been afraid the potion she drank would inhibit his desire, if only by slowing hers. He saw now that he was wrong.

He gathered the reins and mounted. She stood perfectly still, which seemed like a miracle with the swirl of beautiful colors dancing abstractly through her dazed mind. A hand slowly reached to touch her lips, where she soothed the strange sensations. She wished he could kiss her again. . . .

He bent over, his large hands circling her waist to lift her up in front of him. She instinctively grabbed his upper arms as he lifted her off her feet and to the saddle. Dizziness swirled in her head, and she steadied herself by laying her head against his chest. He checked the horse's dance, and then pulled her face up to his. She could feel the scrutiny of his gaze. "I find . . . I am having a great deal of trouble thinking. . . ."

She smiled as she heard the warm sound of his laughter. "I don't believe I paid for your thoughts, much as I might want them." While he could prefer an unencumbered clear mind for the pleasure, opium, he knew, could enhance a woman's pleasure, drawing it out and leaving it shimmering for hours. Hours would not be long enough for her. "Mary Devon, my beautiful changeling, intoxicated or no, just tell me, are you my willing victim?"

"Victim . . ." Her foggy mind seized the word. She brushed her hot cheek against his clean white shirt and breathed the delicious masculine scent of him. The sensation burst into colors in her mind, a swirling rainbow of pretty colors. "Oh, yes, I am. . . ."

He started the horse forward and felt her tense slightly, her arms wrapping securely around his waist. "Have you never ridden a horse before?"

She tried to concentrate on the question. Horses. A

sweet smile lifted on her lips. "I used to ride often when I was a child." She was speaking too slowly, but the thought disappeared as vivid scenes rose in her mind again, scenes of her father's daily riding lessons. For a long moment she lost herself to the play of pretty pictures in her mind's eye. "My father wanted me to ride better than any boy in the parish. He used to tease me that ... that ... he would enter me in the parish race dressed as a boy, that I would win and as I stepped up to the winner's circle, he would remove my hat and show my face and end the argument that women can't ride ... ride—" She stopped, realizing she was repeating herself. The idea brought confusion; she forgot what she was saying. . . .

She felt as if she floated on a bright white cloud of sensation, so heavy and dreamy. He found himself smiling down at her, his suspicions melting away beneath the lilt of her sudden ease and laughter.

"You have not always been blind?"

She managed to shake her head.

"When did it happen?"

She tried to remember. Why was it so hard to remember? Why was it so hard to think? What was the question? "Oh, yes ... seven years ago ... when I was ... thirteen. Like Mercedes ..." The name echoed in mind.

"An accident?"

His question pulled her back and she nodded with a contented sigh as her finger circled a button on his shirt. She reached a timid hand to his face. Gently, light as a feather, her fingers traveled over the strong distinguished lines of his face, exploring the textures again. She touched his lips and traced the wide and sensuous lines there before touching her own lips and remembering his kiss. "I wish you would ... kiss me again."

Victor chuckled as his large warm hand brushed back her hair, his lips lightly grazing her forehead. "You know, I half wish I had the strength of will to resist you tonight, if only to wait until tomorrow when your haze disappears and I could have all of you, Mary."

She felt the brush of his lips on hers. A heated chill raced up her spine as his lips teased a spot beneath her ear. "But, sweetheart, Christ never had such temptation. I don't think I could wait an hour, Mary. . . ."

Mary. Mary, Mary, quite contrary. She wished he would not sat that name. She wished . . . she wished he would kiss her again. . . .

The horse pranced into his gravel-covered driveway.

The large two-story brick mansion was Victor's town home, used only when he was forced to come into the city and away from his country estate. The attractive house was plastered and whitewashed, and stood as one of the finest in New Orleans's affluent garden district. Large columns dominated the front of the house, giving strength to the foundation and a majestic grace to its appearance. Five long steps marked the entrance that led to broad hand-carved mahogany doors. An extensive balcony and portico encircled both the upper and lower levels. A wrought-iron fence guarded the spacious and well-tended gardens; two tall sugar maple trees and a half dozen oaks towered above the roof. A number of magnolia trees interrupted a smooth carpet of green lawn, this laced with dozens of flower beds.

Jade Terese saw none of it. She felt suddenly confused by her circumstances. She tried to remember her fear but she found it all seemed so distant now, like a nightmare upon waking. And as she thought she should be alarmed by this, as she tried to remember something, the colors returned, swirling through her mind's eye. . . .

A groom ran up. Victor swung off the horse, and gently lowered her feet to the ground, only to discover they no longer held her up. With a chuckle, he swung her light weight up to his arms.

Jade hardly knew what was happening as he carried her into a house. She was only vaguely aware of being taken indoors. Carl, Victor's butler, greeted them as they entered the hall. The small man wore dark formal attire, waistcoat and pressed pants. His dress, the crisp graying halo of hair, the handsome Negro features, all gave him a distinguished air, one Victor often thought was at odds with his irascible character. Presently a dark brow lifted as he stared curiously at the lovely young woman's provocative hair arrangement and the dreamy look on her face.

"Ah, Mademoiselle?" he inquired with a condescending grin, rocking back on his heels, waiting for Victor to let him in on the joke or ruse.

Victor knew Carl only too well, and recognized the mischief in his dark eyes. "Mary Devon," was all he supplied.

Wondering where he had heard that name before, Carl handed Victor a written message as he set the young lady to her unsteady feet. He started to relate the other messages when she seemed to be slipping. Victor's arm steadied her again. In the movement Carl caught a glance of her clothes beneath the cloak, or lack thereof. His eyes widened with sudden mirth. She wore only a corset. He supposed he should expect such increasingly desperate tactics from the multitudes of women frequenting this house. "Mademoiselle"—his grin was all farce—"you must have dashed out in a hurry tonight."

She had no idea he was talking to her, even that he was talking. Carl watched her slipping with alarm, and thought to extend the courtesy of warning Victor. "Perhaps you should catch her up again before she totters."

Victor bent over and swept her off her feet again. He passed quick instructions as he headed up the stairs. "Cancel my Sunday engagements. My father is expected back."

"High time," Carl replied.

Victor cast an annoyed glance at him.

"There are a few other messages."

"Tomorrow, Carl . . ." At his bedchamber, Victor shut the door. He carried her to the enormous four-poster bed and set her gently on the velvet coverlet before turning to open the balcony doors. The room was so warm. She unclasped the cloak and laid back, luxuriating in the softness and velvet. So happy to be in a bed. Like her parents' bed.

A smile came with the thought . . .

Two lamps threw gold light into the beautiful and lux-
uriant spaciousness of the unusual room. Done in rich
blues and dark greens, the room had heavy furnishings
made of smooth ebony, cut in straight lines and shining
like black velvet. The furniture had been brought with
great care from the Orient. Stunning seascapes hung on the
walls: pictures of magnificent, bold ships sailing violent
and stormy seas . . .

He stood for a moment in the now open balcony doors,
then turned to remove his vest. "Would you care for dinner, or a small supper—" He stopped as his gaze came to
rest on her. He released his breath with a soft curse.

She drifted on a dreamy haze. In this haze of colors and
pure sensation she knew no fear. There was no past or future or indeed any time at all. There were only brilliant
colors beneath her closed lids. . . .

She did not know how long she laid there before she realized someone stood over her. He was saying something.
". . . you look like an angel and taste like the heavens . . ."

She reached out for him with a beckoning smile.
"Please . . ."

She felt the backs of his fingers caress the hot arch of
her cheek before sliding back to remove the pins in her
hair. Her long hair tumbled over the bedclothes. His fingers traced a line over the curve of her breast. Heated
shivers gathered there; she reached for and found his hand.
She kissed it tenderly as she begged, "Kiss me . . ."

Never in the whole of his life had he felt so tempted and
teased. Like a dream she was, the slender figure shrouded
in golden light, more beautiful than anything his ample
imagination could possibly have created, beckoning with
her own desire. "Mary." He released his breath with the
sound of her name. "Desire manifest in flesh . . ."

She smiled at the whispered words, then felt his weight
come to the bed. He gathered her into his arms, position-
ing her slightly beneath him so he might peruse the beckoning curves of her slender figure.

At first the sensation of his huge warm body pressed

against her brought a rising panic; an idea struggled to come up through her foggy consciousness. She tensed with the shocking feel of the hard length of him. Yet the tension erupted into shimmering, heated shivers. She did not want to feel so helpless but the sensations grew. Any sense of will melted into a warm sea of feeling. His body was so much larger and harder than hers and so warm . . .

Blindness had long ago enhanced her senses; the potion carried them to a heightened plane. His fingers caressed her throat, traveling down to her breasts.

How strange this desire! He let his hand smooth the silky softness of her hair, marveling at his control. His need had felt strong from the beginning, but now, with her soft supple body against him, the taste of her warm breaths against his chest, the rich perfumed scent of her skin, the long dark hair spread over his arm, it soared and urged. . . .

"You'll never have to ask twice, Mary. . . ."

Mary . . . The name registered vaguely in her mind, then disappeared as his lips moved slowly up her neck to her ear, where his warm breath, the tip of his tongue, played. She felt a tremor of delicious pleasure as his moist lips moved to her closed lids, then her cheeks. He touched his lips to hers once. He drew back, his mouth hovering just over hers as the caress of his fingers parted her lips. The kiss deepened as he tilted her head back and drew her against himself, needing to feel her with the same urgency he needed breath.

He felt the yielding pliancy of her lips beneath him, the soft relaxation of her slender curves as she freed her hands to slide them around his neck. He was hot and hard and ready for her, his hands curving around her buttocks to draw her into close alignment with his male hips, the crux of a finger sliding beneath the flimsy corset, over and over, while his lips played against hers, teasing, soft as a whisper, then demanding . . .

Chills rushed to greet the tender play of his lips on her neck and ear. A soft cry escaped her lips as she arched dramatically. A tingling congestion grew deep inside. She drew a shaky uneven breath and the tension erupted in warmth. A sweet pulsating warmth that matched the hard thud of her heart and made her arch her back again. She felt so restless and dizzy and she wanted very much to kiss him again.

She timidly sought his mouth. . . .

"You kiss like a novice, sweetheart. Don't tease me with that tongue. . . ."

The words hardly registered but the kiss conveyed the message. As if to show her, it was hot and stirring, drawing on a slow lazy restraint that in turn seemed to draw warm moist fluids from every recess in her body.

The shivering turned to shimmering; a rainbow of color glistened in her mind as she lost herself to the demanding power of the kiss, feeling the deepest part of herself opening, rising to greet the strange compelling tide sweeping her. Some small part of her struggled desperately to make sense of this, certain it was all wrong, but all thoughts kept dissolving beneath a growing tide of pleasure, a need much too powerful to resist.

He rocked his lips over hers as he studied the feminine velvet of her dark brows and lashes, her lips, the flush staining her cheeks. He whispered words against her ear. "I want this off. . . ."

She hardly knew what was said as his hands were sliding over her shoulders and his thumbs brushed the sensitive skin above her breasts. She held perfectly still, listening to the pounding of her heart as his hand deftly worked the laces of her corset.

He had never cared for corsets, the way the undergarment teased by accentuating, yet hiding, a woman's charms, and he always did his best to remove them quickly. He parted the garment down the middle and in a single motion pulled it from beneath her, tossing it to the floor. He stared at the lush temptation of the large dark pink tips of her breasts, as his hands gently caressed her head, combing through the long silky length of her hair. His lips came to her face.

She felt a tingling rush of chills follow the teasing play of his lips.

"Mary," he said as his hand moved over the curve of her waist to brush her breasts. The light touch washed her in sensations so tantalizing, they passed through her in feverish shudders. Her head swam with the sweet onslaught of sensations, all of them: the flat of his palms moved to the small of her back, where they lightly caressed back and forth over the curve of her buttocks, the warm moist lips molding hers, the heady taste of his brandy and the teasing play of his tongue, the tingling warmth between her legs that made her writhe against him. . . .

Those hands slid from her back to court her hip and, moving whisper soft, he grazed the satin skin of her side before covering her breasts. Shivers, a thousand tiny sparklike shivers, erupted where he touched her. She gasped with the hot pleasure of it, the pounding of her heart dropping as his palms circled the sensitive peaks. Her soft gasps taught him the right movement as he caressed her with ever-deepening strokes. He watched with wonder and no small amount of pleasure the sensuous color drawn by the erotic pattern of his hands. He was whispering words, heated love words, as his seeking mouth found her breasts.

The shock of it crashed into her dazed consciousness. The sudden fear and tension erupted into hot slashes of pleasure as his lips moved softly back and forth over her nipple, his tongue washing her form with a hot pleasure. Rainbow colors burst in her mind: orange and red suns and exploding gold stars.

The warm surge of voluptuous sensations tumbled through her and she didn't know her fingers curled into his hair as if to keep him to her or that she cried softly until his mouth met hers again. . . .

The erotically probing kiss dissolved her will to breathe, yet filled her with need. She felt bathed in a honeyed warmth, pulsating and spreading, then constricting like the hot center of a newborn star.

Her heart pounded wildly. She didn't know what was happening, only that it was; the way he began touching her, kissing her, brought an onslaught of whirling colors bursting in tiny ripples of pleasure. A journey he repeated over and over, each time carrying her higher and higher. She felt a surging dizziness as his lips circled her navel, over and over and lower . . .

She threw her head back and forth and arched her body, moaning softly as wave after wave of shimmering pleasure peaked and fell away only to rise higher again and higher. Just as she felt she would burst like an overripe fruit, he came over her flush form again, his legs pushing hers helplessly apart.

"Please," she whispered feverishly, confused, scared by this change, some loud warning bell ringing in her mind. "Please . . . Oh, please . . ."

"Yes . . . Now, Mary—"

A whispered denial escaped her lips at the exact moment he thrust himself deep inside her. A searing hot pain ripped through her, the bright colors vanished and she slipped into blackness only to return and feel him still and unmoving inside her.

He felt it, a slight tear, and her incredible hot tightness left little doubt. He tried to collect his senses, and using all his will, he withdrew from the hot sheath. With his weight on his arms, he glanced down at his engorged shaft, shiny with her wetness and—

"Blood. My God, you're a virgin!"

She heard only the frantic pounding of her heart. She reached a trembling hand to touch his face, needing to see him but helplessly unable to. He did not let himself think now, if only to keep her from the violence of his thoughts, and his hands parted her thighs, helplessly open to him. She frantically shook her head as though that was enough to stop this madness. It wasn't. She felt his weight return as his lips found her closed eyes, her mouth, and he slipped slowly back into the moistened sheath.

She tried to make him stop; her clenched fists hit his chest. Understanding her fear and alarm, he gently forced her arms to the bed and held her still. "No, sweetheart," he said softly. "It's too late now .... It's far too late .... Let me have you, sweetheart. ..."

Tears sprang to her eyes and instinctively, unable to stop, she tried to twist from him, but he lifted and thrust himself slowly into her, his enormous size forcing her open to him.

She closed her eyes and he filled her, forcing the pain away, pulling completely from her before slipping back, flooding her with a hot searing warmth. With each slow movement, her breath and pulse raced and she clung to him desperately, trying to keep him to her, frightened by the force of it. That ache grew again, swelling to an unimaginable height as he slowly drove and glided, in and out, over and over, building a momentum her body greeted with a warm sweeping rush of heat. She cried out with a hot burst of exploding ecstasy, drowning her in rapturous spasms that sent her into blackness.

She was vaguely aware of him sliding off her, of his hands reaching under her arms, pulling her back to him. They laid perfectly still and he held her tightly. The warmth of his closeness consumed her; it was both intense and complete, physical and emotional.

She teetered between life and eternity then. ...

She gradually became aware of the swift beat of his heart, the tender and soothing stroking of his hand, the rhythm of his breathing, and from somewhere far away she heard rain falling against the earth.

She always loved the sound of rain.

Memories stirred in her tattered consciousness. As a young child, her parents let her sleep in their bed on rainy nights. Every detail of those nights remained a bright image in her memory; the unique, familiar smell that was a blending of her mother's flowery perfume and her father's tobacco, the steady drumming of rain against the window, the feeling of warmth and security.

How she had tried to fight sleep then, to stop it form stealing those precious moments, and all the while her mother tried to bribe her, lure her to sleep with silly songs or stories. Inevitably her father became so amused he'd start laughing, then she and her mother would fall into a fit of giggles. Then they had been like three children instead of one.

All love lost . . .

Lost to his own emotions, Victor felt her small frame begin to shake with silent tears. How the hell did that Madame think she could get away with a stunt like this? Had that woman hoped he wouldn't notice she was a virgin, or had she assumed he wouldn't care? Or perhaps she had not known herself.

In any case he supposed he'd have to kill Charmane.

He ignored how much he wanted her again, a nearly impossible task. Only an idea of what she must have been put through made it possible to resist. A conversation waited. Yet as he found himself tenderly kissing away the last of her tears, he felt a sudden tension seize the small body, a quick escalation in the beat of her heart.

"Sweetheart, can you talk now?"

She shook her head, burying her face closer to his chest. Dizzily the facts of her circumstances began to pile into her consciousness, gathering there with a near-hysterical panic: she had lain with him, Monsieur Deubler might be dead, Maydrian was surely dying, and she needed to descend from this drug-induced heaven to return to an all too living hell. "I'm so scared, I—" She couldn't breath suddenly; an excruciating pain grew in her chest and each breath seemed only to aggravate it.

"I do not wonder why," he said. "You have been badly hurt. I need you to tell me what has happened to you."

She felt ill, her consciousness fragmented, foggy, dazed. She drew air too fast into her lungs, then held it to take stock of these much changed circumstances, releasing it in a rush.

She had to get up.

Remember it, remember it, remember it. . . .

Watching her struggle, he rose from the bed, stealing the last of the warmth. She shivered uncontrollably, trying to catch her breath long enough to maneuver through her drugged and abused senses. Her once-warmed blood now vacated every limb. She felt numb, devoid of all sensation past feverish chills. She could not speak. She wanted to hide forever.

Then he was suddenly there again. "Easy, sweetheart." He gently laid her back against the cushions. She cried as a moist cloth came over her face. She protested weakly against such intimacy, but a strong hand held her still as the cool cloth was passed over her warm skin. He lowered the cloth between her thighs, wiped a small stain there. "So, love—now what the hell—"

A knock sounded at the door. Victor set down the cloth and moved to the door. "What is it?" he asked Carl as he stepped outside.

"I thought you'd want to know that two men came to escort the lady back to a place I can hardly believe she came from," Carl said with a dramatic lift of brow, stopping for Victor to explain the curiosity.

"What did you tell them?"

"I merely said she was engaged presently and that in any case, I was convinced the young lady had enough use of her faculties to know when she should leave. Though of course she obviously has no use of her faculties. I assumed, though, you might decide the issue. I added that if she should leave, you would provide an escort, and when they insisted on speaking to her, I had them shown out. I don't think Isaac meant to hit the bastard so hard, but, well . . ." Carl sighed. "One should anticipate such accidents in this house."

"Yes," Victor agreed quietly. "Carl, I need a cup of

strong coffee, some brandy and then a call to arms to my men." He paused. "For a lynching party."

"Now?"

"Within the hour."

Victor shut the door and went to the closet to fetch a robe. He needed to hide that body of hers from sight or change his plans. He gently lifted her up and placed the robe around her shoulders, pulling the sides around before he began rolling up the sleeves. He watched as she struggled up from her drugged consciousness. Tears hung in a thick mist over the lovely eyes as she seemed to alternate between confusion and panic.

She bit her finger as if to stop from crying. "I . . . I must leave. . . ."

I hand came under her chin. "Get that out of your mind. I won't let you go anywhere, least of all back to that house."

"You don't understand . . ." Her words were slightly slurred.

He sat down on the bed, leaned against the headboard and pulled her over onto his lap. "I know you're in some kind of trouble. That woman forced you—"

She grabbed her head as it spun. "I'm not in any trouble; no one forced me. I—"

"Then you'll have to explain how a virgin's managed to work in a whorehouse for over a year, or what compelled her to offer herself on the block."

She shook her head in negation, desperately trying to keep her wits above a rising panic. Mercedes, Mercedes, Mercedes. She tried to focus on the name. Mercedes had warned her about this, that it was very bad, that no one must know she was a virgin or—"It would be so much worse then," Mercedes had said. "It won't matter afterward and if there's any sign just say it is your bleeding . . ."

"I'm not a virgin—"

"No, not anymore."

"No, I wasn't, it was only my . . . my bleeding."

"You can believe, love, I have enough experience to distinguish a virgin from a whore—"

"It doesn't matter," she cried, scrambling quickly away. Instantly, he caught her arm and held firm with frightening strength. "Please, just let me—"

"Are you going to tell me or do I have to force it from you?"

"You don't understand. Please, you must let me go! Oh, please—"

He reached over and pulled the servant's rope again, stunned by her sudden panic, the tears filling her eyes, as she desperately tried to pry his hand from her arm. Victor found himself becoming very angry.

Someone was going to pay for her terror.

Carrying a tray of coffee and brandy, Carl stopped outside the door when he heard the young lady's cries. A woman's cries coming from this room were quite common but never cries of desperation or pain. He suppressed his surprise as he slowly opened the door, allowing Victor every chance to order him out.

"Sir?"

Jade froze at the sound of Carl's voice. Victor didn't look up; his eyes never left her. "Carl, I want a message sent to that woman's house on Canal Street. I want it to say that Mary isn't coming back, that she hopes the Madame rots in hell."

Jade's face lifted with shock, tears now streaming down her face. "No! Don't do that! Please, please, don't do this to me. . . ."

Shocked by the force of her emotions, fury changed his face. "What has that woman done to you?"

"I . . . I can't tell you—"

"You have no choice. I'd journey to hell before I'd let someone hurt you now. The message goes or you tell me—and either way, you're not leaving this house."

"You can't help me! If you could help me, if it was just me . . . She has my maid, Maydrian . . . and she's t-torturing her, now, as I speak, and if I don't get back . . . Maydrian will d-die!"

"Shhh, slow down," he said softly, and motioned to Carl to step forward with the brandy. Carl poured a triple shot and handed it to Victor. "Here, drink this in swallows—try not to taste it."

Carl poured himself a healthy shot as well and sat down.

Jade took several large gulps; her extreme agitation, her hazy senses and her emotional exhaustion suppressed the normal response. She didn't taste the hot liquid until it burst in her stomach.

"Start at the beginning."

The beginning, the beginning. Images whirled through her mind: Monsieur Deubler, the fight, the hand coming over her mouth. Carl kept pouring liberal shots of brandy, swallowing them whole as he listened to her broken sentences punctuated by gasps of fear. She told of her confusion upon waking at Madame Charmane's house, how she thought she was in a madhouse. Her voice began choking again as she described the first threats. "I didn't really believe she had Maydrian at first. I heard her screaming but I didn't hear her voice. It seemed too unlikely, too convenient to hold a frail, old woman hostage. But Mercedes, oh, poor Mercedes kept trying to warn me, that it didn't matter, that she would . . ."

To her sympathetic but ever-increasingly angry listeners, she went into some detail about Mercedes: how she was an orphaned convent girl, snatched from the streets and sold to Madame Charmane, and how even if there was a chance to escape, she would be hunted by the authorities, blackmailed with forged papers that said she was a criminal, and worse, there were many other tortures to force compliance.

"I was so scared but I knew, I just knew, that it wouldn't work for me. I am not alone in the world, and I would get a note out and be rescued . . . but then, then—" Her tone heightened with fear and anger both, and the emotions overwhelmed her. She stopped as his arms came around her in a tight embrace.

A cold and deadly thing came to his eyes; the violence of it required all the force of his will to control. He managed, but only because she needed his comfort for a few moments more, and his need to give this to her was every bit as powerful.

"It's all over with now," he whispered, thinking the story was finished. "It's all over with—"

"No!" she cried, looking up startled again. "My maid! She has poor Maydrian . . . now, as we speak, she—"

Victor stopped her, knowing what had happened but not knowing exactly how to tell her. He cursed her wretched blindness, the woman who used the sad fact to advantage. Maydrian, he felt certain had already met an unkind fate. "She doesn't really have your maid. In all likelihood, that woman used Maydrian's name to threaten you."

"No, no, no . . ."

"How do you know? You said you didn't speak with her."

Jade seemed unable to answer at first, then suddenly her whole manner changed—and frighteningly so. She stood very still, her already pale face blanched even whiter, and her empty eyes stared off into the distance, seeing some unspeakable terror.

"When the Madame found Mercedes and I in an embrace, she took me down to the cellar again. I didn't know at first. At first I just sat in a chair. Then I heard a hollowed scream from Maydrian. I tried to discover what had happened; I was so scared! I called for Maydrian but no sound came. Then the Madame ordered me to hold out my hand." Jade's hand lifted into the air with a slow, ghostlike movement. "I thought she . . . she was going to hit me like a schoolmaster or . . . or governess, and I thought . . . I thought that she could beat me till I was black and blue, it wouldn't matter. . . . But she didn't hit me. She put something in my hand, pulled away a cloth and . . . and . . . she c-closed my fingers over it." She seemed to panic, her words rushed forward. "It was warm . . . and wet and I couldn't see what it was! She said to me, 'You don't want your maid to be as useless as you are, do you? Take care not to give me cause to . . . to remove her other eye.' "

She heard a soft vicious curse before he pulled her back, her small body jerking against him, while her fingers dug into his arm as though desperately trying to hang on to something. In a carefully controlled voice, he ordered, "Wake Murray up to sit with her. I don't want her left alone. And bring something up to make her sleep."

She trembled with chills. She tried to rise above her confusion and dizziness, fighting still the lingering effects of the potion, but she couldn't. She felt precariously balanced on the edge of a steep cliff over a dark abyss. She needed . . . she needed . . .

Mother Francesca . . .

He held her tightly in his arms, listening to the crackle of a dying fire tick off the minutes. Gradually he felt her trembling slow, then stop, her eyes closed. He thought she was asleep. He pulled back the covers and gently lifted her up before setting her down again. Just as he was about to turn away, a hand reached out to touch him.

"Please . . . I need, I very much want to return to the convent. . . ."

"The convent?"

"Mother Francesca . . . she will be so worried. . . ."

Dark blue eyes searched the lovely pale face as his thoughts rushed to the mysterious place he found himself in. He knew. He also knew he should have known the moment he discovered she was blind.

"Your real name, love? Not Mary?"

She was falling over the side the cliff, falling down into the dark space where a deep peace awaited her. She struggled through the hazy swirl of darkness to whisper the last words, the important words: "Jade. Jade Terese Devon."

Jade Terese. His father's favorite student . . .

Chapter 5

The two lovers failed to notice the steady rain falling against the window. She dashed around the bed, trying to escape the greediest hands she had ever known. He lunged and tackled her, pinning her beneath him on the bed as uncontainable excitement burst forth in giggles.

"Tell me again!" he demanded.

"You are the best lover I've ever had!"

Sebastian had no reason to doubt Mercedes on this. "Then why don't you let me make an honest mistress of you?"

"Sebastian, you are teasing me."

"I am not teasing; I have never in twenty-nine years been more serious! I want you!" He showered her face with kisses. "Ah, you have bewitched me; I have no doubt of that. You are the first woman I've ever wanted as a mistress, the first I've ever asked. I will have you, Mercedes!"

"I do not believe this is happening to me."

"It is happening. Now say yes!"

"Sebastian!"

"Say yes!"

"I ... I can't, Sebastian."

"Why not? Has this not been the happiest, most wonderful night of your life?"

She nodded; it was only too true.

"Do you not already care for me more than you ever cared for a man?" When she nodded again, he laughed. "God, I wouldn't be surprised if you were already in love with me, but if you are not yet hopelessly overcome by my charm, it will take at most a week! One week and I swear you'll be madly, passionately in love with me. I'll make you the happiest woman—"

Mercedes's eyes filled with tears as she turned away. She would always cherish this one night with Sebastian, the one night in which some god, either from benevolence, pity or both, breathed her most fanciful dream to life and set Sebastian before her. She had this one night of his laughter and love, of his sweet promises of a life she could never have, a life she should not dream of.

Sebastian watched the tear slide from the flushed cheek and found his finger stopping it, gently banishing it from her lovely face. "I made you cry. Why?"

She shook her head, unable to answer.

Jade's words echoed dizzily through her mind. What if God was not punishing her? What if God sent Jade and Sebastian to force her to see how terrible her life had become? Because He knew she could not watch Jade become what she had become. She couldn't! She could not spend the rest of her life dreaming about Sebastian! She wouldn't!

So she had to stop it, she had to . . .

"Mercedes?"

His lips kissed her cheek, but she was hardly aware of the immediacy of Sebastian, the room, the house, as her thoughts rushed in a feverish intensity. Her heart started galloping. She had to do something to make it stop. It did not matter that she was killed in the trying. She was already dead; she could not lose more. She had to make it stop. . . .

"Mercedes—"

"I have to go," she said. "Please. I will be back shortly. Would you wait for me? I think, I am quite sure, I will be needing you very soon. Would you?"

Sebastian twirled a strawberry blond curl around his finger, staring down at the lovely girl. He rolled over, offering the girl her freedom. He watched as she quietly rose and slipped on a chemise and a plain gold muslin dress that laced up the front. She rushed to the dressing water and splashed her face before turning to the door.

She made her way down the hall and to the top of the front staircase. A light shone from a downstairs parlor at the bottom of the stairs.

The Madame was still up. Mercedes drew a deep breath and without making a sound she slipped down the stairs one at a time, her back pressed to the wall for support. The door to the parlor was open. Slipping forward inch by inch, with her heart thudding wildly in her chest, Mercedes peeked inside. The Madame sat at a desk with her money books, tallying up the evening's profits.

From behind the beveled glass Mercedes spotted two men outside guarding the front doors. She darted across the front of the open parlor doors and into the now-dark entrance hall. She went through the doors to the gaming room. She heard a servant humming softly as he went about tiding up in the adjacent room. Bright hazel eyes spotted the still-lit lamp near the bar.

With a slight rush of skirts, she crossed the space.

She lifted the glass off the lantern. Careful to cup the precious light against the rush of her movements, she crossed the space and went into the barroom. Feverish hazel eyes came to the obscene tapestries hanging on the wall before searching the room for an occupant. It was empty.

She wove through the tables.

Mercedes set the flickering light at the very bottom of the tapestry. Small flames leaped to life. She stepped back, her eyes wide and frightened as the flames grew and grew, scorching two copulating nymphs before licking them with bright orange flames. With a swoosh of air the tapestry burst into bright fire.

The lantern dropped to the floor with a crash.

She turned and fled the room.

"Mercedes!"

She stopped halfway up the stairs. She slowly turned to see the Madame standing at the bottom of the stairs, staring up at her suspiciously. "What were you doing downstairs at this hour?"

For a moment she couldn't speak, standing there mute and helpless, listening to the roar of her pounding heart in her ears. Then, from seemingly far away, she heard herself reply: "The Monsieur left his hat in the barroom. He asked me to retrieve it. I did not want to wake a servant for the task."

The girl looked flushed and guilty. There was something afoot. Something, Madame Charmane saw, more meaningful than the fact that she held no hat in her hands. "And where is this hat?"

The Madame watched Mercedes's red hands clutch her skirts tightly. "I lost it," she said. "I mean, it is lost. I asked ... ah ..." Oh Lord—she bit her lip—who was working still? Who?

"Yes? You asked who, Mercedes?"

"Edie to search the kitchen and bring it up if she finds it." She turned around and started up.

"Edie retired two hours ago."

Mercedes stiffened dramatically. Thoughts clamored hard and fast for her attention but none of these louder than the rush of her blood through her veins. She wondered if she might faint from fright—

Sebastian had gotten up and stood listening to the curious exchange from an open door. He didn't understand what was happening, much less the manner and tone in which that women spoke to Mercedes.

He hurriedly set about dressing.

The Madame watched Mercedes put her back to her for but for a moment. She was already in a temper, what with Mary still at Monsieur Nolte's house and a whole two hours late. Her men had yet to return and she had just been about to call Constable Girod to the task when this happened—Mercedes sneaking around downstairs and lying to her about it. "Get down here this—"

The first awful scream sounded from the barroom: *"Feu! Aider! Feu!"*

The Madame swung toward the sound and in the same moment Mercedes ran, dashing up the stairs and down the hall, shouting the only word that would be heard for hours. *"Feu! Feu!"* She pounded on every door. *"Feu! Feu!* Wake up!"

One by one people came out of their rooms, only to panic. Screams sounded from downstairs already. The fire had leaped to another tapestry, which fell to one of the wooden tables nearby, even as the flames continued climbing the wall. Smoke curled on the ceiling, billowing into the entrance hall and filling the staircase.

"Anna! Help! Alert the servants upstairs!" Mercedes shouted orders like a general. "Cecil! Put down those clothes and race upstairs with Anna to get the servants out."

Anna froze as if uncertain which was more important: her gowns or the servants. Mercedes ran to the panicked woman, snatched the clothes from her hands and screamed, "Now! Or they'll die!"

She burst inside her room as Sebastian leapt on one foot, managing to push the other one into his boot. Sebastian didn't think. Not now. Later he would try to discover why Mercedes had disappeared from beneath his hot body to set this house on fire, but now he only acted. For there was no more deadly word in any language than *fire*.

"There are people in the basement—"

He saw the plea in her eyes. "What?"

"Hurry! We must save them!"

Cursing viciously, Sebastian raced after Mercedes. The stairs were swarming with people. A bell kept ringing. Cries and screams sounded. Black smoke continued to pour into the entrance hall. Shouts sounded from the neighbors nearby. Half the house filed down the stairs.

The Madame stood at the bottom of the stairs, directing everyone as they appeared. "Lisa, get the silver in the kitchen! Tara, drop that bag and start taking out the china. Rouge—help Manny with those pictures, and watch out—" She stopped with a gasp as she spotted Mercedes.

Her eyes widened with unnatural fury. "Why, you miserable—"

"Quick!" Sebastian shouted. "There're people in the basement—"

An ugly scream sounded as one of the men's shirts caught flames in the barroom. He fell to the floor with frightened screams. A great cloud of smoke enveloped them all. The Madame closed her eyes and covered her mouth as she coughed, stepping back instinctively. When she looked up again Mercedes and Sebastian were gone. She spotted Lisa apparently rushing out to help them free the doomed wretches in the basement and she screamed, "Don't you dare, young lady. Go fetch my silver now!"

Within the next minutes a chain of people passing bucketfuls of water went from the back well through the kitchen and into the barroom. Mercedes never knew how fast the fire moved. The entire barroom was in flames. Endless smoke poured through the doors.

Mercedes led Sebastian out the front doors. Until that moment she hadn't realized it was raining. Rain fell from the still-dark sky, and seeing it, she stopped for but a second and raised her arms to it with a happy cry. As if it were a gift from God. The fire would not spread. If they saved the people in the basement, if there even were still people in the basement, then all would be saved.

Clad in sleeping clothes, neighbors rushed toward the house. Carriages clamored noisily in the distance, bells ringing out the alarm. Mercedes wasted no time, running as she explained to Sebastian: "We can reach the basement through the kitchen. This way!" They ran around to the back and entered the kitchen. Smoke filled the space. A row of people passed the buckets from the well outside in the back courtyard. Servants—Cecile, Lisa and Evett— hurriedly tried to remove what could be saved. The flames leaped over the door leading to the ballroom. Mercedes shouted for help as she went to the cellar door. Sebastian grabbed a bucket of water and threw it over himself. Then he grabbed a wet blanket from the man at the end of the line, trying to keep the fire from entering the kitchen. "There're people in the basement. Hurry!"

Mercedes was already in the darkened narrow stairway, going down. Below came the sounds of weak, frantic cries. "Sebastian!" She looked behind her. "Hurry! I hear them!"

Sebastian rushed ahead of her. Heavy footsteps sounded from behind as two other men entered behind Mercedes, the Madame's bodyguards. A shiver raced up her spine and she panicked. "No! No!"

She reached her arms up to stop them. One man, Saul, held a lantern up, casting their faces in eerie shadows. "The Madame ordered you to stop the fire—"

The last thing Mercedes remembered that night was the soundless cry of Sebastian's name from her parched throat as she tumbled down the stairs and into the blackness edged by flames.

Sebastian stood in the darkened space of the basement, listening to the weak cries of people nearby, but it was so dark! "I can't see a bloody thing! And what the devil is that foul odor?"

He listened for a moment to the sounds coming from far above: running feet, muted shouts and cries, an occasional scream, attempting to see into this hellish darkness. He cursed himself for not having thought to bring a lantern.

A thud sounded from the stairs. "Mercedes!"

He walked slowly toward the sound, afraid to step into something, when suddenly, like a gift from the heavens, two men appeared at the bottom of the stairs, one holding a light. He swung back around to see the room illuminated, to see where the people were.

He heard the sound of his breath sucked into his lungs. He waited for a comprehensible thought to explain what he stared at. There were none. No human explanation.

Four people sat on the floor, side to side, back to back. Chains circled their bodies. They were naked; two men and two women, and they looked, dear God, half starved. Only two were conscious, staring back at him with fear and apprehension as if he were the devil come to torture them more. The other two were tilted, unconscious. Sores covered their bodies. The stench came from their naked flesh.

The light shifted behind him, briefly illuminating the surrounding walls, glinting off the metal of various weapons, tools, chains and shackles, and still he didn't grasp what he was seeing. The light brightened as he stepped forward. Against the far wall was a queer chair. Two stirrups, with human feet in them, rose up in the air. He saw only her legs at first: the smooth, thin, brown legs of a woman. As the man behind him stepped forward he caught a brief glimpse of the rest of her. He almost screamed. She was mercifully quite dead, one side of her face caked in dried blood falling in black streaks down her body.

Two distinct qualities mixed to make Sebastian one of the greatest swordsmen alive: skill and speed, and it was the latter that saved his life. For as his comprehension dawned and he bent over to retch, the blood vacated his limbs, replaced by a murderous rage brighter than the ravages of the fire above. The light behind him shifted, brightening as the man behind him stepped forward, and in the instant he realized the thud had been Mercedes, that they had killed her and would now kill him.

Sebastian rose, mobilizing his strength for a death blow. He heard the man's hellish cry and felt the piercing sting of the dagger sinking to the flesh of his biceps. Had he not already been moving it would have been his back. Yet it never stopped him. The man jumped back but Sebastian anticipated the leap and moved forward, his saber piercing the man's chest. Using all his strength, Sebastian forced it through the wall of the man's chest and pulled savagely downward. The man made no sound as a broad sword fell from his hand. Sebastian pulled his saber out of the man's chest as he dropped soundlessly to the floor.

The other assailant dropped the lantern and swung around to the stairs. Sebastian showed no mercy; he couldn't. His rage demanded revenge, and certain

Mercedes was dead, he did something he had never done before: he thrust his saber into the man's back and forced the sharp metal down with an agonized cry. A scream sounded, stopping as the man's life left his body.

Sebastian stood still for several moments, panting.

He made not a sound, seeming more inhuman because of it, and not looking, he wrapped his hand around the dagger in his arm and yanked. Breathing hard and deep, he waited in the uncertain light for a coherent thought.

It came with the crackling sound above.

He looked up to see the slowly widening circle of burnt wood on the ceiling, widening like a bleeding wound. He picked up the lantern. He quickly held it up to the wall, trying not to think of what these weapons were used for. On the opposite wall he found what he searched for: an ax. His hands seized it as he turned to the poor wretches on the floor . . .

Within a matter of minutes Sebastian had lifted all but one of the prisoners up the stairs and through the kitchen. He lifted the last in his arms, turning toward the stairs. He looked up as he did so. The basement's blackened roof bled, bubbling like a giant angry sore. Ducking, he raced to the stairs. A furious crackle sounded and the roof collapsed. Fire burst into the basement, lighting the walls like a sudden burst of sun. His bright blue eyes widened as he saw her.

She had been lying on the floor the whole time. Not dead. A strange leap of joy gave him inhuman strength. He leaped up the stairs. He stumbled and hit the wall. Burning hot. He gasped, righting himself, and reached the top. He handed the body to a waiting man.

The man's eyes widened as he took in the naked beaten Negro body. Sebastian had already turned to get Mercedes. "Monsieur! No, no! The stairs are collapsing! Look, the fire!"

Yet it was too late. Sebastian had Mercedes in his arms and was headed back up the stairs, choking on the smoke. No air remained in the narrow staircase. He took a step and the wall on his side collapsed. Flames leaped over the stairway ahead of him, blocking the only exit from hell. Flames leaped onto Mercedes's skirts. Sebastian closed his eyes and with an anguished cry, he pushed into the burning flames. The step collapsed with his weight but somehow he was on the next one and then the next, emerging at last at the top of the stairs. He couldn't breathe. He was drawing smoke hard and fast into his lungs, choking violently. The kitchen was in flames, the other man many seconds gone.

Sebastian emerged into the driving rain.

He dropped to the ground, dowsing Mercedes's smoldering clothing in a puddle of water filling the street. He sat there, holding the still-unconscious beauty in his arms, drawing fresh wet air into his scourged lungs, telling himself over and over she was unharmed. She was mercifully unharmed. Then he looked at the sky as the rain washed his hot body in stinging cold drops.

Victor rode up to Charmane's house and drew his mount up hard, coming to quick stop. With a furious clamor, twenty of his men behind him also managed to stop. The horse leaped up, splashing down in the three inches of water flooding the street. Victor, a number of his men too, had pistols out and aimed at the woman who stood on the scorched and smoldering porch. A crumbling house of flames leaped and smoked behind her.

Sebastian stood on a farmer's cart before a crowd of maybe two hundred people, their torches dancing, flickering in the rain and illuminating their frightened faces. He held the girl Mercedes in his arms. The women and servants of the house huddled tightly together, clasping hands and terrified, uncertain of their fate. Sebastian's shirt hung in burnt tatters from his frame; ash smudges and burns and cuts marked his bare skin. The people in the front could see the blood dripping unnoticed from his arm. Wrapped in blankets, crying and moaning, four Negroes lay in the cart behind him. Rain fell unnoticed on Sebastian's person as his voice thundered louder than the driving rain. "I accuse . . . !" His voice roared as a man, behind him, lifted up one of the beaten Negroes to show the crowd the swollen belly of starvation, the gruesomely protruding ribs and stick-thin legs, the skin marked by months of hideous torment. "I accuse this woman . . . !"

A volatile situation. Victor tensed and held his mount steady as the potential for violence grew with each of Sebastian's accusations. The horrible indictment slowly sank into the disbelieving consciousness of the witnesses, his own as well. The crowd was made up of perfectly ordinary men and women: housewives and servants, bakers, tailors, a shoemaker, one of the town's blacksmiths, innkeepers, a restaurateur and bar owners, the graveyard watch keeper, the proprietor of the flower shop on the corner, longshoremen, free Negroes, and slaves, even drunkards. Yet Sebastian united everyone with the fury in his voice. "I accuse . . . !"

The crowd became one animal who began to understand there was a festering wound on their body, one that must be rooted out and destroyed. A savage low grumble sounded from the people as they turned from the poor beaten wretch to the once-proud woman standing on her porch, her growing terror horribly illuminated as the fire smoked and struggled in the entrance hall behind Sebastian's relentless thrust: "I accuse . . . !"

"No!" Charmane cried out. "No! They are just slaves! I bought them, they belong to me—"

"I accuse you"—he pointed, like an angry preacher damning the damned, each slowly pronounced word emerging from his burnt throat to sound God's own outrage—"of leaving them to burn in your cellar as you tried to save your silverware! I accuse . . . !"

Madame Jened reached into the pool of water at her feet and picked up the first stone. Shouting with rage, she threw it hard. Another and another followed. Charmane cried as the rocks hit her. Victor contemplated the mercy of shooting her dead where she stood. He kicked his mount closer.

Girod and four of his men were pushing through the crowd, shouting in French to disband. People began lifting things from her huge pile of treasures to throw at her. A chair was broken into sticks, hands came over cups, vases, her neat pile of banking ledgers and finally a open box of silverware. As the Madame sheltered her head from the stones and knives pelting her body, she caught sight of Girod. "Girod! Make them stop! Tell them! Tell them that I do nothing wrong, that—"

Girod stopped in the very center of the crowd. He began to deny knowing the woman in rapid French. The Madame's stature lifted with fury as she pointed a finger at Girod and screamed, "God damn you to hell! I always paid you, your miserly protection tax, and you knew full well how I kept the slaves in the basement." She shouted, "You never cared a whit when they were screaming for your mercy!"

Not everyone caught this. As the shouts and screams of the crowd reached a feverish pitch, Girod heard a man near him call for his blood. He called for his men but the call was aborted as a fist swung into his stomach, then another and another. He dropped into the rising water of the street, laying facedown, with no consciousness to make him lift from the watery death. Yet no one noticed as the crowd turned back to the Madame, surging toward her with shouts and screams. The people seized anything they could get their hands on to throw. Victor's horse reared up, nearly unseating him. Madame Charmane took a deadly step back into the house to save herself. A collective gasp sounded as her scream sounded in the burning flames. . . .

Sebastian dropped to his knees. He tilted his face to the heavens. Over the rooftops, dawn stretched dim gray arms through the dark rain. . . .

Victor studied the still-sleeping girl. The dark hair spread against the bedclothes. One arm was lifted above her head, the bed sheet barely covering the lift of her breast. Impossibly, she looked more beautiful in the afternoon light, and as he stood there staring he felt a flood of desire—

He turned away.

Victor pulled open the drapes, flooding his bedchamber with bright sunshine from the hot afternoon, and stepped out onto the shaded balcony. There he stood staring at the lush beauty of the acre or so of land, his land, a vast stretch of exotic landscape purposely patterned after the mysterious dark secrets of the Oriental gardens he loved. Thirty-foot-high bamboo enclosed the garden and obliterated the sight of houses nearby. The colors dazzled. The cherry orchards blossomed pink alongside scarlet gum trees, and towering maple and cypress trees created a dense green canopy over the far corner. Flower beds, artistically arranged around ferns, created a riot of color: especially the red and orange marigolds. Dark green ivy grew up over trunks and covered the garden walls, competing with sweet scented jasmine, a bright pink-flowering vine and the bamboo. Chirping birds surrounded the stone rim of the cistern, filling the air with their sounds. The breathtaking beauty of the garden made him think of Jade and her blindness, the tragedy that had stolen such a precious thing from her. . . .

As it always did, his gaze came to rest on the sculpture garden. Beneath the white-and-pink blossoms of an apple tree sat a large Buddha, smiling with profound amusement. This was one of the few times Victor did not smile back.

Dr. Murray had spent the morning mending and patching Sebastian's wounds, though his scorched lungs would just have to heal on their own. "Two days at most," was the good doctor's guess. Mercedes still lay unconscious, but appeared remarkably unscathed from the ordeal. One could only wonder at the mental scars that would remain forever. As Victor related what he'd learned of Mercedes's history to Sebastian, Sebastian had fallen quite still and quiet, overwhelmed by all that she had been through. Then he had gathered her into his arms. . . .

Victor knew the feeling. . . .

The Ursuline nuns themselves tended to the poor beaten and battered Negroes in the infirmary. The governor and the mayor were holding meetings on the subject of city corruption, as the incident brought numerous people forward to report many more of the late constable's abuses of his position.

Carl was busy answering the endless streams of inquiries concerning Jade Terese and Sebastian. The entire first floor looked like a flower shop. Sebastian was the hero, his name uttered by every mouth in the city as the fantastic story was discussed and repeated, over and over again.

"I accuse . . ."

The trouble was, the woman's richly deserved death had destroyed any hope of discovering who had taken Jade to her house. Was it one man or two? Why had they sent Jade Terese to that house in the first place?

Voices rose from the garden below. His father and Mother Francesca stepped out onto the lawn and Victor watched as they strolled, deep in private communion. The Reverend Mother had seemed so unusually quiet, frightened and confused, when she'd listened to the lengthy explanation of what had happened to Jade Terese, repeating, "Merciful heavens . . . Merciful heavens . . ." to herself in a distracted manner. He kept waiting for the accusation to enter the good woman's eyes as it had with his father—whom he had long ago learned to ignore—but this had never happened. As if the woman did not fault him for bedding the innocent young lady and stealing her virginity with the mistaken assumption that she was a whore. As if the Reverend Mother was too upset to think that far. He had the strangest sense that she knew something—some unspeakable secret—about the whole sordid affair. This had grown to a certainty as he fired questions at her: "Do you know anyone who might want to harm the girl?"

"No . . . who could want to hurt Terese?"

"Has Jade mentioned meeting anyone recently, a stranger or someone out of the ordinary that—"

Again a shake of head. "No, no. Merciful heavens . . ."

His father had sensed it too. If anyone would get it out of the Reverend Mother, it would be the senior Nolte. His father was a great listener, empathizing and compassionate, and yet absolutely nonjudgmental. The man pulled out the darkest secrets from everyone.

His father was well known in Vatican circles, though somewhat of an iconoclast in the Church. Throughout New Orleans and Baton Rouge, his father was the person everyone sought when in need—his humanitarian efforts were famous.

A sad sort of smile lifted Victor's face as he thought of Marie. Obviously she had inherited her mother's gift. She had been so right about that woman, and if this entire ordeal taught him anything, it was never to doubt Marie again. . . .

A slight, whisper-soft stirring behind him drew his attention. Jade Terese sat up, careful to bring the bed sheets over her. Against both his father's and Mother Francesca's objections, he had insisted on being with Jade when she awoke. He had owned her passion last night, and aye, an intoxicated passion it was, but unlike any other he had ever known. While he certainly would never regret a moment of what had passed between them, he had no idea what she would feel upon waking. Fear, anguish, panic? All of these?

He meant to do anything to banish her pain. . . .

Jade waited for a coherent thought to rise above the escalating pounding of her heart. She still sat in his bed. Memories of the night flooded in to her mind: memories of the sensual swirl made of his kisses, the tease of his mouth and hands on her body and how he had—

Oh, my. Oh, Lord. . . .

Color rushed to her face; she forgot to breathe as her consciousness riveted to the ecstasy and wonder of what he had done to her.

Boots sounded softly on the wooden floor. She froze, staring bewildered out into darkened space, waiting to know who was with her.

"It's me Jade. Victor." The words were spoken in a whisper as he came to the bed. She turned to the sound of his voice, a timid hand reached to touch him.

He closed his eyes as he felt the brush of her fingers. When he opened them again, he saw her pain and fear disappear beneath relief. "I'm so glad 'tis you!"

This took him by surprise. Without questioning the intimacy, operating from the simplest masculine need to take back the night, he drew her slender form into his arms.

"Jade Terese . . ."

The feel of his arms was heaven. She closed her eyes and clung to his neck, savoring the embrace, the clean masculine scent, the warmth and security of his arms. "I'm just so glad it's you. I was afraid—What happened? Did—"

He drew back to see her face; gently he brushed back a strand of thick silky dark hair. "I'm afraid I have a story to tell. . . ."

The story was a long one, and he took his time telling it. She listened quitely, relieved at Mercedes's rescue, thrilled by Sebastian's heroics. He quickly explained the terrible end, staring down at the lovely face as she absorbed this. The mechanical clock on the mantel ticked off the minutes as her startling green eyes darted this way and that before stopping and saying the name: "Maydrian? What about Maydrian?"

Victor's long pause prepared her before he said, "Jade Terese, we have not found her yet. Maydrian had not been among the four Negroes found in the basement. No one knew where she was.

She seemed to stare questioningly. "Oh! But where could she be? What could have befallen her?"

"I have a number of men trying to find out as we speak."

"Please to God, keep her safe! You will find her, you think?"

"Yes. I have no doubt—"

"And Monsieur Deubler?"

"He is quite fine after a hard blow to the head. He was the very first, but by no means the last, to send flowers. By twelve noon my study was full to bursting with the flowers being sent from concerned people. You, young lady, are far more popular, it seems, than the good Pope himself—my father's words."

"Your . . . father?"

There came another pause. "You know him well, Jade. If you were not blind you would have known from the start. You see, he, like your Reverend Mother, calls you by your Christian name—Terese. Father Nolte, with your very own Reverend Mother, is most anxious to speak to my luckless heroine."

"Father Nolte? I don't understand. . . ."

"He is my father. Married to my mother until her death. The vows came later."

She drew back with her shock. "You are Victor—"

"Nolte."

Of course, she knew Father Nolte had once been married and that Marie Saint's famous mother had spared his much-loved wife her last precious months' pain. Marie Saint, Reverend Mother, and finally Father Nolte himself had all told her about it. She knew too, that Father Nolte had a son of whom he was inordinately proud. She had heard dozens of stories of this famous son over the years, including how he had run away from boarding school and had lived on ships in the far away Orient. There Father Nolte said his son had learned many strange notions that made them argue about the poetry, simplicity and beauty of the heathen Buddhist religion. This son then made a shipbuilding business, interrupting his success when the war came. He was said to have been a great war hero. She remembered especially Father Nolte's effort to convince him to move to New Orleans and how glad he was when his son finally acquiesced. She knew all this, but the idea that Victor, this man whose bed she had shared, was this much-loved son of Father Nolte was simply too much. "The shame," she said as pale hands covered her face and she threw herself facedown on the bedclothes. "It will burn me to cinders."

He couldn't stop it. Despite everything, the longest night of his life and no doubt hers, he couldn't stop the rich sound of his amusement from filling the room.

"You would laugh at me now. . . ."

"Oh, love." He laughed as he lifted her up and took her back in his arms. This was a mistake. The wild mass of her hair fell over her robe, which opened as he lifted her easily to position her on his lap. He caught sight of the tempting swell of her breasts before she righted the garment and covered her face with her hands.

Hard hot desire shot through his veins, so hot, so fast, he needed a long moment to recover. His struggle made him laugh again, even as he drew her hands from her face and he saw those beautiful eyes pleading with him for help.

"Jade Terese," he said as his lips gently brushed across her forehead, "there is no shame in what passes between a man and a women behind closed doors. Now, I will not pretend to regret what happened last night, and although I had your passion, I know it was against your will. Everyone understands this. My father," he emphasized, "seems especially cognizant of the fact."

She traced her fingertips over the smooth textures of his face, as if searching for something. "With your father . . . were you . . . I mean, were you . . . frank?"

"Very."

"What did he say?"

He chuckled. "Not a word, love, not a word. His eyes, however, spoke volumes."

He watched as her thoughts raced over this. Again she surprised him with a priceless conclusion, one that revealed the startling passion and optimism of her heart.

"And yet 'twas all meant to happen, do you not think so? Mercedes is free! And when I think of that precious soul and all that she suffered at that woman's hands, I am so glad. There is no place for regrets; we must celebrate the happy fact. I would do it all a million times again for her. . . ."

He chuckled again, and she smiled as she raised her arms, gathering the thick mass of hair to push it behind her back. The sound abruptly stopped. She heard his sharp intake of breath and somehow it made her aware of the impropriety of their situation, that she sat on his lap in a robe, naked underneath.

Really, though, what could it matter after last night?

She felt the warmth of his body beneath the thin material. She squirmed and stopped suddenly, feeling that part of him pressed against the curve of her hip and his fingers reaching to the folds of the robe at her neck with a feather light caress.

"What are you thinking now, love?"

The words were whisper soft. The tingling awareness of him seemed to light every nerve. She drew a shaky uneven breath. "I . . . I was thinking I should be getting dressed."

"A remarkable coincidence." He laughed, a sound as rich and warm as his touch. "The idea was pressing on my mind as well."

He closed his eyes suddenly, in a swift movement, he lifted her off his lap and set her on the bed. He glanced at the foot of the bed, where her clothes lay in a neat pile. "One of the Sisters retrieved a set of clothes from your house. A bath is waiting for you as well. The water is cool now but the day is very warm. Shall I send someone to help you?"

She shook her head, fighting the lingering sensations of their intimacy. "No, please. I should like to be dressed before I received anyone. If you could just direct me to the bath and set my clothes nearby."

He brought her to the water closet and showed her the commode. She emerged a moment later and stood silently waiting for directions, listening for his footsteps. "Are you quite sure you don't want a maid—"

"Yes. Please."

He took her elbow and led her to the waiting brass tub, filled with cool fresh water. He watched as she knelt down and ran a hand around the rim before standing. "My clothes?"

"Here. Your skirt is hanging from the dressing screen." He guided her hand to it. "The rest are beneath the bath towel here."

She nodded and stepped back to the bath. She stopped a moment. "You are turned away?"

"Yes."

She turned toward him. "You are not!"

"How can you know that?"

"Your voice would hit the wall before reaching me. It comes directly."

"How's this?"

"Better." She let the robe drop and stepped into the cool water.

Victor smiled unseen, grasping certain unexpected benefits of her sightlessness. For she had no idea of his interested gaze upon her. He could only wonder at the lure of her beauty, more powerful than the tides beneath the moon. . . .

Jade sat alone at the breakfast table outside, shaded from a sinking sun by a fragrant magnolia tree. Victor had left after receiving a note from his father, promising to return to escort Jade home in the late afternoon. Sebastian still slept, and after spending the afternoon sharing her newfound joy and happiness with Jade, Mercedes had left again to check on Sebastian.

Jade's thoughts turned to the Reverend Mother, by far the person most disturbed by all that had happened, despite the happy ending. So strangely silent and withdrawn, the Reverend Mother had left to retire, pleading exhaustion and promising to put Sister Benedict to the task of finding Jade a new servant until Maydrian could be located.

A tall glass of lemonade remained untouched on the table while Jade distractedly tore up croissants and tossed the crumbs to the growing number of chirping birds surrounding her.

Victor, Victor, Victor. The name sounded over and over in her mind. He had unfolded a wondrous mystery to her. A secret part of the world had been revealed. She understood so much more about men and women, love and life. What was to happen to them? Would they fall in love now? Was she already in love?

When would this emotional ride stop to let her catch her breath? All day long she felt intense rushes of unexplainable excitement; she felt those maddening shivers running through her, her stomach tightening into knots while her heart and breathing raced as though she was running, nervous and happy. . . .

Murray and Carl, now both retired to their separate duties, had spared no effort to provide support and comfort once everyone departed, each taking pleasure in feeding Jade's burgeoning curiosity about Victor. Murray now resided here at Victor's house, helping Victor run the shipyard. Seeking to distract her, they told stories of Victor's business success, travels, background and even the remarkable story of how he got his first ship. Still the most surprising information was what she would have known had she been able to see.

"What's so funny," Murray had told her, "is that Father Nolte mentioned you at dinner a few times. He said there was the most remarkable young lady at the convent, that he never met a young lady more delightfully charming or gifted. It seems you're able to play chess without seeing the board. Is that right?"

Many people were surprised by her gifts.

"How did you go blind?" he had asked at one point.

"An accident. I was struck in the head."

"A head injury? That is rare. The back of the head?"

"No. 'Twas the front. Would you describe the garden again. . . ."

Booted footsteps sounded on the tiled patio. She turned toward the sound. She knew it was him before he came to kneel in front of her. She felt a tingling flush of excitement.

"Jade Terese," Victor said as a gentle hand curved around her cheek, "can you please tell me how it is you look more beautiful every time I see you?" He chuckled as a slight flush of color suffused her cheeks. "Add a smile and you all but knock me from my footing."

She did look lovely. She sat beneath the blooming tree in a plain skirt of yellow, and a white cotton blouse that a peasant girl might wear. Tiny chirping birds surrounded her. The long hair fell in a neat line down her back; a straw sunbonnet sat on her lap.

"Who left you all alone, sweetheart?"

The question confused her; her smile faded. It was as if he felt she shouldn't be left alone, which, of course, was ridiculous. "Dr. Murray is napping, I think, while Monsieur Carl is attending his duties. The Reverend Mother, I fear, is still distraught by all that's happened; she begged to withdraw from company."

"I see," he said.

"Did you speak to Maydrian's family?"

"Yes, I did." He did not explain that he had prepared them for bad news, that Maydrian might never be found and if she were, she would probably be dead. "Naturally they are very concerned, and I believe they are prepared to hear the worst—"

"The worst?"

The beautiful green eyes seemed to search his face, unnerving him with the practiced ability to create an illusion of sight.

"What can you mean?" The question was asked whisper soft. "Surely we will find Maydrian? If something terrible had happened to her, do you not think we would have discovered it by now?"

He suddenly remembered his father laughing at some amusing episode with the girl: "You just have to experience the rose-colored glasses from which she views the world to believe it. Ah, she is like a breath of fresh perfumed air. . . ."

"Sweetheart . . ." He knelt in front of her. "It seems the opposite is true, if you think about it. If Maydrian were fine, no doubt we would have found her by now."

Her fists clenched around the rim of her bonnet, a pained expression crossing her face. "I don't believe it. 'Tis true something terrible must have happened to her but it does not mean she has perished. Quite the contrary! We are only ignorant of what has befallen her. I'm just certain Maydrian will appear hale and healthy. . . ."

"I suppose time will tell," he replied noncommittally. He realized quite suddenly how tired he felt and yet there was something he still very much wanted to do. "Jade Terese, as we wait for the carriage that will take you home, it's occurred to me that while we experienced"—he smiled—"the height of intimacy, I've yet to stroll in the garden with you. Would you like to take a turn in the garden while we wait?"

She held out her hands as she stood up. He led her down a smooth stone path. Amidst the exotic setting, she looked like a picture taken from a French romantic painting. Nimble fingers secured the yellow ribbons of her bonnet around her chin. The hat tilted to the side, while her hair fell to the small of her back. He smiled when he saw her bare feet.

She felt the gentle weight of his arm on her shoulder, his other hand in hers. She imagined the sky was red with the sunset over the river. In her mind's eye she saw the shadows lengthening and the rainbow colors of the garden darkening. "It's beautiful, your garden. . . ."

The words stopped him. With humor and surprise, he asked: "But how can you know?"

"I see it perfectly in my mind," she said. "Sister Benedict informed me it's at least two acres, all surrounded by

a thirty-foot-high wall of bamboo and ivy. Over there"—
she pointed toward the corner—"is a grove of old maple
trees, colored bright green now, and she counted three apple trees there, banana trees and blossoming cherry trees."
She closed her eyes and breathed deeply. "Their scent
reaches me here. I can smell the blossoming flower beds
myself: I imagine red marigolds, lilies, fragile bunches of
lavender and wild clumps of jasmine everywhere. She also
described the curious sculpture garden. She even tried to
make sense of it, but its meaning, if indeed it has a meaning, eluded her."

And so he first confronted the poetry of her mind, and
all the while the high musical voice described his garden
he was thinking back to his father's and the Reverend
Mother's poignant questions concerning his intentions. He
had barely refrained from pointing out that if he married
every woman who found herself in his bed . . . well, instead he had answered honestly. He didn't know—and indeed, despite what had happened, they hardly knew each
other.

It had been a long time since he had considered marriage to any woman, and then not seriously. While he fell
in love more often than the seasons shifted, these inevitably proved to be passing infatuations. He had never met a
woman he had wanted to be with for the rest of his life.

The trouble was, and it was apparent to everyone, Jade
Terese was a woman a man either married or left alone.
Leaving Jade alone did not seem possible. It took only a
memory of their night together, of her complete surrender
to him and a passion meeting his own, to shatter that resolution. He might even admit it would be a losing battle
with her except for one thing.

There was no way he could pretend her blindness didn't
bother him. One of his shipmates had once cared for his
blind sister and Victor kept thinking of this now. One
never forgot for a moment the man's sister had been blind:
her blank stare, the hands almost constantly extended to
feel the world before her, and a indefinable stiffness and

caution of movement. Jade had a few of these manners, and when they occurred, she quickly righted herself. Indeed, her manners were a kind of miracle themselves. She must have practiced the illusion of sight for many years, concealing her blindness so well he found himself forgetting even now, as she dragged her hand over silky moss on a trunk, asking for a description of this and that, even pointing, turning her face up to his before offering up the sound of her laughter.

Watching her thoughtfully as they strolled, Victor turned the conversation around to her . "My father told me about your gifts, of course."

"Oh? I can't tell you how much I care for your father. He has helped me so much over the years. Did he tell you how often I visit him? He instructs me in history and philosophy, too, did he tell you that?"

"Yes, he mentioned all that. It seems my father had been quite taken by you as well." She smiled shyly and he continued. "These gifts, Jade, I find them difficult to believe. He says you're fluent in four languages: French, English, Spanish and Latin. He claims your Latin is exceptional."

"It's only because I can memorize things so easily."

"So I've heard. I'd like to hear it, though. Say something in Latin."

Jade asked in that romantic language a question pressing heavily on her thoughts: "Do you think we are going to fall in love?"

His laughter startled her. "That question demonstrates both your honesty and the arresting idea that you've yet to develop the normal feminine pretensions."

"I'm sorry, I shouldn't have—"

"Don't apologize. I'm delighted. I find it refreshing, to say the least."

He led Jade beneath a sugar gum tree, where they sat down on the grass. The garden scents were delicious, the shade under the tree cool. "What languages do you speak?" she asked, trying to change the subject.

"My Spanish and French have never been very good. I also speak some Japanese, though that's a most difficult language. It's nothing like Western tongues, and having no similarity, it gave me the most trouble. I learned just enough to get by there."

Interested, Jade started to inquire further but he was quicker, shifting the subject back. "My father claims that you can add long sums of numbers in your head, that you enjoy putting poems to memory, that you can recite on request most major works and are particularly fond of Shakespeare?"

"You have to understand, I'm not like other people—"

"I can see that." He laughed.

"I mean . . . well, I can't just open a book and read like others, so I have to put it to memory."

"You're very fortunate to be able to do so."

"I suppose I am."

"I'm beginning to understand how much your gifts allow you to compensate for being blind." He looked at her thoughtfully, brushing a mosquito from her face. "But there is one thing I will not believe until it's demonstrated."

"I think I know what's coming."

"I'll bet you do. How can you play chess without seeing the board?"

"I do see the board. I see it in my mind. I only need the positions called out, you know, King to Queen's Knight four and so forth."

"How often do you have to have the positions called back?" he asked, curious, chuckling when she blushed, for the positions had to be called only once. "I shouldn't have asked. I will be looking forward to a game or two."

"I would never play chess with you!"

"Why not?"

"Men seem such poor losers."

"Jade"—he laughed—"you will be sorry you said that. I will show you no mercy. A fact: you could not beat me in chess."

"The arrogance!"

"Is justified," he replied.

The musical sound of her laughter was intoxicating. Too much so, and he rose, then took her hands as he helped her to her feet. Her laughter died beneath his amused scrutiny. The silence made her suddenly shy again. "Victor, I don't know how to thank you for what you and Sebastian did— stopping that woman, saving Mercedes and—"

A gentle finer came over her lips. "I am undeserving, and if I weren't, I have been rewarded royally. As you know."

As he studied her upturned face, time seemed to stretch, broken at last by the soft whisper of her name. A finger traced the contours of her mouth, barely touching her skin. She drew a shaky uneven breath as she heard him say, "I cannot resist this. I am trying but—"

He lowered his head to hers. He first kissed her closed lids before letting his mouth lightly graze, drinking the sweet scent of her. He whispered her name against her ear. Shivers, she felt a rush of tiny shivers, a feverish trail where his lips touched her skin. The pounding of her heart became a roar in her ears, more as the curve of his finger parted her lips for his kiss.

The kiss called a promise to the very core of her being. Like last night, only now she was in no way impaired. So tenderly did he first kiss her, she felt that strange sense of wonder mixed with some small distress. One answered as the sensual press of his mouth deepened, fueling a tingling warmth surging from deep inside, growing, spreading until—

The pleasure magnified as the play of the kiss sent her into a soft swoon, melting and helpless. Yet he was holding her up. He had taken her small hands in his, bringing them behind her back and lifting her as he did so, gently aligning her soft curves to the hard outline of his body.

He broke the kiss but did not part as his moist lips found the soft hollow of her throat, the line of her neck and the curve of her ear, where he whispered her name

over and over. The artful teasing of his mouth and tongue
sent small hot slashes of pleasure through her, her breath
came in small little gasps and—

"Here, sweetheart"—he reached for her arms even as he
was kissing her closed eyes, her mouth—"put your arms
around my neck. . . . Better," he said, rewarding the movement by tightening his arms around her and returning his
mouth to hers, taking her soft pliant lips with tender insis-
tence.

Like a finely planned crescendo, the kiss deepened
slowly. She couldn't resist or think or breathe. There was
no thought past the lips on hers, the heady flavor of his
mouth, the sweep of his tongue, the feel of his body. As
a dream—

Carl found it necessary to contain his surprise upon
finding Victor and Jade locked in such an intimate embrace, kissing and God knows what else, oblivious to the
world crumbling quickly around them. He cleared his
throat and loudly said, "Do allow me to interrupt for a moment."

Victor broke from her and turned. "You make it sound
as though we have a choice."

"I didn't mean to mislead you." Carl smiled. "I only
meant to draw you attention to the fact that the carriage is
waiting; there are worldly concerns to be attended to, to
say nothing of the smaller trifles . . ."

"I get your drift, Carl," Victor said, releasing Jade from
his tight embrace. "I can only say, I found myself distracted."

Carl looked at Jade. "Obviously."

Darkness stretched over the city as the carriage made
slow progress through the muddy streets. Jade listened to
the banter between Victor and his two men riding alongside the vehicle. It was not a large distance between her
house and his, but the streets were still flooded from the
rain, and it was so much easier to maneuver with a horse.

She kept thinking of his kiss.

Her hand gently touched her lips, remembering the sweeping sensations and reliving the startling awakening of her own sensuality. She must be falling in love!

How else to explain this heady excitement, changing the amount of oxygen she needed in her lungs, changing the normal steady pace of her heart to fast, then slow, then fast again. It felt like being atop a wondrous winged stallion of fairy tales long ago told, a creature who gave wings to a flight of secret dreams, so that she now flew through life at a dizzying yet exhilarating pace.

The carriage stopped in front of the small cottage behind the convent grounds. "Wait here, sweetheart," Victor said after a quick glance around told him Mercedes and Sebastian had not arrived yet. He hoped that Sister and the new servant would be here soon, though he would keep two men outside her cottage door for a week or so.

"All right," he began to whisper so as not to be overheard by Jade. He did not want her frightened. "I want everyone in the surrounding cottages questioned. Someone had to have seen the men who abducted her—this whole French section of the city is like a small town; everyone knows everyone's business . . ."

Waiting in the carriage, Jade felt a growing uneasiness at the thought of entering her house again. Why? As if there was something there. . . . She couldn't quite put her finger on it. What could it be?

Hamlet! Was Hamlet still lying there? Victor never mentioned her dog, and in the rush of events, no one probably thought to bury poor Hamlet! She got out of the carriage and with an outstretched arm, she ran toward the cottage.

"Jade!" Victor called.

Victor's voice didn't stop her, and ignoring the scent that should have alerted her, she climbed the steps and pushed open the door. With tears filling her eyes, she dropped to her knees and cautiously began patting the surrounding area.

She moved forward and knocked into something hanging in the air. She gasped, jerked back, but it swung back and hit her in the face, smashing her hat and sending a pain through her. A timid hand reached into the air. She felt . . . a nose and a mouth—

A body hung upside down.

A blinding white light burst in her head and she screamed with the explosion of unimaginable pain in her head, a seizure that claimed her consciousness. . . .

The men raced into the house. Victor's arm shot up in a quick reflex, stopping the other two in their tracks. An old woman, undoubtedly Maydrian, hung upside down from the ceiling. In case the gruesome sight wasn't warning enough, her throat was slit and the mutilated body barely connected.

Jade lay unconscious on the floor.

In one swift movement Victor lifted Jade in his arms and carried her out. It had all gone too far now, much too far.

Chapter 6

S ister Benedict found the Mother Francesca deep in prayer in the chapel at the convent. She interrupted the Reverend Mother and quickly led her out, barely able to speak. "Hurry, do hurry, Mother. Tragedy has befallen us again. Father Nolte and Monsieur Nolte await in your chambers."

The Reverend Mother could not see Sister Benedict's hands until they had passed through the dark narrow corridor and the woman reached for the lever on the door to her chambers. With alarm she saw the tremble there. She stepped inside the room, bracing, as Sister Benedict shut the door behind her—a sound like the slam of a judge's gavel. For part of her knew before the words had been spoken. . . .

Monsieur Nolte stood at the window overlooking the darkened gardens, the extensive width of his back put to her, his head lowered as if he was trying to collect his thoughts. Father Nolte stood facing her. She found concern and worry in his familiar dark eyes and she stiffened visibly, her hands clasping the small wooden statuette she always carried.

The small figure had been carved in Africa. It was a woman shrouded in neat classical robes and a hood. The tiny face was marked by an inexplicable joy, and yet sadness, the very duality of Mary herself. It was a small miracle of human creation. When she had first laid eyes upon it, her breath was literally swept away. In a strange magical way it served as an emblem of her faith more than her rosary beads.

She rubbed her thumbs over its smooth lines now. Dear God, help me. . . .

"Jade's servant was found," Father Nolte said. "Dead. Please sit down. The details are hideous. I must be blunt."

She stared as if he spoke an altogether unintelligible language. She didn't understand how this was happening. Years ago, in the days following the Devon tragedy, she had tried desperately to understand the nature of evil. Finally, after many hours of meditation and prayer, one night she had found herself in a dream: She stood in a dark room, trying in vain to light a candle. She could not. She stood there staring into a darkness that was so deep and dark and impenetrable . . .

Now the candle was being lit.

The Reverend Mother silently went to her desk chair and sat down, terrified to hear of these hideous details . . .

"She was hung upside down with her throat slit, her body discovered in Jade's small entry hall."

Turning around, Victor watched the color drain from the good woman's face. For a moment she seemed to teeter, and he started toward her to catch her fall, but no. She rocked back in the hardwood chair with the shock before she straightened, alerted. Then she lowered her eyes as she placed her trembling hands in the folds of her gown.

She stated as if a fact: "No . . ."

"The worst part about the murder," Father Nolte's strong clear voice rose, "is that Jade's house had been checked this very morning and Sister Benedict, I believe, had been there to fetch Jade some clothes. This means the body had been left"—he paused for a second as a hand went to his forehead—"and arranged in that gruesome manner in broad daylight. The family next door, the Mordants, had been out on various errands, but two servants had remained home. Neither of them saw anything. The same is true of the house behind hers. No one saw anything. There is no explanation possible. And yet obviously we must face the fact that someone, for some unholy reason, is threatening Jade Terese."

Very unholy reasons echoed in the Reverend Mother's mind. She was shaking her head. Jade Terese was threatened and so, then, was she. Perhaps God had not absolved her after all? "I don't understand what's happening. . . ."

Victor and his father exchanged glances.

Father Nolte turned and paced, his boots echoing softly on the stone floor. His eyes were intense and probing, focused hard on the older woman before him.

"These men—whoever they are—are killers. Jade's situation is, to say the least, extremely dangerous and will remain so until we discover just who is doing this and why." He looked at Victor. "My son is extending his protection, of course. He insists that Jade stay at his country estate until the murderers are apprehended. I must say, I quite agree. With only Father Lahey and the convent gardeners here, there is no one who could possibly protect her from a threat of this diabolical a nature."

The Reverend Mother seemed to collapse all at once, the magnitude of the situation hitting her like a blow to the head. She alone knew no one on earth—not even a man such as Monsieur Nolte—could possibly protect Jade Terese from this threat, but then there were no words that conveyed this. No words to explain the inexplicable . . .

"No one must know," she finally said in a whisper of fear. "We must create the pretense that Jade is leaving Orleans for a convent in France or Spain. We will not name the place. I alone will forward her correspondence. No one will know."

At first Victor assumed she meant this to protect Jade's reputation from the impropriety of a young unmarried woman's living in his household, but no. The secrecy was meant to further protect Jade. "Yes," he said. "Of course." He approached the place where she sat. Their eyes locked. Gently he said, "Now, we understand you are naturally distressed but I'm afraid we must ask you a few questions."

The Reverend Mother managed a nod but no answers to these questions could come from her. For she, like the two men in the room, had always believed in a rational explanation of the universe. God himself was the awe of human experience, a small but meaningful transcendence that occasionally and miraculously rose like a brief shining light above the senseless struggle of daily life. She had always believed the supernatural was superstition, a refuge of the ignorant and naive. Until now. Until a dead woman rose from her grave to threaten and terrorize her and Jade Terese.

"I understand Jade's parents died in a devastating fire?"

"Yes." She nodded, clearing her parched throat. "A devastating fire . . . five years ago June. But—"

"June? In the summer?" Victor said, interested in this. "It happened at night?"

"No." She shook her head. She felt a tremble start in her voice and she tried to clear it again. "It happened between morning and noon, an hour or so after their slaves had left for the fields."

"A kitchen fire, then?" Victor assumed, knowing kitchens were the cause of most fires, what with the hot stoves and wood structures.

"No." She shook her head again, her voice still strained and tremulous. "The kitchen was one of the few remaining structures on the plantation. You had to have seen it," she said, staring off into space as she spoke. "A circle of charred earth that raced through the cane fields like a torch from hell—"

Father Nolte begged the question: "If it was a summer morning, no hearths or lamps or even a candle would have been lit. If not in the kitchen, how, then, did it start?"

"No one has ever discovered the cause."

The ominous words hung in the silence.

"And Jade?" Victor asked. "What about Jade Terese?"

"Jade was found on the perimeter of the fire unconscious. She had a slight bump on her forehead, that was all. Yet when she woke up she was blind. And she had no memory of the fire or the hours preceding it."

The Reverend Mother withdrew a set of keys from her

pocket. She separated a tiny gold key from the others. She valiantly attempted to insert it in the desk with a trembling hand, finally managing. Victor stood behind her. The drawer opened. Inside sat a red leather Bible. He watched her hands shake as she withdrew the Bible. Cushioned between the pages was a letter.

Quietly she said, "This is a letter I received from a doctor at Cambridge. It was in reply to an inquiry I made concerning Jade's health."

Victor took the letter and brought it to a lamp hanging over the desk. He ignored the formalities of correspondence and got right to thrust of it, reading out loud for his father's benefit.

"I find the case you describe fascinating and if it is at all possible, I'd very much like to examine the young lady in question. However, having not had such opportunity, I can only offer my learned opinion of the case as you describe it.

"First, it is not possible, as you suspect, that her loss of sight is the result of having seen something frightening, no matter how terrible. Do reflect but for a moment: If that were possible, I daresay, we'd all be blind.

"Furthermore, blindness as the result of a head injury is indeed rare—I have only seen one such case—and contrary to conventional wisdom, it could occur only from a severe blow to the back of the head, not the front. Since the accident caused injury to the front of the young lady's head, I must conclude her seizures—"

Victor stopped and looked up. "Seizures? What seizures?"

"Jade suffers from seizures that send her into a faint. She experiences excruciatingly painful seizures for no reason anyone knows." Softly she added, "She has not had one for over two years now. We are hoping it is a thing of the past . . ."

After a momentary contemplation of this unpleasant fact, Victor continued reading the letter:

"I must conclude her seizures are the result of the head injury and her blindness the result of her seizures. I can only guess that her loss of memory is also the result of the seizures. I have never heard of a similar case and to be certain of my conclusion, I would first have to rule out epilepsy.

"My prognosis is not favorable. I suspect the seizures have caused irreparable brain damage and that the young lady's blindness is a permanent condition. However, upon reading your description of the pain accompanying her seizures, I would recommend you take every precaution to prevent them. Her activities and life should be restricted; she should never be allowed to become overly excited . . ."

"My God," Father Nolte said. "Why was I never told of this?"

"Jade Terese begged me not to ever mention it to anyone. She is always quite certain they are a thing of the past."

With a preplexing look, trying to make sense of this troubling situation, Victor stepped forward with the next questions: "What did you mean by asking if she might have gone blind by viewing a terrible sight? The fire?"

For a long time she appeared unable to answer the question. Indeed, it was the very heart of the tragedy. She finally drew a deep breath and spread her large hands on the desk, to steady them. "I did not know. It was only a feeling I had. The seizures and, you see," she said slowly, whispering, "there are many unanswered questions about the fire. The day after the fire, the mortician, Monsieur Lawler, who buried the . . . burnt remains of Jade's parents, died as well. Madame Lawler had come to me. Her husband was found dead the day of the burial. Sudden heart seizure, the doctor told her. Yet he was a young and healthy man who, as I recall, worked with his father, the senior Lawler. She told me . . . that he had been going to the constable to discuss . . . to discuss the condition of the burnt bodies of Jade's parents, that he was very upset. That's all the poor woman knew."

"Yes? And what was this condition of the corpses?"

She shook her head. "No one has ever learned," she said. "It was all many years ago. The Church, Father Aglae before you, Father Nolte, had prevented a burial desecration. The matter was dropped."

"This is all so very suspicious," Father Nolte said after a moment's consideration. "It sounds as if someone started the fire to conceal a murder."

"Yes." The Reverend Mother nodded. "Indeed, and as if the same unholy hatred that started the fire has now turned on Terese and myself."

"Yourself?"

"Myself. For I do not think I could survive if something were to happen to Terese."

The emotion in the room bid Father Nolte step forward and place a kind arm around the older woman, while his son said with sudden conviction, "You can rest assured I will not let anything happen to her."

The impassioned promise brought tear-filled eyes up again. If she had ever imagined a match for Terese, it would have been a young man, gentle like Terese, well bred, devout, given to books and poetry, living the quietly reflective and peaceful life. The opposite of this man, with his strength, character, and intelligence, the sheer force of will that he exercised in the world, a world many, many times removed from the cloistered sanctuary that was Jade's life. Yet even now, as his gaze did not waver beneath her scrutiny, she intuitively grasped his honesty and integrity, his father's own. Terese's safety was his primary concern.

The Reverend Mother drew another deep shaky breath, and looking at Victor still, she seemed to plead as she asked, "You will keep her safe?"

"Upon my life . . ."

* * *

In the quiet of a dying light Victor was explaining the whole thing to Murray. He handed Murray the letter. With a furrowed brow, Murray read the letter twice again.

"The whole thing is a life-threatening mystery and I don't have the first bloody clue," Victor said, and looking at the sleeping young lady, he asked, "She doesn't remember her accident or the fire because of these seizures, which then made her blind. The doctor says she should never get overly excited. What do you make of it?"

"That lass must not have them anymore. After what she just passed through, well, it seems to me, if she still had them, we would have seen one—"

"Yes, but perhaps that's what happened when she found her maid. Perhaps she is recovering now from one—"

Murray shook his head. "That is odd about the blow to her head. The surgeon is absolutely right. The center of sight in the brain is behind, not in front."

"The whole fire is suspicious," Victor replied as he sank back into the chair. "And this mortician's death—"

"That could must be an unfortunate coincidence."

"Not if it happened as he was heading to the constable. We have to dig up her parents' graves."

"Bones often don't tell much of a story, you know."

"It's worth a try. I'll have to investigate her father's debts and have my agents make inquiries into her family's history. And," he said, deep in thought, still staring at the beautiful young lady in his bed, "I'm forced to put the maid's murder down to a connection to her parents and to the fire that in all likelihood concealed their murder. There must be a connection to her parents' death if only because it's impossible to imagine why anyone would want to threaten her. Jade has no fortune, no enemies, no relations; she has nothing, it seems, but the love and affection of an entire city."

"Aye," Murray agreed, nodding. "That's true. Everyone loves the lass—Creoles, Spanish, free coloreds and the working slaves, everyone. I stopped at the tobacco shop today and there was Monsieur Jessen and a handful of his customers talking about Sebastian and what a bloody hero he is, and how, thank God, he had saved Jade Terese. They talked like she was a saint! They went on and on about how she had solicited half the funds for the Negro infirmary as well as the Negro girls' school, as well as a scholarship fund for poor students. They all joked about how impossible it was to resist the young lady's honeyed pleas, how now, as soon as they spot her heading toward them, they just remove their billfolds."

Carl heard their quiet chuckles as he opened the door to inquire about a late supper. He first caught sight of Jade stirring in the bed, and he called Victor and Murray to her side. They came immediately but only to see she was not waking but rather dreaming . . .

Small black boots raced up the carpeted stairs. The long plaits of her hair, the ruffles on her gold frock, bounced with each step. "Mama! Mama!" She ran down the hall and stopped at the wide carved door to her parent's bedroom. Her small hand touched the latch and pulled down. The door opened to a blinding white light—

Victor grabbed Jade as she bolted upright, her hands bracing as the fierce blast of pain shot through her head. Jade's face blanched white, her whole being stiffened before she fell limp, collapsing in his arms.

"Jade!" Victor shook her but she remained unconscious and stunned. He laid her gently against the pillows. Murray checked her pulse, her breathing and then shook his head, startled by it.

"My God. There it was."

Victor and Murray were still in the room, quietly discussing the situation, when she woke less than an hour later. She sat up in bed, wearing only a chemise, her arms crossed over herself. She waited for some external sign. Where was she?

"Jade?"

Victor. She reached out for him like a lifeline as he sat on the bed, taking her into his arms. "How long have I been here?"

"It's the middle of the night. You've been here since the afternoon. How do you feel, sweetheart?"

"Were you here? Were you here the whole time?"

Victor and Murray assumed she was asking if he saw Maydrian too, if what she'd felt had been real. "Yes, I was there. I stayed the whole time, save for a visit to your Reverend Mother with my father. Since then I've been waiting for you to wake. Jade—"

"Did you see . . . I mean, did you . . ."

"Yes, Jade, I saw it."

The shame of it turned her face away. Quietly she asked, "I suppose it frightened you."

Victor Murray shot confused glances at each other.

"Please don't concern yourself with it. Heavens, but it's been so long since I had one, I half thought I was through with them. God knows why I should suffer one today, but with a little luck, 'twill be years again before I have another."

"Jade, are you talking about your seizures?"

She nodded.

"Do you remember what caused it?"

"Remember what?"

A shadow moved through the open doors of the balcony and stood there staring at the sleeping woman. She was dreaming. A dream that would change to a nightmare . . .

In this dream Jade danced with her arms outstretched and her face tilted to a summer sun. Her laughter burst into a song that made her twirl and twirl. In her dreams she could see. She could see the world in all the glory and magnificence of creation; a world made buttery sunshine, the rainbow colors of wildflowers and a rushing waterfall into a cool swimming hole. A world made of a child's simple joy.

There was no evil in this world. . . .

Victor watched her, laughing too. He started forward. Excitement burst into laughter; she ran. He leaped after, catching her, lifting her up before he swung her 'round and 'round in his arms. They fell to the soft cushion of grass. Then he silenced her laughter with a kiss.

She couldn't breathe, and she wondered wildly why she wasn't fainting as her mouth, her mind, her every sense melted beneath the sensuous press of his lips. The kiss deepened as he added more pressure. Then she was breathing hard as her head swam dizzily and a great heat burst deep within herself. A hot rush of chills followed.

The kiss broke with the sound of his name.

Jade bolted up suddenly in bed. Small beads of perspiration laced her brow. She drew deep, quick breaths as she tried to slow the racing of her heart.

A gold lamp still burned, softly illuminating the spacious room she could not see. She listened to the haunting rhythm made by a warm breeze lifting and dropping the curtains.

The erotic dream had made her skin feel hot. Her hand brushed back the loosened strands of her hair. She fell against the bed pillow with the whispered sound of his name: "Victor ..."

That one night together haunted her sleep, weaving the memories into erotic dreams. Never before could she have imagined a passion that stole thoughts and transformed dreams! It was so consuming, so powerful! His every word, the sound of his laughter, every slight touch, sent her heart pounding with a strange and new excitement.

Being with him had become a furious battle to keep her mind from the memory of his hot hard body against her skin, the feel of his lips on hers, and somehow when he drew close, all she could think about was his touch. It was all much worse at night. . . .

Her other problem was far more maddening and baffling. Everyone was so afraid for her! Victor rarely strayed from her side unless Sebastian took his place. Victor stood by her during the tearful partings with all her friends, Maydrian's funeral, meetings with the two Sisters who would take over her music classes, the packing. Like a mother cat he was, watchful, questioning everyone as if he might find those men who had murdered poor old Maydrian among the circle of her friends. She just didn't understand why everyone thought she was in danger still. She didn't understand why Mother Francesca, Father Nolte, even Sebastian and Mercedes, were so certain she would only be safe far away at his country estate, and why it was necessary to tell everyone that she was withdrawing to a convent in France. She was quite certain those men who had ruthlessly kidnapped her and murdered Maydrian were a thousand miles away by now.

Not that she minded going to stay at Victor's country estate. Mercedes would go with her and it sounded like a wonderful holiday. Father Nolte and Reverend Mother had both absolutely insisted. Victor had insisted. "Jade, I will keep you protected until we are absolutely assured of your safety," he had said.

Now Mercedes and her trunks were packed and waiting on board a ship. Tomorrow they would board this ship, which Victor had discreetly arranged to have stop some fifty miles downriver, where they would meet him and Sebastian for the roundabout journey to his estate. What else could she do? She supposed time would make them see there was no hidden danger—

A slight creak in the floorboards alerted her. She froze, listening intently. "Victor?" Another creak sounded. It was him! He was teasing her. She would feel his arms before she heard his voice.

Anticipation made her swallow her laughter.

An odd scent alerted her. Dried herbs and burnt wood. Not Victor. Not Mercedes or Dr. Murray. Not Agnes or Belle, the two upstairs maids. She stiffened, drawing the pillow against her chest. "Who is it? Who's there?"

There was no answer. The scent grew more pungent. Someone got onto the bed. Jade waved her hand in front of herself. "You are scaring me—"

A curious hiss of a whispered voice sang:

"Run, little girl, run
Your mother is hanging,
Your father used a gun,
Run, little girl, run . . ."

Jade's screams died in her throat as she clasped her head against a blinding white light and unbearable pain. . . .

Victor climbed the steps of his house. Carl opened the door. "What happened?"

Carl just shook his head, looking quite stricken. "You should hear it from Mademoiselle Mercedes."

He opened the door to his bedchamber. Dawn was just stretching into the room through the open balcony windows. Jade slept in bed. Sebastian, Mercedes and Murray gathered around her sleeping form as if she were on her deathbed. Mercedes wiped her eyes, clinging protectively to Jade's hand.

He came slowly to the bed.

In a controlled whisper: "What happened?"

"Oh, Victor." Mercedes shook her head, still trembling with the aftermath. "Jade and I had retired early, so excited were we about tomorrow. I was just getting up for a glass of water—the water pitcher in my room was empty. I was passing this room when I heard Jade speaking to someone inside. I knew 'twasn't you, you said you would be at the shipyard through the night. She was saying, 'Who is it, who is it?' I reached for the doorknob. And then, then I heard this voice . . . singing a song, like a child's nursery rhyme, only—I opened the door and a man was kneeling over Jade. I thought he was going to kill her! I screamed—"

Victor's gaze flew to Sebastian.

"We didn't find anyone," Sebastian said. "We searched five blocks. Nothing. He got away."

Fury filled Victor where he stood, a bright murderous rage that had no outlet, and it only got worse when Murray said: "The words, you have to hear 'em. They sent the lass into a seizure; she's out cold and ten to one she won't remember a thing on the morrow. Tell him, Mercedes."

She shook her head, tears sprang into her eyes. "I can't . . . say it again."

Murray repeated the words flatly. " 'Your mother is hanging . . . your father used a gun.' What the hell does that mean?"

Victor's gaze widened with outrage; he swore with soft viciousness as he turned to the wall and braced his long arms there. A man broke into his house, into his bedchamber, bent on tormenting Jade with a sick string of words before he killed her?

"What the devil does that mean?" Murray asked in fear. Yet there was no answer.

"All I know is that someone is threatening her now, that someone broke into my home, into my bedchamber, and attempted murder!"

An impotent violence rose inside Victor and he swung his arm back and rammed his clenched fist hard into the wall with a resounding rumble. The wall cracked, and he withdrew his fist with a curse.

The violence stunned Murray. He had witnessed that kind of anger only once before in Victor, the time he was told that sweet young Tessie had been raped by one of his stable hands. Most men would not think long on one of their colored servants being raped in their house, but Victor responded as though Tessie was his own daughter. The man was held in a small cagelike room until Victor arrived at the country estate. Without ever saying a word to the man, he kicked him once in the groin with such violence that the man passed out. Victor then had him stripped and sent into the bayous, to the middle of the swamps, miles from civilization. it was not likely the man survived. "To live like the beast he is," Victor had said, adding to the other workers, "this is not ever to happen in my house again."

Victor did not even stop there. Every once in a while, when he stayed in he country and had a free hour or so, he called Tessie out to the lawn and gave her instruction in the strange Oriental ways of self-defense. Sebastian, Murray, Carl and the other servants rolled with laughter until the lessons began to work. Tessie, a skinny slip of a girl, had learned how to throw a grown man from her person. More important, Victor's concern—so much like a father's—made Tessie feel safe again.

If only there was some way to protect Jade. . . .

Jade stirred as the ugly words sang in her dreams.

> *"Run, little girl, run,*
> *Your mother is hanging,*
> *Your father used a gun,*
> *Run, little girl, run . . ."*

A scream sounded silently in her dream. . . .

A warm sun shimmered over the levee and the marketplace as Victor wondered if half the town had not appeared to say good-bye to Jade Terese. Everyone but Mother Francesca, who had had a private audience with Jade in her chambers. He watched carefully from the ship rail with Mercedes, who was still quite shaken from all that had happened. Jade's music students gathered around her, each girl dressed in a crisp white school frock as Jade went from one girl to the other, smiling and kissing each caramel-colored cheek, many of these wet with tears.

"They love her so!" Mercedes said.

Dozens of shopkeepers and store owners crowded around her, the gens de couleur. Jade Terese embraced Madame Deubler, then her two daughters, and stood for Monsieur Deubler's kiss, her smile and manner as bright as the summer sun above.

She remembered nothing. Mercedes had begged them all not to tell her of the intruder. Victor had resisted the idea until Jade Terese had descended the stairs, full of happiness and excitement over the beginning of this adventure, a happiness that affected him physically and made him understand Mercedes's inclination. Indeed, it felt impossible to ruin her gaiety and replace it with fear and apprehension. And what if, dear Lord, it brought on another seizure?

She would be safe now. . . .

Your mother is hanging/Your father used a gun. . . . The scenario suggested that the intruder was quite disturbed. He wanted to make Jade suffer as much as he wanted to kill her.

Victor's father had arranged for a grave digging. Perhaps the remains of her parents' bodies would lend a clue. At the very least it could confirm the terrible suspicion. He had three agents investigating Philip Devon's debts. In time he would get close to the answer.

In the meantime he would keep her safe.

Upon my life . . .

Victor's gaze scanned the crowd, watching as the beautiful young lady moved from the gens de couleur to where Lucretia Josset stood with a handful of Creole ladies waiting to say good-bye, Jade passing blindly from colored to white. Literally. The other night she had explained it was impossible for her to make the distinctions everyone else made instantly, and while at first she had been scorned for her many trespasses: for taking tea at Monsieur Deubler's, or singing with the colored chorus, attending a baptism or wedding, always sitting in the wrong section—as at the opera—soon everyone came to accept that somehow, by some unspoken consensus, she was exempt from these conventions of society.

Jade knew many people by their scent: Mother Francesca smelled of the rose oil used in the church's lanterns; Father Nolte of his tobacco, ink from writing and the faintest musky scent of old books; Marie Saint smelled deliciously of flowers; and Sister Catherine, too, of roses, for she tended the convent rose garden herself; and so on.

Madame Lucretia's familiar scent of spicy herbs and a lingering trace of perfume reached her as they grasped hands, growing as the lady leaned over and whispered:

"Why is it such a secret where you are going in France, cherie? I want to write to you," she said, "and share all the delicious gossip, no?"

"Oh, please do!" Jade laughed, drawing back a bit. "Mother Francesca will forward all my correspondence. I'm afraid the convent is in the French countryside far from any society; I shall enjoy any letters you might send."

"Very far from society?"

The pale blue eyes watched Jade's response as Madame Lucretia twirled a pink parasol—no sun ever touched her skin. She looked unquestionably beautiful. Her straight dark hair was lifted in a neat chignon: the crown of hair covered in a loose net of pink, this sprinkled with tiny pearls and even smaller white flowers that matched perfectly the tiny flowers embroidered on her lovely day dress of pink cotton. No lines marked her flawless complexion; it was impossible to guess the age of the mayor's wife, even when she smiled.

Jade could not see her, but she had a picture of her in her mind. Madame Lucretia was reputed to be the belle of all balls. Jade knew better than anyone that people wore their physical beauty in their voices and manner. The woman's attention, like so many people's, had always flattered her. Jade counted all the attention and love bestowed upon her by the community of friends as one of her greatest blessings.

"Indeed. I can't remember the name but please, Mother Francesca will be very good at seeing I receive everything. "Good-bye, my sweet lady . . ."

A small Negro girl ran up and placed a string of dark red flowers around Jade's neck, then slipped something into her hands. "A good luck charm for a safe travel, Mademoiselle," she said in a singsong Creole patios, then spun around and ran off before Jade knew who to thank.

"What is it?" Jade asked, holding it in the palm of her hand.

Madame Lucretia bent over and examined the gift. "It is

a tiny pouch made of white crepe. Oh, it smells delicious," she said. "A good luck amulet, for a safe journey and a quick return. She placed it around Jade's neck and kissed her good-bye.

Soon Jade was waving to the small crowd from the plank of the ship and she felt strangely she was waving good-bye to a part of her life: a chapter closing and a new one beginning. Things would never be the same again; she could never be the same again. For she was in love, for the first time in her life she was in love. The emotion shone on her face as Victor came to take her to Mercedes's side. . . .

"Spiders!" Mercedes screamed. "Jade, there are spiders on those flowers!"

Victor reacted before Jade could. He yanked the flower necklace from her neck, while brushing the offending creatures from her white dress. "They're all gone, sweetheart."

"Oh, thank goodness," Jade said, drawing a deep breath, recovering from the fright. She did not see how carefully Mercedes examined the neat pile of her hair to make certain. "It's the one of the worst parts about being blind. Not seeing the little beasties . . ."

Not seeing the evil, Victor thought.

Chapter 7

What a fetching picture the two ladies made in the open-air carriage!

Murray smiled, enjoying the lovely sight as much as he enjoyed entertaining them with outrageous stories of his adventures at sea, stories constantly interrupted by Carl's humor. The two young ladies were dressed for summer and travel. Jade wore a cotton Spanish-style skirt with a bright red-and-gold pattern, and to Victor's enjoyment, a plain white peasant blouse that fell off her shoulders. The white crepe amulet still hung from her neck, blending in magically with her blouse. The thin red ribbon that tied the amulet looked like a small bloodstain against her blouse; Mercedes had even touched it as if to make sure. A wide red ribbon was tied around Jade's straw bonnet. Mercedes wore a plain gold-and-cream short-sleeve day dress, accented with lots of ruffles and flounces, all set off by a matching parasol.

"What do you think Victor and Sebastian are talking about up there?" Mercedes asked.

"About Dr. Murray. Something he has to do, I can't hear what. Victor says his father made arrangements with . . . Kiton. Kiton?" she questioned, confused. "Isn't he that queer old man who guards the cemetery? I know him from church! Well, how very odd. I can hear them perfectly. I can even tell Sebastian is eating an apple."

Mercedes quickly thought to change the subject, making a mental note to warn Victor of Jade's superior listening ability. "Sebastian," she said, "looks gallant and handsome riding the gray-and-white horse, though a bit ridiculous. He is wearing only black breeches and a wide-brimmed black Spanish hat as if he sprang from the pages of *Don Quixote*. Did you read that book?"

"Oh, yes! Well, Sister Gabriel read it to me. Father Nolte made me a present of it." They enthusiastically, though briefly, discussed the book before Jade returned to the more pressing subject. "What of Victor? What does he look like?"

"Victor is wearing white cotton breeches, sailor pants, I think, and those . . . Indian boots . . . moccasins. He has no hat, though there's a red scarf tied around his head for a sweatband. He looks so . . . so—"

"Yes? Handsome like Sebastian?"

"No, not handsome like Sebastian," Mercedes said slowly, staring at Victor's proud, muscled back, his bronze skin, the ease with which he carried himself. Like most women, she knew the exact word to describe Victor, but she chose the more delicate statement. "He is so attractive," she said. "It is difficult to describe but there is something so . . . so magnetic about him."

"Magnetic," Jade repeated with a small smile.

The hot midday sun beat down on the carriage. How much longer could she last? How did the others nap? Jade perspired profusely. Small trickles of sweat ran over her skin, tickling her all over. She removed her bonnet, twisted her hair into a knot and stuffed it back into her hat. One hand fanned her flushed face while the other wiped a moist cloth around her neck and over her bosom.

Watching from above on his horse, Victor groaned, irritated that he could be teased by such innocent gestures. Arousal was becoming a permanent condition around her. It was all he could do to stop himself from carrying her off into the surrounding woods, showing her just how much that beautiful body of hers could perspire . . .

"Goodness," Jade whispered, more to herself, "I do believe I am melting right into this seat."

Victor couldn't take it, not a second more, and with an alarming chuckle, he leaned over the side of the carriage and pulled her up, lifting her over his mount in front of him. Jade gasped, then laughed as her arms wound around his bare waist for support.

Victor found himself in fierce battle for some semblance of control. Did she sense it? Was that why alarm crossed her face, why she quickly positioned herself to put some distance between them? Yes, she must know. She began chatting; asking questions about his background and travels, especially the Orient.

They soon dropped far behind the carriage, slowing as the world dissappeared past the reach of their arms.

Victor kept his gaze carefully on the surroundings, more out of habit than from any threat to her now. Indeed, she would be safe from now on and they all felt it. An easing of tension occurred as the day wore on, Jade's safety assured by the knowledge that no one but his father and Mother Francesca now knew where they were.

Jade was obviously enthralled by his stories of the Orient, and he watched her relive the tales in her head, expressing fear, amazement, excitement and often amusement. Encouraged by her laughter, and without even realizing it, they forgot their acute consciousness of each other. For a while they knew only laughter and enjoyment. . . .

"No, I don't believe that!"

"I'm afraid it's all true." He smiled. "I have the scars to prove it."

"Where?"

Victor took her hand and placed it over the scar on his back, took her other hand and placed it on the gash on his chest. "It is true," she said, running her hand lightly over his skin, remembering having found the scars before.

The horse stopped as Victor knew only the touch of her hand on his skin, the small drop of moisture slowly sliding between her breasts, seeming to collect around the odd decoration that hung there. A tease to which he was particularly vulnerable. He slowly placed her hands back in her lap. Jade felt her hot cheeks flush even more, and from out of the blue, she became acutely aware of the shimmering heat. She could hardly breathe. Moisture slid down her neck, tickling again. She reached a hand to her face, first wiping, then fanning. "Goodness, but it's hot out."

Victor chuckled as he shook his head, pulling a water cask from his saddlebag. "Here, this is water. Tilt your head back," he said, putting his arm around her to keep her from falling. Jade felt the cask come to her lips, a blessed relief as the cool liquid slid down her parched throat. She tried to sit back up but he held her back as the water came over her flushed face, pouring down her neck and bosom.

With the music of her laughter, Victor watched the water spill off her. She was turned to the side, almost facing him. He could no more resist the tease of those lips than he could stop the tide from rising. A hand reached to her hair, gently tilting her head back as he brought her small body against his hot skin and pressed his mouth to hers. His body permitted no protest but then she offered none, surrendering as the kiss deepened—

His muscles tensed all of a sudden and he broke the kiss. A strange scent assaulted his senses, coming from the girl. He looked down at her neck to the amulet.

She wished she could see his face. "Victor?"

Suddenly she smelled it as well. "Victor, there is a foul scent . . . I can't identify it—"

She felt his hands lift the amulet. He jerked it from her neck. "It's this thing," he said, looking at it.

"Oh my! So it is! A little girl gave it to me as a parting present—for good luck on the journey."

"Good luck and foul scents," he said with baffled amusement. Yet, as he examined the amulet closer, a shape emerged beneath the crepe. His smile disappeared. "Here, let me put you on your feet for a moment." He swung off his horse and lowered Jade to her feet, gathering the reins in his hands and giving them to Jade to hold.

"What is it?"

"I just want to see what's inside this thing." He pulled

off the thin red ribbon gathered at the top of it, then unfolded the sides. For a long moment he stared, just stared.

"What's inside it?"

"A bit of powder is all," he lied, staring at the dark green powder, the color of her eyes, tiny burnt crystals, a large dead spider and—

Victor picked up the tiny piece of black wax, no larger than a child's nail, and examined it up close. The craftsmanship was a marvel, an absolute marvel. For the wax formed a perfect human skull, its eyes empty holes and a jagged neck, as if it had been severed. . . .

"I'm lifting you back up," was all he said as he reached for the reins. He lifted her easily to the saddle and mounted behind her. He pulled his horse to abrupt attention, kicking him into a gallop. The hot wind slapped her face and before she could lift back her hat, they flew past the landscape, dust rising where seconds before he had kissed her.

Victor caught up to the carriage, already stopped at the lake where they would spend the night. A forest, shrouded with thick blankets of moss, surrounded a small freshwater lake. The long, spindly branches of the trees stretched wide, providing a mercifully pleasant shade. A tributary of the Mississippi ran through the lake and kept the water cool, fresh and filled with catfish to be caught and cooked in the open air for supper.

The camp was already set up. The matting, brought specifically for Jade and Mercedes, had been rolled out beneath the trees, crushing the lush carpet of ferns, and mosquito nets had already been hung over the mats from the overhanging tree branches. A huge blanket had been spread out, a pile of firewood gathered. Wine cooled in a bucket of cold lake water. Carl slept under another mosquito net and Murray sat against a tree, reading a book.

Victor swung off before lifting Jade down.

"We were wonderin' what became of you two." Murray smiled. "Glad you could finally make it."

"Sebastian and Mercedes?" he asked, bringing Jade to sit by the doctor.

"They already have their poles out, just down yonder."

Jade stretched her arms, savoring the cool shade. Victor left to water his horse, while Murray thoughtfully described the surroundings to her. He handed her his water cask and she drank again.

"How far are we from the lake?" she asked.

"Oh, about fifty, sixty paces. Carl's napping over there. I imagine you're exhausted from the journey and the heat. You can nap if you want. Sebastian arranged a pallet and a mosquito net for you. Supper won't be for some time now."

"Yes," Victor added as he returned, thinking of the horror of the night, the seizures, the doctor's letter. "After our long trip, perhaps you should rest."

Rest? Exhaustion? "Oh, dear," Jade said. "I see now what has happened. The Reverend Mother must have read you a letter from an English doctor who said I shouldn't be excited or overly taxed, am I right?"

Victor cast a glance at Murray, then knelt down beside her. "Yes," he said softly, "and Jade, when I think of what happened to you—"

Jade's hand stopped him. She gently laid fingers against his mouth. "Victor, please do not worry about that, about me. It is true I am blind, but I assure you, my constitution is not as delicate as that doctor suggested. Why"—she spread her arms and laughed—"there's nothing at all delicate about my constitution. I'm as fit as a fiddle and I'm not in the least tired. I want to go down to the lake!"

"But your seizures, Jade?"

All gaiety fell away in the instant as she shook her head. "That doctor was wrong. The seizures don't come from being excited. They come from . . . from being reminded of the accident. . . . From thinking—oh, please!" Fear changed her face as she grabbed her head. "Don't make me talk about it."

Murray stared hard. The startling information made sense, it made perfect sense. . . .

Jade's sudden panic left no question, and Victor instantly understood her warning. He lifted her to her feet, asking if she thought she could sit quietly enough for fishing. Jade nodded quickly, and he added, "Very well, Jade. Wait here just a moment. Murray, I need help with some things in the carriage. Would you?"

The two men walked some distance away.

"It makes sense, Victor," Murray said in an excited whisper. "This whole thing is beginning to make sense. I believe she's right—only it's not a fire."

"What do you mean?"

"She had a seizure when she came across her maid hanging, when the intruder sang that song. She thinks it's a fire, even the way she refers to it as 'the accident.' Only it was . . . it was a gruesome murder. My God, Vic, her parents must have been murdered and the fire started to conceal it and she must have witnessed it. She went into shock and fell down. Her seizures don't cause her blindness, they probably have nothing to do with it."

"I don't understand?"

"Her seizures are what make her forget. Every time she's given the slightest reminder of what happened, anything to do with hanging, she's jolted with a pain so great she falls into unconsciousness, then she wakes with no memory of the reminder."

Victor held the doctor steady in his gaze. "How can that be? I never heard of anything like that. How can someone make himself forget?"

Murray sighed with a shake of his head. "I don't know. All I know is that it seems to be what we're dealing with here. Her parents were murdered and she saw it, and yet to ask her about it sends her into a seizure. She wakes up with no memory. It's as if, as if her mind made a bargain with her heart, that what she saw was just so terrible—" He stopped, realizing how farfetched it was. He had never heard of anything like it either. "I don't know. Maybe I'm wrong, but it does seem to fit the pieces."

Victor reached into his pocket and withdrew the fetish. "Here. Look what was in that charm she was wearing on her neck." He held out the tiny piece of black wax.

Murray picked it up and brought it close to his eyes. "Vic," he said slowly, feeling the hairs on the back of his neck lifting from the ominous talisman, "it's like you say: this beastly person seems to want to torment the lass before he does the unholy business. . . ."

Victor took the oddity back, dropped it to the ground and with the heel of his boot, he crushed it into dust. "He'll never get the chance," he vowed. "I will kill him before he ever comes close again."

The air was still and hot, the shade felt like heaven. "What are you doing?" Jade asked as she sat on the blanket he spread for her on the edge of a grassy bank of the lake. She heard an odd pounding noise above the pleasant hum and buzz of insects.

This was one of his favorite fishing spots: the overhanging branches of trees shaded the dark pool of water. Snakes were the problem. He was beating the ground with a stick to rid the surrounding area of snakes. "Oh, nothing." He grinned as he discovered yet another benefit of her sightlessness.

"I'll take a dip before going off to find some bait," he told her, shrugging unseen from his breeches and moving to the water's edge.

"How many paces would you say the water was from me?"

"Less than five. You are sitting right on the edge."

She nodded, unaware that he no longer looked at her. He stretched once, his smooth bronze skin pulled tight over muscles that displayed a frightening power in his tall frame, before he dove into the cool depths of the water.

Jade laughed and heard him come up, heard him throw his wet hair back with a toss of his head. "I'll bet that feels wonderful." She smiled, knowing she could not resist for long. She'd wait until he left, and then just pop in and out before he got back.

"'Good' cannot describe it." He smiled back. She looked like she was drawn from the pages of a fairy tale with her skirts spread all around her and the wide sun hat tipped slightly. She took off the hat and began pulling the pins from her hair until the thick mass of it swung down her back. He swam to the other side, back again, and climbed out of the water. Jade laughed again as he shook himself over her. "You wait right here," he said. "I'll be back in a few minutes. Don't move . . . or anything."

She heard his footsteps move through the bush, then disappear altogether. She did not hesitate. She slipped off her blouse, skirt, petticoat and chemise, her cotton undergarments, and cautiously inched her way to the water's edge. Once there, she stood up and moved slowly out until the water reached her waist. She knelt under and swam gracefully out.

She never thought she shouldn't. No lady should ever swim, let alone with a man, especially a man one was not married to, but these prohibitions never entered her mind. She and Victor had already traveled very far out of the established conventions and propriety. Then, too, her parents had never emphasized proper decorum as the measure of morality, but rather they had attached inordinate significance to acts of charity. That alone was probably enough to create a free spirit, and the tragedy and its result only added immeasurably to her dauntless ability to toss conventions away without a care or thought.

As a young girl she and her mother had gone swimming almost every day during the relentless heat of the summers. They had a water hole near the plantation. Sometimes her father joined them, too, though he had lost his brother to the bite of a coral snake and he had an exaggerated fear of swimming in Louisiana waters. Still, every once in a while her mother's gentle coaxing could bring him out. Dilsey, their cook, always packed a huge lunch in a basket. Oh, 'twas such fun then. . . .

Nothing felt better than submerging her warm body in the cool depths, feeling the tingling wetness touch every inch of her. With slow, graceful movements, she swam out farther. Determined to touch bottom, she began diving, swimming down and under, laughing as she popped up to gasp for breath.

With a whistle, Victor came out of the forest, took one look and stopped dead in his tracks. He saw only her head pop up from the water before she submerged again. He said her name in a panic of fear. "Jade! Jade!"

He dove in to save her. He swam with all his strength, and quickly reached the spot. Taking one look at the vacant surface, he dove under. Straining his eyes to see a glimmer of white through the darkness, he swung his arms in wide circles, not thinking, just acting, knowing each second under could be one too many for her.

Returning to the surface for air, Jade suddenly felt his hands around her waist. He pulled her quickly to the surface, careful to hold her above the water, but after a toss of his hair, he looked at her and was stunned.

She was laughing, the sound came as an assault to his taut nerves. Demonstrating how completely mistaken he was, she arched back, presenting him with a devastating view before her belly and her legs followed her head and in an amazing acrobatic water display, she disappeared altogether.

Drowning, he thought she had been drowning! He cast a quick glance at her discarded clothes on the bank and he was furious. He had never even heard of a woman who could swim!

Her heart raced with a wild delight. She finally emerged a few feet away, careful to keep her nudity beneath the water.

"Just what the hell do you think you're doing?"

"Why, I'm swimming!"

"I thought you were drowning!"

"Drowning." She laughed. "Men! You think you're the only ones who can do anything!" And to his utter surprise, she took a mouth full of water and sprayed him, somehow hitting him right on the head. Before he could catch her, she ducked beneath the surface.

He was going to kill her. . . .

With that objective, Victor submerged and swam quickly to the spot, only to find she'd emerged a good distance from him.

Victor chuckled, low and threateningly, before warning, "You better not let me catch you because—"

"Catch me! You?" She laughed and quickly dove under. Cleverly, she swam straight down and held herself still for a long minute, knowing he would assume she swam away from him. She came up as Victor swam past her, took one gulp of air and submerged without being seen. The hardest part became stopping her laughter under water.

Victor stared with surprise, amazed by the strength of her swimming and how she managed to elude him. After his third attempt, he emerged, cast a quick glance over the vacant surface and began treading water, waiting for her to emerge.

He closed his eyes for a moment, shocked by the force of the pleasurable tightening of his loins and quickening of his body, triggered by the idea of what would happen, what was happening. The physical response rocked through him: his heart raced, his sex swelled and hardened and his blood ran hot. Yet he knew, too, just how much he didn't want this. . . .

If only he could stop it. . . .

She came up for air, but only for an instant, before going back under. This was repeated three times, as each breath brought her closer to him.

Jade finally came up and, treading water, she listened. It was so quiet. She heard her own labored breaths, the race of her heart a loud roar in her ears, the gentle swish of the water as she treaded. "Do you give up now?"

Aye, he thought, grinning as he watched her escalating fear.

She heard no answer.

She panicked, ducked under again but only to feel his hands snake around her waist from behind as he pulled her hard against him. Like two children lost to their play, their laughter sang in the still afternoon air as he pinned her arms to her sides to stop her struggle. She fought valiantly to escape, laughing with wild abandonment until—

Until she felt the press of his hard wet body against hers. His huge chest cushioned her back but her consciousness riveted to the press of his hard sex against her buttocks. She gasped with the sudden heat there and tried to slip away but he held her firm. He said nothing; whether he smiled or frowned she did not know. His feet touched bottom and he turned her around, pressing her against him.

She felt the hard swell of his sex on her stomach. Her next breath came with a rush of heat through her limbs. Like their time before. Like her dreams. More potent though, far more potent. There was no drugged lethargy in her limbs nor sleepy haze to subdue and quiet the effect. There was nothing but the moist cool water of a forest lake.

"My God, you are so beautiful . . . but surprised, I see." He let his lips graze the curve of her neck. Heated shivers rushed from the spot and she gasped, breathless, as his lips found the sensitive lobe of her ear, where he whispered, "Jade. Jade, didn't you know or couldn't you guess what this madly ill-advised play would lead to?"

Her heart galloped in her chest. "Victor." She said his name in a soft whisper that echoed the distant flight of a bird overhead. She knew that he stared down at her, that her breasts floated just above the water's edge, and the idea that he was watching her nudity made her breath halt, color suffuse her cheeks, another rush of heat spread between her legs.

"No . . . I—"

He gently took the earlobe between his teeth and bit.

Chills dashed down her spine and she gasped. Anticipation tingled in her breasts from the touch of water. He watched the effect on the tightening buds and his next breath fanned the hot desire pumping hard and fast through him. He slipped his large strong hands over her buttocks, lifting her up. A lick of fire leapt through her loins.

She reached her arms around his neck to steady herself. A small surprised cry issued from her lips, which he caught in his mouth. He kissed her once. "Do you want to stop me, Jade?" His mouth stayed close. "You could. Theoretically. I suppose it's possible. . . ."

Actually it wasn't. Not now when the dark hair was pulled against her head, so that the haunting beauty of her eyes, lifeless, sparkling like gems, was dramatically accented. Moisture lined her parted lips, soft and pliant and beckoning. The lush lift of her breasts was a tease as potent as the feel of her soft supple form again his hardness.

Heated shivers raced through her, gathering in a tight coil in her abdomen, small bursts of fire. His mouth caressed hers, teasing, taking her lower lip in his two lips, gently kneading it. "Say it, Jade. Say you don't want me to stop now. . . ."

She shook her head slowly, an ambivalent answer. She realized this distantly and wanted to correct it. She certainly felt no ambivalence. She wondered wildly if it were not because she was blind or if all people felt this explosion of the senses, this tingling excitement racing through every nerve in her body. No, she did not want to stop. She timidly answered the demand by pressing her lips to his. He rewarded her with a slow and maddeningly unhurried kiss, a kiss that seemed to warm the very water between them as it drew heated serums from the most unlikely places. She felt dizzy with it, the kiss, the touch of their hot skin beneath the warm water, the hard press of his sex as he held her tighter.

He broke the kiss with a husky chuckle, a whisper against her ear. "A confession: I lied. For I could no more stop myself than I could change the course of the sun crossing the earth. Jade." He said her name as he brushed his lips across hers and caught her small cry in his mouth. His hands slid under her breasts, his fingers lightly spanning her rib cage, stopping there, only to slide sensuously back.

"Victor," she whispered against his lips as he found her mouth again. The melting heat of his kiss, shimmering like sunlight on water, collected tight and hot inside her.

The pleasure was sharp. Her yearning grew. A small cry died in their joined mouths as his hands slid back and forth over the small round curves of her buttocks, finally sliding up to caress the slender arch of her back, stopping to rest again beneath her breasts. He broke the kiss to say her name, his lips sliding sensuously along her ear. She gasped with the teasing nicks this gave, like tiny pinpricks of magic. . . .

Her heart pounded crazily and her head fell back as his lips found her neck and she felt his hands lightly massage her breasts, teasing the peaks until she sounded soft surprised cries. She heard his sharp intake of breath and then he was kissing her again. . . .

His hands slipped under her arms, coaxing her back until he was presented with her breasts. She cried softly as he drew on one rosy tip, teasing it with his tongue, listening avidly to her cries as a pink flush spread over her small form. . . .

The world was made of a swirl of water and searching lips. Nails dug into the hard muscled back as rushes of warmth gathered tighter and tighter until she felt like she would burst, only to tense more as he lifted her higher. She was suddenly clinging to his neck, her legs wrapped tightly around him as she felt water rush into her warmth as his shaft moved back and forth. Burning sensations licked through her abdomen, gathering into a hot swell that made her cry helplessly for him, his help, his answer.

He slipped long and hard into her moist sheath. He stopped and closed his eyes as the hot tight pleasure spilled into him. Then, moving with deliberate slowness, he lifted her from him, slid almost all the way out before plunging back hard.

There was a wild, untamed carnal element to the mating, coming less from the surrounding wilderness and more from the unleashing of desire, a momentum of hot sensations climbing and climbing, intensifying and reflected by her cries. Her fingers dug into his back as his desire soared to a harder and faster pace until he felt the slender form stiffen and she clung to him as ripples of triumphant pleasure washed through her. He made a last stabbing thrust into her, the intensity of his release rocking violently through him. . . .

He was kissing her mouth as he held her to him, their hearts beating erratically as they spiraled slowly downward together. "Don't let me go," she whispered, frightened by the intensity of his lovemaking as she felt the shuddering echoes of the aftermath. She needed to feel his arms more than she needed her next breath.

"Never," he said, his voice curiously subdued and humbled by the force of this thing overcoming them, overwhelming him. Love. He did not want it and for the first time in his life he felt as if an act of will could not stop it. It was as if he had stepped inside a long dark tunnel that had no light shining through it, and had turned, only to find the entrance gone, vanished, there no more. No way out but forward into darkness. Like her blindness itself. It scared him. Why? He'd never let anyone or anything hurt her—

He shook the feeling and knelt down, so his shoulders disappeared in the water, lowering her as well. She dipped her head back to draw the tangled mass of her hair away from her face.

He was not surprised by how quickly he wanted her again. This was not as alarming as the force of his desire, for even now as he kept her to him, he felt only a temporary satisfaction. For a moment he understood the distant fear, then there seemed to be no boundaries to his desire; to have her once would be to want her always. . . .

"I want you again," he said with feeling as he tenderly stroked her back as though to atone for the force he used. "And again, Jade Terese." He kissed her mouth; the kiss, so tender, so sweet, elicited small sparks of a new desire. "I had you once with a drugged passion and once with water between us. I want all of you now with nothing and no one between us. Jade, I want you again. . . ."

Jade struggled up through her scattered senses, feeling the water slipping over her flushed skin as he stepped toward the shore and then lifted her in his arms. He carried her to the mossy bank, where he lay her down on the soft blanket. He dropped to his knees, his gaze focused on the lush beauty of her nudity.

Her long hair fell in a wet rope to the side and she turned her head to hide her eyes as she uttered his name in a question. Her full breasts thrust prominently upward, their soft firmness crested with rosy pink tips. His next breath came with a sharp gasp as his gaze traveled to the flat narrow waist, the sensuous flare of her hips and down the inconceivably long legs.

Like Eve before the Fall she was, and surrounded by the same untouched bounteous wilderness. A blue sky arched above the canopy of trees, their branches bending as if with the weight of impossibly green moss. Ferns shot up all around them, enclosing them in the rich fragrant scent of earth and all its creation.

He came partially over her and let his mouth touch her moist lips, before he drew back to stare into the darkening pools of her eyes, the long hair trailing like a river of black. "Dear God," he whispered, "I don't want to fall in love with you . . . and yet, and yet . . ."

The anguished words sparked a tremor of alarm. The green eyes moved aimlessly about, seeing nothing as a question struggled through the pounding of her heart. "Why don't you want to fall in love with me?"

She could hear each breath punctuating the silence as he contemplated the answer. His hand grazed the slender curve beneath her breasts. Tiny pinpricks of pleasure erupted everywhere their bodies touched. "It has to do with the mystery in your eyes ..."

"The mystery?"

"Aye. When I look into your eyes, their beauty mixes with the haunting emptiness brought by your blindness," he whispered, "and your eyes threaten to pull me into a depth I'd never willingly trespass into." He let his lips caress the sweet moisture on her neck, teasing slowly, feeling a hot shiver race through her body as his large warm hand rested beneath her breast. "It's a surrender, love. ..."

Drawing on her uncanny intuition, she whispered, "It frightens you, this surrender?"

"Aye," he said with feeling. "It frightens me. I think it's different for a woman. Surrender is natural and easier because of it. When a man loses a part of himself to someone else, he loses control." The lingering sunlight fell like kisses across the paleness of her skin, a dance of shadow and light. He followed the shifting light with his fingers. "That's not an easy thing to lose."

She reached her hands to his face, where she let the sensitive pads of her fingertips explore the lines and forms. She found the dramatic arch of his brows, the long curve of his nose and his mouth, a tender yet somehow troubled smile there. Softly, wisely, she told him, "Control is but an illusion, don't you know?"

"Nay, love. Fate is no more than the will of man," he said with masculine simplicity. "It is the name for facts not yet passed under the fire of thought, facts made by nature and the will of men. ..."

A haunting sadness came over her as she thought of her mother and father, the love that had been stolen from her. She turned her head from him as if to hide. "I wish I could believe that but I can't. It is a trick managed only by the most fortunate. Fate is the great director here; irrational, chaotic, and such a great destroyer. She can sweep down and in the space of minutes change the very essence and shape of our lives. And with utter indifference for the casualties."

He thought she spoke of her blindness. The loss, its profundity, had much to do with the intensity of his feeling. His gaze found a bruise on her hip and another on the slender reach of her arm, still another on her knee. Light as a feather he traced his finger over the soft curve of her waist. Her extreme vulnerability, fragility and, aye, her dependency were not qualities he'd willingly choose in a woman he loved. He did not like it and yet he could not stop it from inciting some deep masculine answer from him. The idea came to him that it was this very thing, her blindness, that made him feel as though he were stepping into the blackness of the tunnel. Against his will . . .

Fate. He thought of the darkened theater, its rows packed with maybe four hundred people and in this sea of bodies, his gaze had come to her and then stayed with a mystical compulsion he found, even then, irresistible. Fate.

"I am so sorry, Jade. . . ."

The whispered words echoed the sadness inside her and yet she guessed he thought of her blindness, rather than the death of her parents. Her blindness. It was impossible for sighted people to understand that the loss of vision was little more than an inconvenience and as she had learned to maneuver through the dark space, a diminishing one at that.

What had she actually lost? Sightlessness in no way impeded her music. In the deepest sense it had enhanced her love and appreciation for music. She had a perfect ear and could play almost all the celebrated classical pieces as well as popular ones by ear. She missed reading but was lucky enough to belong to a class that spent the evenings reading out loud, so instead of being the reader she was the recipient.

Her imagination created beautiful sunsets and fields of flowers; she missed them not.

"Please, Victor." She gently touched the soft shape of his feelings on his mouth. "How my misfortune pales alongside others; I am most undeserving of sorrow. For I am blessed. . . ."

Her smile changed the beat of his heart. "Are you now?"

"Yes, I am." She laughed.

Dear Lord—he smiled—how the sweet music of the sound lifted his sorrow and tossed it away. She raised an arm lazily above herself, unaware of the effect this had, which was rather dramatic. He felt it as a pleasure dangerously close to pain.

"For I am blessed with a rich and colorful imagination and this precious blessing paints rainbows in every sky. . . ."

The words made him laugh. "Rainbows . . . Jade," he asked as he kissed her mouth, smiling down at her, "do you see these miracles of color when I touch you?"

"No." She shook her head, and laughed. "Oh no. When you kiss me, when you touch me, it's rather more like exploding stars made of red, yellow and gold."

The warm sound of his laughter went through her like a caress. She shifted, smiling as she whispered, "I want to touch you."

He felt a sensuous tease brought by her hands on his body. Circling his head, her fingertips combed his thick hair before gliding light as a feather down his neck and over the wide breadth of his shoulders. The innocent pleasure of her hands on his hot skin made a mockery of any thought of will.

Nor had the intensity of his release subdued his response now. He felt the unmerciful urgency of his desire. He had to close his eyes and count, and not since he was thirteen . . .

"You feel so hard and strong and"—an image emerged in her mind—"sleek, like a great Bengal tiger."

He chuckled at the innocence and fancy of her words. "Your skin feels too vibrant to be pale?"

"It's not."

A golden color flashed across her mind as she continued. He felt her hands sliding over his back and buttocks. She heard a groan and felt his hard flesh tremble beneath her touch. She hesitated before knowing to repeat the gesture. She slid her hands forward, over his flat muscled abdomen and slightly curved chest, teased by the pricks of his hair and the catch of his breath, her hand lingering where she felt the race of his pulse. He didn't know how much he could take and he caught her hands in his.

"No, please," she whispered. "I can't see you. . . . I don't know what you're feeling."

"Pleasure," he said simply. "Intense pleasure. Love, here, let me show you . . ."

She flushed as his huge wet frame came on top of her. He pinned her arms to the ground and with his weight resting on his arms, all she felt was the soft burning pressure of his sex on her belly, the tips of her breasts teased by his chest.

Desire was born anew. As his lips met hers, she, too, abandoned herself to a passion too great to resist. "And when I kiss you," he whispered, keeping his mouth close, so very close, "I feel the force of my will slip from my grasp—"

A sweet tingling awakening raced through her. "A surrender . . ."

"Aye." He kissed her again. "I surrender. . . ."

To fate. The fate of two lovers whose uncertain future stretched far ahead. Even as passion rose, orchestrated by an intensity of feeling and pleasure as new to him as it was to her, he felt, somehow he knew, that he had in fact stepped into that long dark tunnel. And there would come a time when no light would make rainbows arch across their sky. . . .

A thousand bright stars, the white ribbon of the milky way filled the black night sky. The campfire burned red, and large flames threw up light like wild Gypsies dancing in the darkness. Murray sat on a blanket, waiting, watching, listening for signs of Victor's return but hearing only peaceful sounds of the forest: a hum of crickets and other insects, night creatures scurrying over brush and then their own camp's sounds: the crackle of fire, horses shuffling feet, sometimes whining or snorting, Carl's muffled snores from the carriage. Carl never would sleep on the ground like the others.

As carefully as Murray watched, he jumped, startled when Victor appeared. No sign or warning preceding him, suddenly he was just there. Like an Indian warrior, Murray thought, the impression reinforced by the long bow and arrows swung across his bare chest, a game bag over his shoulder and his dark bronze skin in the shadow of the firelight. He looked a fright all right, and Murray smiled. "You give an old man another start like that and you're likely to lose him."

Victor grinned as he lowered his frame to the ground. In an effort to feel out his mood, Murray asked, "What you catch there?"

"Two ducks, two pheasants and a quail. They're cleaned. I just need to string them up." He rose to fetch the rods and caught sight of Jade sleeping under the mosquito net with Mercedes. Sebastian slept nearby, alone. "What's this?"

"Sebastian went off looking for you and the lasses just fell asleep together. Mercedes, you know, is like a watchful mother cat around the lass. She is very protective."

"Aren't we all," Victor said.

He walked over to the mat, where he stood staring down at the two sleeping women. They looked so young and childlike, sound asleep, curled up together. They are too young, he thought. Too young to have gone through what they have. . . .

"Come on," Murray whispered. "I'll heat up some supper for you while you string up the fowl."

The two men's longstanding friendship gave Murray the freedom to ask, "You're fallin' in love with the lass, aren't you?"

Victor glanced up from his food, shrugged, and then smiled. "I've been in love too many times to take it seriously."

Murray chuckled softly at that, then shook his head. "I know you too well for that. Aye, you've been in love a hundred times, and not once has it been serious. Jade's not like any one of the others. Lord, Jade is the kind of woman who can make the old feel young and the poor feel rich—she is the damnedest, brightest, loveliest—"

"Spare me the list," Victor interrupted quickly. "Believe me, I'm acutely aware of her charms, of which"—his voice lowered—"the sum of the parts is less than the whole, especially in the case of Jade Terese."

"Well now, that's just my point. It's plain as day she's in love with you. And little wonder, too, after what's happened. She's in a dream, all smiles, nervous and excited, asking us one question after another about you while you were off."

Victor glanced up, letting his expression speak for him. "What's the problem, Vic?"

"I don't want it," he said, softly, seriously. "Let me rephrase that: I won't have it."

Enlightenment slowly dawned on Murray and momentarily, he felt taken aback. "Because she's blind."

"Yes," Victor said after a pause. "I wish I could say it doesn't bother me but it does," he said gravely. "Of course, I'll take care of her throughout this ordeal, until we find this man and as long as she needs me afterwards. Yet, the more I think of it, the more I know it won't work. I'm not sure I even want a wife; I know I don't want a blind wife." He added softly, "No matter how much I might come to love her."

"I don't get it. I don't see how it matters. One hardly knows she's blind unless she's making her way somewhere new—and even then . . . why, I'm always forgetting it—"

Victor's eyes narrowed as he agreed with a nod. "It's amazing how she manages to deceive people into forgetting such a thing—quite a theatrical trick." His tone rose with anger as he expanded. "Today when we were walking, I forgot. The way she'd look out over the land pretending she actually saw it, the way she returned her glance to me when I spoke. I forgot until she tripped over a log, after she lay flat on the ground. And God," he added, "there are bruises all over that beautiful body of hers. . . ."

Murray stirred the fire with a stick. "She does her best. I think she does a hell of a job making up for it."

Victor shook his head, pushing his plate away distractedly. "She doesn't compensate; she can't make up for it. I don't care how bright she is. How much worse this whole thing is because she can't see. I'll be damned if I'll spend the rest of my life waiting to hear about the next accident I couldn't protect her from: a fall down a flight of stairs, or a man getting into my bed because she thought it was me, or a child, my child, being hurt by something those lovely eyes didn't see." He shook his head. "No thank you, I don't want it."

On the heels of a thoughtful pause Murray said: "One doesn't always get what one wants."

Victor suddenly grinned as he rolled on his back to gaze at the stars beyond the trees. "You're right, of course, and unless I find a way to keep my hands off her, it will be too late. So far"—he laughed,—"I have been only too unsuccessful, and now, after today—" He shook his head, stopping himself from even thinking of what happened. . . . "Well, I didn't last a day with her, not one bloody day."

"You are in trouble." Murray smiled. Time would tell. It was an old story, as ancient as the very earth itself: few beings were capable of resisting what obviously had sprung between Vic and the lovely lass, and Lord knew how many months she'd have to be with him. . . .

"Vic," he said, switching subjects after a moment, "I've been thinking. I think you ought to question her, real gentle like, about what she does remember—"

"Yes. I was thinking the same."

Jade and Mercedes slipped out from the tent, trying to stop their excited laughter, both wrapped in blankets. Mercedes gathered soap and clothes and then took Jade by the arm, heading for the lake. Victor watched them run off through the gray light of predawn and then got up.

Coffee, he needed coffee.

They were unaware that Victor watched from the shoreline. Against the soft colors of early dawn, the two young women looked like erotic nymphs playing in the water, figments of the imagination. Victor smiled to himself, amused by the unexpectedly innocent and sensual scene. He watched as Jade swam out, under and around, while Mercedes, far more timid with water, remained waist deep, laughing at her friend.

He stopped smiling when they emerged from the water and Jade began sliding a bar of soap over her skin. He turned full around. To say the least, voyeurism—passive participation—was decidedly against his nature. He forced himself to endure such torment from necessity: while Jade swam like a fish, and she was certainly safer in the water than out, Mercedes couldn't swim, and should she slip or fall under, Jade could not provide any assistance.

The two young women had already slipped back into the water when Murray and Sebastian joined him, thankfully bringing a hot cup of coffee.

"It seems our ladies are providing some morning's entertainment," Sebastian observed with a grin. "While you might be content to merely watch," he accused Victor, "I am not. I've always preferred helping women bathe." With that, Sebastian's black breeches dropped to the ground and both men chuckled as he ran to the water, naked except for a wide-brimmed black Spanish hat.

Victor chuckled as Jade ducked under and cried, "Sebastian! I'm naked!"

Sebastian laughed at this too, and spread his arms. "What an alarming coincidence!"

Victor chuckled and shook his head, turning away with a new appreciation for a single word, *temptation.*

Later, as they were preparing to leave, Victor came and knelt beside her. She reached a hand to touch his face. He lightly kissed her fingertips. "Are you staring at me?" she asked.

"I'm always staring at you," he said, smiling. "As a matter of fact, I was hoping you would ride with me, so I don't have to stretch my neck quite so much in the process."

She laughed as he guided her to the horse. He mounted first before bending over to lift her up. She fit easily in the saddle between his arms and they were off. A conversation sprang up between them as they rode along. She began asking him about his shipbuilding business, about his new flatboats specifically. He was surprised, not just by her interest but by how much she knew about it. It seems his father had been telling her all about the discovery and its progress. He described the ship and its first journey upriver to Natchez—making a whole three miles an hour. How it had made three successful trips before the boiler blew up. He was making three more.

"Your father says it's a miracle that will revolutionize the world."

He chuckled. "If not the world, then trade along the Mississippi. That is if the new ones preform as well as the old one," he said as he stopped the horse to remove his shirt.

Alarm changed her face; she lowered her eyes. "Victor," she interrupted him to whisper apprehensively. "Please, I don't think . . . I mean we shouldn't—"

"We shouldn't what?"

She blushed, "You know . . ."

"Know what?"

He was making her come out and say the words. "I don't want to make love again."

"You don't? Then why are you thinking about it so much?"

"I wasn't . . . well, I was, but . . . I—" She grew flustered, more so as his laughter sounded. "Are you, I mean, were you taking me—"

"To ravish you?" he interrupted. "I wasn't planning on

it, but if we keep talking about it much longer, my plans will definitely change. As a matter of fact, there's a lovely glen to our side—"

"No! No!" she said quickly. "I won't mention it again! My lips are sealed."

The morning dawned bright and beautiful again. Victor kept his horse just ahead of the carriage, and they continued talking easily, which was his intention. She had to be relaxed and comfortable before he questioned her about her parents' deaths. The conversation shifted and flowed effortlessly as they rode along, though each subject became the backdrop for wild flirtations, teasing and laughter. They had ridden a good distance before Victor finally asked, "Tell me, that lovely melody you sang for everyone yesterday, were you thinking of your mother and father when you sang it?"

"Yes."

"I imagine you still miss them very much."

Jade turned her head against him, felt a gloved hand lift from the reins to gently brush through her hair. "It's been five years," she began so softly he barely heard her over the horse's trot. "People say that one's heart heals with the passage of time, but it's not been true for me. Sometimes, when I think of them, I miss them so much . . . I'll start crying right in the middle of something—mass or prayers, during chorus or even school. And it feels as if I'll never be able to quit. . . ."

Victor stopped the horse, drawing him up tight as he pulled her to him, his tenderness always plain. "They must have been very special."

"Yes, they were."

"Jade, I want to ask you about their deaths."

"Their . . . deaths?"

"Yes. Do you remember anything unpleasant happening before they died? Something that upset your parents?"

"Well . . . no." The question seemed to surprise her. "Not really. My parents were very much in love. . . . They hardly ever fought and those few times they did, it was always over my father's slaves. That's how my mother referred to them," she explained, "as my father's slaves. Being English, she was naturally disturbed by the idea that we owned slaves. 'People!' she'd say. 'Philip, how can you own people? Has no one in America read his Bible lately?' Then she'd quote every relevant passage. Oh, yes." Jade laughed lightly as she remembered the fierceness of her mother's arguments. "And my father used to tease that all of England was little more than a breeding ground for eccentrics and fanatics, that he had had no idea my mother was so . . . intemperate and opinionated when he married her. He'd say that she'd charge hell with a bucket of water. It got to where no one ever brought up the subject of slaves in front of her."

He studied her intensely. "Anything else? Anything else that upset them? I'm thinking of a specific incident before their deaths?"

Upset them. A distant memory emerged of her mother falling into her father's arms crying over and over. "Voodoo. My mother became very upset about the voodoo practices among the slaves" She shook her head. "I suppose voodoo makes most people uncomfortable. You should hear Monsieur Deubler go on about it, and your own father gets very worked up when the veneration of the saints crosses that magical line from Catholicism to something else. We have had many arguments about it," she told him. "I've never understood why everyone becomes so concerned about it. Why does it matter if a person gets a headache cure from a penny at Mary's feet or a clump of hair from the tail of a white horse?"

This was close. "Were your slaves practicing voodoo?"

The questioned spurred a memory. "Yes . . . some."

The memory spun through her mind with a hot wave of panic. Cara, the upstairs maid, was making her parents' bed. "Fetch the pillowcases in the linen closet, cherie, no?"

She had opened the drawer. They lay on the crisp white sheets. Two dolls made of black wax. The smaller doll wore a piece of cloth taken from her old green riding habit. 'Twas a special one her father had given her on her tenth birthday and it had finally been discarded when the material could not be let out anymore. There was no face on the doll. The eyes, the terrible eyes, were hideous dark holes. A long strand of her hair stuck out of the head. The larger one wore a piece of her mother's old gowns, a pastel cloth with pretty green and blue flowers on it. Her mother had given it to the church's charity drive just last week. This doll had a clump of her mother's hair stuck in its head. At first she had thought they were fantastic, like toys, and she reached for them—

"I am too hot, I think—" She looked away, as if searching for an exit. "Perhaps you should set me back to the carriage—"

"Jade, were you remembering something unpleasant?"

She nodded, looking quite pale suddenly.

"What? I want to know."

She shook her head as if to rid herself of the memory. "I remember finding two wax dolls in a closet once—and how it upset my mother, that's all. One wore a piece of my old riding habit and the other wore cloth from a dress of my mother's." Her thin dark brows crossed with consternation. She hadn't thought of it since . . . since before the accident . . .

Her heart started pounding. Lord, 'twas so hot. . . .

"Jade, what do you remember about the fire?"

For a long moment, she didn't answer and he thought she might not have heard the question. "Nothing," she whispered quickly. "I don't remember anything." She pulled away from him, fanning her face. "My, but already the day's hot. You better put me down now."

Victor watched her curiously, not knowing how far to push. "Jade, does it bother you to talk about it?"

"No . . . well, yes. Yes, it does, I—" She bit her lip and a pained expression came over her face. "No one's ever asked me about it before. I mean, I've never spoken to anyone about it. I guess my seizures, and . . . and I just never think about it—it was so terrible."

"Jade, what do you remember before the fire? That day—"

"Nothing." She shook her head. "I don't know. I . . . we were going to a music festival in the afternoon. I was out riding in the early morning and I came home and—"

"Yes?"

Jade seemed to drift off and Victor asked again what happened. "I . . . I don't know!" Vague images danced quickly through her mind: a splattered fish, three ravens lifting from the empty stables, the unusual quiet as she raced into the house.

She drew breath hard and fast, her head spinning.

They were a good deal behind the carriage now and Victor had stopped the horse. He had to know. "Did you see your mother?"

"I don't know, I don't know! I woke up and I was in a bedroom at the Taylours' plantation, our neighbors. Mother Francesca was there and she was telling me. I . . . I don't know. I . . . I—" She held her head; her words came in sudden gasps. "She said my parents died in the fire but I didn't believe her! I couldn't see, and all I knew was, oh God, if I could just be with my mother, if I could just touch my mother, I could see—" She stopped, her temples pounded, she couldn't breathe. "I can't talk, I—"

A memory submerged, faded quickly into darkness, then whirled and whirled, suddenly bursting! She heard Victor's voice thundering above her, becoming that voice, Mother Francesca's voice! Mother Francesca calling out to her! She could not see. . . .

"They were murdered! Your mother is dead! Dead! You saw it, you saw it!"

"Nooo! No! I don't see! I don't see! I don't—"

The small black boots on the stairs, the bouncing plaits on her gold frock, the long hall. The door. A hand touched the latch. The door opening. A blinding white light burst in her mind as she grabbed her head against the pain. . . .

Chapter 8

A hot Louisiana sun beat down on the small wood shack, beat through the shade of tall cypress and oak trees, beat to the very roots of the marshy land. A slight murmur of a breeze blew from the Gulf, but the air was still hot, muggy, unbearable at the afternoon hour. Dogs draped themselves around the yard like moss on the trees, each beast still and sleeping, waiting for a cool evening that always came.

Hotter than a two-dollar pistol on Saturday night. . . .

With the morning chores finished, old man Tom leaned back in the porch chair, watching the heat shimmer in waves all around him. With thumbs tucked under his suspenders, he drifted in and out of a light sleep. Like his dogs, he waited for the heat to recede, for that pleasant hour when day meets night and the fellows gathered on his porch, to shoot the breeze over whiskey and tobacco.

Two or three dogs growled, then barked, and old man Tom looked up to see a tall white man, an uptown buckaroo, riding a fine black steed. Tom whistled twice. Nine dogs came to a quick attention at his feet. The man stopped outside the yard to study the small shack, Tom's dogs, and finally Tom.

Tom's bright eyes scrutinized the man. "What can I do for you?"

"I was told you're the man to see about a dog."

Tom smiled, sizing up the visitor as he swung off his horse. "Well, now, you'se told right. I got me plenty of dogs, all kinds. I got large and small, trained dogs, huntin' dogs and pups. I got two bitches out back, just thrown litters. What you be lookin' for?"

"I know exactly what I want. I want the largest, smartest, and toughest dog you have. The best. A puppy, though; it has to be a puppy."

Tom twisted a straw around in his mouth and grinned, taking in the man's long, muscled frame, the buckskin breeches, the two ivory-handled pistols hanging from a black leather shoulder harness and the knife hanging from his belt.

"Know much about dogs, mister?" Tom asked, grinning still.

"Naw, not much," Victor admitted easily with a shrug, bending down to pet one of the dogs. "I only had one dog as a boy." During the happy days when his mother was still with them. "I guess I've traveled too much."

"Uh huh." Tom smiled, twirling the long straw. "And what kind of dog was it?"

"Oh"—Victor laughed—"just some dog I came by. Not much, I suppose." Not much to anyone but himself. He had loved that dog for seven long years, his constant companion. "But this time," he said, returning to the old man, "I need the best dog you have."

"The best," the old man drawled. The trouble would be in keeping a straight face. "Uh huh. Well, I do believe I got just the one."

He led Victor around the back, where he kept dogs in shaded pens. Victor examined both litters: the first litter seemed to be shepherd-type dogs, while the second seemed of a short-haired hunting breed. Thinking of Hamlet, he took a second look at the shepherd puppies when the old man motioned to come look at a puppy in a small pen, separated from the others.

The puppy had been brought to Tom by a Cajun fisherman, who in turn had taken it from a riverboat man. The riverboat man claimed to have found it abandoned in a forest up north. The pup's mother knew the puny thing was not worth keeping alive. Both Tom's nursing dogs rejected the pup outright, but since he never could bring himself to kill animals, especially dogs, he was forced to care for it himself. It was not even weaned yet, and Tom, with years of experience, knew a belly-up dog when he saw one.

Tom held the small bundle of blond fur up for Victor's scrutiny. "This here be your dog."

"This thing?" Victor questioned.

"Yes sir, this is an honest-to-God golden mastiff."

"A golden mastiff?"

"The finest dog you can get."

"Geez," Victor said uncertainly. "It doesn't look like much."

"You ever seen one of these here dogs full grown?"

"No, I can't say I have."

"This be one of de largest, strongest dogs in the world," he said with authority. "They been known to pull sleds up north carryin' mayhaps five hundred pounds and"—he paused for effect—"the golden mastiff is the only dog able to take out bears."

"This little guy?" Victor pointed.

"Little now, but with some milk and some care this little thing will grow at least this high." He indicated an impressive height, and added, "Hey, they ain't nicknamed 'golden giant' for nothin'."

A lift of Victor's brow indicated he was impressed as he took the small bundle in his arms. The puppy looked at him, yawned and fell back asleep. Victor smiled. "Well, is he also loyal? He's got to be very loyal."

"Mister, all dogs is loyal by nature. A body don't have to beat it into him like you do with folks. Obedience be their nature."

"Yes, I suppose you're right," Victor replied, gently stroking the soft fur. "And this golden mastiff is a smart breed?"

"Smart?" Tom questioned, slapping his thigh with a chuckle. "Man, I tell you, the golden mastiff be the sharpest and quickest kind of dog. Why, all a body's got to do is rustle a little in a chair and this here dog is at your side, waitin' for you to get up. These here dogs pay attention to their masters."

"That does it, you just sold me. He sounds perfect for her."

"Her?"

"Yes," he said, his voice softening. "I'm getting him for a very special lady who's blind. To help her, you know. To watch out for her." He thought of the man coming into his bedroom and poised to kill her, and his muscles tensed involuntarily. If a dog did no more than warn her and the household of an intruder, it would be a blessing.

He gently petted the little puppy. "She's going to love this little fellow."

"Blind . . . ah, maybe this ain't the dog for you after all. These here shepherds—"

"Oh no, I'm convinced. This little guy is just the thing. How much do you want?"

"How much?" Tom repeated stupidly. "Ah, no charge mister," he shook his head. "No charge for a blind lady."

While Victor appreciated such sentiments, he insisted on paying something. After mounting his horse, he tossed the old man a gold piece. Tom looked at the shiny gold coin, and while it was more than he normally got in three long months, he'd like to see it turn to cold, stone lead. "If 'in' anything goes wrong, you come back now to pick of any dog you want."

What a kind-hearted old man, Victor thought.

He turned his mount toward Shady Manor, returning from the stay in New Orleans, a necessary trip to handle his business in the city. He also needed time away from Jade.

They would soon be digging up the Devon graves. His agents were still investigating Jade's father's business affairs. They had not a clue, past that it was someone who had had a connection with her parents, someone who practiced voodoo. In desperation he had appealed to Marie for help, laying the whole thing at her feet.

He had concealed his own alarm upon witnessing her fear. "The amulet is gris-gris," she said, alarmed, but trying not to show just how much. "The curse of death . . . Not an easy death. Death through terror."

Marie had promised to help him trace down the citizens who practiced the voodoo arts, a shockingly huge number that seemed to include the whole of the colored and Negro population of New Orleans. Yet Marie had assured him only a very small number would know the gris-gris magic. Marie had not wanted to help in this way, as she found the whole "voodoo religion" extremely distasteful, that to "trespass into darkness was to be drawn into its abyss."

Yet for Jade Terese she would.

"Jade Terese," he sighed out loud, "You are irreversibly entangled in my life."

Turning his mount from the road, Victor stopped by a small stream to give his horse a drink. He dismounted and set the sleeping puppy on the moist bank before splashing the cool water on his face. Then, leaning against a tree trunk, he stared unseeing at an afternoon sun slanting over the running brook.

It was not bad during the day. Work consumed both thought and energy as they now had three years worth of orders, and the orders kept coming in. Expanding the ship building company was not only worthwhile but necessary. He had begun to recruit labor from as far away as Hannibal, and this part of his dream was as rewarding as anything he had previously imagined.

The nights were difficult, to say the least. Unaware of any danger, Jade's enthusiasm for life, her charm, laughter and even her beauty seemed to blossom under the country sun. She constantly surprised him. Who would have suspected that hidden within her damnable femininity was a young lady capable of holding her weight in any argument or discussion on politics, religion, philosophy? He had never enjoyed a woman's intellect as much as he enjoyed Jade's; his firm rationalism waged a continuous war with her exaggerated, at times unbelievable, idealism.

Last week he had returned to his study early. He overheard her in the adjoining drawing room, one voice among others. Curious, he had opened the door. The room was filled with his house servants, including Tessie and, even, Chachie. Each pair of dark hands held a bible. Jade quoted passages as they followed along.

Mercedes, Tessie, indeed all of them, looked at him with guilt and fear. At first he didn't understand it until his eyes found the chalkboard. It rested on a mahogany table, leaning against a prized picture of a ship on the open seas. He later learned Carl had paid for that board himself. Written on the chalkboard were beginners' words: man, woman, cat, dog etc. It seemed half the lesson was spent going over the spelling of these beginning reading words, the other half spent reading from the Bible.

She was teaching his servants to read.

And damn if Carl wasn't, suggesting none to politely, that he ought to build a proper school house somewhere to accommodate the number of free people living in the country and their children. Carl wanted a school ready as soon as Jade Terese could be returned to society.

There were many other ways Jade had found a place in his household; and everyone's growing fondness for her both amused and alarmed him.

By far, the worst of it was resisting the temptation of that lovely body of hers—and that was at all times sheer agony. He had only to think of the sweet mercy her slender figure offered his flesh . . . of kissing her lips, parting her from her clothing, and taking the luscious tip of her breast as he parted her thighs and sunk into the hot moist sheath.

The sound of her name had the power to heat his desire. And he was forced to see Jade in all manners that a man sees his wife: They shared the same roof, table and friends and she slept in the adjoining bedroom. He felt her presence at all times; there were numerous near disasters—encountering her while she dressed, or worse, undressed, in a bath. The other women he carefully kept in his life, hardly helped or even distracted . . .

He understood there would come a day when he had to

let her go and somehow, the idea presented itself with the thought of another man in her life. That idea brought him such a swift violent rage, it made him grasp what was happening to him. While he was still unable to get past the reality of her blindness, the alternatives were felt on a deeper level, a level that manifests in a powerful possessiveness. A physical thing, as if she belonged to him and to him alone.

He had to get past this. He did not want her love.

He shook his head with a soft curse. The puppy looked up at him and cocked his head, as if curious about the sound. Deciding he liked it, the dog came bounding back to Victor. Gentle hands came over him.

It had only been a month, one lousy month. Just how did he expect to last until the danger was mute, until he could return her to the convent and her former life.

"Marie help me now . . ."

A thin, brown hand wrapped around a white one and Jade asked, "Can you see it now, Tessie?"

"Uh huh, I'se see it."

"Describe it to me again."

Tessie obligingly began a description of the country estate as they returned from a long walk. "The house be the prettiest and grandest manor a soul's ever laid eyes to. It be shaped like the letter L. Tall cypress trees shade the round circle in front. The drive is made of rocks sparklin' like gems in the sun. Sometimes if I squint my eyes just so, it looks like a road made of diamonds. The house be two stories high, five picture windows on top and four larger ones on the bottom, all the storm shutters be painted green and it be plastered and white washed. Can't see the kitchen to the side or the whistler's walk—" This referred to the well worn path connecting the cookhouse with the main house, the path that servants took from the kitchen and in most houses, a path where a body had to assure anyone nearby they were working and not eating what they were carrying. "But you can make out the stables nearby, all of that is covered by ivy. I'm looking through a whole passel of trees all around it, and lord, the bougainvillea, be turning' scarlet now, and it's climbin' all around it, too. Ivy started up the right side, too—Carl says the whole house will be covered by summer next and—" She laughed, "he says he's looking forward to all the amusement brought by a house full of spiders. If'in you look to one side, you see a stretch of forest, lovely, dark and deep and if'in you look to the other side—"

"You can see a crystal blue lake shimmering beneath the summer sun," Jade finished for her.

Tessie did not correct her. The "lake" was a large green pond surrounded by woods—no one could see it through the trees until your feet got wet. Victor had set the men chopping a small stretch of one side, that was all. She and Mercedes sat there while Jade swam in the heat of the afternoon when most all the house was restin'.

"I wish you could see it. You'd a know how pretty it be."

"Oh but I can see it, and it is beautiful!"

Could life be this perfect? Or was Mercedes right when she said they were dreaming? They must be dreaming, for it was all too good to be true.

She loved teaching in the mornings, loved the afternoons spent in leisure—swimming, picnics and long walks—and most of all, she loved the evenings when Victor and Sebastian returned, and they all dined together. Sebastian was building his own country estate on the property bordering Victor's. He was just settling the land purchase this week and construction would begin within the year, and until then Sebastian and Mercedes would live at Shady Manor. Sebastian was to take Mercedes back to Austria to marry her—Mercedes kept saying she woke from a long terrifing nightmare to find herself in a fairytale dream and all her anxieties and horrible obsessions were gone, dissipating beneath the love and security Sebastian gave her.

Mercedes, Sebastian, Murray, Carl and Tessie became

the family she had lost, filling an empty part of her heart again, an emptiness she only now realized had been there. Thinking of it, Jade's fingers tightened around Tessie's hand as they walked back. Tessie smiled at her, seeming to know her thoughts. Tessie's carefree, lively and unrestrained personality complemented Jade's, and as her maid and helper, they were nearly constant companions.

The best part, unfolded more each day, was this love blossoming in her heart, arching like a bright warm sun over her life.

As they gathered on the patio to await the evening meal, Murray thought Jade sparkled with a cat's contentment. Wearing a pretty cotton rose dress and with flushed cheeks, she sat on the ledge of the patio, her fingers flying through her knitting. Mercedes and Sebastian sat at the table playing a game of chance together, while Murray completed his book work.

Still fascinated with Jade's gifts, he called out long series of numbers to her. Without interrupting her knitting, Jade totaled the numbers in her head and called back the answer. After a shake of his head, he wrote the figure down without even checking it, having learned she rarely, if ever, made mistakes.

Victor surveyed the pleasant scene of domestic tranquility and, before anybody could jump up with excited exclamations, he motioned them still.

"Forty hundred and three," Jade said unaware. She heard Mercedes and Sebastian stop their game and she lifted her head, listening, alerted. "Victor!"

Everyone laughed and after setting the box down, he came to her side and kissed her affectionately on the forehead. It was all he permitted himself to do. "How have you been?" he asked, brushing his hand over her face.

"Fine! But I'm so glad you're back. I've missed you."

"What's this?" he asked.

"Knitting," she guessed.

"No, this bruise," he said eying a nearly black bruise on

her thin arm. The bruise covering at least six square inches around her elbow.

"What bruise?" she asked, confused. She felt his hand gently touch her elbow. She hadn't known there was a bruise there.

"How did that happen?"

"I don't really remember . . . I suppose I just turned into something—"

"I think that's when you slipped from the carriage step," Murray suggested.

"No, it wasn't that." She touched Victor's face, finding a frown and said, "Don't worry so. It doesn't hurt at all."

"I do worry." Last week she had been climbing a ladder to reach the hay loft in the stables to "see" a new litter of kittens when she fell over ten steps to the ground, bruised but miraculously unhurt. Before that she had slipped in spilled water in the kitchen, spraining her hand. "You must be more careful."

A number of servants came outside, forming a circle around them, to see Jade when he gave her the gift. Victor finished a quick exchange of greetings to the others and after briefly relating recent events in the city, he turned back to Jade.

"I've brought you a present."

"Me?" she always asked.

"Yes, you." Alarm lifted on her features and he chuckled. "Don't tell me I've found a woman who doesn't like presents?"

"Oh, why no . . . I'm sure I'll like anything you might give me," she lied, not at all sure actually. He had given her too much already. A single gift more would be too many. She also felt a little apprehensive about what he might choose to give her. "What is it?"

"Guess," he said.

"A new sun hat?"

He was going to enjoy this. "No."

"Is it something to wear?" she asked.

"No."

She thought it must be jewelry then and somehow, jewelry seemed the worst kind of present he could give her. "It's not a piece of jewelry, is it?"

"No."

"Well what is it?"

Victor reached behind him and lifted the puppy out to the whispered murmurs from their audience. He set it on her lap. Jade's hands come over it and she gasped. Victor chuckled with the others at the heart-stopping look of astonishment and joy on her face.

Jade brushed her hands over the smooth, soft fur, then lifted him to the air and buried her face into his fur. And when the puppy answered her with a small whimper and a kiss, tears filled her eyes.

Victor watched, first with disbelief, then damning himself for his thoughtlessness. "I should have known it's too soon after Hamlet. Oh sweetheart—"

Jade managed to shake her head.

"Victor," Mercedes interrupted with a tender smile. "These are happy tears, joyful tears."

Victor stared at her for a moment and when he saw it was true, he chuckled, feeling a swift rush of emotion. He stood up, swung his leg around her on the patio ledge, drawing both Jade and her puppy onto his lap to the happy applause of the crowd.

Jade held the puppy to her face. "He is the best, most wonderful present I've ever received," she whispered because she couldn't manage anything more. "I can't believe you thought of . . . Oh Victor, thank you."

Everyone gathered around to take a close look at the new puppy, throwing possible names back and forth. But Luke, one of Victor's best workers, took one look at the face, eyes, ears and knew. "Ah, you made a big mistake Vic. That's no dog."

"What do you mean? This is a golden mastiff puppy, the man said he was one of the best dogs in the world."

Luke chuckled as he shook his head. "I never heard of

that, but that pup there, ain't no dog. That's a wolf cub if ever there was."

"A wolf?" Jade asked. "He's a wolf?"

"Yes ma'am, that be a wolf, though I ain't never seen such in Louisiana Territory."

"How do you know?" Victor asked cautiously.

Luke pointed, "Look at them eyes, them ears. If that ain't a wolf, then he sure got wolf in him."

"He's right," Sebastian said, petting the puppy's head. "He does look rather wolfish."

"Now that you mention it . . ." Murray mused out loud.

Victor took the innocent looking bundle from Jade and held him up for closer examination. The old man had said it was a Golden Mastiff. He thought back over his interaction with the old man. He suddenly saw it in a different light. He laughed, "I think I've just been had."

Jade wasted little time in taking the puppy back. "It doesn't matter, he's still the cutest, sweetest—"

"Sweetheart, I can't let you keep him. Wolves aren't domesticated. He's a wild animal. I'm sorry but—"

She stood to her feet. "Wild now, but I shall tame him—"

"Jade . . ."

He said her name in that tone, an unpleasant one. Intuition spoke to her, suggesting the tactic that could not fail. Holding the puppy against her bosom, she stepped forward and silenced him with a gentle finger to his mouth. She ran a finger over his chest, looking up at him with wide eyes and while she didn't see anything, those eyes were perfectly capable of pleading her case.

Victor found his fingers suddenly twirling a loose strand of her hair. Mercedes winked at Tessie, knowing well the signs of a man weakening.

"Please," Jade whispered. "If you take him from me now, you'll break my heart, I swear it. Just look at him, does he look like he would ever be mean?"

Victor's gaze lowered to the bundle of fur held against

her bosom. She heard a groan, a pause, a deep sigh and finally a chuckle.

"I relent," he said. "But reluctantly and on the condition that if he does become too rough for you, you turn him over without a protest."

Jade threw her free arm around him and laughed before kissing him with gratitude. The women left for the kitchen to fetch food for the puppy. Watching them march away in triumph, Murray sighed, "Women will never stop believing in their God-given ability to tame what's wild."

Sebastian smiled, "And it's a good thing, too, for if they ever did, civilization would grind to a halt and we'd all soon be the savages we once were."

Victor shook his head. "Sometimes, I think I'd prefer those good old savage days."

"By the way, when's the grave diggin'?"

"Wednesday night. Next week."

Late that night Jade stretched out on the bed, still fondling her tiny wolf as he basked in his new, tender and loving care. Victor's cook, Chachie, had taken one look at the puppy's teeth and said he had been too young for weaning, but if he lived—something of which Jade was certain—the puppy would consider Jade his mother. Jade smiled at the idea of being a wolf's mother.

The room where she slept was large and spacious. Tessie said the bed clothes, the velvet coverlet and the gossamer draperies were colored dark blue, with a green and maroon paisley pattern, that it matched perfectly the adjoining room, Victor's bed chambers. She saw it perfectly in her mind. She had felt around the dark mahogany furnishings: the dresser and vanity, the bed posts, the sitting chairs and table, and she had known immediately it was the work of old man Lamana.

Old man Lamana had a shop off on the corner of Chartres and Beinville and there was no finer artisan in the city. He gave large monthly stipends to the Negro girls' charity school, and all because he had gained his freedom by learning to read. When he was a boy, his master kept finding him staring at the words in the Bible and had jokingly promised him freedom if he could ever read a page in the Bible. That was all it took. The young boy went to every prayer meeting, memorizing the passages and verse, later looked them up and studied and matched the words until he could read. His master had been so dumbfounded and surprised, he had kept his word, signing his papers and paying for his apprenticeship.

She heard Victor enter his adjoining bedroom. Murray had been sleeping in the room while Victor was away, and though it was never mentioned, she knew someone always shared the adjoining bedroom in the event she had a seizure. Thankfully, she had not suffered another. She felt safe again.

Intent on demonstrating her puppy's progress to Victor, she swept him into her arms and carefully, slowly made her way through the adjoining dressing room. She paused outside the open door and asked softly, "Victor? May I come in? I want to show you something."

Undressing, Victor smiled to himself. Since she received the puppy, Jade was not to be seen; she had even missed supper. "Come on in," he said.

Jade came through the doors. He took one look at her and froze. She wore only a thin, white cotton night dress; the transparent material merely shaded the slender shape beneath. The short sleeves and neckline barely covered her shoulders, while the long dark hair had been lifted back, and plaited, revealing every part of her to his scrutiny.

"Watch this." She smiled.

"Oh, I'm watching."

Jade set the puppy down, retreated four steps back and then knelt on her hands and knees. The gown dropped an inch or so from her person, displaying what he often found himself imagining, and with her in a pose so provocative, he stiffened, drew a sharp breath and released it in a groan when he could not turn away.

"No, wait," she said, misinterpreting his groan. "Come

on, Wolf Dog, come on!" she called excitedly. The little wolf dog rose unsteadily to his feet, wobbled the four paces, and she laughed as she swept him back into her arms. "See, already he'll come to me! Are you impressed?"

"Very."

"Oh, I know he's going to be a fine dog!" she continued excitedly, superlatives gushing from happiness. "He is the very best present I ever received in my whole life, and, oh, Victor, if only there was some way to thank you enough."

This made Victor shake his head with a chuckle.

"I still can't think of a name for him," she admitted, petting the furry head.

"I'm having a great deal of difficulty thinking right now," he confessed.

"Oh?" She looked suddenly confused. "Are you tired? Yes, of course, you must be after the day's travel. I didn't mean to keep you up—"

That did it. Victor fell back on the bed and roared with laughter; it was too much, it was just too much. His laughter brought Jade a quick understanding, a blush went to the roots of her hair and she could not leave fast enough.

Vintage Jade, he thought.

The rain pounded on the balcony outside. Jade stepped quietly into her room. She set Wolf Dog in his small basket, petted him until he fell asleep and before undressing, she lay down on the bed to listen to the rain fall against the windows.

She loved the sound of rain against windows. . . .

Victor turned off the lamp in his bedchamber. Darkness surrounded him. The light from her room seeped through the door, and yet he was suddenly listening to the rain against the house. Haunting images of their first night together took shape in his mind. Without fully knowing his intentions, he found himself moving through the door, the adjoining dressing room, and then just standing in the doorway. She lay on the bed, seemed lost in her thoughts.

What was she thinking?

He remained motionless, watching, studying her, unable to turn away and yet unable to go to her.

Jade sat up with a sad kind of sigh and began undressing. Confidently, she moved to the closet, though one arm remained outstretched as necessary protection. He smiled as she struggled with the buttons, buttons he could undo so easily. She hung her dress, removed her petticoat, and when he saw the chemise coming off, he grasped the danger and forced himself away.

Lured by the soothing sound of rain, she soon fell asleep. Perhaps an hour or so passed before she drifted into the now familiar dream that wreaked havoc on her sleep. It was always the same dream, spun from a memory of a hot afternoon by a lake. Some nights the dream became so startlingly vivid that it woke her.

She'd awaken to find her nightgown clinging to her front, a moist sheen covering her body, her nipples erect, wetness between her thighs. She'd fall against the pillows, desperately trying to think of anything but him. . . .

Victor was still awake, anxiously turning thoughts over in his mind when he heard a soft cry from her room. Thinking it was a seizure, he flew through the doors.

Yet, it was not a seizure.

He took one look at her sleeping figure, tossing and turning with a dream, the nature of which was all too apparent

His weight came to the bed. She felt his strong body come against her, his hand pulling the nightdress over her flushed form. She woke, landing on the very real shore of her dream.

"Victor?"

"It's a dream, Jade Terese," he whispered, kissing her neck first, his breath catching with the potency of the feel of her soft slender shape beneath him, his huge body tensing with hot pleasure. "It's only a dream . . ."

"Victor . . ." She whispered his name before she felt his lips on her mouth and he was kissing her deeply. A kiss that made each breath drawn into her lungs fill her hot body with the sweet fire of desire. He turned on his side, freeing his hand, watching her as he ran his hand over the smooth soft rise of her breast, teasing her there with light brushes of the warmth of his palm before traveling over her flat stomach and lower, his hand slipping between her legs until she arched back with a cry.

Only to feel her sex swollen like a budding rose and wet with the sweetness of her willingness. Their lips melted into each other, and tongues sparred, teased, aroused. All the while he kept his weight from her, a prisoner to his pace, his pleasure. The pleasure made a whirl of color in her head as his mouth lifted over hers and words were whispered against her flesh as his lips moved down her neck to one breast.

His mouth took the nipple and rolled it in his tongue, pulling it with his teeth, playing, teasing until she tossed her head back and forth. Her heart pounded wildly and her thighs opened themselves before his tongue found her navel, slowly circling it over and over until she trembled with it, and his kisses moved over her belly and lower.

Tremors shot through her flesh and she cried helplessly as she let him lift her thighs, feeling a melting surging dizziness spread outward as he orchestrated a previously unimaginable pleasure. Hot waves slashed through her, rising and falling in shimmering tides, building higher and higher each time until she thought she would ... burst at the slightest touch. ...

When he tried to pull away, she reached weakly to draw him back, but he came over her again, her own scent on his mouth. She breathed his name as his lips found hers again. His groan died in their joined mouths. He felt her small arms wrapping around his neck as she returned his kiss with a burning passion that matched his own, and he slowly slipped into the hot waiting sheath of her femininity and thought he would die. ...

Jade stirred, turned in the pillow. The bed was empty. She came fully awake with a question. The hot blush on

her cheeks, an ever so pleasant exhaustion and his lingering scent answered the question. She fell back against the
pillows and smiled.

She remembered after his arms had wrapped around her,
enclosing her in that irresistible exhaustion, she had asked
if he was going to marry her. She had said, "You should
because I love you." Either he made no reply or sleep had
invaded the remaining sliver of consciousness because that
was the last thing she remembered.

Later Carl told her Victor had left for the city.

The tightly corded muscles on the three men's backs
tightened and relaxed, tightened and relaxed, as they
rhythmically lifted moist dirt in the shovels, and tossed it
onto a growing mound at the graveside. The air still felt
warm and perspiration streamed from the shirtless men,
though this stilled night was rich and heavy with the
promise of rain. Again.

Sebastian circled the graveyard with three other men, to
make certain no passersby came close enough to understand that graves were being dug up and desecrated.

Victor stopped a moment. Breathing heavily, he wiped
the perspiration from his brow. This was their only hope.
His agents had found nothing of interest in Philip Devon's
affairs. Most of the documentation had been kept in a
bank; the files were easily gotten to. Inheriting a fair-sized
fortune of the estate and property, unlike most plantation
owners, Philip Devon had had little outstanding debt. He
seemed to neither gamble nor drink much, the most common curse of his class. Yet, for the last four years, the har-
vest had fallen short of balancing the books. Jade had
inherited the property, which the Church, Mother
Francesca acting as her guardian, had deeded to the bank
to cover the family's remaining debt. He had owed only
five businesses the year he died: the seeding company, a
general merchandiser, a carriage maker, a local cabinet-
maker for a house full of new furniture, and a relatively

small sum to the bank for a loan from a crop failure about five years before.

They had gone over every transaction going back fifteen years. Nothing. Nothing unusual. Philip Devon had kept a mistress briefly before his marriage, but there had been no dependents issued from the liaison. After all the debts had been paid, Jade had inherited a small yearly amount, enough to keep her from poverty, that was all.

There was no trace or sign of anyone who would be seeking vengeance on Devon's daughter. And the mystery deepened the more Victor came to know the young lady Jade Terese. For, as Mercedes said to him one night, to know her was to love her. How true that was. . . .

"There it is," John said, reaching the brass cover of the casket. He leaped down in the hole and brushed the remaining dirt from the coffin. Steffan tossed his shovel down and leaned over, drawing deep breaths into his lungs as John uncovered the other coffin as well. The brass caught and reflected the dim light of the lamps hung on the overhanging branch of a dogwood tree above.

"They'll need a crowbar to 'em," Murray said, glad he wasn't the superstitious kind as his gaze swept the dim white crypts gleaming dully in the darkness. Two oil lamps lit the spot and gave life to the shadows. Even the incessant murmur of insects was banished from this place, strangely silent. . . .

"Let's open them up," Victor said, jumping down at John's side. A light rain began falling from the darkened sky. The warm drops hit his bare back. He looked up. "How's that for a bit of luck?"

"Ain't no luck in a graveyard." John laughed.

Murray handed him the crowbar. Victor clasped it firmly in his hands and put it to the first casket. "Who does it say there?" Murray asked, squinting to see the name carved in flowing script on top of the casket. He reached to unhook the lantern and the light illuminated an eerie scene.

Lord, his heart kept thumpin' like a tired ole mule!

"Philip Devon," Victor said.

A chill raced up Murray's spine, for no reason he knew.

Victor pried the lid open. "Well, here goes," he said as he pushed it back and looked inside.

A collective gasp sounded as they stared.

The light gleamed and blazed over an empty coffin. . . .

He found her in the empty church. Golden sunshine streamed through the tall windows and fell over the place where she knelt in the front pew beneath the altar. Her eyes were closed and so deeply was she lost in her prayers that she never heard the quiet approach of his footsteps.

"Mother Francesca . . ."

She turned to him. For a moment she studied the uncommon strength of his tall frame clad in a gentleman's gray riding pants, knee-high black boots, a black vest over a white shirt, an ivory-handled pistol secured in a shoulder harness. Not even he, Monsieur Nolte, could keep Terese safe. His presence here was proof.

She clutched the small precious statuette tight in her fist before asking: "What has happened?"

Victor made a list for her, including all their suspicions, the amulet, the empty graves of her parents, the terrible hunch that Jade saw a murder, that her seizures somehow blocked her memory, that this murderer was trying to kill her now because of what she had seen.

"Yes," she surprised him by saying, "I, too, harbored the same suspicions. I once tried to force her to remember her parents' deaths but—"

"She had a seizure," Victor finished. "The seizures somehow keep her ignorant. I know you know something more about her parents' murders. I need you to tell me. I must know what has happened to her." Softly, with feeling, he added, "For Jade."

She stood up slowly and took a seat on the pew, wondering wildly how he would react when she finally answered him. And yet how could she respond to those questions? "What if I said that I once knew who had committed the murder?"

"What?" His voice echoed like a profanity through the empty church.

"You are shocked, I see."

"To say the least! Who?"

"A woman named Juliet Lalaurie."

"A woman?"

"You must wonder why I have not told you sooner." She raised her hands to stop his objections. "I beg for your patience, Monsieur. I believe you will understand my hesitancy by the end of it."

The Reverend Mother paused as she studied the painted statue of Christ, but saw only a carved block of stone. For the first time in her life her religion was failing her.

"It began long ago with Jade's father, Monsieur Devon, a Creole gentleman, a young man, unmarried—it was on the eve of his inheritance. Three years, I believe, before the senior Devon died, leaving him, as the only son, with the plantation. And this sad story begins when he went to the quadroon ball—" The good woman's voice rose with sudden bitterness. "The quadroon balls where mulattos and octoroons sell off their precious daughters to the highest bidder. With the unholy sanction of our entire society. Men take these girls as their mistresses, a kind of 'dark wife,' as they say. 'Tis a hateful practice, keeping these young women from the true sacrament of marriage and all that means to a woman and her children. I think especially of these children."

"It was her, Juliet Lalaurie. She was barely fourteen when he . . . he initiated the liaison—with her mother's full consent, of course."

"Her father's mistress?"

"Yes. I knew the girl. She had attended our school for many years. She was a strikingly beautiful young woman, a colored girl who could easily pass. She had long brown hair and even, blue eyes. She was uncommon in many other respects. Her mother was an octoroon, a onetime beauty herself and quite well off. She paraded the little girl around as if she were a princess."

She shook her head. "We have had few girls like her. She was willful, impetuous, headstrong for her position and age—I think the result of all the admiration she had gotten over the years for this uncommon beauty. She was finally dismissed from our school for a rage she fell into, brought on when another girl was picked for a solo in a musical recital.

"Juliet was introduced at the quadroon balls when she was only thirteen. Thirteen . . ." The Reverend Mother shook her head. "At the time I had spoken to her mother, desperate to dissuade her from presenting the girl so young. I demanded that she wait a year at least. I will not relate the shocking details of her mother's response to my plea. It is enough to say that she did not wait.

"Juliet was the star of those balls that year. Monsieur Devon made his offer. The mother accepted. He arranged generous living conditions: Juliet was given a house with two servants, an impressive allowance. And as often happens to such women, he became her life. She was passionately in love with Jade's father."

"Yes? What happened?"

"Within a year Monsieur Devon left, like so many young men of his class, for his sojourn to the Continent. He was a young man of twenty then. He was gone for two years. Juliet had one of our sisters, Sister Benedict, pen a letter every day to him. Every day. I was not aware of the situation. Sister Benedict felt that this attention from one's Negro mistress was ridiculous, and she never posted a single one of these heartsick letters. He had never written once to her; she had disappeared from his mind as soon as he had shut the door to her little house.

"And yet he lived and breathed in her heart. She created the impression in her own mind—as well as others—that Philip could not live without her. She was so young. She had even convinced herself he would never marry because of her.

"Yet Philip had met Elizabeth in Paris. In a picture gallery. She was the only surviving daughter of a Lord and Lady Avington, a respected English negotiator on trade issues between the two countries before the war."

"Jade mentioned her grandfather . . ."

"Yes. Her mother had talked a good deal about her family. They had refused to allow the courtship. Monsieur Devon was French, untitled, and while propertied, the holdings were in New Orleans—all quite unacceptable." She waved her hand in dismissal. "Courtship, like marriage, was out of the question. So the two lovers met in secret for the year that Elizabeth's father was positioned in Paris. The month her parents were preparing to leave Paris, Elizabeth and Philip eloped.

"Jade's grandparents died within two years of each other and without ever forgiving Elizabeth, a thing of great hardship for her. Even after Terese was born, they refused to answer any of her letters."

Victor's gaze dropped to the Reverend Mother's lap as she paused and he watched her pale hands whiten more as she clutched her small statuette.

"So, Monsieur Devon returned with his new bride. I don't believe he saw Juliet again. . . ." She paused before adding, "He severed the liaison through his banker. . . ."

Victor swore softly at this.

The Reverend Mother shook her head. "A banker's note. Juliet went . . . insane. Juliet considered herself bound to Philip forever more, a liaison that was her life. In the beginning it was constant suicide threats, and the priest involved convinced Philip not to intervene for her, that it would only make it worse. He was beside himself, understanding too late the error so common to his sex: the masculine dismissal of a woman's love. . . .

"It seemed to become worse the year when Elizabeth gave birth to Terese, the same year Juliet's mother passed on. At some point Juliet turned to a voodoo witch doctor. Dr. JohnJohn, I believe he was called. This man was said to have introduced Juliet to the voodoo arts. Over the years Juliet became ever more involved in the heathen worship and evil practice.

"During all this time her hatred for Elizabeth grew and thrived. Elizabeth was the demon. Elizabeth was the evil one who stole her only happiness. Elizabeth had put an evil spell on Philip. Amulets and threats and voodoo fetishes appeared regularly on the Devon plantation. The threats kept escalating, then suddenly for no reason anyone knew, they'd stop. Years might pass relatively free from Juliet's relentless hatred and torments. Then, again with the same capriciousness, suddenly they would start again. Elizabeth sought my advice when finally one of her prized mares succumbed to a mysterious ailment that could only be poisoning.

"You'd have to know Elizabeth to understand how she tried to resolve this sordid situation she found herself in. She had long since forgiven her husband, whom she loved very deeply. She was a women of refined taste and sensibilities, and yet headstrong, forthright, characteristics many people in our community found refreshing in a woman, while others, well—" She shrugged her shoulders. "No matter that now."

"Well, what happened?"

"The horse. Elizabeth finally became frightened. She demanded that either Juliet be deported to a faraway place or that Philip return with her to England—which was out of the question, of course. His family had owned the plantation for nearly fifty years and it was his life. He began the arrangements to have Juliet deported—illegally—in the dark dead of night. She was to be transported to Brazil. . . .

"A week or so before this desperate plan was to be launched, Terese found two wax voodoo dolls. The smaller doll had its eyes burnt out, the larger doll had its head severed—"

"Jade told me about that."

The Reverend Mother closed her eyes. Her pounding heart was a loud roar in her ears. She clung tightly to her statuette, and on the heels of a long pause, she confessed, "The fire occurred one week later. . . ."

Victor braced for the end of the story. So it was a woman and her insane attendants—voodoo practitioners. How he loathed the superstitions and idiocies of the ignorant. They would just have to find where she was now and force a confession, he supposed. . . .

"And this woman," he said. "Where is she now?"

"You don't understand," the Reverend Mother said, her voice near breaking. "Juliet drowned shortly after the fire. Juliet has long been dead. . . ."

"Marie, what are you telling me? There are only two people who could have made that amulet and yet neither of them did?"

It was both a statement and a question. Marie did not know how to explain it differently to Victor, who would neither understand nor believe.

They sat alone in one of Marie's anterooms. The windows opened onto the courtyard. A profusion of flowers below threw a riot of perfumed scents in the air and he closed his eyes, breathing deeply. He turned back to Marie. Colors softened beneath the setting sun, casting her in a lovely light as she sat across from him on a maroon velvet meridenne. "Marie . . ."

"It is all I can tell you. It is all I know and the only thing I know. My servants have spoken to the current queen—a madwoman often seen at the market, a woman named Malvina. She is harmless. She mostly just cures people of their ailments or arranges love matches. They've also contacted the voodoo doctor, Tars, who I believe you know of—and these are the only two people who could make that amulet."

"And this Dr. JohnJohn?"

"Buried six years ago."

Marie paused, her dark eyes lowered, her thoughts spinning around the difficulties here. She wanted very much to help him; she was certain to fail. She did not tell him that she'd had the spell removed. For he did not believe in spells. Yet she knew well the awesome power of gris-gris. The mind and the imagination were omnipotent and it was from these mighty sources that the spells and potions and curses worked their magic. "So, no"—she shook her head—"they did not make this terrible thing. I know them both and I am satisfied with their testimony."

"Marie, somebody made it!"

"Yes, of course." She searched for another way to say it, but found none. "The people talk of a spirit that is appearing at secret ceremonies held at Lake Femae. This spirit woman is said to hold great powers: the power of death—"

"Back to spirits?" Victor shook his head and said slowly, "Marie . . . this is not helping."

"No," she agreed. "I do not believe I can help you. For how can I make you believe what I know? The person who is threatening Jade Terese is not a man. It is a woman. The woman is dead."

Victor did not believe any of this. He swallowed his drink whole, setting it with a clink on the table. He knew he was wasting his time now, but because he cared for Marie, and deeply, he did not follow his first impulse to storm from the room in frustration.

Marie's gaze was unwavering.

"Marie, a dead woman did not make that amulet or throw Jade into that whorehouse, or break into my house. And Marie"—he paused for effect—"a dead woman did not hang her maid upside down with a slit throat."

She did not know how to answer. "I am as baffled as you. Perhaps more because I know the truth."

"Marie . . . I want . . . I just want her safety."

Hearing his agony, agony born of his fear, Marie rose and stepped to him. She reached to touch him, her lovely eyes serious: "For you, for your piece of mind, *mon amour,* I can tell you that she will be safe as long as she is with you."

He wanted badly to believe this. And he did, especially considering all the facts: the relative isolation of his country estate, how no one knew she was staying there, how someone was always with her.

Then too, that dog. He was still just a puppy, but the other night Sebastian wanted to show how very remarkably the dog protected her. Once everyone had retired, they stepped outside her door. Nothing happened until Sebastian put his hand gently on the door. Sure enough, a low puppy growl sounded from the other side.

"You know, I got her a dog—"

"Yes, I do. Not quite a dog, is he?" Marie asked, smiling when Victor looked quite surprised. "He is a very noble creature." She said in a whisper, "I have seen him in a dream. He will save Jade's life—twice."

She had seen a picture taken from the distance future. Jade was sitting at a cluttered desk. Victor stood behind her when two boys came running into the room. They were so beautiful, their sons. The boys were excited over a find in the woods. They led both their parents out. Then they were kneeling over a fallen creature.

Jade dropped to her knees and buried her face in the fur. It was the wild dog. An animal would appear in Jade's dreams. An animal that would draw her outside in the dark middle of the night when the moon was up and the shadows fell over the dark woods where she imagined she saw the creature watching over her. She'd call his name over and over until finally Victor would rise and enclose her with his love and sympathy, as he moved her back inside.

It was Wolf Dog.

As the startled boys stared at their mother, Marie heard Victor explaining to his sons that here was the dog that saved their mother's life. More than once, he told them, more than once. As he took Jade into his arms and as his sons crowded around to comfort their mother, Victor gently stroked the wolf dog's fur. "We owe our lives to this dog, our very lives . . ."

Remembering this magical dream, she said to Victor, "Jade is your mate; she is the blessing in your life."

Victor's gaze searched Marie's with fiery intensity. "No," he whispered, his expression filling with unspeakable pain. "No ..."

Chapter 9

"I be right back," Tessie said as she met Jade at the water's edge with a towel. "Chachie's got some bread baking. Should be ready by now."

Breathless from her swim, Jade sighed with exasperation. "Tessie, there is no one in the world who eats so much but for whom food does so little."

"Yes, ma'am." Tessie said as she broke into a run toward the house.

Wolf Dog saw some fun as Jade picked up her chemise. Grabbing the cloth in his mouth, he bounced away with it and growled. "Oh, you rascal, you!" She called him back. He came immediately but not with the chemise. "Wolf Dog!" She carefully searched the ground, then again, and once more before finally giving up. She slipped back into the water to wait for Tessie's return.

Knowing trouble when he saw it, Carl took one glance at Victor and stopped himself from asking how things had progressed in New Orleans, stopped himself from asking anything. Victor wore beige breeches, black boots, a canvas vest. Two days' growth of beard and a threatening scowl had changed his face and made him look as villainous as a backwoods bounty hunter. . . .

Hands on hips, he asked, "Where's Sebastian?"

"Just back from the fencing academy. Now I believe he is fishing at the river with Mercedes. Murray is napping."

"Jade?"

Carl looked past Victor's tall frame. Victor turned to see Tessie coming through the front door. He normally greeted

Tessie affectionately. She seemed to stop as she waited for it.

"Where's Jade?"

"She's down at the pond. I left her to fetch some food."

"You left her alone?"

Tessie nodded as she lowered her head.

With a pointed finger and a stern tone: "I've told you once: you are not to leave her alone. Ever. Unless someone is with her, you are to be by her side."

"Yes, sir," she said with a pounding heart. Nothing could be worse than Victor's scolding. This was her first. "I'se run back right now."

"No, it's all right. I have to talk to her anyway."

Victor quietly approached the scene. For several minutes he just stood there staring. It seemed to epitomize his struggle; Jade Terese floated in the shallows, her face tilted to the sun, naked, vulnerable to anyone or anything and totally oblivious to all.

Jade felt the hot sun on her face, the soothing warm water surrounding her. She had not a thought. Slowly, rhythmically, she sank beneath the surface, took a mouthful of water, popped up and squirted the water into a fountain, smiling as it splashed back on her face.

As she squirted the next mouthful of water, she sensed the coolness of a shadow falling over her. She nearly choked. A cloud? A person!

She bolted up, swung her arms in a wide circle and touched a boot. "Who's there?" She scrambled back as her arms protectively covered herself. "Who is it?" No answer. She screamed, ducked under the water but too late. Two strong hands caught her at the waist.

She screamed again as he threw her over his shoulder and knocked the wind from her. Adrenaline shot through her limbs. She kicked and screamed, her fists pounded into his back but this did not slow him down let alone stop him. He threw her onto the blanket and lowered himself quickly on top of her, pinning her arms to the ground and her body beneath his.

"Victor!" She said his name in a cry as her stomach turned in leaps. "Victor! You scared me so! You scared me—"

"I meant to scare you! Just what the hell do you think you're doing out here, naked and alone? God, girl, where's your sense?"

"I . . . was . . . Oh, Victor, I—"

"There is no excuse for this! What is it going to take to make you realize . . ."

His voice thundered above her and on and on he yelled, but she could barely comprehend, swept as she was with relief that it was him. It was him. Thank God. . . .

Heavens, did he have a monstrous temper! A monster that emerged anytime he imagined she was hurting herself, or anything having to do with her blindness. He did not seem to trust her ability to get around sightless. . . .

A scene drawn from recent memory floated dizzily to mind: She had waked to discover Wolf Dog was not in her room. She imagined the puppy had fallen off the balcony and she had flown in a panic, ringing the servant's rope, over and over, but it was taking too long. She raced into the hall and flew down the stairs, falling in her panic. She just sprained her ankle but for all of Victor's fury she might have broken her neck. "I could have lost you over a dog, a goddamned dog . . ." and on and on he had yelled then.

His weight crushed her unmercifully and she squirmed, interrupting the torrent of words. "Victor, please let me up."

"Not a bloody chance."

Quite suddenly the whole situation changed.

"If you don't let me up . . . I'll . . ."

"You'll what?"

"I'll sic Wolf Dog on you!"

His chuckle was one of plain masculine scorn. He took

one glance around and spotted the puppy sound asleep under a tree. Sleeping through the attack, wolf or not, no better than a cat. "Something like, 'Get him boy? Get him?'"

"Yes! Yes! Wolf Dog, Wolf Dog! Help!" Wolf Dog awoke at his name, perked up, and came bouncing over to them. "Get him, Wolf Dog. Get him!"

Wolf Dog showed Victor how terribly wrong he was: The little puppy, already four hands high and still growing, was more than willing to rescue her. He bounced over to Victor, yelping as his little head shook back and forth, a demonstration of how he would tear Victor apart.

Victor rolled over with his laughter.

Once released, Jade sat up and swept her puppy into her arms. "My brave little puppy! You showed him! You showed that monster that he can't take advantage of us! You showed him, my brave little Wolf Dog!"

She seemed so beautiful then, holding the puppy against her bare skin, laughing and praising his fine show. The long wet hair fell over her, curling in a wet heap at her hips. Her face was flushed from the sun and her enchanting eyes sparkled as if reflecting some inner light. And that body of hers. Never had he wanted a woman so much; never had it been so physical. Like a thirst it was, his body seeking—nay, needing, demanding—the erotic play and release brought by that slender form against his.

Dear God, what was he going to do?

He fell back and stared at the sunlight filtering through the leaves. She was tearing him in two. Everyday his love grew, like a wondrous winged creature flying higher and higher, soaring to a previously unimagined height. And with this miraculous love came the certainty that it was not enough. Love was not enough. Marriage to her would bring regret, perhaps even resentment, a thing that could not destroy the love but could change it from a heavenly bliss to a poison. He had to start distancing himself, somehow—

Laughing and playful, ever so alive, Jade threw herself on top of him and his unpleasant thoughts disappeared with the irresistible lure of her happiness. He had neither chance nor choice; he never had. His body was already hot, ready, waiting, greeting the music of her laughter, the long wet hair lapping over his hot skin and the thrilling feel of her bare breasts against him with greedy enthusiasm. He gently turned her onto her back. He would have her now, on a marshy bank under a canopy of a bright blue sky. . . .

Mercedes and Sebastian rode up to the entrance just after the carriage swung around the center circular drive. "Our dresses! Our dresses have finally come!" Mercedes cried in excitement. "Tessie! Where's Jade?"

As excited as Mercedes, Tessie watched the progression of box after box be carried into the house. "At the pond!" Mercedes did not pause. She reined her horse around and pushed the spirited mare into a gallop.

Jade had dreamt of this kiss. As his warm firm lips touched the corners of her mouth with a tender pressure, he molded her mouth to his, his tongue sweeping deeply, insistently, into her as her wet moist body pressed against his hot skin. Warm desire swept through her and she reached her hands around his neck. . . .

Victor looked up to see the horses galloping up. Before he even turned, he pulled the blanket up and over her. Seeing Mercedes and Sebastian and remembering passing the carriage on his way back, he felt a relief almost as intense as it was painful. "I believe Mercedes has come to fetch you."

The two riders reined up and took in the scene. Sebastian smiled. "It must be the sunshine . . ."

Numbed and overwhelmed, Jade sat in a chair, listening to Mercedes's and Tessie's wild exclamations as they inspected one dress after another. Was there no end? A pale blue day dress, a green-and-violet ball gown, a flowered silk dress, matching pelisses, a pale apricot one, another flowered one, and on and on, and after an endless parade of dresses came lace and ruffles, petticoats, hats, scarves, slippers, night dresses. She was going to cry. . . .

Victor entered the room to find Jade sitting in the chair as still and pale as a porcelain doll, buried in a pile of new dresses and looking, dear Lord, as if she were about to break down. He motioned for Mercedes and Tessie to leave them.

He took the clothing from her lap. "Jade, what's wrong?"

"Victor, it's you," she said, wiping her eyes quickly. "No . . . nothing's wrong."

He chuckled affectionately. "Then why are you crying?"

"I just . . . I can't accept all this. . . ." She waved her arm around the room.

"You're crying because you can't accept my present?"

She bit her lip and shook her head. How could she tell him that she did not want his presents, that it scared her to receive gifts like this? All she wanted was for him to tell her that he loved her, that he was going to marry her. Such generosity might be acceptable afterward, but arriving before any declaration, it made her afraid.

"You're so generous," she said softly, knowing it was an understatement. "But I really can't accept all these lovely things."

"Why?"

"It . . . it just wouldn't be proper."

"Proper?" He laughed. "Don't tell me you're going to deny me the pleasure of seeing you in some pretty new clothes because of some ridiculous sense of propriety."

"Victor, it's just that you have given me so much already—you've helped me, kept me safe from some imagined threat, taken care of me. I live in your house and . . . and now, all this." Again she motioned across the room. "It makes me feel . . . well, I don't have any way to repay you."

"Repay me?" A curious emotion sprang in his gaze. "What are you thinking, sweetheart? That if you accept my gifts you'll have to accept my lovemaking?" He smiled when she tried to deny it. "I knew you wouldn't think that," he said softly, seriously. "Operating on such a simple, shallow level of reciprocity makes a mockery out of us and all we've shared together. It's beneath you and, I assure you, it's beneath me. I don't have to buy or even win your favors; I've never had a woman who gave herself so completely or freely to me."

On the heels of a troubled pause she asked, "The night you left . . ."

Victor brought her to her feet only to enclose her in his arms. "It was only a dream, Jade Terese."

"Did you hear what I said to you then," she whispered, afraid to turn her face to him. "You never said . . . I mean, I want to know—"

"If I've fallen in love with you too?"

He received her nod before his arms tightened around her, his lips brushing her forehead. "Yes Jade, I've fallen in love with you. I've known you such a short time and when I realize how much I could love you . . . it scares the hell out of me."

Her fingers lightly traced the contours of his mouth. He said what she had longed to hear, but with anguish. The surrender again. She wondered if it would ever be easier for him. "Then are you to marry me?"

The day would arrive soon when he'd have to answer that question, but not now, not today. He said simply, "The question of marriage is one that a man asks, in his own time and at his own choosing."

Jade accepted this, content with his declaration of love. It was enough for her, enough for now. "But Victor"—she smiled—"what if a man seems to be taking a very long time about it?"

His gaze held fondness, and he smiled then too. "Just

where did you learn to be so forward? I know it's not something they teach young ladies at the convent."

Jade laughed, but before she answered, he slipped apart from her. After looking over the clothes, he separated a green silk dress from the others.

"Do a poor man a favor and wear this for supper." And without another word, he handed her the dress and left.

Jade looked lovely in the new outfit. The green silk gown was perfectly simple. It accented and flattered her beauty, especially her eyes. The dress had a low neckline with short sleeves falling off her shoulders, a fashionable waistline and folds and folds of rich material. The gown might be worn at any gala, and thankfully, supper was a markedly formal affair at the country estate. The days might be spent barefoot, but for supper, everyone, even the men, wore formal attire.

Remarkably good with a brush, Tessie was wrapping Jade's long tresses in matching green ribbons, then lifting the locks into soft swirls for a crown. Mercedes watched at her side. Jade, distractedly, ran her hand over Mercedes' gown, attempting to get a picture of it in her mind.

"What do I look like? I mean, how would you describe me?"

Tessie winked at Mercedes. "Oh, you be plain as a pumpkin. I be just talkin' 'bout you to Chachie; I says my mistress, well, she be sweet as honey but my, I ain't never seen such a face as hers. Her eyes be rather too large and green, her lashes too long and dark, her nose too straight and her skin! Lord, that skin as soft and smooth as a baby's. That hair too, just too dark and shiny, too much and too long." Mercedes started laughing, and Tessie added, "And her lips, well, ain't a soul alive who deserves such a dark red color without addin' rose oil to 'em. Thank the Lord she's got that smile like a burst of sunshine after a week of rain to make up the difference."

"Tessie, you're impossible."

"Yes, ma'am."

* * *

The men gathered on the patio waiting for the ladies, engaged in a heated debate over the congressional reenactment of the habeas corpus laws. Victor had been furious when Congress had suspended these essential laws that forced the state to prove a citizen's guilt, and he and his father had lobbied extensively to have them reenacted. Presently he and Murray were trying to explain why this was so important to Sebastian. Sebastian seemed unable to grasp the principle; he had no difficulty distinguishing the good from the bad, the criminal from the law-abiding, and so it seemed to him any magistrate acting for the state could be expected to have the same common sense. . . .

The last light of day stretched gold arms across the land, while the lingering warmth filled the early evening air. The flames of the festive lanterns and even the candles on the table hardly stirred. Mercedes guided Jade down, through the long hall and out onto the patio, presenting her like a personal creation.

Victor turned to confront her, took one long stare and turned away with what Murray thought was a look of total anguish. Sebastian, however, was already at their side, making each of them turn a pretty circle before complimenting first Jade, then Mercedes, and with all the flamboyance of which only he was capable. Murray needed no prodding to join Sebastian.

Oblivious to the stir she created, Jade was far more interested in showing Victor Wolf Dog's new trick. "You must see what he can do now," she said excitedly, calling the dog to her.

Victor turned back around. Murray knew his trouble intensified by merely looking at her, for Victor's expression seemed an exercise in conflicting emotions.

"Are you watching?"

"Yes."

After determining Wolf Dog was standing, Jade ordered the puppy to sit, and petted him affectionately when he complied. "He is the most wonderful puppy! Hamlet never learned as quickly as little Wolf Dog. Tomorrow, I shall start leash training."

Victor knelt down beside her. She was so just alive. Everything about her sparkled with a rare gift of enthusiasm; she showed excitement at every little thing life offered. How was it possible when she lived in a totally debilitating darkness? And dear God, what would she be like if she weren't blind?

"You are so beautiful."

"You like my dress?" she asked, misinterpreting his remark.

"Yes, Mercedes has done your beauty a great justice." Victor turned then to Mercedes. "And you, Mercedes, you look like a princess."

Mercedes smiled, then felt herself blushing. Victor's rare compliments affected one in a way no one else's could. That masculine charm of his, the way he tossed the simplest words like a casual shrug, almost as an afterthought, made one self-conscious and aware of his sincerity.

As the party sat down, Murray was admiring the way the green dress set off Jade's enchanting eyes. Jade leaned forward as she took her seat across from him, and as she came towards the candle, her pupils constricted.

What the devil was that?

He peered closer, seeing the unbelievable. For he was watching her pupils dilate as she receded into the chair.

He had never noticed before!

The doctor did not hear what Sebastian was saying, though everyone stopped talking as he leaned forward with the candle in his hand and moved it toward and away from Jade's eyes. Jade turned her face to the side in confusion, and reached her hand into the air, knocking the candle over. "What— What was that?"

"I was just holdin' a candle to your eyes, darlin'," he explained. "Did any of the doctors who examined you mention that your pupils dilate and constrict?"

Jade nodded slowly.

"But I thought you said you were completely blind, that you don't see any change of light?"

"No, I don't see any light or colors or anything. I wish I did, it would help a lot. Sometimes when I wake up, I can't tell if it's morning or not, and honestly, I can't tell you how many times I've gotten up and dressed, thinking it was close to morning, only to have to wait hours and hours."

No one noticed the doctor's confused distraction as he tried to reason this through. And while the dinner was served and he continued to dwell on this, his suspicions mounted, suspicions that led him to the first of many startling conclusion's about Jade and the nature of her blindness. He'd send for those books tomorrow. . . .

It was the first of many horrible nightmares drawn by a truth much too painful to know in the light of a waking day. Victor stood above her, disgusted by her. He would have no more of a woman who could not see. She begged him, pleaded with him, frantically trying to show him all the things she could so without seeing. "It's no use, you're no use! You're useless, Jade Terese, pathetic, just like that woman said!"

She bolted up in bed.

Panicked, breathing hard and fast, she did not think. She parted the mosquito net and slipped from her bed, making her way through the dressing room and to Victor's chamber. He woke as she climbed onto the bed. He took one look at the tear-filled eyes, the lovely face changed with pain and fear. "Jade," he whispered. "Sweetheart, what's wrong?"

"I want to be with you. . . . I want you to love me."

Victor suffered no hesitation. There was no thought of his relief when Tessie had informed him that yes, Jade had a bleeding while he was away. There was no thought of his relief that very day when Sebastian and Mercedes had interrupted them. There was no thought of his vow never to take her to his bed again.

He could never deny her. He was vaguely aware some dream had frightened her, far more aware she sought a reassurance that he loved her. God knows he did love her and would always love her. For their short time together, he could love her.

Jade felt his arms gently lay her on her back. His lips brushed the wetness from her cheeks. When he kissed her, it was with a tenderness that spoke to her emotions.

"Yes, Jade Terese," he whispered, slowly sliding the thin straps of her gown from her shoulders. "I will love you. Now and forever, I will love you."

Jade's emotions soared, and as she felt her gown removed, his hands come over her body, tears fell from her cheeks. He did love her! He would never turn his heart away because she could not see. It had been only a nightmare. . . .

In the dark shadows of the night, love was spoken as never before. He kept passion to a slow pace, savoring a slow and sweet building of the momentum of her love. His hands barely touched her skin, yet he ignited every part of her. His kiss, like his touch, lit a warm fire until her body trembled and quivered with the first rise of those delicious flames. He caressed, then massaged, knowing exactly where his touch should dance lightly over her skin, where her desire begged for more, all the while he whispered words of love.

She felt those waves of rapture rise and build, gently washing over her as he parted her thighs and slowly entered her, letting her feel each burrowing inch of him joining her to him, forever and again.

He spun love and desire until like the promise of a cloudless dawn, a bright radiant sun burst inside her and she was soaring, soaring, unaware of his last thrust, unaware he held her collapsed body tight against his. She clung to him, breathless and humbled, barely able to feel her body beneath him.

An eternity or two passed.

"Again, my Jade Terese? Shall I love you again?"

"Yes . . . yes, again . . ."

Passion rekindled and desire sparked anew and their bodies moved together to this timeless music, love burning bright through the long dark hours of the night. . . .

Murray sat beneath the tall, longleaf cypress trees. His old medical book was spread across his lap, and he skimmed, then read. He knew he'd read that case years ago at Science Academy in London. He was sure of it. It must be in his other books, left in the house in New Orleans. He'd send for them.

The morning sun made its way across a cloudy sky. The air stirred with a slight breeze. The day felt pleasantly cooler, though still muggy and humid. A storm must be headed in from the Gulf.

Murray noticed none of it.

Carl appeared with some lemonade and mentioned that, unbelievably, no one else was up yet. "I do hope the two couples find the strength to make it down for supper."

Murray chuckled and said something about being glad for his sunset years, no longer being kept up all night, and anyway, not ever remembering having been kept up this long by anyone. Carl readily agreed with such sentiments.

"Carl, when's the next trip back to New Orleans?"

"Well, Tripoli just arrived this morning with Victor's business affairs and I should think he'll be leaving again this afternoon, as soon as it's cool enough to travel."

"I need some books at the house. They're buried in the library there. They'll have to be searched for." The doctor gave specific instructions and then said, "I want them back as soon as possible. Send someone out on a special trip if necessary."

Murray returned to his troubled thoughts of a blind young lady who suffered from terrible seizures at the mention of an accident, and a murderer still at large, the perplexing puzzle of just how a seizure could wipe away a memory . . .

"I'm going to have to get Luke to help me cut down

that tree today," Victor said as he came up behind the doctor, carrying Jade's puppy and noticing the tree Murray sat beneath for the first time. "I never noticed how close it was to the house. A good lightning storm will send her into flames."

"Well, you finally saw your way to getting up."

"I had a very long night," he said, as he smiled in reply.

Victor looked relaxed for the first time in long weeks. He sat down beside Murray and let little Wolf Dog run free on the ground, grinning as the puppy bounced down the hill, then back to his arms, then away again. Carl returned with coffee, more than his usual amount of insolent comments, and presented Victor with a stack of letters and envelopes from the city. "Carl, find Luke and tell him I need him to help ax that tree there, fetch the axes and the saws. I don't think I want to wait a day."

Victor began going through the mail. Most of it was commodity bills for his company, but there was also a letter from John, who was overseeing the hiring, what little of this there was. John had managed to find only six men. They needed five times that many. If things didn't get any better he'd soon be forced to purchase indentured servants.

"No news," Victor said after perusing the contents of the last envelope. He quickly read through Jade's stack of letters. He scanned them, searching for something, anything unusual or suspicious. Most all were from her faithful students and the convent sisters, the Reverend Mother, a lengthy letter from Monsieur Deubler and his wife. He read the one from Madame Lucretia, the mayor's wife, more carefully.

The letter said she was soon debarking for Paris for a long-denied visit to relatives and friends. She would be gone until the next season, almost a year. There were instructions on where Jade should forward her address, so as to arrange a visit. . . .

Jade had more than enough time before she had to answer the letters. Mercedes had devised an elaborate calendar for Jade's correspondence to maintain the appearance of Jade's residing in France. Jade would have nothing to do with it. " 'Tisn't just that I find it so difficult to deceive my friends, and I am quite certain it is all so unnecessary . . ."

If you only knew, Jade Terese. . . .

Victor wondered how the mayor could possibly get by without his wife, wondered if there was anything more odious than a hen-pecked husband. The man seemed to have trouble putting on his pants without her careful instructions. Claighborne often complained that it wouldn't bother him so much if he could just present the situations that required a joint effort between New Orleans and the Louisiana legislature directly to Madame Lucretia, instead of first presenting them to her husband and then having to wait for that poor bastard to get his wife's authorization.

He had never liked the woman. Less because she kept so many lovers and more because she pursued them so flagrantly, often as her husband watched, appearing as if he didn't have a clue what she was doing.

The woman certainly seemed to like Jade. . . .

Well, he supposed that was not unusual. . . .

He leaned back against the thick carpet of needles. "No news and for some reason, I don't care. I don't care about anything today."

Perspiration glistened from the two masculine frames, one bronzed, one black. The task was difficult and dangerous, and Luke was one of the few men Victor trusted with the arduous, backbreaking labor.

They finally set the saw aside and picked up axes. Victor swung back as Luke swung forward, each man slamming his ax into the meat of the tree, pulling out, and then slamming back again. They moved in a perfect, exacting rhythm, and when Carl called, neither man stole a glance up, though Victor called back, "Not now, Carl!"

Carl turned inside and passed Jade on her way to the

patio. He took her arm and guided her to the door, commenting on how pretty she looked in that color. Jade thanked him, not bothering to mention she had no idea what color it was she looked so pretty in. She vaguely remembered Tessie saying it was an apricot dress, but she could not be sure. The new clothes were still new.

Carl, always thoughtful, took a moment to explain what the men were doing and cautioned her to stay on the patio and not to interrupt their work. In anticipation of their thirst, he had just brought out water, and he asked Jade to tell them when they were through that it was on the table. "Don't interrupt them now."

Jade shook her head, smiling, a smile that seemed to light up her eyes. She felt lost in a dreamy bliss spun from Victor's lovemaking last night, wrapped in the security of his love. She thought she would try to start Wolf Dog's leash training. The wide-open space of the patio, its smooth tiled floor and clearly defined, familiar limits, seemed the best spot to begin training Wolf Dog.

Victor, assuming Carl was still there to see the thunderous crash, ordered in between swings, "Fetch some water."

Jade stiffened, alarmed and alerted. Had she heard right? Yes. He wanted water and he told her to fetch it. It was the first time he had ever asked her to do anything. He was finally beginning to trust her ability to do things!

Carl had said the water was on the table.

Jade set Wolf Dog to the ground and, knowing it was about fifteen paces to the wall, she turned with an outstretched arm and walked until she reached it. Using a hand on the wall to guide her, she walked the next twenty or so paces to the right, first hitting the serving tray and then the table.

Her hand moved over the table and found the large crystal container and two glasses. She was debating whether to take only the glasses, or both the container and glasses on a tray. She decided on the latter and lifted the tray into her hands just as Luke yelled, "Timber!"

She stopped, waiting patiently for the great crash. The wood cracked and cracked, then came a long whooshing sound of wind, and finally the huge trunk crashed to the ground. Jade smiled as she moved toward them carrying the tray, listening to their hearty laughs, self-congratulations and slaps on backs.

Jade had learned to carefully slide her feet over the ground to discover any object that might cause her to fall. She wished she had remembered to put on some slippers! The tiles were hot. She lifted to tiptoes to escape the burn.

A long, neatly coiled rope lay directly in her path.

Victor and Luke spun around on their heels at the sound of a halted scream, glass smashing against the tile, and in a flash of an instant, they were running. She had fallen facedown, her bare arms catching her fall and taking the worst of the shattered glass. Glass stuck in her. There was a brief glimpse of white skin before blood, dark red blood, covered everything.

"Don't move. Just don't move," Victor said, and then to Luke, "Get the doctor." The calmness in his voice pacified her, pushing both panic and fright away. She didn't move and felt no pain, felt only slight stinging sensations.

She heard Wolf Dog's whimper and felt his anxious nuzzling of her face but Victor reached under her and lifted her, carrying her inside. He lay her carefully on the hard tiled floor in the house. In the same calm voice, he instructed: "Don't move an inch. Hold your arms up. It's going to sting, sweetheart, but try not to flinch."

He began taking pieces of glass out, starting with a tiny jagged piece sticking into her neck mercifully far from her jugular vein, trying unsuccessfully to control his raging emotions, trying not to look at her small quivering lip.

"Is it very bad?" she asked in a halting voice. The sensation of warm blood streaming down her arms flooded abruptly into consciousness, and with it came the magnitude of what had happened.

"It's pretty bad but you're going to be all right. Don't speak now."

Murray, Carl and Tessie, followed by everyone else in the house, came flying into the room. "Oh, my God!" Murray cried, almost sliding into her. "Carl, I need hot water, bandages and my bag. I'll need a needle and thread, she's going to have to be stitched up. Tessie, fetch a pillow for her."

The doctor had plenty of experience with all manner of accidents and he worked methodically, his manner efficient and competent, while at the same time his gentle instructions and explanations helped calm her. Victor worked on the other side, both men pulling out the glass shards first.

"It's a darn good thing you don't see, lass. You're a sight, all right, but believe me, these glass cuts always look a fright worse than they are." All the glass was finally pulled and the bandages were brought. "Vic, wrap this around her arms tight now and hold your hands around the worst cut until it stops bleeding."

Victor and Murray each took an arm, wiped it with a wet cloth and then began wrapping. Tessie was at her head, gently and lovingly wiping her forehead.

"What the hell happened to you, lass?" Murray asked.

"I fell—"

"What were you doing carrying a tray of glass, Jade?" Victor growled.

"I was bringing you the . . . water you asked for."

"You were what?" He stared incredulous, but just as he fully grasped what had happened Murray shot him a warning glance that could not be ignored.

"Now, lass, you're going to be fine, just fine. I'm going to have to stitch you up on this one arm. It's a lot better than it first looked. I'll try to do the tidiest job possible on you. How are you feeling?"

"I really don't feel very much. It stings a little in places but that's all."

"These kind of cuts sometimes don't hurt much."

"I was so surprised when I heard you ask me—me!—to fetch water for you, Victor," Jade said. "I knew you were finally beginning to trust me and it meant so much. You're always so worried and cautious about me and . . . and now this. I'm so sorry."

Hearing this, Victor's expression seemed to hold the anguish of the world. Murray shook his head sadly, then whispered kind words of comfort to Jade, seeing that Victor could not trust himself to speak.

Jade sat up in bed with Wolf Dog on her lap. She had been told to rest, sleep if she could. No one was permitted to disturb her. One cut had required stitches, that was all. There were many smaller cuts on each arm and one tiny prick on her neck. All in all, she felt fine now, certain too much fuss had been made about it.

She wanted to explain and apologize again to Victor. She needed to assure him she was fine. Accidents were bound to happen. Why, they should even be expected! She was always fine in the end, wasn't she?

Victor's respect for her ability to get around sightless meant everything to her. She could not help but be proud of her accomplishments, accomplishments that might seem small to some, but ones she knew only too well required patience, determination and strength. How hard she worked to lead as normal as life as possible! And she did; she did far better than most. Surely his trust would not be ruined by one foolish accident.

Musing over these concerns for the better part of an hour, Jade finally decided to make her way downstairs, hoping Victor wasn't too busy to talk to her. Tessie had spread her clothes over the bed and she stood up and dressed, moving carefully. The tight stitches pulled her skin if she moved too quickly. Once dressed and with the faithful wolf puppy at her side, she made her way through the door, down the hall and stairs to his study.

Victor's voice raised with anger as she slowly approached. What was it? She paused outside the open door to determine if she should wait for another time. Victor's anger surfaced quickly, he spent it even more quickly, and it was over within minutes, and she thought—

"It's not just that she's blind. Though God knows, that in and of itself is bad enough. It's that she insists on pretending, acting as though she's a normal woman. I could not believe she pulled a stunt like that—carrying a tray full of glass, thinking that I—I—asked her to!

"God, I came so close to shaking her, forcing her to accept her utter, damnable helplessness. The worst mistake of my life was allowing myself to fall in love with her. The agony that girl causes me every blessed day . . ."

Jade slowly leaned against the wall.

At first she didn't feel anything. To save herself, mind, body and soul went numb. It was like taking a leap into frigid and cold waters. She knew only one thing. She must retreat, first from the hall, then from the house and then from him, forever. Retreat.

She moved slowly down the hall, back up the stairs and to her door. She grabbed the door handle tightly, needing something to hang on to. Seconds passed as she felt with horror a hand that could not turn the handle. She clasped her hands together tightly to stop their trembling, finally managing to push the handle down just as her knees collapsed and she fell inside.

Quiet fell over the great house in the afternoon. Most of the servants napped through the heat. The men had left. She had no idea where Tessie or Mercedes were, but she imagined they were either napping, too, or at the lake.

Nor did she have any idea of how she might leave. She could only try and keep trying until she was successful. She knew someone was leaving today for New Orleans, for she had written a letter to the Reverend Mother, and Tessie said it would be leaving this afternoon. It would be her first try.

She took only the clothes she was wearing, a pair of sandals, her mandolin and Wolf Dog. She made the bed to look as though she still slept in it, left a short, simple note of explanation under the blanket, and gathered her things. One hand held a parasol.

The first time she had ever used a blind stick. . .

Chapter 10

"**T**he master don't never send womenfolks out in no cart!"

"Oh, but didn't he tell you? No? There just wasn't time to make other arrangements. You don't mind, do you?"

Tripoli looked around uncertainly, removing his wide-rimmed straw hat to wipe at his brow. Last night's rain done already dried up. Not a body in sight; the heat, like hell itself, chased away all mortal folks. 'Ceptin' for a pretty white lady with a strummin' board askin' an old colored man if he minds none.

He looked back at the girl. He just couldn't figure it. The master treated his ladies like they be queens, givin' dem all that finery, jewels, fancy dons and all. Why, he once gave a lady her very own carriage and four fine geldings!

"Oh, please!" The cry came with soft urgency. "I won't be a bother at all. This is all I'm carrying and, oh, if you would?"

A graying brow rose with shock. "Please" from a white woman? He swallowed, then nodded vigorously. "Yes, ma'am! Ain't no bother at all. Ole Tripoli here be the last soul bothered by a lady with a strummin' board. My pleasure, ma'am."

Yet an hour or so down the hot road Tripoli knew he had spoken too soon. Casting an anxious glance at the pale, tear-streaked face, he cracked the reins over the old nag's back, hoping for a little more dust. Weren't no pleasure in it, he sighed. A mite more pleasure at a funeral dig. She couldn't talk none and just sat aside him cryin' and cryin' like the world's come to end and they all be goin'

221

to hell for bein' such sinners. Every time she settled some and tried to give him a song, she gets halfway into it afore she chokes up and starts bawlin' again.

Lord, she was a-breakin' his heart.

Twilight inched slowly into the landscape.

He focused on the passing scenery, staring at the long crooked branches of the trees, dark and shadowy in the falling night, stared until they became something else. Uh oh. That one looks like an ornery ole witch and that one looks like a bear as mean as a bee-stung dog. That one looks a fright, like a scarecrow come to life.

It raised his gooseflesh somethin' good. Lord, he might have been a runaway nigger with paddyrollers chasin' him, it spooked him so bad. He fetched his tiny salt shaker—one he always carried—from his pocket and shook it over his left shoulder before trying to settle his gaze on a shiny half moon brushed with clouds as he listened to the creaks of the cart, the steady clop of the old mare pullin' them along.

All the while she sat there sobbin' so quietly . . .

He finally gave up and withdrew his whiskey cask from his bag. He pressed it into her hands and begged her to share the cause of such grief. He could hardly believe it. A darn sad tale she told as they passed the whiskey back and forth. Seems her aunt and uncle were livin' just fine till an accident put the aunt in a chair and makes her a cripple. Her uncle couldn't take it, couldn't bear to see someone he loved so much in pain and struggling and all, so he just up and run away.

Jade took another swallow of the hot liquid. "Isn't it one of the saddest things you ever heard, Tripoli?"

"Yes, ma'am!" He shook his head. "That be a sad story for sure. I'se real sorry for your folks and all. I suppose hangin' be too good for a man who up and leaves his wife crippled like that. No sir." He shook his head again, quite certain. "Hangin' be too good for that fellow."

"Oh, no, Tripoli," she said with feeling, clutching the

cask tightly. "I know how he feels. He just couldn't bear to see her in pain. It hurt him more than it hurt her."

Tripoli was not convinced. "Still . . ."

"I know how it is, Tripoli, I know. I know 'cause I'm blind. Did you know I was blind, Tripoli?"

Kind dark eyes focused hard on the girl. "You mean you don' see nothin'?"

Jade shook her head.

"Well, glory be!" He just stared, amazed. "I never knowed. Youse never said nothin' 'bout hit."

"No one ever knows. Why, I can walk into a roomful of people and fool all of them. You see, Tripoli," she expanded philosophically, "seeing is normal for you but being blind is normal for me. It hardly ever bothers me. Why, I can do most everything others can do: I can walk, swim, talk, I can sing, play chess and count sums. I can do most all the little things for myself: dress, eat and everything like that. I have a system for everything: I know exactly where my brush and hairpins and clothes trunk are; I know how many steps from the patio to the dining room, how many stairs there are. Why, it's as though I can see. I can walk into church and down the aisle and sit in my pew without touching anything.

"And you know, Tripoli, I hardly ever miss seeing. Sometimes it's even better. My imagination creates pictures of the world for me to see and these pictures are better than real life. Women are more beautiful, men more handsome, the sky is bluer, trees are taller and greener, the flowers more radiant and colorful. Why," she added in an impassioned whisper, "I can make rainbows whenever I want. . . ."

"I kin see how that might work out."

"Do you know what the worst part is, Tripoli?"

"No, ma'am, I don't reckon I do."

"The worst part is the person I love. He thinks I'm helpless and suffering, and I'm not Tripoli, I'm not! Accidents are bound to happen but . . . but it's like they happen to him and not to me. Oh, Tripoli, I love him so much! So much I just can't bear it." She cried as her head fell on his lap. "My heart is breaking, Tripoli, I can feel my heart breaking. . . ."

Shortly after the second sounding, Tessie still tossed and turned in her bed. Sleep eluded her. Something bothered her. Not just Jade's accident. She felt like a feather tickled her brain, trying to tell her something. . . .

Jade's room emerged in her mind. She had checked in on her numerous times. Jade had slept straight into the night, but the doctor said this was to be expected. The trauma taxed the body, he said. So, what could be bothering her. . . .

Wolf Dog!

Tessie flew from her bed and, not bothering with slippers, shawl or even a candle, she ran out from the servants' quarters, along the path around the kitchen and up the wood stairs, and into the back door. She took the stairs three at a time, lifting her thin cotton nightdress over skinny, brown knees, all the while trying to stop from calling alarm until she knew. Yet, she did know, she did!

Tessie opened the door, took one look at Wolf Dog's empty basket, and then stumbled to the bed discovering a pile of clothes beneath the covers, a note she could not read and no mistress.

"Master Sebastian! Doctor Murray!"

Dawn broke through the clouds. A warm breeze blew steadily from the Gulf when Victor passed Tripoli's cart on his way to the city. He spotted it off the main fairway, sitting under a willow tree just after Barataria in Jefferson parish. He thought nothing of it. Tripoli was taking a brief nap before continuing on to the city. . . .

A light rain fell from the smooth gray sky. A piece of canvas covered the back of the cart where Jade slept, deeply, dreamlessly. Wolf Dog was curled up beneath a tree trunk. A breeze swayed the branches and sent fresh drops of moisture over the puppy's coat. He looked up with a growl. He stood and shook himself, moving to the cart where Tripoli slept.

Tripoli woke when the damp fur came against his skin, but when he tried to lift his head, his body rebelled with the powerful, dull ache of what his woman always called the Lord's revenge. He found his water cask, and after taking a long drink, he laid his head down again and fell back to sleep.

Riding up to New Orleans from Port Sulphuro, the five riders had almost passed the cart when Morrel's loose stirrup gave way. He stopped his mount, cursing his stirrup, the horse, the day, the world, and he dismounted to attempt a quick repair. Glancing up, he spotted the cart.

A broad grin spread over weathered features. A fresh bit of luck, he saw. He knew the cart, knew the colored man under it. He had passed the man about two months ago on the very same road, and after one glance down at the old man's basket of food, he had reached over to help himself to the fried chicken, honey and rolls, sweetmeats and stuffed eggs. 'Twas a sorry day when a bloody nigger ate better than he did.

He cinched the knot. This whole damn city treated their niggers like they were better than white men! Them quadroon wenches up there in that ballroom, not lettin' no man through unless he be fancy and fine—as if his money weren't good enough for a nigger wench. All them niggers owin' stores and houses, walkin' about with their noses stuck in the air. The whole damn lot of 'em ought to be whipped and sold off. . . .

Morrel mounted and turned his horse off the road, heading toward the cart. Wolf Dog growled, jumped to his feet and barked warning. To no avail. Tripoli didn't stir. Reining his mount alongside the cart, Morrel bent over and lifted the canvas . . . only to find himself looking at something far better than a basket of food.

Wolf Dog jumped on top of Tripoli to wake him, barking frantically. Tripoli sat up, dazed, took one look at the four legs of the horse alongside the cart, and scrambled to his feet. Only to watch Morrel fire a pistol into the air to call the others back.

Jade bolted up, too, dazed, confused; the pistol fire no louder than the pounding of her aching head. With a startled gasp, she covered her head.

What was it? What was happening?

Taking in the scene at a glance, Tripoli cursed with tangible fear. "Youse just keep them hands off her, you hear?"

"Oh, I hear you, nigger boy. What I want to know is what the hell is a colored man doin' with a ripe piece like this?"

Tripoli's muscles went rock-hard rigid with the danger. Up the creek without a paddle, he knew, and while he could not stop this man, he'd die trying. He tried first to warn him. "The lady belongs to my master. I'se a-takin' her to him now. You be knowin' Captain Nolte?"

"Nolte?" Morrel questioned incredulously before chuckling. "Boy, if you be lyin' to me, I'll blow your bloody face against that—"

"No sir! I ain't a-lyin' to you!" Tripoli shook his head. "I'se a-tellin' you, my master will kill the man who lays a finger on her; I swear he will!"

Morrel's horse danced as he threw his head back, shook his wet hair like a crazed animal and laughed long and hard. "Let me tell you, nigger boy, the wench that be fine enough for Mr. High-and-mighty Nolte be fine enough for me."

Jade froze, just froze, color draining from her face like life from her blood. She dropped to her hands and knees, braced for the terror and prayed for a quick death. The sound of other riders approaching felt like Saint Peter's trumpets.

A rescue! Mercy in heavens—

She knew it was a rescue. Wolf Dog barked furiously as the four riders quickly circled the cart.

"The man says she's Nolte's wench." Morrel smiled.

Don Bernardo pushed his mount up alongside the cart, reached in and grabbed a handful of Jade's hair. Jade cried as her head was jerked back. "Madonna, blessed Madonna, she's Nolte's all right." A howl of laughter sounded, long and hard. "This is the bloody wench that started all the trouble at Charmane's the night it burned!"

Jade screamed as hands came around her waist, lifting her up and throwing her over a saddle. The wind was knocked from her lungs. She pounded fists and feet violently, fighting with all her strength, ignoring the painful tearing of her stitches, a sick dread rising with bile in her throat. "Stop it! Let me—"

Desperate to save her, Tripoli lifted a long branch high into the air. Just as he was about to crash it into Don Bernardo's side, a bullet exploded in his shoulder.

Tripoli dropped like a discarded rag to the ground.

"Tripoli!" Jade screamed. "Tripoli!"

Don Bernardo only chuckled, swatted her buttocks affectionately, and pushed his mount into a gallop. The men left, though Morrel paused, searched a moment, and after lifting the basket of food, he laughed. "Sweet dreams, nigger boy. . . .

Victor,

I have left to return to the convent after overhearing the agony I have brought you. If you care at all for me, please do not follow, or ever seek me there.

I will always love you. . . .

I wish it were enough. . . .

                                              Jade Terese Devon

They read it twice, then three times, and then it took over an hour to determine that Jade was nowhere on the grounds. Desperate and crying, Tessie thought of Tripoli and they guessed how Jade must have left. A heated discussion followed: would Victor find Jade with Tripoli on his way to the city? Surely he'd have to pass them. What if he missed them somehow? Would Jade be safe with Tripoli?

Not willing to take the chance, Sebastian left immediately.

Sebastian rode a young black Arabian mare, half wild and barely green broke; he rode with the wind's speed through the dawn and early morning until he came upon the terrifying sight.

The abandoned cart rested in a quiet glen beneath a willow tree. Underneath the cover of the cart and out from under the rain lay Tripoli. A middle-aged colored woman and two gangling young children surrounded him. The woman's apron was unfolded and she used it to stop the bleeding while the little girl held Wolf Dog in her arms. There was no sign of the dog's mistress.

Sebastian flew off his mount and rushed to the scene, his long black cape lifting with the wind. The woman retreated in fear, gathering her children around her, watching warily as Sebastian dropped to Tripoli's side. "Tripoli! Dear God, Tripoli!"

The old man lay unconscious. Bright red blood soaked his shoulder and chest but he was breathing still.

"What has happened? Jade—"

"He got shot, mister." The woman glanced up at him. "Me an de chilins' be headin' to de market and we see him laying here. I'se tryin' to figure what to do."

"You don't know who shot him? Did you see anything?"

"I ain't seen a soul, 'ceptin' for you. He your man?"

"Yes, he had a lady with him—"

"I ain't seen no lady neither. He came to a while ago and alls he says was a 'a Spanish pirate' or somethin' but I ain't seen nobody—"

Sebastian grabbed her shoulders. "He said what?"

" 'A Spanish pirate'—and somethin' bout gems is all. I reckon he got himself robbed."

"Gems? Jade, you mean Jade! Did he say 'Jade'?"

"Yes, he says 'bout de Jade and a Spanish pirate—"

Sebastian did not pause. He tossed her a money bag and told her to wait for a carriage a couple of hours down the road. There would be a doctor inside who would tend to the man.

"Mister, I don't need no coin for—" But the man was already on his horse, racing off toward the city.

Victor stood on the platform before the ship construction, discussing the new welding method for masts with John when a young boy raced up and wordlessly, handed him a note before rushing away.

The Black Crest. Hurry!

Marie Saint

Victor studied the strange note for a full minute. What? The *Black Crest*. Hurry? Hurry to what, the *Black Crest*? Could Marie be in some kind of trouble with Don Bernardo? No, not possible. What then?

He was just about to send someone to obtain a clarification from Marie's house when Sebastian raced up the gangplank. Then he understood Marie's message all too well.

The captain's quarters of the *Black Crest* were simple and neat. It had paneled wood walls and floor, of course, a long square table in the center, a bed, a trunk and maps, that was all. The orderliness of Don Bernardo's servant waged a continuous battle with the captain's chaotic life, and the cabin showed evidence of both sides. A tossed dagger pinned a torn scarlet curtain over the porthole, the pirate's desperate attempt to stop light from entering one morning during a particularly bad hangover. Small gold daggers stuck in various spots on the wall maps, marking places for reasons long since forgotten. Hanging on the wall, the wine rack held a dozen or so bottles of Maderia, one bottle cracked halfway across, its dangerously jagged edges left unnoticed. Clothes lay in disarray on top of the trunk and the bedclothes were in great need of washing. On the other hand, the floor was swept, the table wiped clean.

Left alone on the middle of a bunk used as a bed, Jade held her knees tight against her with her sore arms, so her body looked like a small ball. She shook uncontrollably, trembling as if she had been left in a snow-covered field during a blizzard, though in reality she had fallen into the hot fires of a certain hell.

She was not helpless. She planned to fight in every way possible. "Rape is a violent act, a woman has no defense," Victor and Sebastian had said after they unwisely repeated Tessie's story. "A woman should submit without a struggle to avoid being hurt even worse."

Which made no sense. There was no "hurt even worse." Certainly not death. This was what she counted on. She'd fight tooth and nail; she'd do everything to make the man so angry he would kill her. And if that wretched bastard, who tossed her around like she was nothing more than a feather pillow, did manage to overpower her struggle, she planned to force a . . . a seizure. She was not going to be raped, not as long as she drew breath.

Tessie had told her rape was "a scare that chokes your whole inside."

Oh, Tessie, yes . . .

Rain fell steadily outside. Men rushed noisily about on deck. Blood streamed down her arms from her torn stitches. Voices rose and fell, cursing, shouting orders and sometimes laughing. Hammers pounded louder than the rain. Then she heard that voice—she did not know his name—along the side of the cabin. She stiffened, then forgot to breathe as the door swung open. With a cool burst of air, he stepped inside. She thought two others followed. She scurried against a wall, warily alert and ready.

The two men set trays on the table while Don Bernardo tossed his hat and canvas cape over the trunk. He stood with feet apart and arms on hips looking at her with a bright gleam in his dark eyes.

"Look at her! Nolte's whore in my bed! Leave me. I want to enjoy this alone."

Amidst laughter and lewd comments, the men left quickly. Don Bernardo strode over to the wine rack, pulled down a bottle of Madeira and took a seat at the table. He had many lusty appetites: wine, wenching and killing ranked only after eating. She heard the bottle being uncorked, heard the man take a long draught before he slammed the bottle back on the table. She smelled the stew. He served himself a healthy portion of it as he said: "Take off your clothes, wench."

Jade was about to deliver a flat, firm no when she grasped the means of her first attack. "May . . . may I have some food first? I'm so . . . so hungry."

"Come and get it."

Jade stood to her feet, steadied herself for a moment, and directed by his voice, she stepped timidly forward till she reached the table. Don Bernardo watched her hands, trembling, feel their way across the table till they touched a chair. He waved a hand in front of her face.

"Madonna, you're blind as a bat." He laughed, "Blind, comely and scared! Wench, I'm gonna like you."

She tried to ignore him as she assumed a chair. Don Bernardo took the bowl to his lips, drained the contents, and after wiping his mouth on the back of his hand, he filled the bowl and handed it to her. He took another swig of Madeira before his fingers began tearing off pieces of the roasted duck.

Now for the hard part. Jade lifted the bowl to her lips and with a grimace; she swallowed and swallowed, neither tasting nor chewing, and she did not stop until the bowl was empty. Immediately, she felt the desired effects; her stomach turned in violent protest.

She was going to be sick.

A dark brow rose, a grin followed. He was a bit surprised by her hearty appetite, more surprised when she stood up and reached an arm to him. With a chuckle, he slid his chair back and then pulled her across his lap. Not a second too soon. Just as his hands came to tear at her clothes, she threw up all over his beard, chest and belly.

"Jesus! Bloody Madonna!" He jumped to his feet, throwing her to the floor. He cursed and yelled, desperately trying to rid his person of her mess.

Jade offered no apology.

Plainly disgusted, he stormed to his trunk, tore off his shirt and, seeing there was no dressing water, he grabbed a cloth and left the room in a huff of fury.

Jade desperately wanted to yield to the hysterical laugh that threatened, but she did not fool herself; it was only the beginning. Fear pounded in her breast and after recovering somewhat, she stood to her feet and felt over the table for the bottle of Maderia .

She poured some to the floor to rid the neck of the bottle of his spit before lifting it to her mouth. She swished the sweet wine around her mouth and spit it out on the floor. She felt hurriedly over the food, stuffed whatever she could into her mouth, swallowing it all whole. It had worked once and she would do anything, anything that worked. She washed it down, than drank and drank until she felt violently ill again.

She flew into a frenzy. The devil himself could not have orchestrated more havoc; she threw the duck toward the door, dumped the remaining stew on the floor and then cracked the bottle over the table. Braced and ready, holding the jagged weapon, she backed against the wall and waited.

Sufficiently recovered but still grumbling, Don Bernardo swung open his door. Using all her strength, she aimed at her best estimation of the target and fired. The jagged bottle slammed against the side of his face and neck and he uttered a startled howl of shock before it crashed to the hard wood floor.

Don Bernardo wiped his wound and stood for several dazed moments staring at the blood on his hand. His gaze fell on Jade, cowering against the wall. His huge body billowed like a sail in the wind. He took one dangerous step forward. His foot crunched into the duck hide, slipped from under him, and he fell with a thunderous thud.

Jade, fighting hard to hold back another bout of nausea, didn't know exactly what had happened, only that something had. She listened, waiting like a trapped mouse, but for several threatening moments there was no sound past the pounding tide of her pulse and the labor of her breaths.

It was a great effort to lift himself from the mucky pool of stew, but he did. He did not bother to wipe himself off this time. Rising on all fours, he looked up at his victim, and unbelievably he chuckled. The deep chuckle grew to a growling roar of hearty laughter.

Only Nolte's whore could do this to him.

"I'm going to kill you, little girl." Footsteps approached. "The devil be damned, I am going to stick it to you till your innards spill over my rod and—"

She never heard the rest of the barbarian's savage threat. She felt his hand reach her person and she was so sickened and frightened, she threw up again.

With another startled howl of rage, Don Bernardo tried to step back but received her message over the whole of one leg. A deadly fury filled his small dark eyes as he raised him arm back and hit her hard across the face. The blow knocked her to the floor. Pain shot through her head but she scrambled away. A callused hand snaked around her throat, pinning her to the floor. She screamed as a knife pierced her skin, then ripped through her shirt, down her front. The sharp blade scraped her skin.

She held perfectly still.

The knife cut a neat line up her chemise.

She knew she would die now.

But he abruptly lifted from her to remove his breeches.

Don Bernardo had just pulled his shirt off when he heard a low growl, a bark. He looked down to see Jade on hands and knees, hopping around the cabin, crazed, barking like a dog.

His eyes first widened, then narrowed. What the hell was this? Screaming and crying he could fathom, but barking like a dog? He didn't get it. Was she trying to threaten him? Or was she crazed?

Frantically, Jade shook her head back and forth, growling, barking, her hand scratching the floor as if warning of a charge. After watching her ridiculous theatrics a few moments, he suddenly wanted a drink and wanted it bad.

With a fresh bottle of Madeira, Don Bernardo took a seat and studied the crazy woman. It was the smartest trick she might have pulled, for Don Bernardo lost his violent rage, a fury that surely would have killed her. It was gone. Three-quarters of the way through his bottle, he finally concluded that it was no ploy. She was mad. The little girl had lost her wits.

Well, what the devil did that matter?

Jade, more than willing to continue in this manner, might have done so for another hour, but Don Bernardo, frustrated, having no patience, finished his bottle and stood up to go to her. Her barking stopped as his hands came around her, lifting her into the air. He threw her over his shoulder. Jade kicked and screamed and her fists pummeled his back, but these tactics hardy deferred the bear-like man from his purpose.

Jade was about to be thrown to his bed when she let him have the next-to-last trick. Don Bernardo froze and felt the hot urine spread over his chest, soaking him through and through. The cursing that followed sounded so loud, it was rendered blissfully incoherent. But she had done it, she had been successful. Don Bernardo reached a point of such frustration, rage, and disgust that he could not have had her even if he had wanted to.

Which he wasn't at all sure about now.

Jade did not understand what happened next. She was still on his shoulder, being carried swiftly from the cabin. With an effortless shrug of his shoulder, he tossed her over the side of the ship. Never in the whole of his forty-three years had he ever enjoyed a woman's scream more, stopped by the splash of water.

When she didn't surface, Don Bernardo ordered one of his men in after her. If she hadn't been Nolte's woman, he'd have been perfectly content to let her drown, but when he thought of Nolte, he changed his mind. He wanted her at least once. After ordering another to clean up the mess in his cabin, he chuckled and left in search of his mates to tell a tale no one was going to believe.

It had happened four years before. Riding up from port to town, Victor and Murray approached Moran's tavern, a favorite watering hold of Victor's crew. Old man Moran sat on the steps crying, his face buried in weathered hands. They dismounted and asked what had happened. Moran couldn't utter a sound. He motioned inside the tavern.

Victor pushed through the swinging doors and stood staring at the chaos: tables and chairs knocked over, shattered bottles and glasses, foodstuff and rubbish strewn over the floor. Bullets have been fired into barrels of Madeira and ale behind the counter; liquid still spilled out onto the floor. A man lay dead in the middle of the room; he had been stomped in the chest and face repeatedly, the work of ruthless barbarians.

Scanning the scene of the massacre, Victor's gaze finally stopped at the far corner of the room. He had to force himself to approach. He had only met the young girl once, while she was home for the holidays to visit her grandfather. Moran was showing him a horse for sale and had introduced the shy thirteen-year-old.

"They will be fighting for my little Marianna soon, no?"

Indeed, the young girl had showed promised of becoming a pretty maid. Victor, with a smile able to charm young and old alike, had kissed her hand and asked if she might wait for him. She first blushed, then a hand reached to smooth her long brown hair, woven into pigtails; sparkling brown eyes boldly lifted to him and she giggled before running quickly away. . . .

Marianna had lain on that table. Her skirt was lifted over thin, bloodied thighs and her blouse was torn, revealing bruised and bloodied flesh. She was dead. Murray had gotten sick, just as they heard a pistol fire outside. Moran had fired a gun point-blank into his head.

Don Bernardo's men had been apprehended and hung. But Victor was not thinking of this retribution as he loaded the four pistols. The image in his mind was of Jade's body lying on the table, and it pushed him over the line separating sanity from insanity.

John raced to round up what men he could find to meet Victor and Sebastian at the *Black Crest*. Sebastian raced to get Victor's mount, while Victor positioned two pistols in his belt alongside a long dagger. Carrying the two other weapons, he raced to meet his horse. Waiting with the horse, Sebastian caught both pistols, tossed one after another. By the time he secured both in his belt, Victor had already galloped into the gray day, racing like a madman to hell.

Victor felt his strength, his body, his very soul buckling under, collapsing with a grief that could not be borne, and using all the force of his will, he banished the image from his mind. He did not have a thought.

He merely acted.

His name was Raphael. Strong and mean, he was known for knife throwing and an ability to outdrink Don Bernardo. He stood on guard duty when Victor rode up, and before Victor even reined in his horse, the man tossed a knife into Victor's bare arm, readying another. A warning: the next knife would pierce a more vital organ.

Victor took no notice of it.

The man started to call for help—but too late. Victor flew from his mount, kicked a booted foot hard into Raphael's groin and sent him doubled over with pain. Victor slammed the butt end of a pistol into the man's face again and again. The man fell to the ground. With a knee on the fallen pirate's chest, Victor put the pistol to Raphael's head.

Madness shone from the dark blue eyes. Victor pulled the knife from his arm, tossing it to the side. All he said was, "Where is she?"

Raphael smiled slyly, then spit blood to the side. "Nolte, ole boy, we all owe you. Ain't had a bloody piece as good as your wench in years. Why, it took nearly five of us to quiet her moanin'—"

Victor again smashed the end of the pistol into Raphael's face. A mistake, for with that action he lost what little control he had. Blow after deadly blow followed the first. Knowing only the vicious fear pounding in his heart, wanting only to kill or be killed, he never realized the man was dead.

Sebastian rode up on the frightening scene and flew off his horse, shouting Victor's name as he came up behind Victor. He grabbed Victor's uplifted arm with both hands. Victor swung his free arm around as his body lifted with frightening force, knocking Sebastian into the air. He landed with a slide in the mud on his back.

Victor stared at him in shock.

Sebastian tried to lift himself from the ground but fell back. "You broke my rib, you bastard," he said breathlessly. "For God's sake—no, for Jade's sake—get a grip on yourself!"

Victor shook his head as though to clear it as Sebastian ordered, "Go on, get! The others will be here soon, but I'm warning you, Vic, if you get yourself killed up there, I will curse over your grave. . . ."

Sebastian watched as Victor silently moved up the gangplank and then disappeared in a darkness that was the *Black Crest*. Damn, he would get himself killed! Enduring excruciating pain, Sebastian lifted himself from the ground and cautiously made his way after his friend.

Victor had to knock out two men before he could make his way below deck. He slowly moved down the stairs and into the long corridor. He heard voices coming from the mess hall, recognized them as Don Bernardo's, and he turned the opposite way. He ducked inside the carpenter's room. The small room was centrally located on the ship, and because of the stock of wood inside, it was perfect for his purpose. He grabbed the lighted lamp hanging by the door, dumped the oil over the room and tossed down the lamp. He waited to make certain the blaze took before stepping out and shutting the door behind him. He moved down the hall.

The man coming down from the deck had no chance. Victor sprung upon him with a quick deadly punch to the throat. The man dropped with a sick gasp. Victor moved on, stopping just outside the doorway of the mess hall, listening first to determine how many men were inside.

Don Bernardo swore: "You son of an ale whore! 'Tis not a matter of strength." The prove the point, he placed a bottle of rum between a forearm as large as most men's upper arms and an upper arm as thick as most men's thighs and with a quick flex of those grotesque muscles, he crushed the bottle, then merely brushed the shattered glass from his arm.

"I can kill ten men with my bare hands," he continued, a fact each man there had witnesses. "She is just a little thing and comely, aye, but I swear, Nolte's whore is the devil's handmaiden! I should let you bastards have her so you can know what that wench put me, Don Bernardo, through. She throws up on me twice, tosses broken bottles in my face; she goes crazy like a dog! And finally, when I get her bloody clothes off and just as I am throwing her to her back . . ." He shook his head, chuckled. "Madonna, I still don't believe what the little girl did."

Obscene laughter and comments roared in Victor's mind.

"No, I am telling the truth, *amigos*. I need another bottle before I face her again, and I wager now I will end up throwing her over the side again!"

Blood pumped hard and fast into Victor's head as he

tried to comprehend what was being said. He only grasped that Jade had somehow fought him, that Jade was alive.

She was alive!

Don Bernardo's experience gave rise to other stories of meetings with cunning or elusive women. The party roared with laughter as the other men related similar tales. The laughter died a sudden, instant death as gazes turned to the doorway, where they confronted the barrels of two pistols.

No one moved.

Victor never looked taller, more threatening or frightening than he did standing in the doorway of the *Black Crest*'s mess hall. Clad only in a canvas vest and breeches, not even wearing boots, and with water dripping unnoticed from his person, his barely clad frame radiated the beast he had become. Again, all he said was, "Where is she?"

With boots on the table, and not really surprised, Don Bernardo chuckled slowly, took a long draught from a rum bottle and slammed the bottle back to the table. "Nolte, you got me good this time; the wench has not been worth it. I should have killed the bloody whore."

Victor was not there to discuss it. He fired, the bottle exploded on the table and glass flew across the room. He demanded one more time. "Where is she?"

Silently, a man came up behind Victor. Sebastian might have stopped him before he thrust the dagger into Victor's back, but as Sebastian raised his sword, pain shot through his body and he stumbled, and while he managed to force his sword into the man, it was a second too late. Victor jolted, felt the cold metal dig two inches into his back, and the pistol fired twice into the dead center of Don Bernardo's massive chest.

A cloud of smoke filled the space. "Don't move!" Sebastian warned as he jumped through the door, leveling his two pistols at the remaining men.

Don Bernardo's death was quick and painless, and as Victor reached behind to withdraw the dagger from his back, he regretted that. The men stood up, arms raised.

Outside, John and a good twenty or so of Victor's men swarmed up the gangplank.

"She's in the captain's cabin, quarterdeck."

Victor left first, followed by Sebastian. Vicious flames licked the end of the smoke-filled corridor, looking like the mouth of an angry dragon. They dropped to their hands and knees to escape the smoke. Victor reached the stairs, emerged in the fresh air where men were fighting everywhere.

Numb with shock and exhaustion, Jade curled up in a small ball in the far corner of the room. The smell of smoke to a blind person is the sight of a gray fin to a swimmer, the worst possible threat. She assumed the battle sounds were efforts to put out a furious fire that would surely be her death.

The door crashed open and she covered her head with her arms, thinking that some man had come to either take her away or throw her into the flames. She screamed as hands grabbed her. She tried desperately to kick, twist away, but he lifted her into his arms, crushed her against him. Then she heard his voice.

"Jade, it's me . . . it's me!"

Victor kissed the trembling hand that slowly reached to his face. Tears sprang to her eyes. She didn't utter a sound as she collapsed against him, and he held her tightly against his strength.

She is safe as long as she is with you. . . .

May God make it so. . . .

The fight was over and the ship ablaze when Victor carried Jade down the gangplank. The remainder of Don Bernardo's crew was forced over the side to watch from the water as the ship was consumed by fire, a fire of such wild and eager flames that it only laughed at the rain falling into it.

Victor's men watched from the dock, passing bottles back and forth as they cheered. With the help of two men, Sebastian managed to mount his horse. He handed his cape to Victor. Victor wrapped it around Jade's shoulders before they disappeared into the darkness. With the help of a friend's brandy cask, Sebastian swallowed his pain and stayed to witness the glorious ruin of the pirate's ship.

In the land of the Orient, one is born again—given a new life, a different perspective, a second chance—after having lived through a confrontation with death. Victor had experienced the certainty of Jade's death. He would not waste this precious second chance.

The next day a small gathering composed of Mother Francesca, a number of other Ursuline Sisters, Mercedes, Sebastian, Tessie and Carl stood in the convent gardens. Broken clouds and rain and bursts of bright sunshine raced across the uncertain sky. Smiles lifted the joyful faces and tears filled many eyes as Father Nolte sang the sacred text of marriage. Victor and Jade spoke the vows of love and honor until death, vows that were sealed, liked their fate itself, by a ring. The moment Jade felt Victor's strong fingers slip this precious ring on her finger, a tingling raced up her spine. Everyone assumed the mist of tears in the blind green eyes sprang from happiness . . .

Chapter 11

The room was crowded with men.

Victor conducted most of his business in the room above the warehouse. It was an unfinished room, and while he always meant to set his men to finishing it off, plastering and painting, fitting the windows before adding the carpet and the furniture, he somehow never did. The walls and floor were virgin wood and there was one wide-open window overlooking the yard and the river beyond. They nailed a canvas over it when it rained. A long table made of a thin sheet of wood sitting atop four different sawhorses served as the worktable or desk. Papers covered the top, set down in random piles, and ashtrays spilled cigar butts and matches onto the floor. Maps and engraved ship designs hung on the walls. Stools served as chairs. Men came and went over the sawdust floor.

Victor loved the place. He loved most of all the sound of work: the hammers and saws and shouts of the foremen against the rush of the river water. He loved watching his ships grow and take shape outside his window.

John led the man up the narrow staircase that went directly into the room where Victor worked. The man's tall, well-muscled body was rigid with fear. Perspiration poured from his frame, though it was still only early in the day. The noise and bustle of the room were not a comfort, nor was the mix of colored and white in the room.

A white man's summons could mean only trouble.

"Vic," John called. "Here's your man. Jefferson."

Victor looked up from the drafts. The man's fear was palpable. He was a young man, not yet twenty, and while he stood tall, he kept his eyes cast down in adherence to

242

the unspoken rule: never but never look a white man in the eye. Victor did not at first ease the fear.

"Jefferson," he repeated flatly. "Do you know why I called you here?"

He replied in a whisper. "No suh!"

Victor motioned away two approaching men, and then asked for privacy. Motion and words stopped. A half dozen men gathered up their things and headed for the stairs. Only John remained.

"The matter concerns your mother. The woman named Tara."

Jefferson's dark eyes lifted with surprise. "My . . . mama? Why, my mama's dead now, suh."

She is a dead woman . . . Marie had said, and so she had been right again. Not that he had believed it at first. He hadn't, but just to make sure he had his agents go through the local deaths starting from the day after Jade left for the country, looking for anyone who had a connection to the Devon household. They found Jefferson's mother, Tara. "Yes, I know. I also know you were born on Devon plantation, Galier Manor."

The young man appeared plainly confused. His gaze kept shifting uncertainly about the floor. "Yes suh."

"My wife is Jade Terese Devon."

Jefferson looked up again, his fear dissipating at the sound of her name. He nodded, and though his face remained solemn, his eyes lit with a smile.

Victor had grown accustomed to this response to his wife's name. The whole town loved her. "I understand Jade's mother," he continued, "Elizabeth Devon, took you from your mother and gave you to a another family: the Bozoniers?"

"Yes suh. She done sign my free papers, too."

The soft-spoken words somehow managed to convey the magnitude of this grace. Victor was not unaffected; he would never be unaffected by a man's freedom to sell his own labor. "Yes, so I've heard. Do you know why she sent you away from your mother?"

Jefferson struggled to answer, shifting uncomfortably. Again in a whisper, he said, "My mama was not right. In the head. She saw these spirits everywhere. She talk dem up, upsettin' all them folks that heard. Folks got mighty skeered of her talkin' on like that. . . ." He closed his eyes, remembering the beating spells. It got so that he had been terrified of his own mama.

It was obviously a painful subject. "She was beating you," Victor said, adding the rest. "To get rid of the evil spirits she thought were inside you."

"Yes suh . . ."

Victor had discovered the whole of it. Tara had been freed some five years ago from the La Harpes' household, a colored family, a rather well-known shoemaker in the city. He had bought Tara from the Devon estate when it was sold off, but Monsieur La Harpe was eventually forced to free and dismiss the woman. His complaints were many. She refused to give up her voodoo practices, or to even keep them hidden, and she had begun to influence other members of the household in this unpleasant direction. He also said that she had suffered from terrible dark spells when she communed with these "spirits."

"I understand she hated Elizabeth Devon and she blamed her for turning you away from her. Now"—he paused—"I'd like to hear what happened in the years you were raised with the Bozoniers."

"They treat me fine, like I be one of them own. We be poor but we never even knowed it. Not really. We all be free, thank the Lord. My whole life I feel mighty thankful to Mistress Devon. Mighty thankful. Things be fine 'ceptin' for them times my mama comes around. Got so I'se took to runnin' at of the sight of her." He paused nervously before his voice rose with feeling. "Times she just lay out in the road, a-whinin' and moanin', sayin' the devil done got me twisted up inside, and she curse the demon and whatnot. Not makin' a passel of sense. Master Bozonier finally started takin' to shootin' at her. . . . It got better after that. She don't come round much. When she does she ain't hearin' no spirits. Says she feelin' better, taking in laundry for cleanin' and doin' pretty good. She says . . . I made her proud. I pass her a coin or two when I can." He looked up. "Then she died."

"Yes, then she died. Jefferson, I have reason to believe your mother was threatening Jade Terese before she died. Jefferson," he said with a heightened tone of seriousness, "I have reason to believe your mother actually murdered, or at least was involved in the murder of, Elizabeth and Philip Devon."

The only person more relieved to be at the end of this story than himself was the Reverend Mother. She had been desperately searching for an explanation to how a dead woman could return to torment the living, and while she felt certain Philip Devon's dark mistress, the woman Juliet, had done the actual deed, she realized Juliet might have been helped. After all, the two women shared a connection with the voodoo doctor JohnJohn. The explanation fit the facts as they knew it.

Jefferson's dark eyes were searching Victor's face. He started to speak. He stopped. He looked away as a hand wiped his mouth, but then his gaze returned. "No suh. No suh. My mama be crazy, but she weren't never that crazy. I ain't never met the nigger crazy 'nough to kill white folks—" He stopped with a gasp. Those were the wrong words. "What I mean—"

"I know what you mean, but the facts point to her. She hated Elizabeth Devon; she had reason—however twisted—for doing the deed, and you, yourself, know how insane she was. She practiced voodoo. The important fact," Victor continued, "is that the threats against my wife have ceased since her death."

There it was, the last chapter in the tragedy. He sighed as he glanced away. Why didn't he feel the Reverend Mother's relief? Why wasn't he glad to see the end of this?

He stood up and walked to the window to look out. The

wide moving flow of water became a backdrop for his swiftly moving thoughts.

Since the moment he lost his heart to that girl he'd had the unsettling feeling of some impending doom. The inexplicable sense of foreboding deepened as his love had: the more her laughter and love became the music and purpose of his life, the closer he felt to the waiting darkness. Now that they were to have their first child, the sense had magnified.

He had always attributed it to her parents' murderer threatening her. Only to discover now that the threat was buried, here no more, the sense of doom remained, unchanged, indifferent to the fact. . . .

Jade Terese, I love you. . . .

The silence gathered, ticking off the minutes, and as Jefferson still stood there mute, too stunned to create a defense, Victor found himself asking, desperate to believe that his feeling still owed itself to some irrational, lingering doubt: "Give me one reason to believe she didn't do it."

A memory of his mother during a sane period when there weren't any beatings danced dizzily through Jefferson's mind. Him and his friends were runnin' through the woods with slingshots, pretendin' they be Injuns gone a-huntin'. He never meant to hit that blue bird, never dreamt he actually could. He done carry the bird all the way back home. He don't rightly know why it caused a knot of pain in his stomach when the thing dies, but it does. And he remembered his mama saying, real serious: "All of God's creatures be precious, boy. All of 'em: people or bears or the tiniest ant; they all be precious. They be put here for a reason. Like this here bird. God put him here to teach you it's wrong to be shootin' things you ain't meanin' to stuff your stomach with. It's just plain wrong to kill, boy, and don't you never forget it . . ."

"I ain't got no reason to say, 'ceptin' I know she never be killin' no one. Even her most crazy spell, she never be killin' no one."

Victor was not convinced. He started to speak but stopped. Suddenly none of it mattered. For his gaze caught sight of Carl racing through his working men, the older man's face marred with apprehension. Victor felt it as a physical jolt through his frame, tensing his body where he stood, and he knew before Carl could explain the terrible accident that had befallen Jade . . .

Here at last was the dark and terrible future, the place where no rainbow reached across the sky. . . .

Jade Terese seemed to stare at her reflection in the looking glass over the divan. The glass presented a picture of a lovely young woman seen through the light of a single candle resting on the table. Her face held an expression of haunting, turbulent sadness. The expressive eyes possessed a gloss from tears. Her dark hair was tousled and wild-looking from a restless attempt to find sleep, while her skin looked unnaturally pale, her lips darker because of it. The thin strings of a pale rose-colored nightdress dangled unnoticed from her shoulders, bent elbows kept her robe from falling, while her face rested in her hands to prevent a complete collapse into tears.

Wolf Dog lay at her feet, sound asleep.

She tried to keep her thoughts on the first five months of her marriage. Those months had been blissfully, wonderfully happy! Each day had been a renewal of their passionate and consuming love; their home had been filled with laughter. How he had loved her then!

"What does it mean?"

"Jade," he had chuckled, "it means I always want you. Always. Even when you're not with me, I have only to close my eyes and conjure a picture of you—in the bath or sleeping, laughing at a party, at a moment of ecstasy and surrender, or even bending over to pick up something—"

She laughed as she swatted him playfully.

"And suddenly I'm in pain."

"Pain? Oh, please."

"Sweetheart, it's true. Ask any of my men how many dips I take in that cold river during the day. . . ."

"Does it help?"

"Nothing helps but this. . . ." And then he kissed her even as his hands felt over her clothes, impatiently trying to part her from them as he laid her on the soft cushion of their bed. . . .

Like many men, Victor's shock at discovering she was already with child quickly succumbed to excitement. Sebastian and Mercedes postponed their trip to Austria until the baby would be born, though they couldn't wait to be married. Construction on their country estate had been started, and despite the fact that their home would take over a year to be completed, Sebastian had married Mercedes immediately in a grand New Orleans style, and Marie Saint's prophecy about Sebastian and Mercedes had come true. The wise woman had eliminated all of Mercedes's fears when she had said: "Sebastian is the city's hero: he is titled and rich, young and handsome, and somehow he is always battling our villains. People will consider you the perfect fairy-tale complement to our hero. Yes, some people will inevitably learn of your sad history, but you will never know who these people are, for they will have the decency and manners to pretend as if they never heard it. You will see." And so Mercedes had. Society welcomed, even celebrated, Sebastian with open arms—and Mercedes as his much-adored wife.

Everyone had been so gay then! Every night had seemed a celebration and invitations never stopped— parties, charities and dinners, balls and theaters, those wonderful nights when Jade and Victor had been alone . . .

Blessed were the days until the moment that shattered it all. Although the doctor promised there was no permanent damage, promised that she could have another child and, God willing, more after that, she could not forgive herself or blame Victor. Of course he had been loving and concerned at first, staying with her until she had recovered, but she could sense the darkness that had slipped between them. For a while they had pretended it wasn't there, that nothing had really changed, but they loved and knew each other too deeply to honor a pretense. Soon they couldn't pretend.

He remained at the shipyard or in the country.

Time passed unmarked and she might have even dozed as she sat on the divan, but abruptly, from downstairs, she heard the front door open and close.

Could it be him? No . . .

She refused to let hope burst in a rush of anticipation, refused to feel what followed. Yet Wolf Dog thumped his tail. She heard light footsteps, *his* footsteps, on the stairs. . . . It was him! He paused outside the door.

Please, please, open the door!

The door opened just as a tear slid down her cheek. It was all she could do to stop herself from flying into his arms first.

Victor expected Jade to be asleep, and finding her awake, obviously waiting for him, even after long weeks of separation, brought a swift surge of emotion. Her beauty, shrouded in candlelight, the tears from those translucent green eyes, pierced his heart. He suffered no resistance. Stepping to her, he said what words could not by pulling her into his arms, covering her face with kisses. The first touch of her soft, supple body felt like potent medicine, momentarily overcoming his struggle.

Tears fell from her upturned face. She could not help it. The strong arms that finally held her again, the warm lips that pressed tender kisses on her face, meant too much to her. He had finally came back to her; he did love her. He would forgive her—

Victor took both her hands in his, pulled her to the bed. He gently guided her on top of him, wondering if his love clouded his judgment or if she really was that startlingly beautiful. Her hair fell wildly around her and her night-clothes were in a seductive disarray.

"God, I want you," he whispered, rolling her onto her

back, taking her mouth with a kiss that made time stop, suspended in an embrace that spoke hungrily of long denied needs. His lips spoke what words could not and she clung to him ardently, aware of every sensation she had longed for so desperately. Filled with his taste, feeling the momentarily freed desire consuming his powerful frame, she trembled and all but swooned with his love. His bare chest beneath an open shirt brushed against her breasts, while one leg parted hers, and she felt his long muscled flanks beneath tight suede breeches, the hard press of his desire.

Victor kissed her neck, pressed his lips along the long line of her throat as his hand caressed maddeningly below her bosom, savoring the softness of her mouth, her body, drinking the sweet fragrance. "Jade Terese." His lips and tongue tasted hers. "I have missed you."

She could not stop the words or the desperation in her voice. "I was so afraid you'd never—"

He stopped her instantly. "Never say never. I will always come back. I just needed to be alone for a while. I love you. God, girl, you are in my heart, my blood. . . ." His lips brushed over her face and she closed her eyes, shaken by the words she needed to hear. He kissed her again, deeply and passionately, and began to untie the flimsy laces of her nightdress.

"Victor . . . Victor." She had to tell him, so he knew, so they could start over again. She had to tell him because it was what she wanted more than anything in the world. "The doctor says I can have another baby now. . . ."

She felt the tension enter his frame. A timid hand reached to his face. He gently kissed her fingers but he was shaking his head and if she could have seen his eyes she would have known to be afraid. "I can't go through that again," he said in an impassioned whisper. "I won't go through it again. From now on, I want you to take a potion that will rid your womb of my seed."

"A potion . . . what do you mean?"

"It's a potion women take to force their bleeding so that if they carry a man's seed, it's removed."

She sat up slowly. Uncertain, frightened by these words, she asked, "You mean, if I were to carry our child again, this potion would wash it through me and kill our baby?"

"Jade—"

"No! You can't ask me to do that."

Ignoring the horror and confusion marking her features, Victor rose from the bed and walked over to the bureau. He turned his head back to her as he opened the cabinet and found the crystal brandy decanter. He poured a glass of the amber liquid as he, too, chose his words carefully. "I'm not asking you, Jade. I'm telling you."

Wolf Dog sensed Jade's escalating fear. The lithe, graceful creature sprung onto the bed, obediently assuming a place beside his mistress. His keen intelligence was at all times dedicated to the girl. Full-grown now, he was large for a dog, muscular and gray-blond. His small dark eyes watched Victor warily, unmoved by his affection for the man. Jade clung to him as to a lifeline.

"Please, Victor," she cried in a choked whisper. "Don't do this to me! Give me another chance. . . . It was an accident, I didn't mean to . . . God knows, I didn't mean to!"

Victor turned to face her and a long silence filled the quite room as he stared at the girl and her wolf, watching the tears fall steadily from her eyes. Her blind eyes.

Despite the resolution of her parents tragic mystery, he had learned these last few months that Jade would never be safe. He would have to live with the foreboding, the certainty of another accident from which he couldn't save her. The incidents were many: Jade cutting her finger as she sliced an orange, falling down stairs and bumping into things, the constant bruises and the daily "accidents." He had thought he could control it. He had been wrong.

"You know, Jade, at first I didn't blame you. I blamed Tessie, and while you were lying unconscious upstairs, I had Tessie by the shoulders, shaking her, so furious that I almost struck her. . . . I almost struck Tessie, whom we love.

"And Tessie never did say anything; she was more than willing to let me blame her. It was little Matthew who finally blurted that she begged you not to climb that ladder, that Tessie followed you up only because she couldn't stop you."

A fire fueled his anger; Victor felt the full force of his fury and ignoring her muffled sobs buried in Wolf Dog's fur, he drained his glass and poured another. But he ended up slamming it to the table. In a single sweep, he stood over the bed, lifting her tear-filled face with a harsh hand.

"Tell me, Jade, did it ever occur to you that it might be stupid for a blind person to climb into a child's treehouse to enjoy the view? Did you ever once think of our child you carried! And, damn you, Jade, do you have any idea what it felt like to see you lying on the ground, unconscious and already bleeding! And you want me to give you another chance?"

Victor released her harshly. Trying to control himself enough to pronounce the final verdict, he turned from the sight of her. "No, Jade, I won't give you another chance. It's bad enough waiting for your accidents. I'll be damned if I'm going to wait for a child's as well. You're not going to have any children."

"I won't accept that. . . ."

Victor barely heard her response, but it was enough for him to swing back around and lift her completely from the bed. "What did you say to me?"

"I won't do it! You can't make me! If . . . if you don't want me to bear a child then you better find another . . . another—"

"Woman to share my bed," he finished for her. He stared at her long and hard, unmoved by her tears, her slender frame trembling in his wrath. "Is that what you want, Jade?"

"I'll never, never rid myself . . . kill our child."

"Don't you understand? You already have."

There came a stunned moment of silence before she swung her hand to land a hard slap on the face she could not see. If Victor had not stopped his reflexes he would have blocked her swing and broken her arm, and Wolf Dog, standing on all fours and ready, would have attacked. As it was, the feel of her small hand striking his face shocked him with the realization of how much he wanted to hurt her. He wanted to hurt the woman who was more precious to him than life itself. How long before this anger and resentment destroyed them and the love they shared?

"Jade, I—"

She quickly pulled away from the hands reaching for her. "Don't touch me," she whispered, her face marred by pain. "Leave me . . . just leave me! You've hurt me enough."

Silence.

The door slammed. With that sound, something died inside her.

The music was loud, the smoke thick. Sebastian watched Victor, sitting across the table from him. The cards kept falling in Victor's favor, but he showed no reaction. There hadn't been any emotion for some time now.

Victor had thrown himself into work, pushed his men unnecessarily hard and himself even harder. In an effort to escape, he rose before dawn, spent each daylight hour in heavy, backbreaking physical labor only to bury himself in a paperwork at night until he finally collapsed into a short, dreamless sleep. For a while he met success; his labors prevented thoughts of Jade Terese, and more important, they blocked any consideration of their future.

Victor motioned to the barmaid for another drink. He was drinking heavily. The cards kept gracing him, the stakes became outrageously high, and still he felt bored to the point of distraction. He was well on his way to intoxication when a servant arrived with a message.

There is someone here to speak to you. Important.

Marie Saint

Victor did not hesitate. The thought of seeing Marie felt instantly agreeable. It suddenly seemed Marie was exactly who he wanted to see; he could talk to Marie, and she, wiser, possessing that uncanny feminine intuition, would understand, perhaps even help him sort through his raging feelings.

He motioned to a servant to bring his mount around front while he played out his last hand. After asking Sebastian to see to his winnings, he bid the gentlemen good-night and left.

With concern in his bright blue eyes, Sebastian watched Victor leave. If anyone could help, it was Marie. The passage of time had made his friend's pain worse, ever increasingly so, and with each day of Victor's absence, Jade Terese became more despondent. She valiantly tried to hide it, tried to keep her head up and maintain some semblance of a normal life, but everyone was concerned, worried. . . .

Mercedes more than any other.

Victor rode into the small courtyard, dismounted, and tied the reins, experiencing a fleeting sense of apprehension from the unusual air about the familiar house. Marie's house was normally lit like a tree at Michaelmas and an endless stream of visitors arrived at all hours, while sounds of music and merriment poured from the house to the street. Yet tonight her house sat in quiet darkness. No one—in fact, nothing—seemed to stir inside.

A man answered the door. Having thought Marie had only women for house servants, Victor felt momentarily taken aback by the unusually tall Negro standing in the doorway. Bald and dressed in an odd, brightly colored tunic and loose pants, the man's dark liquid eyes appraised Victor, but with a smile. He then bowed slightly and said in flawless English, "Monsieur Nolte, you are welcome."

Marie had evidently dismissed both her woman and servants alike. Victor slipped into the normally crowded entrance hall, but it, too, was empty and dark. Three glowing candles threw dim light and shadows into the space. The man led him down a corridor into the back of the house. He swung open a door and left without a word or sound, retreating with a quiet grace remarkable in one his size.

Victor's gaze adjusted to the dim light. Three more white candles sat in front of a glass, making them six. A large gold cross hung over the display. He smiled at Marie's pretense of magic. Then he saw her, sitting quietly on a sofa. Her trance was broken by his appearance and she rose, approached him, and the way time stopped as she came into his arms, one might have thought they were still lovers.

He suddenly felt a moment's fear, startled by the sheer force of sensuality radiating from her. She wore the simplest gown of cream-colored muslin; the loose folds completely concealed the voluptuous curves of her tall figure. Her long dark hair, too, tied in a tight knot on her head, accented the beauty of her exotic features. A small ruby hung from her neck, that was all.

It had been his present long ago.

The moment he took Marie in an embrace, lifted her face for a kiss, something inside him broke. The barriers he had so carefully constructed around himself shattered, and his vulnerability became painfully apparent. They said not a word as he held her tightly, savoring the comfort and warmth she afforded him.

Moments later, Victor found himself stretched out on the sofa in the darkened room, his head on Marie's lap, while he bared his soul to his friend. Occasionally, his troubled thoughts sent him jumping up, pacing the floor, but Marie's gentle words calmed his fury, eased his tension, and he returned, starting a new train of thought.

Marie had no qualms about deceiving Victor. It was, she knew, the only way, and so she listened to his struggle, and with an open heart provided what comfort she could, all the while waiting for signs that the potent tea had started to take effect. Most men would have slipped into a deep unconsciousness long ago, especially after so much liquor, but Victor was an exercise in masculine perfection. For a while his strength managed to offset the potion.

With anyone else, Marie knew, it would have been much easier. The woman would have simply bonded to a willing person and spoken her message through the borrowed body. Yet Victor! He would reject such an event without consideration. And he must be made to hear the message with an open mind! It held the essential key to his future happiness, to the very life of the lovely Jade Terese.

His words finally began to slow. Staring up at the dark ceiling, he whispered, "God, Marie, I love that girl so much. . . . If only . . . there was a way . . ." He must have drunk a good deal more than he remembered, for the ceiling seemed to rotate lazily.

"I will tell you something, *mon amour,*" Marie began seriously, softly. "The part of Jade Terese you cannot accept is the very same part that captured your heart so completely. Jade Terese possesses the most beautiful and innocent of spirits. Yes, it forced her to close her eyes, but it also makes her embrace the world with an abundance of joy and life."

Marie's reply felt important, but for the life of him, he could not comprehend the words. The room began spinning faster; at a point it almost spun to a far recess in his mind, then it turned back, slowing somewhat. He tried to lift himself up but his body felt like dead weight. He fell back to the sofa.

"It was the only way she could come to you, *mon amour.* Rest now and let your mind drift."

"Marie . . . I—" His mouth was dry, his throat parched, and words wouldn't form. Realizing he had no choice, his last completely conscious thought was to trust Marie and let this—whatever it was—happen.

He could not say for certain he had fallen asleep. Memories emerged in his mind's eye, some dating as far back as his boyhood in Virginia, and some leading him far into the future. Some images spun crisp and clear, some foggy and uncertain, while some became so startlingly vivid that they might have been real.

He woke suddenly in his bedchamber. He was lying on his bed. He watched Jade emerge from the dressing room. She was searching for something, looking at once confused and frightened. He tried to go to her but he could not move. She walked toward the door but spotted the looking glass, and while her back was to him, he watched her reflection in the glass.

She saw her reflection in the mirror.

His heart started pounding. She was seeing herself for the first time in nearly eight long years. She stared in pained disbelief; her small, shaking hand reached to her face, touched what she could not believe. Her eyes then widened, her face filled with sudden, unspeakable horror, and with a trembling hand she grabbed a vase from the table and threw it hard into the mirror.

Her reflection shattered into a hundred fragments.

Suddenly, it was over. He was back in the room and at first he thought he was alone. Marie had gone. He felt weak still; his limbs felt heavy. With considerable effort, he managed to sit upright on the sofa. Then he saw the woman.

She sat on a chair several paces away, a small candle flickering on a table nearby. She stared back at him, locking his gaze to her lovely eyes, eyes that seemed an opening to an azure summer sky. Lighter brown hair fell in tight ringlets around her pale, troubled face. She wore an aqua-blue cloak, and she nervously twisted a lace handkerchief in her hands. He noticed her ring: a small aquamarine stone surrounded by tiny diamonds; the center stone matched perfectly the color of her eyes.

Elizabeth Devon was as beautiful as her daughter.

Certain he was dreaming, Victor used every ounce of strength to shake the vision from his dazed mind. The attempt brought the realization that he still couldn't move. He failed to lift an arm in the air, to create a sound in his throat. The image of Elizabeth Devon held him immobile, forcing him still to listen to what she'd say.

She seemed to be waiting for his struggle to cease, and when she finally spoke, her voice belonged to the elite English upper class, though it held a faint, acquired French accent. It was Jade's voice, too, soft and feminine and, presently, strained.

"I have come to speak to you about the love we share for my daughter, Jade Terese. Before I warn you, before I beg you, please know that I am aware of your struggle. Love is seldom an easy thing. I do not know why this should be so, only that it is.

"In a very short time, you will be shown a way to restore my daughter's sight. You will, of course, want to do this"—her voice rose with feeling—"not just for yourself and your love, but for my daughter's well-being also. You will think it is the answer to your struggle. . . ."

A fast impotent fury rose in him, startling in its force. He fought to make sense of her words, words that he couldn't believe. Was he so tormented that he had created an image of Jade's mother telling him he would restore Jade's sight? Or was it the potion, drinking, what . . .

"It is this that I must beg you not to do! You must understand; Jade Terese chose to be blind. It is no accident. You and I and a million others would not make the same choice, but for Jade Terese, it was and still is the only way she survives. You must understand that blindness allows her to endure; it protects her from what her heart and mind, her very soul, cannot bear to witness."

His jaw locked with tension as his mind rebelled. Words formed angrily in his head but he still could not speak. He didn't understand! This was an outrageous presumption that Jade chose to be blind!

As though sensing his emotions, the woman dropped to her knees and tears sprang in her enchanting eyes. "Please believe me! 'Tis true! If you force her to see again, you

will destroy her! You will kill her! I beg you. I beg
you . . ."

In the next instant Victor was staring at an empty room,
stunned and confused. He did not know how long he remained motionless, looking at the place where she had
knelt moments before. But there came a point when the
room started spinning again. It faded and then, suddenly, it
was gone.

He stood at the end of a tree-lined lane. A house rose in
the foreground and he knew it as Galier Manor, Jade's
childhood home, from the many descriptions she had given
of it. It was so quiet, though. With a start he realized three
ravens sat on his outstretched arm. Screeching, the ravens
took flight. How terribly strange! He looked around with
alarm, confused, not knowing where he was or what he
was doing until—

A young girl he recognized only too well came to his
side. At first he was so transfixed by the image of Jade as
a child that he failed to grasp what he was about to be
shown.

The young girl seemed excited. She wore a plain gold
frock over a white dress, her long braided hair tied in gold
ribbons. She watched the birds disappear into the darkening sky before she raced through the yard and up the
house steps to the porch. He ran after her, knowing before
he called her name that she could not see or hear him.
"Mama, Mama!" she called in a whisper of excitement as
she ran through the entrance hall and up the carpeted
stairs. She turned down the hall.

He started up the stairs after her. He rushed after her
when he saw her hands on the lever of wide double doors.

Suddenly Elizabeth Devon blocked his path. She was
crying, desperately begging him to stop her daughter from
opening the fateful door. The fateful door? What was inside the room? He looked from the mother to the daughter
and in the flash of a second, he knew what she asked of
him. There was no decision for him, there never would be,

and as Jade reached for the latch, he turned back to Elizabeth and yelled, "No! Never!"

"Please!"

It was too late. Jade's small hand turned the knob. Victor forced himself to remain motionless. The door swung open. Elizabeth screamed as a blinding white light exploded in his head, his body jolted with a violent, unimaginable pain.

He bolted upright. "Jade!"

Startled, he opened his eyes to look dazedly around the room. Sebastian and Murray stood over him, watching him curiously. "For God's sake, Vic"—Murray frowned— "Marie said you had a hard night of it, but this is the first time I've ever heard you yellin' in your sleep."

Tessie sat with Jade on a blanket in the garden. Engaged in her reading lesson, the young maid read out loud while Jade helped her over the stumbling blocks. Reading was still a new experience and she hadn't yet developed Jade's enthusiasm for literature. She liked some stories as much as the next person, she supposed, but frankly, she could spin a much better yarn herself.

Tessie came to a word she couldn't make out. "P-R-O-V-O-K-E."

"Provoke," Jade said. "Like a sad experience provokes tears."

Tessie sighed, her warm brown eyes revealing her pained concern. It was like that with every word. She knew Jade tried hard to pretend everything was normal. But it wasn't, not since the day she lost her baby.

Unbeknownst to the two, Victor stood nearby listening. Now he interrupted. "How about, an unfortunate accident provokes a man's anger, a woman's tears provoke a deep regret and an apology. Love . . . provokes forgiveness."

Tessie wisely got up and left without a word or glance. Victor took her place on the blanket, resisting the urge to draw Jade into his arms. He knew to wait for her permission.

"Can you forgive me, Jade?"

Jade lifted her face to the sky in an effort to hold back the tears. Resisting the urge to fall into his arms required all her strength and will, a struggle that changed her breathing and pulse. She had to, though; she didn't want to spend the rest of her life crying.

"It is I who needs forgiveness," she said in a whisper. Victor reached for her, surprised when she pulled quickly away.

"No, please ... I don't want to. I—" She stopped, gathered her thoughts, but was so distressed that she blurted with anguish, "I think we should get an annulment."

She couldn't see his response. Cold blue eyes held her steady in their gaze for a good long minute. "I'm surprised you would give up on me so soon. Jade," he said slowly, "does our love mean nothing?"

Jade nodded her head, wiping the lone tear that managed to escape. "It's not working, no matter how much we love each other," she said with an inexpressible sadness. "You can't accept something that I can't change, and if we keep going on like this ... the day will come when you don't come back."

Had Victor given any credibility to his wild night of visions, he might have thought she could change what he fought to accept. But he didn't. His intelligence closed the door offered to others who assigned credibility to visions. A person created visions to fulfill unmet needs, and it was no surprise that he dreamt Jade's mother said he'd be shown a way to restore Jade's sight. It was even less of a surprise when one considered what Marie placed in that tea. As for the house and the door—that was a vision spun from the terror.

Victor paused, seeking the means to his end. He could accept her blindness, but he refused to accept her method of coping with it: the denial that led inevitably to accidents. This wasn't the time for such a discussion, as it would only result in another argument, and right now he wanted only to have her in his arms. He wanted her with each and every breath, for the long rest of their life. He loved her. . . .

"Jade, do you remember when I told you there'd be times when it would be difficult for me?"

Jade nodded slowly.

"This is one of those times. It won't last forever." When she shook her head, he stated flatly, "An annulment is out of the question. It's not to be mentioned to me again. You're my wife and that's one thing I have no intention of changing."

Jade struggled for words, alarmed by his attitude, the show of masculine simplicity. "Victor," she whispered, afraid, terrified to hope again, "what about the accident . . . and children?"

"The accident took something from us we both wanted very badly," he said softly, and then he paused, his arms aching with the need to draw her against his body. "When I learn you're with my child again," he added harshly, "just don't be surprised to find yourself tied to my bed for the duration."

"How can you make light of it?"

"What part led you to think I was making light of it?"

"Tying me to the bed . . . Really—"

"I think tying you to my bed is a fine idea. I don't know why I didn't think of it before." She looked quite shocked, not knowing if he was serious or not, and he chuckled as, unable to resist, he drew her against him. It was too much. Like a dam bursting, she was suddenly clinging. "Oh, Lord," he said as his mouth came over hers, and he was kissing her as if it were the last time he ever would.

And so they began again.

Tessie stood at the bottom of the steps, and for the first time in a month her smile was effortless. Victor and Jade had barricaded themselves in the bedroom for two days. Just like their honeymoon, all they did was eat, sleep and love each other. Every time she passed the door, she heard muffled laughter or the whispers of lovers.

Victor had ordered supper in a basket, for he and Jade planned go picnicking and swimming. Tessie had it all ready: fried chicken, fruit, rolls and honey, with large pieces of fresh-baked cherry pie and a bottle of Victor's best port.

The door finally swung open. Tessie laughed at the sight of them. Victor had Jade over his shoulder. She wore that old Spanish skirt and blouse, with her mandolin swung over her back, all the while trying her best to hang on to her straw sun hat. Best of all, the musical sound of her laughter filled the house again. The sorely missed sound almost made Tessie cry.

Carl joined Tessie, and they watched Victor carry Jade down the stairs, Jade laughing as Victor sang one of the silliest songs ever heard. Wolf Dog raced down after them, barking wildly, and even his barks somehow seemed happier too. Carl handed the blanket to Jade and then kissed her, while Tessie gave the basket to Victor, ran around him and then smacked Jade with a kiss.

"Oh, Tessie"—Jade laughed—"I love you!"

"You look like you love everything." Tessie laughed too.

"I do," Jade cried as she was being carried through the door. "I love everything!"

"It's going to rain," Carl warned.

"I love the rain too!"

Victor chuckled as he lifted Jade onto his waiting mount, then swung up behind her. Carl wore a huge smile and put his arm around Tessie, and together they watched the joyful couple ride off, Wolf Dog running alongside.

Murray burst from the study, waving a letter with excited, frantic motions. "Is that Vic I heard?" he questioned as he ran up. "Did he leave? Darn," he said, catching sight of the horse turning from the lane. "When will he be back?"

"They'll be gone a long time." Tessie smiled. "The way those two have been carryin' on, I won't be at all surprised if this honeymoon lasts forever."

* * *

They tossed their cares to the wind, and after finding a quiet, secluded spot along the riverbank, Victor and Jade spent the afternoon making love, swimming and laughing. The sky filled with gray rain clouds but like so many Louisiana days, the air remained warm, unnaturally still before the storm. The blanket was spread beneath the pendulous green branches of a large willow tree. The weeping branches formed a dense canopy over the two lovers, creating the illusion of a spot hidden from the world and sheltered from time itself.

Jade only knew that her earthly sphere once again had become a heavenly paradise. He loved her and she loved him, and that love would see them through anything life threw in their path. Anything . . .

Victor was less in the heavens as he contemplated far more earthly matters. He insisted Jade dress before they ate, and as he watched the simple act of her dressing, he wondered how he could—after days and nights of doing nothing but sleeping and making love, after making love twice already—how he could want her so badly again.

Victor's sudden chuckle caused a smile, and Jade reached a hand to him as he pulled her on top of his long length. Her wet braid swung over her shoulder; where the damp spotted her blouse, the thin material became transparent. The sight of the tip of her breast, her bare shoulders and, probably more than anything, the laughter on her lips and the smile in her eyes, caused an immediate physical response. Jade felt the hot hard part of him press against her as his hand impatiently pulled the blouse from her skirt, seeking the source of his trouble.

Wolf Dog interrupted, first with a small whimper, then with a wet kiss on Jade's face. Once he got their attention, he raced to the basket and barked at it. Victor laughed, explained what Wolf Dog was after, and she laughed too, wondered out loud what kind of man would starve his poor wife and her dog.

"A man very much in love," he answered as he reluctantly opened the basket.

He watched Jade eat, tossing pieces of chicken to her dog, and without expecting it, the image of Elizabeth Devon floated into his mind. The similarity was striking and he found himself saying, "I had a dream the other night about your mother."

"Oh? My mother?" she questioned, surprised.

"Tell me, did she look like you?"

"Everyone said we looked very much alike. I inherited darker hair from my father, and except for the color of my eyes, everything else came from my mother. Did she look like me in your dream?"

"Yes, she looked very much like you."

"I used to have a pretty miniature of her but ... well, it burned in the accident. How very strange. What was this dream about?"

"Oh, I don't really know." He shrugged. "You know how dreams are—loosely connected images that never make any sense." He'd like to dismiss and forget it, but part of him felt intensely curious. "What color were her eyes?"

"She had the most beautiful blue eyes you can imagine! Just everyone commented on them. They were so large and the blue was so blue—an aqua blue." She fed the last of her roll to Wolf Dog and then pulled her knees up. "Once when I was about nine, my mother's birthday was coming up in a month or so and I wanted to get her something special, not just the lace handkerchiefs I always gave her for her birthday. But I had no coin of my own and I didn't want to ask my father for it. The only day of the week I wasn't with my mother was Sunday. My mother never did convert from the Anglican church, except for the marriage, and my father went to church infrequently, so I normally joined the Taylours to go to mass in town.

"Well, for five Sundays in a row I told the Taylours that I was attending an ill friend during mass, keeping her company and reading to her and all. Then I skipped barefoot over to Congo Square. I played my mandolin, singing for coins for the crowd. When it was time to leave I'd race back through the streets to the church." She laughed. "People thought I was a Gypsy girl."

Victor was enjoying the story, listening with mild amusement until she arrived at the conclusion.

"The last Sunday I was there, guess who rode by and spotted me in Congo Square singing to a small crowd for coins like a beggar?"

"Your father." Victor chuckled.

"Oh, Victor"—she laughed nervously—"he was never more furious at me than that moment. But he just couldn't be mad at me after I told him why. He took my coins—I had ten or twelve reales saved by then—and we went that day to a jewelry shop. He told me to select my mother's present, that he'd make up the difference. As soon as I saw the ring, I knew it was the one. I picked out this delicate platinum ring, tiny diamonds surrounding an aquamarine stone that was the exact color of my mother's eyes. And you know, she never once removed that ring. She wore it every day of her life."

"You must have told me that story before," he said quietly.

"Oh, did I? I don't believe I've thought of it for years." And in the same breath she shrieked, "Victor, it's raining!"

Nightfall descended with lightning speed and they were caught in a torrential downpour. Wolf Dog raced into the house first and shook his fur all over the freshly polished floor. Carl tried to be kind. Jade and Victor followed, soaked to the bone. All Jade wanted after such a perfect day was a hot bath and a warm bed, and not surprisingly, Tessie had anticipated just such a desire. The bathwater was being heated.

Victor had just finished drying himself when a knock came at the bedroom door. Murray stood in the hallway looking strangely agitated and excited.

"I have to speak with you about the lass," he whispered

so as not to be overheard. "I hate to interrupt you, just when you've come to your senses and I hear laughter comin' from the two of you again, but it's important. I'll be waiting in the library."

Victor spent many of his working hours in the library. The room was dark and masculine; books lined two whole walls. A green-and-gold carpet spread beneath a long sofa and two chairs, while his large mahogany desk dominated the other side of the room. A painting of a brave clipper ship battling a stormy sea hung over the desk.

Dressed in a blue robe, Victor entered the room and noticed that Murray had already lit the lamps and started a fire beneath the brick mantel. He had also poured a warm brandy for Victor. He looked grave and concerned.

"What is it?" Victor asked, taking the brandy, swirling the gold liquid as he sat down.

"I don't know exactly where to start now that I've finally got you here."

"How about the beginning?" Victor grinned, not yet alarmed.

"The beginning, well, that would be some time ago. It would be a night Jade wore a green silk dress that set off her eyes. It was because of the color of that dress that I noticed Jade's eyes worked just fine, despite the fact that she's blind. Since then I've seen it a hundred times.

"I never told you, Vic, but her pupils dilate and constrict, which means they adjust to shifts in the light. Eyes don't adjust unless they actually see light, and Jade should—at the very least—be able to perceive changes in light."

"What are you saying?" Victor asked slowly.

Murray paused for a moment, trying to decide the best approach.

"Let me explain it to you as it happened," he decided to say. "I was suspicious then. I started through my old medical books, though I never did find the article I was looking for. I finally posted a letter to Cambridge and had someone search through the library there. I just received the answer today."

The doctor began reading a case history taken straight from a medical book, making a mistake in assuming that Victor could follow the language. It was as indecipherable and as foreign to him as Hindustani. After several minutes, Victor barely grasped the subject, let alone the point.

"Spell it out, Murray, and in English. The only thing I grasped was that some young lady was mute."

"It's a case of a young lady who had abruptly lost her voice, for no apparent medical reason and with no other symptoms. She couldn't utter a sound for over ten years, and then, on the day her mother died, her voice returned. Not only did her voice return, but a memory as well. It seems the day she had lost her voice, she had opened a door and discovered her father compromising the maid. She ran downstairs and was just about to tell her mother what she saw and she lost her voice, just like that—" He snapped fingers. "And in that same instant, too, she lost all memory of the coupling. Voice and memory returned only after her mother died."

Victor stood slowly and moved to the mantel. He stared at the fire through his brandy glass, resisting any connection between the story, his bizarre night of dreams, and hope. Patiently, Murray let his words sink into his friend's mind, but several long minutes passed before Victor spoke. "God, don't give me some false hope. I couldn't take it right now," he whispered. "There must have been dissenting medical opinions as to the cause of that lady's muteness."

"Aye, there always are, Vic, but I've been over them real careful and they're sewn as loosely as fishing nets. No, Vic, that young lady lost her voice solely because she couldn't bear to hurt her mother. And if a young woman can lose her voice because she came across her father compromising a maid, a little girl could lose her sight because she saw her mother hanging from a rope and her father shot in the head."

"We aren't even absolutely certain that happened!"

"Aren't we? Vic, the pieces fit together perfectly. Jade's head injury was in the wrong place to cause blindness. Her eyes do function. We already know her seizures don't cause her blindness but rather block her memory. There is no physical reason for her blindness."

"I can't believe that! How could she make herself blind—how could anyone look at something, no matter how horrible, and make themselves blind because of it? I just don't see how it could be possible!"

The doctor paused, knowing this was the most difficult aspect to explain. In many ways the answer to Victor's question could never be understood completely. He'd do his best, though.

"You see, Vic. I think it probably went something like this: The moment Jade saw her mother like that, she closed her eyes and shut the horror out. Just like that it was gone, and somehow, it's as if her mind struck a bargain with her heart and said, So long as you keep your eyes shut, so long as you're blind, you won't have to see it; you won't have to remember it."

Victor greeted this phenomenal situation by first trying to deny its possibility, and yet as his mind turned it over and over, he couldn't. It was all true. They knew no reason for her blindness. She had no memory of what happened, and yet they knew something monstrous had occurred, something too horrible for a thirteen-year-old girl to ever assimilate into the sanity of her mind.

His heartbeat escalated when Murray said slowly: "I believe that it can be reversed."

Victor saw, already knew, as Murray explained the logical conclusion—if Jade was forced to remember, forced to have seizures until she remembered, if she ever did remember—she would see again. The prophecy of his dream would come true. He was being shown a way, at least a possibility, of restoring Jade's sight. It was not just that her blindness and subsequent accidents threatened their love; he believed her blindness conceivably could threaten her very life at some future point. Just as in his dream, he never hesitated. There was no choice for him.

One does not get anything in life for nothing; there is always a price. Victor knew the price was proportionate to the gain. The price he would pay to make Jade see again would be heavy, perhaps the heaviest price he had ever paid, for he would be the one to force her into that pain.

"I never told you, but that night at Marie's, I had a dream about Jade's blindness." He waved his hand as if to dismiss the very possibility, a dismissal contradicted by his next words, the very race of his thoughts. "Not only did I dream of her mother telling me this would happen, that I'd find a means to restore Jade's sight, but I dreamt ... I dreamt of her house. It was so vivid, as if I was really there. There was something wrong with the house, a scent in the air or something, a feeling of terror about to happen."

Victor told Murray his whole dream, concluding with, "She opened the door and this blinding light exploded in my head with a hot burning pain. I can't describe it but it was ... bad, very bad. And I'm wondering if that is the pain I'm going to make her feel?"

After a long contemplative pause, Murray said simply, "You have to, Vic."

"Aye, I have to."

They discussed what had to be done long into the night, examining it from every conceivable angle. The unknown variable in the equation was the number of seizures Jade would have before she remembered. They made no mistake on that point. It would not be two or three, but closer to twelve and perhaps as high as twenty. Years of darkness simply could not be undone easily. He'd have to force one seizure after another, wake her from unconsciousness with smelling salts before forcing a seizure again.

He selected a day. Tomorrow.

Chapter 12

❧

Jade felt a lingering warmth and a trace of the clean masculine scent she loved where he had slept, and she smiled, wishing he were still there. Dressed only in his shirt, she got up and made her way into the dressing room.

"Wolf Dog?" Where was he?

A fire crackled in the hearth, its small warmth unable to fight the morning chill. After finishing in the dressing room, she dashed back to the bed and buried herself in the covers. Just two more minutes of warmth, she told herself.

Watching her sudden flight from a chair, Victor stood and moved to the bed. Jade heard his footsteps and sat up. "Victor?" she asked as his arms came around her. "Where's Wolf Dog?"

"I took him out to give him a bone."

She smiled. "You were watching me?"

He said what he always said to that. "I'm always watching you." And he was. For a long moment he lost himself to the study of the lovely upturned face, the pale soft skin, as soft and smooth as rose petals, the feminine velvet of her thin brows, the rush of color on her cheeks, and the thick mass of dark hair falling over his arm, and all the love there, as if a great beacon of light shone from within.

Forgive me, Jade. Forgive me . . .

His lips came to hers, gently, tenderly at first. He had, she knew, as many ways of kissing as the sun had of shining, and as the kiss deepened and deepened more, a tremor of alarm passed through her. One sensation emerged through the sweeping onslaught of emotion: desperation, that born of fear. But the feeling dissipated, vanishing beneath the shimmering heat of this kiss. His strong hands

271

slid under her shirt to draw her tightly against the steely strength of his body. Oh my, oh Lord, the kiss stole every last thought as her arms circled his neck, searching for a lifeline as she felt herself swooning.

He broke the kiss but kept her close as he closed his eyes. "Jade, I love you. . . ."

She felt his fear. She stretched out a hand to find his face. "Victor," she asked in a whisper of concern, "what's wrong?"

"I am afraid, Jade. I am so afraid. . . ."

He wrapped her in a quilt and guided her outside to the breakfast table on the balcony, lifting her to his lap. He poured her a cup of coffee. Murray, who would be waiting downstairs all day, had cautioned against allowing her to eat any breakfast.

"Tell me what's wrong."

Victor stared out over the garden. The rain had stopped, though the sky was still washed with gray. The land held a moist dew in the storm's aftermath, sparkling with colors of green, crimson and gold. How beautiful the world was! He wanted to share it with her. He wanted it more than anything in the world.

"What if I found a way to restore your sight, but in order to do so I had to hurt you, perhaps even badly. Would you want me to do it?"

"What?" she whispered.

"You heard me."

The next breath brought a wave of alarm and in its wake was dread. Here it was again. Again. So soon. This was a nightmare. Now he had fantasies about making her see.

"Victor," she said with soft yet vicious seriousness, "I am blind. I will always be blind. You can't seem to accept it—"

"Answer my question."

It was the first show of the monster born of her resistance. She refused to cooperate. "I will not answer this—"

She started to get up but he stopped her movement with

his arms. With force. Alarm changed to panic as emotions welled inside her, threatening, rising—

"I won't answer you! I don't understand—"

"You don't have to understand. I won't threaten you, Jade. Answer the question, yes or no."

"Victor, I—"

"Answer me."

"Yes, yes, of course I would want to see again, but—"

"Even if I hurt you by causing your seizures?"

She went very still, alerted to something she didn't understand. "Seizures? You would force me to have a seizure? You don't really think you could make me see again? You're just saying all this—"

"I *do* think I can make you see again."

"Nooo!" She tried to get up and away from him, but he held her effortlessly. "No . . . please, let me go— What are you going to do to me?"

"I'm going to make you remember what happened when a thirteen-year-old girl opened the door to her parents' bedroom and saw something—dear Lord—something so terrible . . ."

She never heard the rest. She first seemed not to hear any of the words, her eyes stared off blankly and her face lost all emotion and expression. The images started in her mind. Her temples pounded, her face drained of color, and he released her arms just as she grabbed her head to brace against the blinding burst of pain.

A scream sounded in the still morning air.

Tessie was on her way to Jade. "Oh, Lord!"

Murray caught her halfway up. "Tessie! Stop!" She paused and turned. "You're not going in there today!"

"But . . . Jade!" she screamed. "A seizure! She's having a seizure!"

"Come back down, Tessie, and I'll explain it to you."

Tessie hesitated, turning from him to the door, obviously confused by his order. "Come on, Tessie. Vic's in there with her. I'll explain what's going on."

Victor had lifted Jade to the bed and stood over her with smelling salts, still startled by the ferocity of the seizure. It took over half an hour with the salts before her eyes opened. She sat up, looking confused and disoriented. He reached a hand to her, which she quickly grasped. "Oh my," she said, holding her head. "I had a seizure in my sleep. . . . It's been so long now, I—"

"No, Jade," he said. "You didn't have a seizure in your sleep. We were out at the breakfast table when I told you I was going to make you see again by forcing you to remember the accident. The real accident." And he repeated his exact words: "What happened when a thirteen-year-old girl opened the door to her parents' bedroom and—"

She had four more seizures. Each was the same as the one before: he never even let her out of the bed before he threw the words at her, watched the same progression that led to the burst of white light, the violent jolt of pain, and her collapse into unconsciousness. When she regained consciousness, confused and disoriented, she thought she had just wakened, that the seizure had occurred during sleep.

After the seventh time, he was able to wake her after just five minutes. She opened her eyes. The first thing she heard was, "My God, you're weakening!"

Fear changed her features. Before he touched her, she panicked and scurried to the far end of the bed. Before he said anything, she covered her ears with her hands and shut her eyes tight.

Seizures! He was making her have seizures! How? Why? The pain, oh Lord, the pain. She'd not survive a single time more!

Victor stepped around the side of the bed, but as he reached for her, she scrambled away.

"Don't touch me!" She covered her ears again and said, "You're s-scaring me, you're making me—"

Victor leaned over the bed, effortlessly lifting her from it. He brought her backside against him, holding her arms tight. He felt her tremble and he closed his eyes.

Her fear was his own pain.

"Do you know why I'm scaring you?" Breathing fast, she squirmed desperately, but he held firm. "Do you, Jade?"

"Nooo . . . No. I—'"

"Because I'm going to make you see again. All you have to do is remember seeing your mother dead. Remember opening the bedroom door—"

That was as far as he got. She swallowed once before her mind went blank and her head exploded with the white light, and she cried out weakly, collapsing unconscious in his arms.

Mercedes twisted a handkerchief in pale hands and said with conviction, "This is a mistake! I do not believe it. I have no faith in this program. He is hurting her—"

"Mercedes . . ." Murray started to speak but stopped. One hand to his forehead, he continued pacing. Another muffled scream sounded from upstairs and he stopped. Anxiously his gaze watched Mercedes and Tessie, their disbelieving faces focused on Carl's and Sebastian's brandy-filled glasses. Glasses that had stopped in midair as the scream had sounded, and now went to the men's lips.

Carl rose to pour another round.

Murray resumed pacing, staring uncertainly at his black boots, stepping over the green-and-gold carpet.

They waited downstairs in the study. Which is not to say everyone expected Jade to descend at some point to see their faces for the first time. Murray had explained as best as he could what Victor was doing and why. For nearly an hour Mercedes had desperately searched for a fault in the reasoning. She had no faith in the basic preposition that Jade made herself go blind; it was quite impossible. Her certainty increased with her anxiety at each distant scream.

And each scream was weaker than the last. . . .

Few words were spoken. Carl had dismissed all the

other house servants and he and Sebastian were already well on their way to intoxication.

Mercedes and Tessie sat together in a chair, leaning against each and holding tight to each other's hands, oddly alienated from the men in the room. Unlike them, brandy hadn't dulled their senses and the women could not hide fear or horror each time Jade screamed.

The next scream broke Mercedes. Like Victor upstairs, Jade's pain became hers and it was unbearable. Jumping from the chair with a rustle of skirts, she dropped to her knees before Sebastian. "Do something, Sebastian! I beg you! It's gone too far! He cannot be helping her, it cannot be working!"

Concerned blue eyes bored into the soft hazel ones and Sebastian pulled Mercedes into his arms when the first tears appeared. He held her tightly, gently taking her hand in his as he turned to Murray. "What if she's right? I mean, how do we know?"

"We knew it was to be like this," the doctor replied softly, gravely. "A young girl doesn't make herself blind and stay blind for all these years if it could have been changed easily. We might be waiting all night."

Mercedes shook her head at this, collapsing against her husband. It was hard on all of them—and, Murray knew, hardest on Victor. "Sebastian, you better take the ladies out."

"No, no," Mercedes said, lifting her troubled face. "Murray, can't you just go up there to see? Please?"

No sounds came from inside the room. Murray knocked softly. Victor swung open the door. He showed all the signs of his hell: disheveled clothes and hair, a strand of it falling over strained troubled eyes, a creased brow. "She's out right now," he said, stepping aside for Murray to enter.

"What's happening?" the doctor asked as his gaze fell to the bed, where Jade lay unconscious.

Victor's eyes met Murray's and his voice held his heightened emotion. "It is working! It's going to happen.

At first she woke up and had no memory of what caused the seizures, but this last time she woke, she was afraid. She knew I was causing the seizures. And more important, after each seizure she regains consciousness quicker than the last time."

Murray walked over to the bed and stared down at her stilled form. "So her defenses are falling," he said out loud, abruptly grasping what the measure of approaching success was to be. The closer Jade came to seeing the terror, the more desperate she'd become. He quickly explained his suspicions, concluding, "I'll wager anything she starts fighting—fighting tooth and nail."

"Jade? Fighting? You mean physically fighting?"

"Yes, any way she can."

Victor looked down at Jade, unable to imagine her fighting. What she had managed to do to Don Bernardo had always shocked him, for Jade had not a vicious or violent bone in her body.

She was unquestionably one of the most feminine of women he had ever known; her femininity manifested itself in almost everything. Little things, daily things: Jade's horror when he moved to swat a spider or insect on the wall, not the horror most women feel, but rather horror that he would kill it. She always made him catch it, toss it outside or over the balcony.

"Our mistake was in starting in the morning," Murray commented, interrupting Victor's musing. "We should have started at night when she was already tired. It's just going to be a question of wearing her down. So let her fight you. You might even *try* to make her fight you." His last piece of advice before leaving was, "Do anything to wear her down."

Victor pressed smelling salts beneath Jade's nose. At first she showed no sign of waking but her eyes suddenly began moving beneath closed lids, and just when he thought she was coming to, he knew the images began playing in her mind. Sure enough, her body jolted and she collapsed from sleep to the peace of unconsciousness.

That one broke him. He pulled off his shirt, laid down beside her and gathered her soft form tightly against him. his hand brushed lovingly through her loose hair as he whispered, "Forgive me, Jade. God, forgive me. . . ."

Jade woke before the smelling salts were pressed to her face but she stayed perfectly still, keeping her eyes shut and showing no sign of waking, forcing the scream in her throat down. She felt confused; her thoughts felt fragmented. She tried to slow a rising panic enough to grasp what was happening to her.

Where was he now? Was he looking at her? Was he still in the room? And what—dear God—was he doing to her?

She refused to accept the obvious evidence that he was purposely and maliciously hurting her. No, he had gone mad.

That pain, oh God, no . . . please . . .

Like a trapped and tortured animal, her desperation grew and her poor heart beat wildly against its destiny. As a dark river sweeps by under a lightning flash, she felt her life swept from under her. She must escape, and before he caused that pain one more time. Escape and get someone to stop him, to explain that it wasn't working, that it wouldn't work, that he would kill her. . . .

She heard a small clink from the balcony, a glass set to the table. If he stood on the balcony, his back would be turned from her as he stared out at the garden below.

She slowly slipped from the bed, and without making a sound—with the noted exception of a violent pounding of her heart—she cautiously moved to the door. Her hand felt for the knob, she turned the handle and opened the door.

Downstairs . . . get downstairs! She grabbed the rail and fled, the sudden rush of movement freeing an overwhelming fear.

When she was halfway down the stairs, Victor yelled her name from the top. "Jade! Stop!"

She heard his pursuit and she screamed, then cried. "H-help m-me. Somebody please h-help me!"

Sebastian instantly jumped up to hold back both Mercedes and Tessie, while Murray and Carl rushed into the corridor to confront the heart-wrenching sight: Jade had collapsed in a tight ball on the bottom step. Tears streamed down her face. She tried to cry for help but trembled so violently the words choked her. . . .

Seeing her like that nearly destroyed Victor. If only Murray was right, if only she'd come up fighting, angry, furious, he'd be safe. He could handle anger. But this, such fear and desperation, jolted every fiber of his being. All he wanted was to sweep her into his arms and chase away the fear. . . .

Victor just stared, for a long moment. Continuing meant it would get worse. Much worse. Yet how could he ever rest if Jade was blind and he had the means, a possibility, to make her see again?

He closed his eyes and forced his mind to create a picture of Jade falling down the stairs. . . .

The picture destroyed any last thought of stopping. He rushed to her and swept her up into his arms. She cried weakly, calling in choked whispers of fear for help.

He quickly ascended the stairs and brought her to the bed, where he set her down before turning to the door. He locked it and placed the key in his pocket. There would be no more escapes.

Jade sank to the floor, so frightened she could only beg, "Please, Victor, don't do this to me. . . . You're going to kill me. . . ."

Victor lifted her, moving to a chair where he held her on his lap. She was stiff, yet trembling, while her breath came in huge gulps. He sought a different route to the same goal and he first tried to ease her terror enough to listen to him. With a calm voice, he coaxed her into taking deep breaths, until, while she still trembled, she finally stopped gulping in air.

"Tell me what I'm doing to you," he said.

"You're ... m-making me have s-seizures."

"Why am I doing that?"

"You think I'll ... see again b-but I won't. ... I won't."

"And you don't know why I think that making you suffer these seizures will make you see again, do you?"

Jade shook her head frantically back and forth; it was the source of her confusion.

"Listen very carefully. I want you to understand one thing: you can't understand why I'm doing this because any attempt to explain causes a seizure and makes you forget. Each seizure makes you forget. Can you understand that much?"

Made her forget what? She struggled to comprehend, trying desperately to understand enough to show him where he was wrong, very wrong. He believed she couldn't understand something, but what? What was she missing?

Fear pounded so loudly in her heart she could not think to save herself. She heard the words but comprehension eluded her. It was excruciatingly frustrating, like catching a feather in the wind; she grabbed for it, only to find it blew farther away, that to catch it she had to jump ahead, anticipate its leap through the air. ...

Jade grabbed her head and cried, "No ... no, I don't understand. ... I can't. You're wrong, wrong! I can't see; you can't make me!"

"I can make you and I will. We won't leave this room and you won't eat or sleep until you do remember. I don't care if you have a hundred seizures, Jade; you're going to remember."

"Remember what? What can't I remember?"

"Remember what you saw behind the bedroom door."

The door, that door. Her plaits and jade cross bounced as she ran up the stairs and to the door. She felt a mounting terror as she reached that door—

"What's in the room? What do you see, Jade!" Victor's voice thundered into her head. "Open the door, Jade! Look!"

"No!" she screamed as the door opened: opened to the blinding white light, the pain exploding through her body. She screamed again, collapsing unconscious in his arms.

She woke to the smelling salts. Like a violent wave crashing to a rocky shore, consciousness mobilized her body. Seized with a desperate instinct to survive, she came up fighting, and despite Murray's warning, she caught him off guard.

Before she even opened her eyes, she swung her clenched fist into him, smack in the side of his arm, and hit his face hard with her other hand. She managed to land two more fists in his neck and face before he responded. Stunned, Victor's first inclination was to push her to the bed, pin her flying arms down, but remembering what the doctor had said, he jumped up from the bed instead.

With her heart pounding and her eyes filled with fury, Jade mistook his retreat as first triumph. She wasted no time, flying from the bed.

Victor watched her with a lift of brow. So, she had some fight in her after all. Without making a sound, he stepped away from her, knowing she was waiting for some sign to determine where he was.

"Are you going to fight me now?"

"Yes! Yes!" she cried as her hand felt over the night stand and she grabbed a book and flung it at his voice. Victor caught the book, dropped it to the ground and thankfully managed to catch the vase that followed before it crashed to the ground.

"I'll not let you do this to me! You . . . move one step toward me . . . and I'll, I'll—"

"You'll what?" Victor asked, taking a step toward her.

She sprung at him, managed to land right on him, and went wild. She pounded with her fists, landing blow after blow against him. Her frantic craze prevented her from grasping the frightening truth; Victor was not fighting back, indeed, he was holding her waist, knowing that if he let go of her, the furious motions would send her tumbling to the floor.

Yet the exertions began to exhaust her.

"Surely you can do better than this?"

Anger joined her fury and she renewed her efforts with strength and vigor. He lifted her off the ground, kicking, pounding, screaming at him to stop. He sat down on the chair and held her across his knees as she pounded her fists into his legs and kicked in the air, screaming, trying to twist around, wanting to scratch him, to hurt him—

"This body of yours can certainly accommodate a man, but I don't think it was made to fight a man."

The cruel comment and its profane humor caused a sudden cessation of movement. Once she stopped, she became aware that he held her with one hand. One blasted hand! Using his other hand, he had poured himself a glass of water. Water. He was drinking water while she fought . . . for her life.

"Let me up! Let me up!" Seeing that she had realized the futility of fighting, Victor lifted her to an upright position on his lap. She shook from the violence of her fight but she managed to ask, "Give me some water too."

Victor held her with one arm while his free hand passed the glass into both her hands, and he failed to detect the maliciousness of her intention until it was too late. She took a few swallows, threw the remaining water into his face, and in the flash of a second, smashed the glass against his head.

In one movement, Victor pushed her to the floor and stood up, the shattered glass falling around them. He would never underestimate her again. She lay panting and crying on the floor.

"What's behind the closed door, Jade?"

A minute later she was unconscious.

Victor lifted her to the bed and pulled the servants' rope. He stepped into the dressing room, dampened a cloth in the dressing water and pressed it against his head. He stepped in front of the glass and, after wiping away the blood, he saw only a small gash.

Carl straightened the room and swept up the glass while

Murray examined Victor's cut. As the door shut again behind the two, Jade began to regain consciousness. He quickly slipped the key in his pocket and waited, not knowing what to expect now. He sat back in the chair to watch.

A trembling hand quickly wiped a tear from her cheek, and she used all her strength to push back fear. She was desperate. She could not fight him. She had always been acutely conscious of the power and strength in his masculine form but she had never experienced it like this. He had never seemed so strong, or herself so helpless. She had only a last desperate ploy. He could not love and hurt her at the same time.

She got up on her hands and knees on the bed, listening for him. "Victor? Are you still here?"

"Yes, I'm right here," he replied, trying to repress his normal response to the sight of her like that: her slender figure barely concealed in his shirt, posed so seductively, her long loosened hair falling about her, making her look wild.

"What's going through your head?" he asked slowly.

"I'm thinking," she said, coming off the bed, "that if you loved me you wouldn't, couldn't, do this to me." She stepped toward him and every part of her body, every movement, radiated her intent. "Can I make you love me?"

Victor stood up and moved in front of her. She lifted her face, showing dark green eyes filled with tumultuous emotions. He remained motionless, permitting her hands to gently caress his chest, his shoulders and arms, still motionless when her hand moved to his breeches.

She could not be so foolish ... but then, he had never shown her how a man takes a woman and remains emotionally unaffected by it. She had no such option. He'd exhaust her physically and emotionally; he'd steal her small strength—

"Will you love me?" she asked, sliding off his breeches, taking his hard flesh in both hands, hearing his breath catch and a shudder pass through his tall frame. "Will you?"

Victor took her hands, forced them behind her back, and pulled her against him. Before his lips crushed against her mouth, he said simply, "No, Jade, this will not be an act of love."

He allowed her a brief moment to struggle before forcing her head back, her lips open to him, and in that moment, a silent scream rose in her body, protesting what she had started, protesting what would not be pleasant and what she was powerless to stop.

Trapped tightly in his arms, she felt his kiss hungrily devour her, purposely giving as much pleasure as pain, and she became limp, weak-kneed and senseless. A savage passion radiated from him, at once engulfing and enraging her.

His mouth left hers suddenly, and she drew a gasping breath. As he released her arms to remove her shirt, she darted back quickly in a surge of defiance, out of his reach.

"Nooo ... please, I—" Fear threw her off balance, and she stumbled to her hands and knees. He lifted her from the ground, turned her backside against him and stopped her flinging arms. She squirmed. "No, don't do this to me—"

"Fight me all you want, Jade Terese."

He lifted her hair from the sweep of her neck and pressed moist lips there. Chills raced along her spine, and then, with his lips on her neck, his hand ripped open the buttons of the shirt. Helpless tears spilled down her cheeks as his one arm kept her powerless and his other hand gently, methodically began massaging her breasts to swollen peaks, forcing a fire to spread through her loins. His hand wandered over her, finally circling her belly, moving lower and lower until she cried out with joyless anticipation.

Humiliation burst upon her and she cried again, squirmed in rage, dug her nails into his arm and clamped her legs tightly together but only to hear a growl. The force of his body, the threat she squirmed against, his very passion, soared, flamed and permitted no struggle. His leg forced hers apart and his hand slipped between her thighs with a touch like fire, causing her to cry, tremble, moisten.

He lifted her to the bed and allowed her no choice of position, though she tried desperately to twist around to face him. He held her hips firmly and she closed her eyes, biting her lip till she tasted blood, as his hand parted her again, lifting her higher. She felt the length of him slowly caress her sex, opening her for a hard thrust.

His body pounded into her, forced her to tighten with each forceful push, the tension building and building despite the act of violence. And while each movement carried her ever closer and closer, she was hurt by it, praying for the end that finally came. She stiffened and jolted; the tension exploded inside her, washing those ripples of intense pleasure over her, waves that left neither feeling nor strength in their path. His hands tightened around her, holding her to him for his last hard thrust, and his violence exploded with unexpected force, ending it. She collapsed, feeling nothing but a debilitating, numbing exhaustion.

He had closed his heart to her struggle and would not open it now, though he lay down on the bed and pulled her unresisting body against him. His emotions would remain sealed until the moment she opened her eyes and saw him.

He held her for nearly half an hour. She cried softly, trembling slightly despite the intensity of the warmth between them. He listened to her heartbeat spiral slowly downward, seeking a peace that came with sleep, a peace he'd not permit her. Just as her breathing spoke of a final collapse, he brushed his lips over her flushed face and his hands began a slow caressing.

Jade opened her eyes in panic and her body stiffened as he forced her on her back and said what she dreaded most, "Once is never enough with you. Again, Jade Terese. I will have you again."

"No!" she cried, and pounded her fists into his chest as

he moved over her. He pinned her arms to the bed and his leg parted hers, his body effortlessly subduing her assault. "No. Please! I—"

He stopped her protest with his lips, a kiss almost gentle, a kiss able to bring life back into her body. He would not let her passively participate in an exercise of his desire. He forced her desire to meet him, and moved slowly, with purpose, awakening every strained fiber of her being to pleasure again. His lovemaking always stretched endlessly after his first release, and this time he kept her carefully at the peak of exquisite agony and forced her to relinquish everything to him. He held back his pleasure until he was certain he couldn't push her over the thin line that separated her from ecstasy a single time more. And only then did he allow himself to spill his seed inside her.

The room was dark when she finally felt his violent shudder, the low groan of his final release, signaling the end to his claim on her body and the start of her nightmare again. For a long moment she didn't move, overwhelmed by the horror and helplessness brought by this nightmare. A dark nightmare of terror.

It was only a matter of minutes, just minutes, and she never knew if it was a dream or a vision but suddenly she was transported away. She stood in a dark world and at first there was nothing, no shape or even light in this dark space. Then suddenly she saw it.

It was the most beautiful thing she had ever beheld. A huge ball made of transparent rainbow hues. Rays of color shot out from it. Glittering transparent color. Somehow she knew it was part of her, the essential part of her soul.

As she stood there in utter awe and wonderment at this miracle of light and color, Victor emerged. He appeared as a shadow. He held a stick. She screamed as he raised the stick in the air and swung hard at this magical ball of light.

She cried out as it shattered.

She awoke from this vision to feel the warmth of his body leave her. "No, no!" She reached for him, placing her arms around his neck. He closed his eyes but for a moment, and she clung to him desperately, sobbing. Gently, he forced her arms from him and left the bed. She collapsed into a pillow, shaking in tears.

It was gone, alive no more.

Victor lit a fire and the lamps before putting on a robe, grabbing hers from the closet and returning to her. He lifted her limp body from the bed, covered her with the robe. He said nothing, pulled her hair out from the dark green silk, and even tied the sash around her waist for her.

Jade dropped to her knees, lifting her tear-streaked face to him. "Please, Victor, please . . ." She could not see the emotion on his face, but she felt his merciless strong hands lift her upright, then lead her to the chair and put her on his lap. After making her drink a glass of water, he began.

"Would you like to know how this all started?" he asked in a deceptively calm voice. Jade shook her head and covered her ears, and he noticed the change as he forced her arms to her side. She had almost no strength left. "I'll tell you how it started. It started with Maydrian."

"What? Maydrian?"

"Remember when you ran into your house looking for Hamlet?"

She nodded, wearily aware that he was playing a trick on her. "You didn't find your dog. No, you found Maydrian hanging from a rope with her throat slit. You must have bumped into Maydrian's body. We suspect it reminded you of something—"

It was too late. She heard him, the words forced a memory of boots, small boots swinging into her face. Maydrian hanging . . . a door opening to see—

Jade's body suddenly convulsed with effort to draw breath, and she gasped for air. . . . He held tight as she screamed, her small body jolting with the pain. She collapsed.

Victor stared at her, stunned. The change was immediately apparent; her pain was less than before—he felt certain of it! Her body could no longer generate as much pain to hurt her.

He woke her in less than five minutes and instantly asked, "Do you remember?"

Dazed and confused, she managed to say, "I . . . Victor, I—"

"Do you remember?"

"Yes . . . yes, but it . . . it doesn't make sense. I—"

"Finding Maydrian's body reminded you of what's in the bedroom. Was it your mother, Jade? Did you find her dead—"

She went very still but her mind had already begun the progression she could not stop. Her body braced as she saw the door, her hand on the knob. It swung open and for one brief instant she forced herself to look at the burst of white light, but immediately she was hit with pain, and then, mercifully, darkness.

Victor forced four more seizures, his excitement growing after each one. There was no question: the pain lessened each time, as did her period of unconsciousness.

The end was coming.

Jade was unaware of it. She became more afraid each time she woke. It was like watching a guillotine fall to your head in slow motion, the terror of death connected with a quick extirpation. She screamed, struggled, cried with each and every breath, but he had never felt so forceful to her. Her growing fear fueled his power and he became stronger as she became weaker.

Then it happened. As she opened the door, bracing herself for the burst of light and the pain. It happened in a split second; the light burst in her head, but just as the pain jolted her, she caught a glimpse of dark shapes forming from the light.

She cried with an unknown terror, the first scream not caused by pain. The jolt had been but a brief shudder, and for the first time she remained conscious.

"Jade!"

She couldn't understand what had happened. Fear defined her being and it was all she knew. A trembling voice told him, "I'm so s-scared. I'm ... so scared. ..."

"I know you are, sweetheart, I know," he whispered, enclosing her protectively in his embrace. "I'm right here. I'm right here."

Those words sparked a sudden insight, and intuitively he knew how to bring her through the last time. Just as in his dream, he could be there when she opened the door for the last time. It would work, he knew it would work.

"Jade, listen carefully. We're going to do it one last time, but this time I'm going to be there with you. I'm holding your hand as you open the door—"

Jade bit her lip, closed her eyes and shook her head, a last futile effort to stop the image from taking hold in her head. She was looking at the door. This time was different. She really stood there, reliving the fateful day so long ago.

He was not there with her.

No one was with her. She stood at the heavy wood door for a long moment, her last. A small pale hand reached to the brass latch, pulling it down. The door swung open. There was no blinding white light to save her. There was no pain to save her.

She did not scream; she felt no terror and indeed she had not even moved. She never knew how long that one moment lasted, a minute or an hour, it could have been either or anything in between. She had no awareness.

It was a blink of her eyes. At some point, she simply blinked, and as her lids closed over her eyes, she discovered the scene ceased to exist. It was gone. So, when she opened her eyes, there came a flash of blinding white light, an unbearable pain jolted every fiber of her body and threw her back into the hall.

There was no such miracle this time.

"Look at it! Look at it!"

Her father lay on the floor. She looked up at her, blood covering her hands.

She could not see her father for all the blood. Blood everywhere. Over the bed. Stains on the wall. A bright pool under her. A red chemise. A thick rope tied to the ceiling beam. Tied to her mother's feet.

Her mother's hair dripping with blood.

No one ever forgot Jade's last scream. It would sound in their nightmares for the rest of their lives: the scream of a thirteen-year-old girl confronting a scene of unearthly terror. . . .

Chapter 13

A vague memory pervaded Jade's sleep. People whispering. Concerned. Exciting. A tender hand gently stroking hers. "We'll see in the morning. . . . We'll see in the morning. . . . We'll see in the morning. . . ."

The words echoed in her mind, over and over again, until she slipped into a deep dreamless sleep.

An uncomfortable sensation stirred her awake. She turned over, hoping it would disappear. What was it?

Light. . . . Light filtered beneath her closed lids.

Her heart started pounding. She shut her eyes tightly, holding her breath, but colors—blood reds, velvet blues and purples—burst like fireworks in her mind.

There was no escape. She opened her eyes. There was no period of adjustment. No blurriness to ease this stunning transition.

The world came into sudden sharp focus.

She stared up at the whitewashed beams of the ceiling, the tops of two shiny black bedposts, then patches of the green-and-blue satin of a comforter.

She sat up. Victor lay sound asleep beside her on his back, and as had happened every night of his life, at some point during his sleep he had became too warm and had tossed off the covers. A single sheet barely covered one leg.

She felt an odd dispassionate interest in this first look at the man who was her husband. He seemed at once familiar and so very unfamiliar. Once, after the theater, Mercedes had expanded her description of Victor: "There is just something so . . . so magnetic about him, and to say simply he is attractive doesn't really do justice."

Now she understood what Mercedes had meant. It came as a mild surprise that he differed markedly from the picture she had formed of him in her mind. Simply put, the man she had imagined fell short of the reality. Every part of him was more than she had thought.

How? How could that be? She had touched every part of him, every inch of his skin. How could she have been so misguided, so inaccurate, so wrong?

Even things like his height, a specific measurement she had arrived at without seeing, suddenly seemed wrong. He looked taller than she had imagined, and it was a curiosity to see that he must be a whole foot taller than she. Why hadn't she realized that? Yet his height was hardly the only curiosity.

What could she say? The blatant masculinity of his naked body scared her. She had never thought of him that way before. She had felt over every part of the lean body hundreds of times, explored those hard muscles wrapped around the calves and thighs of his long legs; she had felt the wide expanse of his bare chest and shoulders; she had felt those bulges in his arms. Now that she saw him, it came as no surprise that he had held her kicking and screaming with one hand while calmly drinking a glass of water with the other.

There were some things she couldn't have imagined. The bronze color of his skin, the lighter brown color of his hair. Hadn't he always said his hair was dark brown? Until yesterday she had never imagined that hard and cruel lines could dominate his face. She had never imagined those muscles on his hard, flat stomach, either. And she felt nothing but shock, then panic, at the sight of his flaccid manhood.

Nervously, she lifted her gaze to the room, seeking something comforting, familiar. Here, too, though, familiarity joined unfamiliarity. She had known the room through other peoples' descriptions and the limited information of her remaining senses. The room looked beautiful, and while she would expect it to be so, seeing the heavy shiny black furniture, the polished wood floor, the blue and green colors and those startling tapestries forced her to realize just how limited her perspective had been.

She was stunned. Details, everywhere she looked details flooded into consciousness. Small and large details—things she had never known or realized—flew at her from all directions: the intricate pattern of the veiled lace of the curtains, the sweeping length of the green velvet drapes, the whitewashed ironwork on the portico and balcony seen through the hand-carved French doors, the pattern on the damask-covered chairs, the oil lamps, the shiny brass of the candleholders, her toilet articles on the divan, the pile of books on the night table, and even the ascetic symmetry of the whole room; its spaciousness that seemed to be collapsing, closing in . . . and—

She grabbed her head, pressed her pounding temples and wished it would stop. She wished she could find something, anything, one thing that didn't hurt to look at.

Why was her heart pounding so?

She rose from the bed. She spotted her robe folded neatly over a chair. That alone felt peculiar. She calmly walked to the chair and slipped the robe over her shoulders. She should pretend everything was normal. She would soon grow accustomed to the change. She would pretend it was just a normal day. . . .

She stepped into the dimmer light of the dressing room and nearly swooned. Immediately, the darkness acted as a security blanket, comforting and protective and familiar! Feeling a momentary relief, she was able to catch her breath.

Why was she breathing so hard?

It didn't matter. Just pretend it was a normal day.

With this understanding, she finished her toilette and though she would have loved to remain in the dark dressing room all day, she forced herself to leave.

What would make everything normal? She usually had her breakfast in the garden. Fine. It did not sound so difficult. She could do that, couldn't she?

She started toward the door. A movement flashed before her. She swung toward it. She stared in the looking glass. She stared at a strange young woman.

She froze with the shock. Blood vacated her limbs as if called to an emergency; she went numb. This could not be her! She couldn't look like this! She was much . . . larger and . . . stronger than this fragile and frightened-looking creature.

She reached a trembling hand to touch her face. The reflection shimmered like a mirage, then disappeared completely.

She stared into a room washed in blood. . . .

A scream stopped in her throat. She reached a trembling hand over the nightstand behind her. Her hand seized a vase. She threw it into the glass.

Victor woke to the shattering of the glass. He bolted up to confront the vision of his nightmare. Jade stood in front of her reflection broken into a hundred fragments. With a startled cry of anguish, she ran from the room.

"Jade!"

After giving the matter considerable thought, Mercedes had decided they should all await the momentous occasion in the garden. Jade would be seeing them for the first time. While no one knew what to expect, it seemed obvious it should take place in a lovely setting.

Seated at the breakfast table, Mercedes allowed her gaze to dance delightedly over the exotic garden. How fortunate for this lovely day! The morning held the bright promise of spring. A cloudless blue sky hung over a bathed earth that sparkled with fresh dewy moisture. Lush growth sprouted everywhere and trees and flowers waited to burst into magnificent blossom. The buds on the plum, apple and sugar gum trees looked like decorative pink and white ornaments! Marigolds of all colors, sweet peas, jasmine, violets, red crocus, scarlet bougainvilleas and begonias, each in various stages of bloom, created a luscious riot of color. It was perfect!

She squeezed Tessie's hand.

Almost perfect, she realized. Last Michaelmas Sebastian had bought Victor two peacocks affectionately named Mister and Misses. The exotic birds were a perfect touch for Victor's garden. Mister and Misses were always strutting around somewhere. Wouldn't it be just splendid if Mister could be coaxed into spreading his fine feathers for Jade?

And where were Micky and Mary, the two squirrel monkeys that also lived in the garden? Micky had been some neighbor's runaway pet, a feisty little fellow who had decided to make the garden his home. As with all animals, Jade first won Micky's favor, then one morning she had Carl take her to the market, where she bought Mary, another squirrel monkey, to keep him company. Just like the birds, Micky and Mary choose to visit only when Jade was there. Something about Jade, her patience and gentle nature, won the affection and trust of all animals, tamed or wild. . . .

"I'm as nervous as a groom on his weddin' night," Murray suddenly commented, interrupting Mercedes's eager musings and the group's harmonious silence. He shifted uncomfortably in his Sunday best clothes. "Imagine, to be seein' us for the first time." He waved his arm to the garden. "And all this for the first time."

"She will be like a small child discovering the world for the first time," Sebastian proposed fancifully.

"Aye, she'll be thrilled," Murray reasoned. "Maybe overjoyed, but I for one think a little stunned with it all. She'd have to be."

"I don't reckon she'll be surprised at all," Tessie said. "Why, she always knows everything goin' on around here!"

"I wager she shall be disappointed," Carl said. "I can't tell you how many times I have started to describe something to her and halfway through she interrupted to finish the description with her exaggerated superlatives—superlatives that spring from that rich imagination of hers." Having all experienced the phenomenon, they each smiled. "The real world is bound to seem pale compared with it."

Sebastian recognized a sudden concern in Mercedes. "Mercedes? What do you think, darling?"

Apprehension replaced Mercedes's excitement. How thoughtless they were being! Foolishly and stupidly thoughtless! They were only thinking of the miracle of Jade's seeing again! But what of the price Jade paid yesterday? They had already moved beyond it, but could she?

"We've all forgotten yesterday's horror." She paused, the whispered words filled with apprehension. "We've all forgotten her past."

Terrified witless, and filled with a frenzied desperation to escape, Jade had flown down the stairs and raced through the hall, looking into each room, searching frantically for something, anything, one thing she could look at without fear. Her eyes and mind raced in a swift continuous panic. Details flew at her like winged bats in a nightmare.

Watching from the top of the stairs, Victor saw Jade race through the hall and turn into the back corridor leading out to the garden. Not knowing what to make of it, he charged down the stairs and followed her.

Jade burst outside and stopped abruptly. Victor came up behind her and like everyone else, he remained silent to wait her response. They each straightened and forced a smile, praying, hoping against hope, that Mercedes had been wrong.

Breathless, panting, Jade stared from one face to the next. Familiar and not familiar, familiar and not familiar. Carl's skin was too light and he looked ageless, much younger than his fifty-six years. His eyes were larger because she had not felt the depth of those sockets, nor had she imagined the effect of his high Negro cheekbones or the flattened Negro nose on his face. Tessie looked too dark and much skinnier than she had imagined, too skinny. Her two pigtails stuck almost straight out, seeming at once ridiculous and bizarre. Then Murray—older, his hair looking grayer, longer, more unruly, and those kind brown eyes too small for his long, weathered face. Mercedes shocked the most; she had known Mercedes was pretty but not as beautiful as this young lady with strawberry blond curls tumbling about a pale lovely face. Dressed in a bright yellow dress, she was a young lady staring back with naked worry in her soft hazel eyes. And Sebastian! He looked familiar, very familiar, but not because she had pictured him like that. No, Sebastian looked like a romantic caricature of how she had always imagined the youngest, most handsome, of the Three Musketeers.

The silence was pained, and unable to bear another second of it, Sebastian spread his arms and grinned. "Jade, what do you think of us?"

Jade's eyes widened, her terror abruptly blatant. Victor reached a hand out to touch her, his fingers jolting her like a lightning bolt. She swung away. "No! Don't touch me! Don't ever touch me!"

"Jade!"

She backed away from him. Desperate eyes jerked from one thing to the next. The world began spinning. Everywhere she looked—a window, the table, their faces, a tree, the ground—became the background for the terror of her mind. She dropped to the ground and shielded her head as if stones were being flung at her. "Mama . . . Mama! Mama! Stop it! Stop it!" And when it didn't stop she could only scream. . . .

During the long weeks that followed, Jade discovered that the world settled only when she lay very still, closed her eyes and emptied her mind. The less interference the better. If only they understood this; if only she could explain it to them.

There were many things she'd like to say, but the thought of speaking frightened her and felt dangerous. The sound of her own voice broke the quiet she struggled so hard to find, shattering what little peace she had managed to feel.

Words had become empty and meaningless.

Wolf Dog brought one of her only comforts. Before her mind produced the vision, she could close her eyes, bury her face in his fur, and somehow the familiar feel and scent allowed a momentary escape. So, the worst time of day was when Carl came morning, noon and night to exercise Wolf Dog, and the best part of the day was when Wolf Dog returned.

Mercedes and Tessie seemed always in the room. They talked quietly between themselves, sometimes sat silently, and occasionally Mercedes read out loud. They kept trying to engage her, and unfortunately they did so frequently, repeating the same things over and over. Their remarks struck her as singularly ridiculous.

"How do you feel, Jade?"

She felt awful, couldn't they tell?

"You're looking much better!"

This felt difficult to believe. . . .

"The Reverend Mother's here again."

"Have you seen yourself today?"

No, she avoided that.

"Would you like to take a stroll?"

This forced her to shake her head. . . .

"Would you like anything?"

She wanted so very much to be left alone.

Sometimes she wanted very much to die. . . .

"The Reverend Mother's here again."

The Reverend Mother did not bother her like the others. The Reverend Mother came in the afternoons and sat with her. Jade could lay her head on the familiar lap, listening as the Reverend Mother told her about life outside this bedroom. Gentle hands stroked her hair with tenderness and love, and talk was of quiet things: her students' progress, the construction of the new orphanage, the exciting secret encounter with a group of Quakers who were trying to establish a line of the underground railroad this far south, the last letter sent to her from Madame Lucretia in Paris, a description of Monsieur Deubler's grandson's baptism.

The Reverend Mother did not understand that Jade did not care about these subjects, but that did not matter. For somehow the quiet familiar voice of the Reverend Mother was a comfort. It was the loving voice that had carried her through the desperate and sad days after her parents' deaths, and it was a voice connected to Church and God and blindness. The Reverend Mother never expected her to speak. She alone seemed to understand that words did not work anymore, that words did not matter.

Jade refused to eat, though three times a day Murray forced her to drink a glass of milk with an egg, lard and molasses mixed in it. Murray always sat on the bed to tell her she was getting better—and soon, he kept promising, she'd be over the shock of it.

She would like to believe him. Could he find a cure for seeing her mother hanging upside down with her throat slit? Probably not.

If Murray admitted there was no cure, maybe he'd stop making her drink the liquid that kept her alive. The idea of shrinking, of getting smaller and smaller, thinner and thinner, until finally nothing remained seemed not at all unpleasant. Did he know that?

Victor made her the most uncomfortable. It was hard not to panic when he drew near. She stared at his arms and remembered how he had held, trapped and forced her; she remembered how hard she had struggled and fought, how she had begged and cried. Did he remember that day, too?

She watched him cautiously, suspiciously, as he sat on the bed or sometimes even lay down on it to talk to her. He always told her how his day was going. He didn't seem to understand she did not care. Then he asked the same stupid questions: "When are you going to get better for me?" She had no idea, though she felt certain that if she did get better, it would not be for him. "Why won't you talk? Can't you say anything, sweetheart?" She didn't want to say anything, and to tell him that would be to say something. Talking interrupted her hard fight for peace. What was the point anyway? Talking hadn't worked that day, why would it work now? "What are you thinking, sweetheart?" She actually thought very little. That was the whole point, didn't he understand that? Didn't he know, or couldn't he guess, that when she thought at all it was so unpleasant that—

If she wasn't so afraid of him now, she would have liked to ask him some questions. He seemed caring and kind now, gentle and concerned, sympathetic and compassionate. Why was he like this now when she neither needed nor wanted it? Where were these qualities the day she needed them more than the air she took into her lungs? The day she had begged him to stop killing her?

There were things she might tell him, too. She didn't want him to touch her anymore, or to sleep with her anymore, and she especially didn't like it when he gathered her into his arms and pressed his body against hers. He must know that. The first time she felt that hard hot part of him, she had known fear. When she tried to move he had held her to him. "Come now, sweetheart, I'm not going to hurt you. I know you're not well enough yet to make love. I just want to hold you, that's all." She did not want to be held, but to tell him required more energy than the suffering.

If only he'd leave her alone . . .

The Reverend Mother's grief felt profound, palatable, as if she alone understood the terror and anguish that Jade now had to live with, and she did, she did. For it was her own as well. The sun streamed through the balcony windows as she sat on the bed this day, watching as Mercedes slowly shut the door, leaving them alone. Jade shifted ever so slightly, so that her head lay upon the smooth black cotton of the Reverend Mother's habit. She closed her eyes, drawing in the familiar scent of oil and ink, succumbing at once to the tenderness of the weathered hands combing back her hair. The silence told Jade the Reverend Mother finally understood completely that she could no longer care about the roses or the collection or the new church music.

The Reverend Mother did understand, and the realization caused the stone fortress that was her strength to crumble. In a whisper she said, "I killed her, you know."

Jade nodded ever so slightly. She did know. She remembered now the day the Reverend Mother told her she died. It was as if she had known then. But of course she hadn't. . . .

"After. Weeks later. We met on the levee. It was dark and late and so quiet. Only the rush of water. I begged her to confess. She pretended not to understand me. Then she laughed at me and even more than the profanity of that sound, 'twas her eyes. I couldn't bear the utter emptiness of her eyes . . . as if God had long ago left her. When my hands squeezed the breath from her, it felt like nothing. Like nothing. It seems so strange to me now. As if it hadn't happened. And after I pushed her body into the river and dropped to my knees to pray to God for forgiveness, I felt like I was pretending. I only went through the motions of asking God's forgiveness because I knew God didn't care. . . ."

Jade shut her eyes tightly.

The Reverend Mother was crying now.

Tears for her; tears for her mother. . . .

Each night after supper Victor left to visit the one person he always sought when he was troubled and unable to see his way through a situation. Weeks after what Murray termed Jade's breakdown, and for the sixth night in a row, he arrived at the spacious thatched-roof cottage nestled in a grove of live oaks on the outskirts of town.

Manny, his father's only servant, showed him through the neat and noticeably bare rooms to the back patio. Victor assumed a seat at the table beneath a thatched awning. On the table sat a chessboard—a game that had always been between him and his father—along with two glasses and a bottle of port. Once again he had to wait for his father—the only person he had ever known who was busier than himself.

Insects flew around the lamps. The long chirping of crickets became the backdrop for his unpleasant thoughts. He was afraid. He was afraid he was losing her, that in fact he had lost her. . . .

The nights were the worst. She woke up screaming two and three times before dawn. Dear Lord, if only he could save her from the nightmare of the door opening to a room washed in blood. . . .

Victor glanced up at the sound of his father's approach. His father wore priest's robes only in church. All other times one found him in a tailored black suit and usually with the coat discarded and the sleeves of his shirt rolled up over strong, tanned forearms. The Church forgave—or rather, overlooked—his unconventionalities, for his work spoke well for him and the Church.

The handsome older man assumed the wicker chair across from Victor with only a nod of acknowledgment passing between them. Victor's gaze rested on a mirror image of himself—separated by only the twenty years' difference in their ages. They both shared the same sharp features: the bushy arch of brows, the dark blue eyes, large nose and generous mouths, though his father's hair was graying at the sides, something that only added to his distinguished features. He tilted his pipe, one of his few indulgences, and first opened the game. "Jade?"

"The same." Victor shook his head. "It's been almost three weeks now and I'm . . . I'm—"

"Afraid she has truly lost her wits?"

Victor nodded, his gaze solemn and filled with this fear. "She still hasn't spoken and she won't eat, but the worst is her eyes, those beautiful eyes. The pain there . . ." He sighed. "The only things that seem to bring her comfort are her dog and, somehow, I think, the Reverend Mother."

"Victor," his father said kindly, "you want to attack the problem head-on, as a panther pounces its prey. The point is that Jade has every reason to act as she has been and no reason to change. It is true that she is suffering from shock; I suppose she is rather like a soldier suffering from battle fatigue. Blindness protected her from that tragic truth for many years until you forced her to see it."

"I know all that," Victor protested impatiently. "I also know that you know something I don't. I'm not going to lose her." Quietly, in a plea: "I need your help."

Unmasked admiration showed in his father's gaze as he considered his son. "It's your willfulness, Victor, this restless impatience with the world, that prevents you from fully grasping what has happened. It all makes perfect sense when you consider Jade and the startling uniqueness of her person.

"You know, I could not have imagined a daughter-in-law whom I might receive with more affection than Jade Terese. There is no other woman I'd be happier to see you marry, and in many ways I consider it a perfect match. The one sense in which I thought you two ill suited is that Jade's startling innocence is often at odds with you and your world. Of course, the trouble is that Jade's innocence is at odds with anyone's world." He paused, drew on his pipe and smiled. "Do you know what one of the Sisters used to say about Jade?"

"Let me guess. Probably something about Jade's not realizing we fell from grace."

"She said Jade was like Eve before the bite of the forbidden fruit—that Jade had been born without original sin. We were all aware of it here and it caused almost everyone to embrace Jade with abject fondness.

"Jade could never bear any ill—social or otherwise. I don't believe she has ever felt any ill feeling for anyone or anything. But, Victor"—he paused gravely—"you've changed all that. You've opened her eyes literally and figuratively. I daresay she will never be the same. No, let me finish," he added quickly, stopping Victor's protest before it was uttered. "You did what anyone would, I know. Jade will eventually emerge from this a stronger person. Reality will no longer slap her in the face, so to speak. But, Victor, your battle—or rather, her battle—is far from over. It has, in fact, just begun. In the same way her blindness protected her, she is attempting to protect herself now by withdrawing from life. She could never bear any animosity, and she still can't. Presently she is desperately trying to protect herself from feelings that she can't stand to own."

"You mean her mother's death?"

"Certainly the terror is part of it. But there's more, Victor, much more. I saw it the first time I visited after it happened. Frankly, I was shocked, and only after some reflection could I come to understand it." A subtle light flickered in the dark eyes as he reached the most difficult point. "Surely you must have seen it, Victor? You must have recognized it in those lovely eyes of hers when she looks at you?"

Victor held his father steady in his gaze until suddenly he understood. He had seen it, though until this moment he had failed to grasp what it meant. While a majority of the time, Jade's eyes, her expression and manner, showed only that disturbing emptiness or unspeakable pain, every once in a while her eyes flashed with a fierce emotion before disappearing beneath closed lids.

Victor looked away and began to speak almost apologetically. "I don't think I've ever done anything that would shock you—"

"Don't be so sure about that."

"In any case, that day would have shocked you. I was . . . brutal, and God knows, I did hurt her badly. Repeatedly. But I've gone over it in my mind, looking for a way I might have made it easier for her, less painful or terrifying and—"

"Your conscience is clear," the elder man finished. "You did what you had to, I know."

"She has every right to be angry." Victor looked directly at his father. "But she's still not getting any better."

"Why should she?"

"What do you mean?"

"Well, now that you understand what she's trying to hide from, I feel at liberty to discuss the matter in which you and yours are treating her. You are allowing her to withdraw, tiptoeing around her as though she is an invalid, as though she has truly lost her wits!"

"I had assumed she needs rest and peace."

"Victor, you don't grasp quite how dangerous the situation is. Don't you see the mistake in letting her hide from life? Then you do run a risk of losing her completely."

"What do you suggest?"

"You tell me. What would you take as the sign of her gaining health?"

"Anything! If she began eating again, coming to dinner, talking, going for walks, anything!"

"Obviously, she's not willing to do these things."

It was a loaded statement, and one that Victor understood only too well. He swallowed the last of the port, as though to help him face the unpleasant fact. "I should force her."

"I know that after what you've been through, you want only to win back her affection and trust, but I'm afraid right now she needs your strength even more than your love." He leaned forward and said solemnly, "Of course, you know she is getting better when she finally asks who did this hideous thing."

"Yes," Victor said. "I am ready for it."

Joanie and Agnes, each carrying a brass pail of hot water, followed Tessie into the bedchamber. The two women smiled at Jade, nodded, and went about preparing the bath.

Jade turned away as they left. It was curious to see the faces of the two maids whom she knew so well. Joanie, the upstairs maid, who also helped in the kitchen, and her younger sister, Agnes the downstairs maid; both women were dark and plump, with smooth skin, dark luminous eyes and wide white grins.

Mercedes cast an anxious look at Tessie and pleaded,

"Please, Jade Terese?" Victor had said to insist and be firm, that if they failed, he was to be called up. "I promise you'll feel better."

Jade lifted her face from Wolf Dog's fur and stared at her two friends before shaking her head. She didn't want a bath, and really what did it matter if her hair were dirty? Once upon a time she went out of her way to see that such an awful fate never happened. It no longer bothered her at all. Unfortunately, Mercedes and Tessie seemed quite upset over it.

"Jade Terese, you just must!" Mercedes abruptly threatened. "We won't leave you alone until you do."

Jade looked at them with distrust, her suspicions aroused by Mercedes's anxious tone and threat. They really weren't going to leave her be. Something had changed. What?

She struggled for a moment to comprehend their motive, but it was too difficult to think. She shrugged, reluctantly submitting to the bath only because submission was easier than protest.

Mercedes and Tessie exchanged smiles as she stepped over to the shiny brass tub, discarded her robe and sank into the hot lavender-scented water. She closed her eyes and suffered not one unpleasant thought as Tessie's familiar hands gently worked her hair with the thick lather, rinsed it and then applied the sweet-scented oil to soften the long locks.

Once her bath was done, Jade threw herself on the bed, feeling suddenly confused, very confused. The bath had made her feel better. Oh, why, if she felt better, did that make her frightened? It didn't make sense. Yet it was true. . . .

She sought the comfort of withdrawal, the quite peace of solitude. But it eluded her, and the harder she tried to calm herself, the more panicked she became. Panicked, frightened, confused! What was happening to her?

Victor's footsteps sounded on the stairs. Wolf Dog thumped his tail, casting his gaze toward the door. She shot a betrayed look at her dog for this small show of his affection and suppressed an urge to scold him for it.

Victor entered the room. She lifted her attention to him and stiffened as she felt a sudden and intense surge of fury and resentment that came like a floodgate opening. She resented everything about him: his looks, his height, his strength, the way he moved with such damnable ease and confidence in the world, her world, and even the way he walked. She resented his clothes: the tight black breeches, his tailored white silk shirt and the black boots that made him even taller. The intensity of the emotion scared her, and she lowered her eyes.

Victor stepped over to the bed. A hand came under her chin, lifting her face back up. "Is there something you'd like to say to me, sweetheart?"

She could not look at him. Emotions stirred, welled, cresting as she felt herself grow hot beneath his scrutiny. Her lips pressed to a hard line. She shook her head.

"That's strange, I could have sworn that look precipitated words. Well . . ." He shrugged indifferently. "No matter. I have a few things to say to you. Come, I want you to sit up."

The fierce struggle to control the avalanche of emotions coursing through her left no room to object to the hand on her arm, guiding her up and to a chair. Victor strolled to the mantel and paused briefly as he considered her. "Last night I visited my father. As a matter of fact, I've been visiting him all week after you've gone to sleep. As you know, it's my father's nature to listen passively, to guide people to their own conclusions, understanding, solutions and so forth, but last night—either owing to his expansive mood or my desperation—he helped me understand what's happening to you better. He made me see that you're not getting any better, and that in fact it's dangerous to allow you this solitude—your withdrawal, if you will.

"I have to agree," he continued, ignoring the anxious gaze that just shot up to him. "And I'm afraid I'm going to insist on a few changes. I know you want to be left alone but I'm not going to ask for very much. I want you to start dressing and joining us at the table for supper, and I want you to start taking walks during the day."

Jade shook her head.

Victor stepped quickly to her chair and leaned over. "That's another thing, Jade. No more nodding or shaking your head. From now on you're to answer me yes or no."

"No!"

Victor smiled at his triumph. "Yes," he corrected.

"No, I won't! I don't want to! I can't!"

"Yes you will, Jade." The infuriating calm of his voice felt far more upsetting than his words. "If I have to dress you myself and carry you to the table, I will." He watched her comprehend the threat. Tears formed in her eyes, glistening like gems caught in sunlight. For a moment he was transfixed. Her lips trembled slightly with the effort to suppress words, all the unspoken words.

She remained silent.

He turned to leave. "Dinner is in an hour."

Anger, that pure and liberating emotion, welled inside her. Like a violent surge it brought her to her feet and burst into sudden words. "I loved you! I trusted you! And you did this to me. You hurt me, you—" She spun around, unable to look at him as she tried to put words to this sudden torrent of emotions. "Do you have any idea of what you've done to me? Of how badly you hurt me? Did you ever think of me at all?"

"Did I ever think of you at all? Oh, aye, I thought of you. Dear God, girl, only a hundred times a day. The mixed curse and blessing loving you had become! Loving you more every cherished day and being terrified, terrified of what that might someday mean. I'd look out the window at work and I'd see Tessie or Carl running up and I'd suddenly be gripping the table to stop the shake of my hands. My hands, Jade! Shaking like an autumn leaf in the wind, so scared I was, so certain you'd had another accident, that you were lying unconscious or worse. Or worse!"

Her face tightened with anger, her fists clenched in the folds of her robe. Those accidents, all those stupid accidents, that's all he ever thought about. He couldn't stand not being in control, not being able to bend reality to his will. And for that, he had done this to her.

"This precious gift of sight has come at such a cost. My sanity, I have lost my sanity! A thing far more precious than food or shelter, the very breath one draws in one's body, and this precious thing is replaced by a madness that makes me live in terror. I live in a nightmare without end. I can't think anymore. I can't eat or sleep. I have fantasies of melting, melting away to nothing. I have fantasies of the mercy of death—"

The last statement drew a sharp gasp. "Jade, no. Dear God—"

"My only comfort is when I close my eyes, and still all of a sudden my heart and breath will start racing and I'll see her, my mother. Victor, I see my mother everywhere. . . ."

"Jade," he said, gently now. "Jade, this terrible scene of your parents' murder is a shocking horror. All that has happened to you will take time to assimilate—"

"Really?" She turned back to face him. "How I pray this is so. That in time I will . . . assimilate the picture of my mother and father washed in blood, though 'tis very hard for me to guess how it is possible to assimilate this terror into the daily pictures of our happy domestic life, how to set that scene alongside the flowers blooming in the garden, our friends gathered at the table, the pictures in the gallery. But perhaps you are right. Perhaps in time my sanity will return."

She turned away again as the worthless words cost her much. A hand went to her mouth as if to stop the torrent of emotion. He started toward her but she spun around, her arm shooting out to stop him. "No." She shook her head. "Oh no. Don't touch me."

For a long moment she stood there staring at him, her beautiful eyes shimmering with tears. "That day," she said in a whisper of words, her voice filled with a haunting sadness, "that day as I was lying on the bed, waiting like a chained pig for the slaughter, waiting for your torment and the pain, I must have fallen asleep and I had a dream. In this dream I was standing in a dark room. There was the most lovely symbol there. It was a huge ball of transparent light. Rainbow light. Rainbow shots flew off it. It was the most beautiful thing I had ever seen. . . .

"Then you appeared in this dream. You had a . . . a club in your hands. You raised your arms and struck it . . . and, and . . . it shattered in a thousand pieces. . . .

"So now I've lost my sanity. And even if my sanity returns someday, and in time I learn how to look at the world without it changing into a room of terror, even then I will suffer the loss of the one thing, the only thing in the world, more blessed to me. Because you see . . . that magical ball of rainbow light was . . . Victor," she whispered as the tears gathered in her throat, "it was my love for you. . . ."

The handsome face changed with the pain of these words, and she could not bear seeing it. She swung around and did not see his fist clenched with the effort he put to stopping himself from going to her. She heard the boots turn softly toward the door. The door open and shut. A wordless good-bye. For no words could make that magical symbol whole again.

Chapter 14

The bedroom was dark when Victor finally entered and found Jade sound asleep in the bed. One lamp threw soft light into the chamber. She was curled up at the very edge of the mattress, some unconscious display of her animosity and alienation.

He stepped to the side of the bed and knelt by her face. A troubled expression sat on her lovely features, even in her sleep. His hand gently brushed back a long wisp of her hair and he could only wonder at how beautiful she was. He could only wonder at how desperately he wanted to love her again.

The extent and desperation of her struggle alarmed him, alarmed them all. She still would not speak to him and rarely spoke to others. He insisted she go on walks but someone always had to be with her. She suffered from random fears, an indescribable affliction where the world suddenly raced at her as if it were attacking her. At the end, the sight of the room washed in blood emerged, leaving her trembling and shaken. One never knew when it would happen.

This afternoon his father sent word that yellow fever had broken out in his parish. They had no choice but to close the house and leave for the country. Jade was not well enough to travel and had been visibly frightened when he told her of it, but they had to go. She, with her frailty and weight loss, would be particularly vulnerable to the fatal disease. . . .

Despair hit him where he knelt, staring down at her. He stood up and turned quickly away. Within minutes he was undressed and lying against the pillows. She started tossing and turning in her sleep. As the minutes ticked by, before the next bell had sounded, she was pressed against him, wrapped securely in his arms. It was only this curious sleeping progression from the edge of the bed into his arms that brought him hope. Hope that in time he would know how to mend the light to make that magic ball. . . .

With the maddening tease of her scent, the soft curves of her slender form pressed seductively against his hard hot body, they slept and he suffered. Suffered from the effects of a thousand erotic memories playing through his dreams. He was filled with lust. He was dreaming of the sweet lavender scent surrounding him, those lips beneath his, her body warm and soft and maddening as he parted her thighs and slipped into a mercy—

She screamed loud and long, she screamed as the door slowly opened and a thirteen-year-old girl stared into a room washed in blood.

The new day had begun. . . .

"Everyone's leaving," Tessie whispered as the carriage moved through the still-dark streets. As the carriage passed through the wealthy American district, servants were seen busily stuffing trunks and boxes into carriages. Anyone who could leave the city was going—within days the streets would be empty, the market closed.

Jade kept her head on Tessie's lap, her eyes closed against the world and its constant bombardment of details, fighting the panic threatening to engulf her. It would be over soon, she tried to tell herself. She had made the trip dozens of times. Dozens—

The reassurances crumbled beneath the escalating pace of her heart. Yet they had to go and she had to go with them. Yellow fever, like the bubonic plague of years ago, could rush through the city and take thousands of people to their graves. Deaths that separated mothers from children, husbands from wives, friend from friend.

The Reverend Mother suddenly emerged in her mind. . . .

The Reverend Mother had lived through countless yellow fever scares. Countless. She'd make it through this one—

A chill washed over her, frightening in its intensity. Jade never knew how she knew, but she did. As if it were a fact.

She slowly sat up. "Victor!"

Victor looked back into the carriage where Jade sat. "Yes?"

"I want to see the Reverend Mother before we leave. Please, may we stop at church?"

He could hardly refuse. "She would be still sleeping—"

"No. She always rises before the dawn. She'll be at church for morning prayers."

She kept her head on Tessie's lap as they turned down Rampart Street to the church, not daring to look yet, though one could see little of the city when passing through at night: only shadows lit by the dim light of the two night lanterns swinging on each side of the carriage. Sebastian and Victor rode alongside the carriage, Carl drove, while Mercedes slept with her head on Murray's lap, in the seat across from Tessie and Jade. Wolf Dog slept on the floor.

The carriage stopped and Jade sat up. Victor swung down to help her descend. "Shall I go with you?"

Jade shook her head as Tessie withdrew a modest cotton scarf from the traveling bag and handed it to her. Jade tied it neatly under her chin, the white of her pale skin nearly the same color as the cloth. They watched as she rushed quickly up the path and through the doors, swallowed up by the morning quiet and darkness of the vestry.

An inviting warmth greeted her in the vestibule. She stared into the huge hallowed darkness and understood the sanctuary of the church more than at any time in her life. Candles lit the tabernacle of the main altar far down the aisle, where she saw the lone figure kneeling in prayer.

She quickly dipped her fingers in the holy water, genuflected, and stepped quietly down the empty aisle, her eyes adjusting to the light. But she stopped as details of the familiar space flew at her: the darker color of the wooden pews, the old worn tiles of the floor, the impressive height and architectural design of the ceiling. How strange. She saw that it was different from the picture she had held throughout her blindness, and seeing it now sparked the memory of it that predated the accident. Memories of her mother floated through her consciousness: the day of her first communion, when her mother had come to church. . . .

She was suddenly breathing hard and fast. The statue of Christ hanging on the cross above the altar drew a small inaudible gasp from her. She closed her eyes tightly against the assault, swallowing her panic as a shudder passed through her like a violent caress. It was just the church, just a statue. She forced herself to proceed, more slowly, careful to keep her gaze focused on her small boots as she went.

"Reverend Mother . . ."

The older woman turned and beheld Terese. She wore traveling clothes, a plain green skirt and blouse, looking, dear Lord, so painfully frail and thin. The lovely ivory of her skin gleamed in the dim light and appeared translucent, its paleness accented by the bright flush on her cheeks and the feverish intensity of her eyes.

"Terese . . ."

She did not seem surprised to find her here in the predawn darkness. They approached each other, one's hands reaching to clasp the other's. They kissed on each cheek as the Reverend Mother searched Jade's eyes, eyes filled with inexpressible sadness and anxiety.

"I came to say . . . good-bye."

That was all she said and yet it was so much. Time seemed to stretch as meaning passed between them without words. The Reverend Mother closed her eyes for a moment, not realizing she clasped Jade's hands even tighter, not even aware that they still held hands.

"Yellow fever?"

She opened her eyes to watch Jade nod, slowly, her eyes bright with sorrow and anguish. Jade said, "And we are leaving now. . . ."

She was leaving. The Reverend Mother closed her eyes and withdrew her hand, reaching with it into the folds of her habit until she found the tiny statuette. She clasped it tightly, letting the blessing of her faith wash over her and sooth the pain of this good-bye.

"Here, I have something for you." She pressed the small statuette into Jade's hand. "A parting gift."

Jade's gaze lowered to the token she now held in her outstretched open palm, and when she saw it, her vision blurred. She had held it many times before, feeling its smooth lines as she contemplated the small miracle of Mary's appearing to an African savage from the dark continent, where no Christian walked. She had always imagined it to be beautiful, and so it was, but disconcertingly, it was far more beautiful than she had imagined. The revelation was carved into the tiny features staring back at her.

She wiped at her eyes, peering closer. "Oh, look," she whispered. "It has a tiny scratch. . . ."

"It's always been there."

"I never saw it before."

The tiny scratch was nearly worn smooth by the touch of the Reverend Mother's hand, and Jade closed her own hand around it. She looked back at the Reverend Mother. "I'll treasure it always. . . ." Her lip trembled with emotion. She caught it with her teeth, trying to tell herself it wasn't so, that this would not be the last time she'd see the old woman she loved, and yet—

"I shall miss you, Terese. . . ."

The emotions swelled as Jade shook her head. "I don't want to part from you now! I need you—" She fell into the older woman's arms, clinging to her as if it was the last time she ever would.

"The parting is not forever, Terese."

These were whispered words of faith, faith in the reuniting of all love under God. Jade nodded slowly. "I love you." She mouthed the words because she no longer had a voice. Victor stepped into the still, dark church and Jade heard his boots. She shut her eyes tightly and forced herself to move away from the Reverend Mother. She clutched the small treasure tightly, cast one last look at the older woman, who had turned toward the cross to hide her own tears . . .

"Oh, Jade," Tessie beckoned in a whisper as the carriage passed on to the country road, "you gotta look, just for a spell. The day's a-gonna start as pretty as it ever has."

She sat up, slowly. The sadness of the good-bye had passed through her, leaving her curiously numb and exhausted. Tessie's smile was filled with youthful levity and enthusiasm, the only way she knew to answer Jade's sadness. Refusing to let her withdraw again, she snatched Jade's pale hand in hers, pointing to the dawn's light breaking with a magnificent sunrise.

The sun slowly rose into a patchy blue sky broken by gray cotton clouds. It was just a dawn, an event that had occurred all over the earth every day for millions upon millions of years, and yet it was the first one she had witnessed in eight long years. It was not pleasurable. The colors were sharp, almost too painful to view. One hand went to her forehead to shield her eyes from the assault of changing light and shapes. She stared at a tree, a simple tree, one of the most common shapes on earth, and yet it took a full moment to know what it was she stared at. A small shock would pass on the heels of this queer delay.

The most ordinary sights struck her as bizarre or obscene: the way Murray's brows motioned like hands as he talked, the trickle of juice running down Tessie's face as she bit into an apple, the excessive love on Mercedes's face every time Sebastian drew near to inquire how they were doing. Even swatting at a bothersome fly felt singularly peculiar, jolting her with that sense of familiar and not . . .

She remained unaware of someone who watched her so closely. Victor's eyes rarely left her person as he, too, was living his most precious dream. Jade was blind no more, and—dear Lord—he felt like singing his joy for all the world. . . .

In mounting discomfort she tried to fix her gaze on the steady movement of the horses' legs, but they blurred suddenly. She rubbed her eyes.

Mercedes watched this with alarm. Jade rubbed too hard. She reached across to catch Jade's hands in her own and gently draw them away. "Jade, darling, look at the pretty bluebells there."

A trapper's shack sat at the edge of a clearing. Surrounded by trees, a carpet of flowers spread out, the velvet blue petals opening to the warmth of the sun. Tiny white moths fluttered in the sunlight. She stared at the enchanting picture and—

Her heart started pounding. Harder and faster as her chest constricted. She was suddenly sucking in air, her breath choking her as trees, moss-laden branches, bluebells, the very sky, rushed at her. Her eyes widened to accommodate the terrifying bombardment of details, a thousand too many of them, and just as she felt faint, it stopped and she was staring into the room washed in blood.

Tears filled her eyes and she was shaking, unaware of the skinny brown arm holding her tightly, Murray shouting for Victor, Mercedes's alarmed cry.

Gloved hands fitted under her arms, lifting her quickly up and over a saddle. Victor held her tightly against his chest. "Easy does it, sweetheart. . . . Take deep breaths, that's it. It's all right now . . . I've got you. . . ."

Then it was gone. She gradually calmed down and looked over the settled landscape. She watched it wearily with mistrust, afraid it would start flying at her again. Then she closed her eyes and gathered her strength to part from him.

"I'm fine. . . . Please . . ."

He did not want to release her. Like a hunger it was, the need to hold her, different from desire, and almost as strong. "Are you sure?"

She nodded curtly.

"Perhaps I should just keep you—"

Fringed in wet black lashes, the green eyes shot up to him, her expression a piercing blow. He set her back in the carriage seat. The unspoken agreement. She let him comfort her only during an attack, only during the dark dead of night when consciousness and will disappeared in sleep.

Carl started the horses off again. Murray attempted to get Jade interested in a chess game, but she did not feel up to it. Mercedes, thinking she could not resist, withdrew a picture book from her bag. It was a gold and leather-bound book of Russian fairy tales, and although it was written in Russian, the pictures were astonishingly beautiful exercises of fanciful imagination. It had been Sebastian's Christmas present. Jade just shook her head and turned away.

Only she wasn't gazing at the passing scenery. Her heated gaze rested on Victor, riding ahead with Sebastian. She could not explain it to herself and did not try. She felt powerless to turn her gaze from him, as if the violence of her emotions demanded the visual source.

Murray was watching Jade intently, shocked by what he saw. Despite Father Nolte's belief on the matter, that she was not mad, it was there. Brief flashes of pure madness in those furious green eyes, flashes that were as unmistakable and plain as day. She was not well, not even close. . . .

Jade withdrew as the carriage moved on. She laid her head on Tessie's lap and kept one trembling hand on Wolf Dog, her eyes closed to the world.

The sun crested the meridian when the carriage reached the familiar rest stop. She heard Mercedes cry out: "Why, look who's here! 'Tis the Booraems!"

The carriage had passed a few other parties along the way, families leaving the city to escape the same yellow fever threat. Anyone who had a country estate and could leave the city was doing so without delay. The Borraems' country estate was about four miles away, and their party had just stopped at a small pond to enjoy a meal before continuing on their way.

Forced to remain in the city for a week, Monsieur Booraem was not accompanying his wife, Helena. Craig Booraem was an older gent from one of Baton Rouge's more wealthy German families. He had tripled an already sizable fortune within a very short time in the New World. Victor had said Monsieur Booraem was one of the wealthiest men in the city, and had the distinction of being one of the few men Victor hated to meet in a business deal.

Jade and Mercedes were both immensely fond of Helena Booraem. She had won Jade's unconditional regard when Victor told her what he knew of Helena's efforts to silence an unnamed gossip concerning Mercedes's history. Apparently, shortly after Mercedes had married Sebastian, at a dinner party they had not attended, someone at Helena's table was about to share what she knew of Mercedes's past. Helena had stopped the other woman before a word had been uttered, and without anyone the wiser, had made it perfectly clear that such malicious gossip was an affront she would not tolerate.

Curious to meet Helena, Jade sat up and peered over Mercedes's head to catch her first glimpse of this good woman. Victor had already dismounted. He stood alongside his huge black gelding, one arm resting casually on his saddle while he talked amicably with someone who could only be Helena.

For several moments as the carriage drew to the spot, Jade watched the woman answer the dark blue gaze with smiles and laughter. The sight was like a hot dagger piercing her heart.

The carriage jolted to a stop. A warm breeze blew through the trees, shifting the afternoon light over the thick carpet of needles. People descended; greetings were exchanged. Jade stood still and ghostlike, unable to tear her startled gaze from Helena.

Jade had expected her to be beautiful, for something about the story of her warmth had suggested that she was pretty. Mercedes had affirmed that idea with detailed descriptions of the dark-haired Creole's beauty. So Jade was not surprised to find Helena admirably proportioned, her shiny dark curls cascading about her shoulders, slightly disheveled from the day's travel. What shocked her was the understanding her sight brought her from one brief glimpse of Helena talking to Victor.

They had once been lovers.

Mercedes had already fallen into Helena's warm embrace. Victor helped Jade descend but she could not hear the women's exclamations over the pounding in her temples. Helena had turned to her, taking her hands. "Jade Terese, I cannot believe the good news! You can see! Everyone is talking about it! Oh, we wanted so to visit you! And now, *mon dieu,* this is the first time you've ever seen me!"

Jade stared aghast, frightened by the woman's hypocrisy. She could not speak. Her mind suddenly teeter-tottered: Helena's lustrous curls, her own dark hair loosely and unattractively contained in a thick knot at the nape of her neck; Helena's warm smile, her quivering lips; Helena's pretty traveling clothes, her own ugly muslin skirt and plain white cotton shirt; Helena's voluptuous sweeps and curves, her own frail frame.

She snatched her hands away and unconsciously grabbed a handful of her skirt, while her other trembling hand nervously pushed loose hairs from her face. Terrified, she was unaware that everyone had stopped talking, that everyone was watching tears fill her eyes. She felt Victor's arm come around her shoulders; she heard him pronounce her name with a question mark.

She twisted from his arms and began backing away. She turned and ran. The world flew past her; trees and spindly branches, the dark of the land thickly covered with wild scratching ferns, flying, all of it flying and then spinning, needles and twigs cutting her bare feet, fire leaping in her lungs, and still she ran.

Victor suffered a few moments of stunned incomprehension before taking pursuit. She had a considerable lead. Her panic and fear produced unnatural speed. Had he not been directed by Wolf Dog's barks he might have lost her completely. He finally caught sight of her disappearing through the trees ahead of him.

Jade screamed as the unmercifully strong arms grabbed her from behind and put a harsh brake to her flight. He lifted her off the ground while her arms and legs still fought wildly to escape.

"Slow down," he demanded. "Just slow down."

She collapsed all at once, and they both fell to the ground.

"My God, Jade! What's wrong?"

"It hurts!" she cried. "Everything I see hurts to look at! I want to die. . . . I just want to die."

And then, dear Lord, he watched as her hands went to her eyes, rubbing, rubbing too hard. He caught her hands and held them protectively in one of his own. "Let me help you, Jade," he whispered. "Stop pushing away from me and let me love you again."

The words crashed through the tumult of her fragmented thoughts, and she stiffened, at once pulling away. "No! Never! You hurt me most of all!"

Victor didn't stop her as she leaped to her feet and disappeared quickly through the trees. He laid back against the ground, stared up at the patch of blue sky he could see through the branches, and for a while he didn't know what to do, didn't know what he felt. Several minutes passed before his thoughts settled.

A conviction first rose above all feelings. He would win this war with her. If it took a month, two months or a year, he would win. He would live to see the day her health and love returned.

That love, Jade's love—how it had captured him so

completely, so quickly! It was a mild shock to realize that not so very long ago his eyes had first settled on the beautiful young lady seated in the theater. The time was a curious reference point, for at any given moment he could conjure a thousand different pictures of Jade, of their life together.

Memories drifted through his mind, each marked by an abundance of laughter and playfulness and joy, many marked by a darkly erotic passion that lit his body and soul with undying hunger. And as he stared unseeing at the darkening sky, he remembered lying on the bed with a book, waiting for her, as she emerged from the dressing room in one of her nightdresses. It was made of transparent silk, and in the light, every ounce of her slender figure had been revealed for his pleasure. She'd slipped onto the bed, resting on her hands and knees. Her hair slid over her shoulders, partially hiding her form. A thoughtful expression sat on her face as she gently touched his cheek to know if he smiled or not, and unable to discern his mood, she had asked, "What are you thinking about?"

"I do not want to upset you."

"Tell me. My imagination will make it far worse than it ever could be in fact."

"Very well. I was thinking of . . . my ghostly lover."

She had looked shocked. "An imaginary lover?"

"Aye."

"Someone you fantasize about?"

"Aye."

"And what does this imaginary lover do that your flesh-and-blood wife does not?"

A low chuckle had sounded as he considered her. "She lives for my pleasure."

"I live for your pleasure. . . ."

"She answers my every command without thought or question past pleasing me with her obedience."

Her breath had caught; her eyes had sparkled. "I, too, answer your every command with neither thought nor question. . . ."

"Oh?" He had chuckled again. "I think my wife is too young, still too innocent for the part. . . ."

"No," she had whispered. "I will prove it now. . . ."

The erotic memory heated his blood; his pulse quickened as he lay on the forest floor. He could not count the ways in which she had proved it, over and over. In a similar way that theology had transformed his father's life, Jade had transformed his. After all he had been through in life, all he had experienced and all he had hoped for, he had suddenly found an exciting and unexpected new meaning in existence. Things seemed suddenly to matter more, to be more important to him. The change in him was not reflected in his appearance, and perhaps the only people who recognized it were his father, Murray and Sebastian. He did not even recognize it until . . . until when?

That day Jade came to him with the news that she carried his child. He had thought little of children before then, and he supposed if he had thought at all about them, he considered them inevitable, and if they ever happened, merely a pleasant addition to life. But oh how that changed with Jade. Suddenly he had not wanted one child; he wanted a dozen of them and not a soul less. He wanted to see that smile on Jade's face permanently; he wanted that flawless figure plump and forever changed, marked by their love. . . .

He felt a sudden sadness he recognized as longing. Longing for her smile and laughter, the bounty of the love she had brought to him, the feel of the soft slender curves against his flesh as he tasted her mouth. . . .

Daylight receded slowly, bit by bit, absorbed and drained by a darkening violet sky. Twilight and its quiet stillness settled onto the land. His body abruptly tensed; his senses stood aware of something. Like an animal alerted to danger. His gaze darted around the small clearing as the words sounded in his mind: "I beg you, Monsieur, you will destroy her, you might kill her . . . kill her . . ." Then Jade's pained declaration: "I want to die! I just want to die. . . ."

He never knew how he knew but the knowledge came as a sharp physical jolt, an unimaginable fear. With Jade's name on his lips, he was instantly on his feet, running.

She stood at the edge of a steep cliff carved by the small tributary below, looking down forty or so deadly feet to the swift-moving river water rushing over smooth, clean rocks. There was no question she wanted to. Leaning precariously forward, she waited only for the necessary moment of courage.

She remembered a Jade who had valued human life above all other things, her own life included. Where was that Jade who embraced life with open arms with all her heart and soul? She had died; she was nothing more than a receding memory. . . .

How curious that the dead Jade would have felt such shame at reaching the edge of a cliff. Taking life was an unpardonable sin—the greatest crime—and taking one's own life, unconscionable. For she had been blessed with all God has to give: she had a husband who had loved her with all the fierceness and possession of his being, she had a family of friends, each of whom had loved and cared for her. She had once had so much love, and an abundance of joy.

But he had killed that Jade so she could see. And so she did. She saw a room washed in blood everywhere she looked. . . .

Wolf Dog howled, low and long, confused by how close she stood to danger. He leaped back and barked, a fierce threatening bark.

She felt no shame now. Only the desperation of a trapped and helpless creature with no way out but this cliff. She closed her eyes, felt a gust of wind flap her skirt and slide tears from her eyes. Then, in an effort to find courage, she took a deep breath and visualized the room washed in blood.

* * *

Victor burst from the forest and stopped dead in his tracks. Jade at the edge of her death, a vision from a nightmare. He couldn't reach her in time. He couldn't voice the *"No!"* in his throat, certain that she would turn and look at him, leaving him haunted by that one last look for the rest of his life. With a previously unknown helplessness, he cautiously moved toward her, praying for something that wasn't to be given, forcing himself to watch a horror that couldn't be borne.

But Jade seemed unable to jump. Her courage inched its way into being and she leaned toward the thin line of balance separating her from death.

She crossed it. Her heart leaped in anticipation of flight. Her arms, futile wings, frantically circled to push her back. Victor shouted behind her even as Wolf Dog sprang in the air.

The dog's leap into the air looked like a devil's cruel push, but jaws clamped onto the bun of her hair, and with an unnatural twist of his lithe body, Wolf Dog fell back to a safer place, bringing Jade with him to the ground. The dog turned on her as if he knew her madness, and stood over her to keep her still for the mate.

Victor fell on top of her. He pinned her arms to the ground, his eyes looked wild and crazed and filled with fear. He stared down at her in shocked disbelief.

Jade, too, was shaken with fear; she was afraid of having come so close, of how mad she was, of how much it hurt. She was afraid of him and what he would do.

Victor filled with a rage the more violent than he had ever known before. The purpose had been to punish him! It was the ultimate revenge and it would have destroyed him as death never could.

"God damn your vengeful heart to hell! I prefer a bullet to my head, girl! We all would. Yes," he said to her confusion. "It wouldn't just be me who would have to live with the burden of that grief. It would be all of us who love you, Jade."

She closed her eyes and shook her head. "I am so scared that I won't get better. . . . It hurts so badly, this precious gift of sight. I hate it. . . . I hate seeing!" The green eyes shot up to him. "And I hate you for making me!"

Victor opened the door. She lay on the bed, her face buried, her long loosened hair spilling over the bedclothes like dark silk. Wolf Dog wagged his tail but, as if he too, felt her despondency, he didn't rise.

She looked up, and he saw her antipathy.

A heart that holds no hope finds no peace. The very first evening Jade had climbed down from the carriage, walked through the doors of her home that she could see for the first time and climbed up the stairs. She found her room. As everyone else crowded into the entrance hall they heard the door shut. Her despondency went deep.

Two weeks had passed—and little had changed.

Then word came that the Reverend Mother had died . . .

It had been the hardest thing he had ever done, bringing her the news. She had looked confusedly about the room, and—dear Lord—those eyes . . . She looked, as if she were being ravished from the inside out, until, finally, they lowered to where her hand held the small, cherished statuette. He had tried to comfort her, wanting to so badly, but she would not let him. "No please. I need to be alone. . . ."

"Jade, sweetheart," he beckoned, "I have a present for you downstairs."

She turned her head away. "I don't want it."

As gently as possible he said, "I insist. Come. Up with you, now. I want you to see it."

She rose wordlessly from the bed, stepping to the door and ignoring the hand reaching out to her. Wolf Dog barked, happily following his mistress down the stairs. She stood in the entrance hall waiting for directions.

"Outside." He pointed.

She stepped through the doors and stopped with a gasp.

Surrounded by Murray, Mercedes and Sebastian, and in the middle of the gravel-lined driveway, stood the most magnificent young mare she had ever seen. More beautiful than Marcella, the last mare she had seen win the parish races. Sixteen hands high, the roan-colored horse was tall and proud, made of smooth muscle and power. Made of magic and wonder. Jade felt an invisible line draw her steadily to the creature who had the awesome force to give wings to her dreams.

"Mine? Is she mine?"

He tried to hide his excitement, her response being so much more than he had hoped for. "Yes," he said.

Jade went to the mare's side. The audience fell quiet, but smiles betrayed their excitement as Jade's pale hands gently stroked the silky coat. The mare jerked the reins from Sebastian's hold as if to get a good look at her new mistress. Jade stroked the beautiful head, drew a deep breath and expelled it into the animal's nostrils, laughing as an excited shiver raced along the huge back. The mare nudged Jade approvingly.

The sound of her laughter made Mercedes squeeze Victor's arm affectionately. Victor bit his lip to stop a pleased smile, and instead said matter-of-factly: "Old Riredon bred her. He does the job without breaking the spirit. Still, she's pretty green, so you'll have go easy until she gets used to the saddle."

Jade ran a hand along the strong back. She'd never put a saddle on her. Never.

"She's a beaut," Murray offered, pleased.

"You can borrow my riding clothes," Mercedes offered.

"Riding clothes. Yes." She needed some riding clothes. Surely Chachie had something. "I'll be right back," she said as she spun around and rushed back into the house, leaving Victor and her friends to whisper excitedly about this first success in drawing her out.

Victor knelt down, and was inspecting the mare's shoes when Jade emerged from the house. He first heard

Sebastian's appreciative whistle and Mercedes's halted exclamation. He slowly stood up, staring. Staring because he had never seen a woman in trousers. He had never imagined such a thing. Jade wore a pair of old breeches, a belt and a shirt. She wore no shoes. Every dramatic curve was accented for his gaze.

Desire, hot and hard, hit him so forcefully it rocked him back. He started to shake his head. "Oh, no, Jade. You can believe I won't—"

"No one will see me. I'll ride through the back swamps and keep to the property line."

The coal-black brows and lashes accented the lovely eyes, the uncertainty there. He knew what she was asking him. For freedom. How badly he wanted to give her this and how easy it would be—if only he had her love again!

"Can't you see? She wasn't meant for a saddle. I won't do it."

The moment stretched as he stared at her. A breeze blew through the towering cypress and the old oaks, shifting the ivy hanging like drapes from the branches. Red-breasted sparrows flew to a nest hidden in the flowering bougainvillea on the first-story eves. The mare shifted her feet, crunching against the tiny pebbles of the gravel.

He nodded.

She bit her lip to contain her excitement. The smile that followed was a lure more powerful than a siren's song. If the way to her heart was through creatures, he'd start buying her every wild animal in the London Zoo, one by one. . . .

Surprising everyone, she agilely vaulted the mare's side as if she had rehearsed the move a thousand times. She leaned forward and took the reins, lifting them over the horse's head.

The horse danced prettily, excited by her mistress's small weight.

"Oh, Jade, your shoes?" Mercedes said, still aghast and only vaguely aware of the fear riding this swift change, a fear somehow focused on her bare feet. "It's dangerous not to wear proper boots—"

"Aye." Murray was still staring. "You could break your foot—"

Jade looked down at their worried faces, her eyes somehow mocking this concern. "It's not something I am inclined to concern myself with these days. With any luck I'll manage to keep my feet intact."

Mercedes felt suddenly desperate to keep her with them. As if they all saw too late what the horse meant. She asked anxiously, "Oh, but what shall you call her, Jade?"

"Ariel," she said as the animal turned in a pretty circle. "The wind spirit."

Then she leaned forward slightly, lightly touching her bare feet to Ariel's side and giving a click of her tongue. Horse and rider were off, looking like a mythological creature from the pages of a fairy tale. Looking like the physical manifestation of the single word *freedom*.

Wolf Dog raced after them, barking with excitement.

Victor stared after her rapidly disappearing figure, hoping the sudden freedom Ariel gave her would be a step back to him, rather than one more step away. Desire still coursed through him, swift and strong, utterly ignorant that it would be left unanswered yet again.

He closed his eyes, and against his will an image sprang to mind: Jade's eyes darkening with passion, the slender figure aligned in his arms, and a kiss that was a reconciliation and celebration both. . . .

Despair hit him like a blow to the head. It must have been obvious, for Mercedes's tender hand brushed his face. "She will come back," she said softly.

He gently kissed the tender hand. He tried to find some hope, but felt nothing beyond the despair born of unanswered desire, a thing his father always named as hell. "When, Mercedes? Can you tell me when?"

"When she realizes how desperately she loves you. . . ."

* * *

Tall black boots, sporting silver spurs, sat on the rose-wood desk top, a writing table sat on his lap. Black blots marked Victor's elegant scroll, the result of pressing too hard on the paper, as if the force of his penned words demanded exclamation points for emphasis otherwise unnecessary in conversation. The letter was to his father; it was a plea.

. . . She leaves at dawn's light, sporting nothing but a shirt and a pair of breeches, passed to her from Chachie's grandson of all people. She rides until afternoon, sometimes not returning until just before the supper bell. Mercedes reports to me each evening on her activities. Jade tells her that she rides through the marshy swamp at the far eastern section of our property, and then sometimes through the southern forest. Yesterday she went as far as the river. Mercedes tells me that she communes with nature, that she has found favorite spots where she dismounts and sits in prayer and meditation. She reports to Mercedes that as the days pass she has indeed begun to feel her wounds begin to heal and while her heart is still burdened by the weight of the tragedy, she reports finding a measure of solace on these long sojourns. I try to convince myself these long hours of freedom from her domestic demands, from me and our home, are a healing force. I try not to interrupt her precious freedom.

And yet this is difficult for me.

She returns in the afternoon and often swims in the pond. Sometimes I quit work to watch her: the pale skin glimmering beneath the sun, the long hair trailing behind her like a cape with each smooth strong stroke. I still love her so much, a love that does not diminish as the days gather into weeks and months of this long and hot summer.

There are many other signs of her recovering health. She has begun reading at night. At times it is difficult for her to hide the pleasure she gets from this newfound ability to read books. Perhaps most importantly, she has begun confiding in Mercedes and Tessie again; the three young ladies have begun their pondside picnics as they used to do in days past. The sound of her laughter has become a prize in our house.

Which is not to say she is completely recovered. Far from it. She still suffers vicious attacks, more vicious for the capriciousness of them; she never knows when they might happen. She has learned to talk herself through them, waiting the moments until they subside, relaxing bit by bit until they vanish and the world goes still again. The nightmares persist; I wonder now if they always will.

Nor has she asked the question. I don't know how she keeps from wondering who it was that murdered her parents and caused this pain and grief. I begin to wonder at the wisdom of your advice not to initiate the subject, to wait until she is ready. More and more I want to take her by the shoulders and look in those eyes and say simply, I did not do it, Jade. I did not do it. . . .

I am more aware than the others of how much she still struggles and the great effort she puts to hiding it. More than once I have discovered she had been crying secretly and silently, and nothing on earth or in hell could tear at my heart with greater viciousness. And still she does not speak to me. At times she is passing courteous, at other times barely civil. Still other times she maliciously goes out of her way to make me angry, occasionally with some success, despite my every effort to control it.

I don't know how much longer my patience can last—

Victor paused and sighed, his hand rubbing the bridge of his nose. How much longer *could* he last? The only time she allowed his comfort was after a nightmare, and had it not been for those nightmares, he would have long ago insisted she take another room. Sleeping with her had become his most excruciating torture. He took care to keep as much distance as possible between their two bodies, to retire after she had fallen asleep and to rise before she woke—and still, most nights he found himself pacing the floor like a caged and crazed animal, staring at her through the darkness of the room while she slept, wondering how much longer he could last, trying to maintain some semblance of control until she—blessed day it would be—came to him. . . .

Desire became a monster he fought. Now it was increasingly difficult to be in the same room with her. Inevitably his gaze wandered to her, memories surfaced, his imagination caressed that beautiful body of hers, and predictably he found himself releasing his breath in a groan, feeling his body stiffen maddeningly.

He had never been good with celibacy, nor had he ever endured it as long. He often half joked that forced celibacy had been the reason he gave up those long sea voyages in the first place. He felt like a starving man denied food; he found himself becoming more and more obsessed as each day of denial wore on, torn between battling with what he saw as his weakness and laughing at his misery. . . .

He returned pen to paper.

> *I hear your voice in my mind.* You shall last as long as it is demanded of you. *Very well. Then let me be blunt. I need you. I believe your company, as it often does, provides incalculable worth, especially to those, like Jade, who are so troubled. The ever increasing pace of the shipyard demands my presence more and more and yet, I am afraid to leave her alone here. For a hundred reasons I do not think it would be wise. Also, Sebastian has been asked to a series of demonstration at the fencing academy, and I know he would very much like to return to the city*

as well. And speaking of a country visit: when shall
you finally finish that book you've promised your su-
periors? A country stay would provide you with nu-
merous hours of uninterrupted peace as well—

A knock sounded at the door. Thinking it was Murray, Victor bid him inside. The door opened and he glanced up. The pen fell on the desk top; he stared.

The change was immediately apparent. Jade's hair had been neatly lifted and pinned, pretty green ribbons woven throughout the crown of her dark tresses. She wore a deep green merino dress that blended, it seemed, with the Dutch landscape painting she stood before. The low-cut neckline revealed the pale ivory lift of breast, the ample wealth there flowed seductively into the bodice. A small black velvet ribbon held a cameo at her throat, a birthday gift from Marie Saint. The black band dramatically accented the long lines of her thin neck.

His breath caught, he forced his heart still. It didn't mean anything, he told himself. A small step, 'twas all. Yet her eyes held every emotion of her heart: uncertainty and fear of the wisdom of being alone with him.

"Jade." His hands went behind his head, a casual and disarming gesture with his booted feet resting on the desk top. "A visit. I'm surprised."

She nodded, nervously glancing down at the tips of her matching slippers. "I was wondering if I might speak to you about something."

The quiet sang in the stilled afternoon air. Her eyes shimmered with emotion. He would be gentle, very gentle.

She felt her face grow hot beneath his scrutiny; it felt very nearly unbearable. And yet she had to say this, to make this truce, because no matter what, he didn't deserve her petulance or childish anger.

Yesterday she had decided to cut her hair. She had asked Tessie to fetch the shears. With horror, Tessie grasped her intentions and raced off to find him. Victor had taken the stairs two at a time, emerging through the door to find her in the dressing room, furiously going through the drawers. "Ah ha! Here they are," she had said, finding his shears at last.

"What do you think you're doing?"

"I'm going to cut my hair."

"Why?"

"Because you love it." She had glanced at him to assess his reaction. The tender amusement in his eyes startled her, and for a moment she struggled to understand. "Don't think you can stop me! Even if you stop me now, the minute your back is turned, I'll do it."

She had pointed with the shears as if threatening him. He closed his eyes, feeling the exasperation of a parent with a misbehaving five-year-old. "I don't suppose I could stop you from doing something like that."

His words surprised her.

"But before you take such a drastic measure, Jade, you should know that it won't work. I'd still want you with short hair. What's more, I'm liable to want to prove it to you."

"What . . . can you mean?"

"I believe the words were plain."

"You would r-r-rape—" The word had caught on her tongue, and she stammered. Color drained from her face, and she felt a curious numbness creeping into her limbs.

"Rape you?" He had shook his head. "Rape is when a man forces a woman against her will. I'd never do that." Her heart stopped as he stepped toward her, his gaze unwavering, penetrating. He calmly removed the shears from her hand and set them on the divan. "And that would be so much worse, wouldn't it?"

His punishment had come as he shut the door behind him and listened to the sound of unspeakable anguish . . .

"You have something you'd like to say?"

Jade tried to banish the unpleasant scene from her mind. She could not look at him. "Yes." The words struggled up from the depth of her despondency. "I've been . . . horrible. No one deserves it, and I'm . . . I'm sorry. In time perhaps I will come to accept all that's happen."

"Jade—"

"This does not mean anything has changed. Not really." A trembling hand went to her forehead. She wanted so badly to escape, escape from him and from the darkness of the passage she had been though. Just looking at him solicited emotions that set her trembling in their wake; it was a constant torment. "Victor, please"—she put her back to him—"I want very much to return to the convent."

Her head tilted to the ceiling as if to stop the tears, and he wondered a moment what power his love might have to heal her heart. What if she let him love her again?

He abruptly realized she was *asking* him for permission to leave.

"No."

The single word rang with a profane echo in the silence. She told herself she had known he would deny her this, that she wasn't surprised. She moved to the door and reached for the latch. "In time I hope you come to understand this would be best for everyone."

Victor found himself staring without seeing the landscape painting, his thoughts racing to the faraway future when he owned her love again. A future somehow farther away with each day that passed. . . .

"Never," he said to the empty room.

Victor was forced to leave for two days before his father arrived for a stay. A group of small farmers in the area had requested his help in destroying a pack of wild dogs that had been running over the land, killing livestock and posing a threat to human life as well, for it was believed the dogs were rabid. Since Victor was reputed to be one of the best shots in the parish, certainly good enough to pick off the dogs, the group of farmers had asked him first, and were grateful when he accepted.

For the two days of his absence Jade knew another, different kind, of release. His absence made her understand just how much energy—emotional currency, so to speak—was required to maintain her air of indifference to his presence.

She rubbed her eyes wearily as she lay down to sleep, not realizing how hard she did it, a part of her wanting to inflict pain at its source. She imagined escaping from him forever. She pictured herself and Wolf Dog running out of the house and to the stables. In this fantasy she leaped on Ariel's back and loosened the reins so the horse could fly her away. Then she'd never have to see those piercing blue eyes again and remember his betrayal. She would never have to remember the magic ball that lay shattered at her feet. . . .

It was becoming an agitation, a source of acute discomfort that she found most difficult to comprehend. She tried to talk to Mercedes and Tessie about it, but both friends turned a deaf ear to any expression of ill feeling toward Victor.

"Jade, how can you talk so?" Mercedes gently scolded her. "Victor is your husband and he loves you, and you would realize how much you love him, too, if you'd just come to forgive him. You will see, you will see! This is very childish, this running away idea. You belong to him and here and to us. Yes, us, Jade! We are your family. The workmen laid the fountation of our house yesterday. . . ."

The afternoon sun had just finished its grand descent from the sky to sink behind the western horizon when Jade returned from a long, vigorous ride on Ariel and wearily climbed the stairs to her bedroom. She smiled when she discovered a steamy hot bath already waiting for her, wondering how Tessie could always anticipate these things. Her dinner clothes had been laid out, too. She quickly lifted her hair, undressed and slipped into the soothing, sweet-scented hot water, determined not to think of anything.

She instantly lost herself to it, drowned out every last

unpleasant thought, and with her eyes closed, she soon rested on that pleasant border, neither sleep nor wakefulness. She never heard him step inside the room.

Victor just stood there, staring. The sheer seductive force of finding her like that rocked him back. Her hair lifted carelessly, strands swept recklessly around her lovely face. Her eyes closed, her wet lashes brushed against flushed cheeks. A thin line of moisture appeared above slightly parted red lips. The steamy water was but a transparent veil over her nakedness.

He wanted her more at that moment than he had ever wanted anything, more than he could have previously imagined wanting anything. Afraid to move in any direction, he was riveted to the spot. Not wishing to make his presence known, he longed for the strength to leave, for he had some small idea of how very vulnerable he was at that moment. Her reaction could send him plummeting to a new hell or lift him to a certain heaven. Yet there was no choice if there existed the slightest chance.

"Jade?"

She opened her eyes and took in the unexpected and unpleasant reality of his presence. He looked frightening, that tall muscled frame clad only in moccasin boots, tan breeches and a vest; a menacing dagger still hanging on his belt. His hair was loose like a savage's, too long to be proper, and two days' growth of beard shadowed the rugged, sharp features. Those fine dark eyes stared back, always bold and unashamed.

She gasped as her arms crossed above her bosom.

He stepped over to the tub, her apprehension increasing with each step. He knelt down and for a moment said nothing as his gaze traveled leisurely up and down her figure. She caught her breath and held it.

"Jade . . . love." His voice was whisper soft, like a caress, yet changed with his desire and his own uncertainty. "I never told you, but I have this dream. Over and over. In this dream I am offering you a present. It is the magic ball made of our love. I am holding it out to you to see; it's alive again and so beautiful. Jade, I am desperate for you to see this—"

She was shaking her head now, her eyes wild with bewilderment and panic. She could never love him again. Never.

The words were spoken by her silence, the shake of her head, the naked fear in her eyes. Victor felt something rip deep inside. She climbed out of the tub and backed away from him like a trapped animal. "No, please, I—"

He rose and turned so quickly she never finished. He didn't look back, but paused at the door long enough to say, "I want you to have your things moved from this room. I don't think I can stand it anymore." He shut the door and she did not see him again for over two weeks.

"I suppose what I did was a terrible sin?"

Jade and Father Nolte sat across the patio table from each other. The chess board lay between them. It was a perfect late summer day. The afternoon air was warm but not hot, and a pleasant breeze blew in from the Gulf, stirring the shade of the ancient cypress trees surrounding the patio.

Jade had just finished exercising her horse and swimming. Her long hair was still wet, combed to a neat rope down her back, and while her face held a pretty rosy hue from the exertion, her gaze held the troubled gravity of a child as she spoke. Her eyes seemed unwilling to settle on anything, darting anxiously to and fro, first from his face—he looked so much like Victor—to the rose garden behind him, then back to the chess board. Nervously, she fondled the carved ivory pieces, giving but token consideration to the game.

He had arrived for an extended visit during Victor's and Sebastian's absence. (The Church had given him leave for three months to complete his book.) Daily life at the country estate fell into a comfortable pattern. He rose before dawn and barricaded himself in a small room adjacent to the library where he worked until mid-afternoon. Murray, feeling more and more the weight of his years, had asked Jade to help him with the bookkeeping, and she had agreed, finding a great deal of comfort in the work. Now she and Murray worked in the study almost all afternoon. Mercedes played the mistress of the house, aiding Carl's supervision of household chores and affairs.

It was a quiet and reflective time for Jade, mainly owing to afternoons spent with Victor's father, who seemed to comprehend the turmoil of her heart, turmoil that oddly increased in Victor's absence, rather than diminished. Not that he was sympathetic to it all. Quite the contrary, he often shed a different perspective on her struggle, forcing her to see things differently.

Like now. "The sin of suicide is in its success," he replied finally. "I daresay, most of us have at one time or another contemplated that alternative. If you are not now among the majority, you certainly are in a large minority."

"Victor thought I wanted revenge. He called it the ultimate revenge, and I suppose there's some truth to that, too." She paused before leaning forward. "But that wasn't what I was thinking of then. I can't really say I was thinking at all, I was so distressed, but if I had to describe how I felt—what had motivated me—I would say it was hate."

"Indeed," he replied, taking a move he thought might finish the game.

Jade looked at the board, saw immediately his intentions and almost without any contemplation moved her queen and thereby placed both his bishop and a knight in jeopardy. Father Nolte smiled. The young lady was a far more menacing opponent now that she could see.

"Perhaps it sounds strange, but I feel as if I understand so much more about people now."

"Oh?"

"I've changed so much; I'm not the same person. I used to never have, well—for lack of a better word—'bad' thoughts about people or things. I'm sure that sounds presumptuous, though it's nonetheless true." Her voice changed. "Now, not only do I think unpleasant things, I feel them."

"Yet these feelings are centered on Victor?"

After a moment's hesitation, she nodded. Victor seemed so different from before. Now when she looked at him she saw his strength and aggression, the calculation he put to everything: the men he hired, the bills he paid, the ships he built, the things he bought, even his friendships seemed calculated programs that related to an ulterior purpose.

He was so different. . . .

Father Nolte's gaze focused intently on the young lady before him. Quietly, he asked, "What stops you from forgiving him, Jade?"

The question jerked her from her ruminations. "Forgive him?" Bewilderment appeared in her eyes. "You weren't there! He destroyed me! He destroyed the woman he loved and she is gone, alive no more—"

"No, she's not gone. She's just changed, different, in many ways better—"

"Better? Because I can see?"

"No. Because you are not blind."

The words were not without impact. For a long moment she stared at him, her eyes shimmering with heightened emotions. It was true, of course. She was not blind, and now she saw the world as it really was: the weathered chips of paint on the house, the broken shutter and the slipping tile, the muddy puddles in the lanes. She saw the dying blossoms in the rose garden, a spider's nest outside the window. There was no crystal-blue lake but rather a swampy green pond filled with snakes and mosquitoes and leeches. She saw the age lines on Murray's face, the thinning gray hair through which his scalp shone unpleasantly, the tired limp to his gait as he made his way from one room to the next. She saw Mercedes's crooked teeth every time she laughed. Everything and everyone she saw was changed, different, unsightly, where once it all was just . . . beautiful.

"Yes, I am no longer blind," she said very softly as she withdrew the small statuette from her skirt pocket, and she stared at the small worn crack. "You don't understand, though. No one does. Once I saw only a world made beautiful by my . . . heart. Skies filled with rainbows. And it was this heart of mine that won the treasure of his love. That's why his betrayal is all the more painful and . . . unforgivable.

"Now I am not blind, thanks to him, thanks to the sheer force of his will pressed upon mine. He opened my eyes and forced me to look upon the world as it really is. And now I see . . . I see a world where my mother was hung in a blood-washed room. . . .

"I never tell anyone but I often find myself thinking of my father lying dead nearby, shot by his own pistol. He loved me, you know. Very much." Her voice broke as the thought of her father's love brought emotion flooding into her consciousness.

Father Nolte tensed, leaping ahead to the place she led him.

"And yet, as much as he loved me, it was not enough to change what he had to do when he saw my mother like that." She looked up at him, her eyes livid with the accusation. "He did not save me, my father. He couldn't live with the sight of her a moment longer. Not even to save me from her. You say the sin of suicide is in its success, but I say that no merciful God would judge him harsh; because, you see, I saw it, too. And I know why he did it. I only wish to God Wolf Dog would have let me leap from that cliff—"

"Jade . . ."

She withdrew in a rush of skirts. For a long while he stared at the black-and-white squares of the chess board, feeling hopelessly inadequate as his mind ran over her words again and again.

Not even to save me from her . . .

What did that mean? The sight of her mother?

Confused by it, he shook his head. He didn't know anything. He certainly didn't know any words that might take back the long dark night or make rainbows arch over the sky again. . . .

Chapter 15

The beginning came in late August on a hot summer afternoon, the day after Tessie's fifteenth birthday, when Victor returned from the city. Samuel ran up to take Tarsman, his tall black horse, watching as Victor withdrew the large package peeking from his saddlebags. Agnes watched from the upstairs window and she called to Tessie, Mary and Carl. Mercedes and Murray rushed to the doors, and by the time Victor stepped into the entrance hall, the entire household had gathered to watch Tessie open her present.

Jade came down the stairs slowly. She had been going for a swim but she stopped to watch the fun, too, greeting Victor with a slight nod before her eyes looked quickly away.

He wondered when he would develop the necessary armor to protect himself from her. A year? Two? He didn't know.

Jade, how I miss you . . .

He turned to Tessie, hanging behind the others, already embarrassed and excited by the package he held out to her. It was wrapped in red paper, decorated with gold ribbons. Colorful penny candies were tied to the ends of the ribbons. Tessie just stared with her mouth wide open, a look of childlike wonder on her face.

They all gathered around with chuckles and exclamations, Mercedes voicing Tessie's hesitation: " 'Tis too pretty to unwrap! What could be finer than the box itself?"

"I'm as nervous as a goose at Christmas," Tessie said as she took it from him.

As if by accident, Jade's and Victor's eyes locked again.

343

Just for a moment, then he looked away, as if it hurt to look at her now. Jade's gaze lingered a moment longer, a questioning bewilderment there. His attention had returned to Tessie and her present. A mild shock went through Jade when she found herself thinking how handsome he looked: his impressive height, the dark skin, the rugged shadow on his unshaven face, the piercing intensity of his gaze. She noticed a cut on his muscled arm and wondered how it had happened—

She looked away, knowing she would never ask him— she avoided anything remotely personal or intimate—nor would he offer the information. The contrast stuck her where she stood. For there had been a time when they spoke of everything; their intimacy went deep. He had been her confidant, lover, mate, and she his; they had kept nothing, small or large, from each other, and every exchange seemed marked by laughter and love.

An unexpected sadness welled inside and she tried to ignore it as she, too, turned to Tessie and her gift. Victor had adopted the satisfied smile of a well-pleased man, a man who knew full well what his present would mean. Chuckling, he said, "Go on, Tessie."

Jade watched as Tessie's delicate brown hands gently tugged at the ribbons, then carefully unwrapped the paper to reveal a plain box. She cast her brown eyes at the excited party before lifting the lid.

A collective gasp sounded.

Tessie lifted up a porcelain doll that was beautiful, delicate and fine. She had large brown eyes made of glass and long curled hair, a Negro's doll with darker skin. She wore a beautiful gown made of layers and layers of pale green velvet and darker green ribbons over voluminous lace petticoats. Tiny green slippers covered her feet, and her hands clasped a matching parasol.

Jade spotted the note. She lifted it up and read out loud: "Here before you, Tessie mine, is your last doll to mark the setting sun of childhood . . . ."

The sentiment was sweet—oh, so very sweet.

Tessie stared at this, her last doll, and when Jade saw the tears filling Tessie's eyes, she glanced up at Victor. He was watching Tessie with unmasked tenderness. Jade's own emotions rose unbidden in response.

"Jade—" Mercedes blurted as Jade fled from the room.

Sometime later Victor opened the door to her room. She stood at the window with her back to him. She tensed as she heard him. Still she kept her back to him.

He knew better than to go to her. "Jade." He said her name. "Something happened . . . just now. The way you looked at me."

"No." She shook her head but it was a lie. "Yes . . . I don't know!"

She closed her eyes and told herself she didn't love him, she couldn't love him again. Never, and yet his tenderness, even now as he considered her in silence, reached across the space between them, beckoning, promising something she refused to believe.

"Please leave me. I . . . I don't know what happened. I don't want to think about it; I can't think about it."

She never saw the anguish in his eyes as the door shut quietly behind him as if it had never been opened.

That night she dreamt of that tenderness expressed in a kiss. She dreamt of his warm firm lips on her mouth, a kiss that was reconciliation and celebration both, and with it her heart took flight, freed to soar like a winged creature through a sky made of blue. . . .

The long stream of summer days continued, interrupted only by Victor's appearances and exits; his stays seemed to be ever brief, lasting no more than a handful of days before he left again. This was what she contemplated as she sat on the patio, peering up over the treetops to the sunset. The sky around the setting sun was painted in blood-red colors. Murray said 'twas a volcanic eruption somewhere in the world that made the sky turn red. She wondered if it could be true that a volcanic eruption halfway around the world had the awesome power to change the color of her sunset. It seemed so fantastic. . . .

Two noisy squirrels clamored up a nearby cypress tree. A lizard darted over the edge of the patio. She reached a hand to Wolf Dog at her side, stroking his head. Victor had promised that the visual world would stop hurting, and so it had. She had not told anyone of the other aspect of the change: seeing things, really seeing them and experiencing a pleasure so intense as to be almost painful. . . .

Despite every effort to stop them, memories of the days of their love pressed on her mind and played in her dreams. She had been surprised, even shocked, the first night she had awakened to erotic yearnings so powerful they seemed another kind of madness. She had thought she buried that with the shattered glass of her love, only to see she was wrong. Erotic memories of his love surfaced like the sleepy long arms of the sun stretching over the cold and dark place where her heart now lived.

They didn't mean anything, she told herself. They didn't matter. She did not love him and would never forgive him. Not as long as she remembered that day. . . .

Victor still did not think she was ready to receive society, which seemed fine with everyone. In truth, she did not feel ready to take that leap. Though goodness, there were dozens of invitations. It seemed the whole city was hosting balls and soirees in honor of Madame Lucretia's return. The thought of rejoining society made Jade panic. Everyone would want all the details of her miraculous recovery of sight, and she still could not talk about it with anyone but Mercedes, Tessie and Father Nolte.

Wolf Dog perked up, his ears upright. He jumped to his feet and raced into the darkening forest. She sighed as she watched him run off. More and more he was leaving her for the wilds, and for longer and longer amounts of time. Victor had always warned her it could happen.

Tonight, she decided, she would retire early. Darkness

fell quickly, and she had no desire to confront the well-meaning company of her friends.

She finally fell into an uneasy sleep. She tossed and turned as bizarre, sometimes unpleasant, visions played in her dreams until she finally found herself at the top of the steps and turning down the hall. Her hand went to the latch. She pressed down. She stood staring into the room washed in blood.

Jade woke with a long and loud scream.

She jumped from the bed and, choked with terror and tears, she parted the mosquito net and raced into his room. The curtains stirred eerily; the bed was empty and the bedclothes undisturbed.

The silence of the room seemed to resonate with her darkest fears. . . .

She knew he was to return that afternoon, for he had to go over the monthly accounts with her before the bank statement went off the following day.

She went about her normal routine and the morning passed slowly. She kept watching the clock, waiting, concerned more that her hair remain neat than that her monthly figures were accurate. She kept glancing at her dress, wondering if he would notice.

It was one of the first dresses he had bought for her, a white cotton-silk with tiny pastel flowers woven into the thin material. The dress seemed just a bit too tight. He had once said it was his favorite but that she wasn't to wear it unless she was asking for trouble.

Oh, why was she wearing it? She hadn't even thought of what he'd said until Tessie had finished the buttons and tied the sash. She should change, she knew, but—

Her head turned as the door opened.

Mercedes stepped inside with a sweep of her green cotton day dress. An amused sparkle lit her hazel eyes as she sat in the chair opposite Jade. "Jade, I just have to read you this letter from Sebastian's mother. Are you busy?"

"No. I have a few moments." She could use a distraction.

"I'll skip the parts about Sebastian's family, his brothers and sister and all his nieces and nephews, and then the pages and pages of Austrian and French politics, Napoleon's exile and the talk of his return and, oh, she goes on for pages! Suffice it to say, Sebastian's parents had just returned from their annual trip abroad"—this meant to Paris, the only city they felt worthy of their presence— "and she reports that she found upon her return that everyone is healthy and happy, except for his older brother, who broke his leg in a riding accident. Anyway, here it is." Mercedes read the letter in French as it was written:

" 'Imagine my delight and surprise to encounter a Madame de Boire at a gala given to celebrate Admiral Cambrie's triumphant return from his famous Italian campaign. There she stood splendidly outfitted in a ruby silk— worthy of the most fashionable Parisian artisan—and being introduced to her peers—' " Mercedes looked up. "She underlined the word. You'll see why." She continued: " 'As the wife of the mayor of New Orleans in America.

" 'Upon being introduced, naturally I refused to suffer the humiliation of announcing my youngest son resides in that part of the new country. How could one explain the phenomenon without it casting the said parents in a most disagreeable light?' "

Mercedes laughed gaily at this, and Jade smiled. Sebastian's mother would never accept the fact that Sebastian actually liked New Orleans, that one of her sons could possibly choose America over the Continent. She saw the entire country as barbaric, a strange unknown place of swamps and dark-skinned people, criminals and savages, utterly provincial and foreign, and definitely not part of the civilized world. . . .

Mercedes continued: " 'I watched the woman closely: surprised at her impeccable manners and dress, amazed by her charm and grace. She did not stumble once, though the discerning eye might notice the coarse rock beneath the polished veneer. You'll understand my amazement more thoroughly when I explain that my friend, Baroness D'Alba, happily swore she was the very same woman who appeared in Paris many years ago on the arms of some stalwart captain. This man—making his living off the despicable importation of human flesh to your hateful shores—was more generally known as a pirate, or politely, a profiteer. Apparently, his pockets were suffused with enough gold coin to buy this woman a place in a house where she would be instructed in the arts and manners of a lady, only to be introduced first in the minor Italian courts and later in Paris as Mademoiselle Lucretia Diale. Somewhere along this unsavory path, the woman got rid of her captain and married the man who is your mayor.' "

"Oh my!"

"Wait, it goes on. She says, 'This woman rests my case. If this is the type of society I could look forward to meeting in New Orleans, I will no longer humor any of your flowery invitations to visit you and my darling daughter-in-law, Mercedes, in that place. You shall henceforth refrain from issuing these overtures.' "

Mercedes looked up as Jade laughed, merriment sparkling in her eyes. "The rest of the letter is the predictable indictment of our modest society here. I shall spare you, Jade. But isn't that astonishing? I must confess, considering my own less than humble beginnings, I find some small measure of glee—terribly wicked of me, I know!—in knowing these sordid details of her true origins."

They talked for some time about the house construction: the new tile, the roof, the size of the stables, the best imported carpets, until finally Victor returned. Mercedes withdrew after a happy greeting. Victor had obviously ridden all the way from the shipyard, for he wore his work clothes: white sailor pants, a vest, and moccasin boots; and when Jade glanced up from her papers to confront him in the doorway, she could not escape a sudden stirring. The white against his bronze skin, the casual ease with which he carried his tall frame, his smile and those finely shaped, ever-so-intelligent eyes.

She felt strangely shy. He greeted her pleasantly but casually, and to her dismay he took no notice of her dress. His eyes but briefly fell on her before he went into another room to confer first with Murray.

Another hour passed before he returned.

"All right, sweetheart, let's get this over with before dinner." He sat down at his desk, swung his long legs on top and leaned back. "Go ahead, shoot. I'm all yours."

With her work in her hands, she rose nervously. "It's all finished, but before I go over it with you, I was . . . well, I was . . ."

"Yes?"

"You were gone all last night?"

"Uh huh." He smiled, but added sarcastically, "Don't tell me you missed me."

"I—" She stopped, the idea striking her as ridiculous. She was relieved when he was gone—except for when she suffered a nightmare, though she would not admit that.

This wasn't going well.

She closed her eyes to collect the tumble of her thoughts, and without warning the image of the transparent light that had once been her love rose with startling clarity in her mind. A warmth rushed through her, but then she shook her head as if to escape the vision.

When she opened her eyes again, it was only to see his distracted gaze. He was spinning the large world globe alongside his desk around and around.

"Well, I was . . . I was wondering where you went off to?"

Somehow his smile mocked her. "Suffice it to say out and I see you're interested Jade," he said. "As if you actually care. Why, I wonder, would you rather I sleep with you?"

A blunt question. It caught her off guard. Her thoughts tumbled in confusion as she tried to answer the question, having no idea the answer appeared in her eyes.

He wanted to show her. "Sweetheart," he began in a deceptively calm voice, "just so you understand completely, let me show you exactly why I flee this place."

Victor walked to her side and stood next to her. He said not a word. He didn't even reach a hand to her; he knew he didn't have to.

Jade tried—oh, how she tried—to control herself. But he stood so close! She focused hard on the tips of her pretty white slippers but she felt his huge body's warmth on her skin and she stiffened with alarm, her heart beginning to pound violently. She couldn't breathe. That sinking, trapped feeling swept over her, and she struggled so hard to fight the urge to step away that she began trembling.

Victor seized her, then—grabbing her arms, pulling her hard against him, stopping just short of shaking her senseless. "There you have it, Jade Terese. A plain demonstration of the sorry state of our marital affairs. I cannot stand next to you without your quaking with that fear. Jade, I want you, and sometimes so badly I'm driven nearly mad—" He stopped, staring down at the growing panic in the wide eyes, and he released her with an abrupt push. "Get the hell out of here."

A smooth canopy of gray clouds served to insulate and absorb the heat, but let none escape. It was hot and muggy, and by the afternoon, nearly unbearable. Jade was on a mission.

So many things lost ...

Wolf Dog sat on the edge of the water, watching the other swim away. Water was the only place he refused to follow her. He hated the water; hated the absence of smell, the painful tickles in his ears, the darkness below in which he could not defend an attack. He also hated waiting for the other, and he did so anxiously, always worried that she could be swallowed by the wet darkness.

Jade swam to the far end of the lake, estimated the spot where she had lost her earring, and began diving. She surfaced, took a breath of air and dove again, having just a few seconds to pat the silty bottom before returning for air. Ten dives later she surfaced and for several minutes rested by floating in the water.

After another round of dives, she was ready to give up her effort. How sad, she thought, feeling her right earlobe, where she touched the two holes. Victor had given her the earrings on the eve of the new year. She had been so excited that she had missed her piercing and made a new hole that hadn't been there before.

A vivid memory filled her mind. When she had showed Victor her mistake—the extra hole she had created—she was laughing at her silliness, but he had leaned over and kissed her ear. His lips had lingered there, his breath caressing her skin, causing those wild shivers and that warm flush. Desire born from his slightest touch . . .

Jade shivered suddenly, her reaction having nothing to do with the cool water. How he had loved her! They has been so happy then. She looked at the water, remembering the first time they made love in a lake, and she grew warm, every part of her body suddenly awakened, straining from the mere memory. . . . Tears filled her eyes.

Her tears went unnoticed, for quite suddenly the small pearl earring seemed more precious than anything else. . . .

Marie Saint woke from a sound sleep.

She sat up in bed, her lovely eyes wide, frightened as she searched the dark familiar room through the veil of the mosquito net. At first she didn't see her. Her eyes swept the divan and the armoire, the large gilt-framed looking glass above the hearth, then past the sitting table and chairs before doubling back. An outline made of light appeared in the looking glass; she heard the faintest sound of a woman crying amidst the steady fall of rain outside.

"Why have you come?"

Marie's whispered words failed to get a response at first. She listened to the soft sound of tears above the quiet tick of the mechanical clock and the patter of rain against the windows. Then she heard: "She is going to kill her. . . ."

"Who?"

"She is trying to reach me still. . . ."

"Who is doing this?"

"Juliet."

"Juliet is dead."

"She lives; she lives. She is claimed by darkness and hate. She lives only to punish me still. . . ."

"No, no!" Marie's long hair swirled about her shoulders as she shook her head. "Juliet has died, long ago she has died. . . ."

The light faded and disappeared.

A chill went up Marie's spine.

The sky was a gray bowl of smooth clouds. The sun was high behind Victor, and heat seemed to rise from the ground like steam, shimmering in a mirage of waves, while the sun occasionally broke through like a scorching burst of heat against his skin. How could she last long in this heat?

Yet somehow she did. She still rode out at dawn every day and returned in the afternoon. The oppressive heat that sent everyone in the house to bed in the afternoon, with the shades drawn and a fan in hand, never seemed to affect her. When he was home, less and less frequently now, he watched her swim in the afternoon. She stepped to the edge of the pond, disappearing behind a bush, and shrugged out of her clothes before stepping into the warm water. Gracefully, so gracefully, like a swan or a water nymph, she glided out, ducked under and then began swimming back and forth across the pond.

"Jade how I miss you. . . ."

He drew his horse up and stopped, wiping his brow before he listened for a sound of the danger. Only the cry and cackle of unseen birds, the scurry of a lizard across the mud-and-moss covered creekbed. This morning just after Jade rode out, the Meeks and the Galliers, along with a handful of slaves on foot, had appeared at Shady Manor. It was not a social visit; the men were upset and agitated. There was another pack of wild dogs. Last night the pack had killed two horses, one a prized mare, both horses corralled in a pasture.

The news had alarmed him. Wolf Dog alone could not protect Jade from a pack. He'd join the hunt just as soon as he found Jade and got her safely home.

He looked back to Ariel's tracks, left in the mossy banks of a moist creekbed. He was getting close now. He couldn't see Wolf Dog's tracks. He scanned the surrounding area but there was no sign of the dog.

He kicked with his soft-skinned boots and his mount continued on. The moss-draped cypress trees created a dense canopy overhead, and the grass-covered ground was still moist from last night's rain. A coral snake slithered over a rotting log and into the swampy marsh to his side. He suddenly wondered at the wisdom of letting Jade ride out alone—

A sound alerted him. He stopped his mount. In the far distance Jade called for Wolf Dog. He kicked his mount into a trot, ducking the overhanging branches as he moved quickly toward her voice. He stopped again and swung off his mount, gathering the reins over his horse's head to walk forward. Her voice called over and over for Wolf Dog.

Suddenly, she stopped.

He raced into the small clearing ahead. The muffled sound of tears came to him before he stepped past a tree and found her. She knelt on the ground, her face buried in her hands. She wore the maddening costume, the breeches and shirt, her hair braided down her back. Her abandoned sun hat laid on the ground nearby. Ariel stood to the side, the small intelligent gaze turning to him.

He dropped the reins and moved to her. "Jade, sweetheart . . ."

She looked up. "Oh, 'tis you . . ."

The pain and anguish in her tear-washed eyes startled

him. If he saw it a hundred times, it would still startle him. "Sweetheart ..." He knelt at her side, reaching a hand to her face. "What's happened?"

"Wolf Dog," she whispered, shaking her head. "He's gone...."

He searched her face. "When?"

"Sometime last night. I looked everywhere for him this morning; I went to all the places we go but he's gone. He's gone...."

And suddenly she fell into his arms. He tensed with the unexpectedness of it, and for a moment he felt fear. He was afraid of what it meant, of feeling hope. Yet the sensation of her small form leaning against him sent an avalanche of emotion coursing through him; his senses filled with the familiar feel of her. She felt so slim and warm, and the faintest trace of her familiar lavender scent excited every strained nerve in his body. He lifted her onto his bent knee only to get a better hold around her as he closed his eyes tightly and thought it was heaven.

Heaven. Jade, I love you....

"I need him.... I need him so badly...."

He could not give her false hope. The dog was no doubt drawn into the pack, and once there, he would be forever changed by the blood, tame no more. He let his hand lovingly comb her hair. "Jade, sweetheart, I am so sorry."

"I loved him.... I loved him...."

He was not at first thinking of the words they said. Love words mixed with a tone and caress, all to comfort and sooth her pain. It began to rain. Warm drops fell against his bare skin as she buried her face against his chest. "He loved you too, sweetheart. He worshiped you...."

"But how could he do this to me? How! To just ... hurt me like this ... when he knows, he knows how much I needed him, I loved him...."

He tensed ever so slightly, his mind understanding when she did not. And though he knew it wasn't true, he said, "He'll be back. He will come back to you."

She shook her head. "No, 'tis done. Somehow I know he is gone, mine no more."

"You don't know that—"

He felt her stiffen. She slowly looked up. Their gazes locked, his searchingly as he brushed a lone tear from her flushed cheek. He was shaking his head, but it was too late.

She stood up, backing away, frightened by the power of the emotions between them. "Why did you have to do this to me? Why couldn't you just leave me be? As once you loved me?"

"I still love you, Jade! With every breath I draw into my body, I love you—"

"No." She backed away more. " 'Tis over now. You might as well have killed me. And I hate you for it. I hate you!"

He acted in the instant as if she had violated a sacred text, and she had, she had. He had heard her say this once before but she had been mad then. He caught her in a stride. His strong hands seized her wrists, pulling them behind her back. She cried out as he pulled her up hard against his unyielding form. She struggled to free herself but he'd give her no measure now. "Look at me and say that!"

She tried to twist to the side but couldn't.

"Look at me."

The force he used brought fury, and, feeling her heart race, and her breath labor, she tilted her face up and boldly met his gaze.

Only to be brought up short by his emotions there. The next breath caught. She swallowed slowly, mesmerized and torn by the wealth of his love, his own worries and fears that shone like a light in the darkness of her turmoil. For a moment it frightened her. Her defenses tumbled in sudden confusion as she still stared, held by the love shining in his eyes.

The rain fell all around them now. An errant lock of hair

lay against his forehead. He was breathing hard; his eyes appeared questioning, uncertain. "I still want you."

She felt her face grow hot. She started to shake her head now. Her head spun as when his lips touched hers. It was as if she had forgotten how it felt to have his warm firm mouth on hers, the heady rush and drive of his tongue inside her, the sheer force and power of his desire sweeping into her limbs, making her blood run hot. . . .

Like a vicious monster the sweep of desire turned to fear. Images drawn from the nightmarish day rose forcefully in her mind: she remembered how he had trapped and held her down, forcing that pain into her weak and battered body over and over as she begged him not to do it. She had begged him. . . .

A silent scream rose in her throat. She tore her mouth from his with trembling violence. She backed away, shaking her head before spinning around and running for her horse. She leaped onto Ariel's back and took off all at once, leaning over to take the reins over the horse's head as the creature was already trotting away. And even as she held the reins tightly in her hand, she stayed forward, leaning against Ariel's strong neck, crying, a hundred too many tears, she cried.

When at last she looked up it was to see only darkness. Night had fallen. The clouds hid the moon and the stars. The forest was quiet, dark and deep.

Like a mirror held against her soul . . .

There was no light to guide her. The light of a full moon hid behind the clouds. No stars pointed the direction to home. The shadows of the towering trees were strangers. Even the sounds were strange to her—unseen night creatures scurrying away, the haunting caw of a hidden night bird, searching for prey. She was lost.

Ariel stopped as if awaiting directions. With a toss of her pretty head, she stomped her foot impatiently, hungry for her oats and hay, the warm dry comfort of her stall. Jade searched the surrounding darkness, looking for a clue as to the right direction, but there was nothing except darkness. She released her hold on the reins, having no choice but to yield to her creature's greater instincts. The slosh of Ariel's hooves as she picked her way through the soggy forest floor, the thickness of bush and trees suggesting the area around the lake . . .

Dear Lord, if that were true, 'twas a very long way from home. A very long way. "Wolf Dog! Wolf Dog," she cried out loud into the darkness.

If only he were still with her!

Her anxiety mounted as the minutes gathered into a hour. She felt hungry and cold and so tired, as if she had not felt the comfort of sleep for days. She closed her eyes and prayed for a sign, some small sign that would lead her home.

Victor's image rose in her mind's eye with such startling clarity and vividness that he might have been before her. He was standing on the lamplit porch, his handsome face torn with worry as he called her name over and over.

Her heart leapt. "I'm here! I'm here!"

The image disappeared with an angry thought and a forceful shake of her head. She did not need him. She did not want him or his love that cost so dearly!

She opened her eyes and gasped. A light shone in the distance through the trees. She stopped Ariel and stared. Voices rose, sounding far, far away. She kicked her bare feet to Ariel's sides. The mare trotted happily forward as if she, too, were relieved by the sign.

Torchlight illuminated a clearing, an opening of the forest floor, marked by three stumps of different heights. Jade drew back hard on the reins, slipping off Ariel's back as she crept through the trees and stared into the lighted space.

She stiffened as if struck by a bolt of lightning.

Dozens of scantily clad people, both colored and white, knelt in a huge semicircle in the middle of the clearing. A whispered chanting rose. A wide circle was drawn around them; tiny candles lit what appeared to be the dark rocks or coal that made up this circle. Three even tree stumps supported a black velvet cloth with a metal box on top of that. Various feathers and candles surrounded the box, too, and she realized as she studied this that it served as an altar. A naked man and woman attended this abomination, their perspiration glistening in the torchlight. Blue sashes were tied around their wrists and waists.

A voodoo ceremony. The vision was so bizarre as to lend it a queer nightmarish quality. As if it would all vanish if she only woke.

A chill raced up her spine. A warning sounded loud in her mind and yet she was held still, mesmerized by the fantastic sight of the sacrilegious, the celebration of darkness. The chanting grew louder and louder still. She felt her heart beat with the haunting rhythm of the rising chant. Brass goblets were passed from person to person, each person interrupting the chanting to partake of the stimulating bile.

Moans began interrupting the chanting.

The queen began writhing. Her long naked legs straddled the box like a lover. The hideous moans became louder. More and more people began writhing, the chants coming faster and faster as their upper bodies jerked with convulsions. A number of the people came to their feet and began dancing obscenely, their bodies gyrating and undulating with the increasingly loud and fast chant.

The queen spread her legs and arched over the box. Four men leaped up; each took an arm or leg, and they spread the queen's limbs wider as her naked body writhed. The king danced around her. A nervous tremor possessed the entire audience. And as if by magic the lid of the box opened and the head of a snake appeared between the queen's legs.

Jade caught the scream in her throat, staring with incredulity, awe and horror. The people went wild. Pandemonium ensued. The dancers spun around and around with incredible velocity, tearing their scant vestments. Bodies undulated wildly in the circle of light before they flung themselves to the ground, panting and gyrating.

Emerging from the darkness, she appeared. A white woman behind the queen. Jade stared at the thick ropes covering her naked body—

No, not ropes. Snakes, slithering and alive. Snakes circled her naked white skin. The blood left Jade's arms and legs in a rush. She didn't know she was instinctively backing up until she hit Ariel's strong flank, shaking her head even as she reached for the reins.

Screams began sounding from the mad audience as if they were surprised by the snake woman. The snake woman's knife caught and reflected the torchlight as she raised the knife and sent it into the queen's body—

Jade screamed a piercing long no.

The chanting stopped, dying like a whisper carried on a breeze as one by one gazes turned in her direction. The snake woman shouted at her. Two men started running to her. The snake woman pointed.

In a terrified panic, Jade leaped onto Ariel just as a hand grabbed her foot. She screamed again and again as strong hands pulled her off the horse. Ariel neighed angrily, turning to bite. One of the men held Jade hard against his body as the other man stuck a dagger in Ariel's side.

Ariel leaped into the air with a frightened neigh, her hooves crashing to the ground as she took off in a gallop. Jade never saw. The men carried her kicking and screaming over their heads into the circle of torchlight. They laid her flailing body over the altar. Four men held her down.

The chanting began whisper soft . . .

The snake woman leaned over her.

Jade froze with terror as she watched the slithering creatures move over the naked flesh. The woman's eyes caught and reflected the torchlight like a cat. Jade screamed again, frantically struggling to escape the hot sweaty hands holding her down.

"You!" the snake woman said. She threw back her head with a howl of laughter. "My power grows and grows, bringing you to my feet!" She stopped as she stared at her victim. "You see now!" She hissed as a snake came off her arm and circled Jade's chest. "You see now!" The woman's hands struck the air all around her. "Snake eyes, snake eyes!"

The chanting grew louder.

Jade could not stop screaming. The world became a blur of terrifying images: of snakes and knives and frenzied bodies. The loud chant turned into her loud continuous scream as the snake woman's face became the one she knew in her nightmares. The snake woman became the woman soaked in her mother's blood as she turned to see a young thirteen-year-old girl opening the door. . . .

"Run, little girl, run . . ."

Chapter 16

Dawn's light crept over a still-gray sky where Wolf
Dog ran, sniffed and ran some more. The rabbit
was close now. Very close. He ran to a tree.

He stopped. He sniffed. There the scent excited him.
The other. The horse.

He barked, his tail waving in the still morning air. He
raced around the trees, searching for the scent. He caught
it. The scent brought him into a clearing. His huge body
tensed.

Blood nearby. Humans.

He barked again, following the scent that grew stronger
and stronger. His eyes drew him to the fallen form. He
rushed over, barking excitedly. He barked and barked. She
did not stir. He whimpered. He stood over her. He licked
her face and barked some more. She still did not stir. He
laid back on his haunches to wait, his tail thumping with
excitement. He sprang up, whimpering, licking her face
again.

The noise of the birds sang loud. The air warmed by degrees. Wolf Dog fell asleep by her side.

A scent woke him. His ears pricked, his nostrils drew in
the scent. The pack. He stood up. Intelligent red eyes circled the surroundings as his hair lifted along his back. Lips
curled over strong white teeth. A low long howl sounded
as they appeared one by one through the trees and bush,
drawn by the scent of spilt blood. Hungry red eyes studied
the snarling wolf.

The leader snarled threateningly.

Wolf Dog leaned back. The other. She was his pack.
They could not have her. He would kill to protect her.

The leader stepped forward.

Wolf Dog leaped on him, his jaws sinking mercilessly into the neck. Four other dogs sprang on him. The death fight was on.

Victor's voice sounded hoarse from calling Jade's name throughout this long night and morning. A distant sound made him draw his mount to a stop. He listened, hearing the snarls and snaps of the wild dogs. His next shout reached through the forest for a mile or more in any direction even as he kicked spurs to his mount and his horse leaped forward with sudden vigor. The forest was thick here. A tree branch caught a tumble of his hair, another caught his shirt and yanked hard, but he hardly noticed as he leaned forward on his horse, attempting to simultaneously withdraw his pistols.

He came upon the terrifying scene in a rush. A half dozen or more dogs in the circle of a vicious fight. He reined his horse to a stop with a loud shout, leaping to the ground only to get a better shot. He fired once. A dog dropped. The smoke cleared. Two other dogs backed away in sudden alarm, turning to run. Three others still fought. He aimed carefully, following the wild jerks and vicious tears until he found a clean shot and fired again. The dog dropped with an anguished whimper. Mercifully Victor fired again.

Another dog ran off. Two dogs left still fighting.

Then he saw who it was covered in blood. "Wolf Dog!"

He shot at the other dog, missed, and then fired his last shot. The dog dropped. Wolf Dog still tore into the flesh, going for the kill with a vicious rip at the neck. Then it was quiet.

"Wolf Dog." Victor stared. Blood covered his muzzle. He stood on all fours, panting, as if uncertain it was over or that he was alive. His eyes lifted to Victor. He howled, then fixed his eyes at a point away.

Victor followed the gaze and saw her. "Jade!"

* * *

Victor quietly shut the door. He paused for a moment and closed his eyes with a heavy sigh. Now this. Now this delusional madness.

I am so scared . . .

Jade, let me help you. . . .

He descended the stairs and moved down the hall and the lower gallery, out to the patio, where Sebastian, his father and Murray waited for him, watching the sleeping dog who had saved her life. Again. A half-devoured cow thigh bone laid next to him—Sebastian's present. Murray had patched and stitched the dog's numerous wounds, and still it seemed a miracle the dog was alive.

Victor knelt by the dog's side, petting his head gently so as not to rouse him. "He saved her again," Victor said with deeply felt emotion. "Twice he has saved her life."

"How is she now?" Father Nolte asked.

Victor looked up, his eyes filled with worry, an emotion that defied his next words. "She seems fine now, trying to sleep."

"Tell him, Sebastian," Murray said.

Victor's gaze turned to Sebastian. He knew, of course.

"Luke, Robert and the others just returned. They searched on foot five square miles surrounding the place. Nothing. No tree stumps, no trampled grass, no blood beyond that of the dogs where we found her. No snakes. Nothing." In a whisper, he added, "She must have imagined it."

"I thought as much."

Murray knelt down to touch the dog. Not looking at Victor, he said, "The lass probably had a nightmare when she fell. Exhaustion, no doubt. Lord"—he sighed, wiping his brow—"she had been out goin' on twenty-four hours. . . ."

Imagined. Dreaming. Victor watched as his father nodded at Murray's conclusion, and yet he felt the probing scrutiny of his father's gaze, indeed all of their gazes, as they watched him, measuring his reaction to this setback.

They were being kind, he realized. Did they avoid the obvious conclusion for themselves, or to spare him?

He supposed it didn't matter.

"It seems fairly obvious," Victor said, "that Jade Terese is still not well."

"That poor lass. That poor, poor lass," Murray said with a shake of his graying head. "Snake women, voodoo ceremonies, naked people in the dark night, the stuff of madness and nightmares . . ."

Victor did not want to think of the rest of the conversation that night as he climbed the stairs. Swiss sanitariums and London doctors mentioned but briefly. Before he could even collect the words to level an adamant refusal, Sebastian did it for him. "Absolutely out of the question. Mercedes would never hear of it. I daresay I could not even mention it. None of us could. If Jade needs rest and care her entire life long, she will get it under this roof and get it with the wealth and blessing of our love."

He opened the door. The bright light of a full moon streamed in through the open balcony doors. A single lantern lit the space, bathing the room in a soothing gold color. He crossed to the table and chairs, where he began undressing, his thoughts troubled and his heart weary, heavy with this frightening turn of events.

He got up to pour himself a drink. . . .

With brandy snifter in hand he stepped to the balcony, staring off into the moonlit garden and the forest beyond. His gaze rested on this darkened space and it might have been his heart. He never heard her enter the room—Jade could move more quietly than a cat crossing a starlit field.

For a long time she stood nervously behind him. He wore only breeches, his tall form bathed in shadows and moonlight. Her eyes traveled up the tight narrowing of his lower back to the width of his shoulders, his long hair tied neatly behind him.

She closed her eyes a moment, feeling the heaviness of his heart. Because he loved her so dearly, she knew. Because he felt she had slipped ever so far from him. Because he felt the bright spring of their love—the days of laughter and joy and passion—would be only a memory. . . .

"Victor . . ."

His back stiffened, the huge muscles flexing as if with alarm. He turned to see her there. He drew a sharp breath. The moonlight caressed her lovely features, bathing her in a haunting light. She presented an illusory picture of angelic innocence dressed in the thin white gown. Her eyes were wide, misty, filled with emotion and uncertainty. Her long hair tumbled over bare shoulders down her back and hid the two thin strings that held her gown. Strings that would require but a slight tug to snap and break. He didn't wonder why she seemed more beautiful and desirable than ever before. The reason was obvious.

His heart and pulse quickened as he stood staring; he felt the rush of heat to his groin and he closed his eyes for but a moment, trying to gain some measure of control. His next breath brought to him the faintest trace of her lavender perfume. He opened his eyes. He tried to sound casual. "Jade. I thought you were sleeping."

The huskiness in his voice reached her. She drew a deep uneven breath, looking away. She knew what she would say. She had no idea how he would react or what he would reply. "I . . . I need something. . . ."

"Oh?" He put the drink on the wood railing, his gaze settling on her eyes, dark now in the moonlight and yet sparkling with an intensity of emotion he didn't understand. A breeze stirred the length of her nightdress, lifting it over her bare ankles. Somehow the brief glimpse of those thin delicate ankles made him aware of her fragility. Softly he asked, "What is it, sweetheart?"

"I need you to believe me. I need it very badly."

She waited for his response. She saw he was surprised, perhaps alarmed by this, for he didn't understand what it meant to her.

She turned away suddenly, stepping to the bedpost, which she clasped as if needing support for these next words. "You see, I didn't tell you everything that happened," she said softly. "Before I came across those people in the forest, I had closed my eyes and prayed for help. I was so scared and alone, hungry and—dear Lord—so very tired. So very tired," she repeated softly. "And you came to me. Like a vision, I saw you so clearly in my mind. You were torn with worry for me, calling for me over and over. I felt my heart lurch. All my buried emotions burst inside of me. I wanted you! I said your name. . . ."

On the heels of a pause, her tone changed, filling now with confusion and doubt. "Then I felt angry . . . at myself for it. I told myself I didn't need you, that I didn't want you. I could never forgive you. Again and again I say that to myself. And so I banished your image from my mind. . . . And when I opened my eyes, I saw their strange and awful light through the forest."

He had come into the room to stand near her as she told this tale. "Jade . . . what are you trying to say?"

She sent the long hair tumbling about her shoulders as she brought one hand to her forehead. "I don't know!"

That was a lie. She did know. "Those people, that snake woman, 'twas all so hideous and terrifying. 'Twas the opposite of all things good, 'twas the absence of joy and laughter, tenderness and love. Victor"—she swung around to face him—" 'twas evil I saw. I know you think I was dreaming or imagining it or mad. Maybe you're right. Maybe I am mad enough to imagine such a terror. But you see, it showed me something."

"Jade . . ."

"Your father once said the deepest truth lies in metaphors. This afternoon as he sat at my bedside and I asked him if he believed me, he asked whether it mattered whether it happened in my mind or in fact, for it happened. Because, you see, it was showing me a choice." She clasped the bedpost behind her, staring up at him. His hand reached out to brush back her hair. She closed her eyes to slow the wild gallop of her heart. She had to say the rest. She looked back to search his eyes, eyes that were intense and probing. "The choice, Victor, was life with the blessing of your love, or life without it."

His heart pounded hard and loud in his ears. A grown man in his thirty-second year, and he felt afraid. "Jade ..." His fingers lightly grazed her cheek and she closed her eyes and held his hand there. "Jade, don't do this to me. Don't lead me here if you can still turn away."

She shook her head, holding his large warm hand against her cheek as she studied the intensity of his gaze. His strength and warmth threatened to overwhelm her. If she but leaned forward she'd fall into his arms.

He released his breath with the sound of her name. "Jade," he whispered, afraid, so very afraid, of this, of coming so close again. "This fear of yours? When I draw close—"

"I used it; I used it badly. It was to stop myself from forgiving you. Because forgiving you meant accepting. Accepting the very painful idea that I had made myself blind, that I had caused myself so much pain because I wasn't strong enough to face the terrible reality."

"Jade—" He stopped as she shook her head again.

"You can neither save me nor spare me from the understanding. And you see, all of sudden, after this thing that happened, nothing seems more frightening to me than the idea of a life without your love.

"Victor," she said as tears filled her eyes, "just now I was wakened from a dream. In this dream you stood in a dark room. You took my hand to lead me to something. There was such joy on your face. Then I saw it. Shining like a beacon in the night. A large beautiful circle. A magical sphere made of transparent rainbow light ..."

She did not have to say the words out loud. Yet no words would ever be more important. "I love you. I need you to love me again."

"Jade ..." The name sounded like a prayer over and over as his arms went around her, and he closed his eyes, lifting her off her feet, letting the feel of her slender form molded against him resonate through his mind, body and soul.

"Jade, I love you. . . ." The words were simple and inadequate, and yet they had the magical power to transport him from a cold, dark and lonely place to stand beneath the warmth of a summer sun. "Jade, I love you. . . ."

He was holding her up, tightly, as if he might not ever let her go, and she might have fallen if he had not held her, because the shock of the embrace at last had obliterated her very will. Obliterated the pain and agony and madness. Obliterated the entire world outside the reach of his arms.

And then he was kissing her. There was no place for fear, not the way that first kiss, the touch of his body, brought desire sweeping into her limbs, consuming her to the depth of her being, causing her to swoon almost violently in his arms.

He could barley control what was overwhelming him, and he broke off the kiss with a shudder, though his lips never left the lavender sweetness of her skin. He felt her trembling and tasted the tears escaping from her closed eyes.

Pain, hurt, anguish were released in their passion. He was kissing her, dissolving her tears as he hungrily took her mouth, the unleashing of the emotional intensity in the joining of their lips, and he lowered her feet to the carpet only to get a better hold of her. A kiss without end.

The pleasure felt sharp. Love and desire, so long denied, flowed through her. She couldn't think to know that her feet had touched the floor, that her nightgown had fallen around her feet, or that her head was held back as his mouth dragged from her pliant lips to her neck, over the hollow of her throat and lower still, seeking and finding her breasts. She swooned beneath a pleasure too great to describe as his tongue flicked over and around the straining peaks.

The music of her heart sang against his whisper of her name. A tingling pleasure stole every last thought, and her arms circled his waist before climbing up the hard muscles of his back, desperately searching for a lifeline as her knees collapsed. Yet he was holding her up again as his mouth found hers, and he was kissing her with all the passion and tenderness of his being.

He broke the kiss and swept her up in his arms only to carry her the short distance to the bed. Moonlight bathed her nude beauty. Her dark hair, darker than the night, spilled over the pillows, and her arms beckoned impatiently, unnecessarily, for her eyes sparkled with the bounty of love and desire reborn.

Reborn. He had never wanted anything as much. It was like a dream. He shrugged out of his breeches and went to her opened arms, his hand brushing through the silky gloss of her hair. His lips gently kissed the spot on her neck where her pulse fluttered wildly. "Again, Jade Terese. I would hear it again."

She felt the rage of emotions adding to the tumult of desire coursing through her. "I love you." Tears blinded her. "Now and forever, I love you."

She could not think, not as he kissed her again, so tenderly at first. His hand played over her, drawing up her softness through his fingertips, brushing her skin with fire as the kiss became wild and hungry, the enormity of his desire flooding into her. He was devouring her; she was drowning, until she felt the shudder pass through his huge body and he broke the kiss. "Jade, Jade," he whispered huskily against her skin, "I want you so badly. I am afraid—"

He never finished. He didn't have to. His hands and mouth moved over her, causing and celebrating a crescendo of need. His tongue found her breasts again, and she tensed, feeling flushed, feverish, as he drew them softly, then urgently, into his mouth. The hot swirling patterns made her breathless, then dizzy, helplessly wanton with yearning, increasing as his hand stroked the dampness of her desire. Her creamy breasts swelled with passion. A sheen of moisture appeared on her silken skin as she arched against this pleasure with each ripple of ecstasy.

All she knew was the pleasure spilling into her body. Soft cries escaped her. Her hands grazed the muscles of his back and arms, a touch part clinging, part urging, before circling his dark curls, as softly, shakily, she was kissing him again.

He answered the sound of his name and moved over her. He cradled her head lovingly, staring down at her passion-flushed face, her closed eyes. He felt the impatient writhing of her small form beneath him. "Victor . . ."

He smiled as kissed her lips, a tenderly erotic kiss able to draw hot serums from her anxious body. He broke the kiss with the sound of her name. "Jade." He did not move. "Look at me, Jade. I want you to see me."

She opened her eyes, lovely eyes darkened with passion and filled with the intensity of yearning brought by her love. She locked her feverish gaze to his as he joined her to him. And the blessing of love manifest in a physical pleasure that was ecstasy and rainbows . . .

Dawn's light poured through the open balcony doors and drawn drapes when sleep at last claimed them. Wrapped in each other's arms, they drifted into the world of dreams. By mid-morning dark clouds covered the sky and threatened rain.

Worried about her friend, Mercedes first checked Jade's room only to discover she was not there. Peering quietly through the adjoining door she beheld her wrapped in the warmth of her husband. The sight riveted her to the spot; for a long moment she couldn't move. She felt as if life, so profoundly generous, had decided to grant her every wish. Sebastian's love, and now Jade and Victor's happiness at last. An overwhelming joy brought tears to her eyes; she almost fell to her knees with gratitude.

She turned with a tremulous smile and with a sweep of her skirts, she left the room, quietly shutting the door. She found Carl and asked him to give instructions to the other servants not to disturb Victor and Jade until they rang the bell.

By noon it was raining, and still they slept, deeply, blissfully. Drops fell into a brandy snifter left on the balcony ledge. A cool breath of wind blew through the open balcony doors and into the bed, lifting the heavy drapes. Jade snuggled closer to the warmth. The rain began pounding on the balcony and the windows, and in her mind's eye it became the familiar thump of her plaits as she raced up the carpeted stairs and turned down the hall.

Her hand touched the latch.

"Don't!"

She turned to see Victor standing behind her. "Don't go in there anymore, Jade."

"Oh, but I must! I must!"

She pressed down on the lever and opened the door. Terrified green eyes took in her mother, hanging upside down with her throat slit, her blood in a pool on the floor, covering the bedclothes, spread across the wall and on the rope that held her at her feet, up twenty feet to the wood beams of the ceiling.

Her father lay on the floor, shot in the head.

The snake woman knelt at his side, blood covering her hands. This time Jade saw the pistol in the woman's hands as the hideous creature turned to see her standing there. Her terrible eyes, like blue ice, showed no emotion. All emotion had emptied with her mother's still warm blood.

> *Run, little girl, run . . .*
> *Your mother is hanging*
> *Your father used a gun*

"No!" Jade screamed. "You shot him! You shot him!"

The snake woman whispered, "They think you're mad! I'll make you mad!"

> *Run, little girl, run.*

Victor bolted up with the sound of Jade's scream. Instantly he drew her tightly into his embrace, securing her in his warmth and his comfort. A loving hand soothed the tousled mass of dark hair. She drew deep gasping breaths as she listened to her heartbeat slowly ease from the terror of her nightmare into the security and warmth of his arms.

A sudden gust of cool wind blew through the open doors. He felt the shiver pass through her and, mistaking its source, he rose and shut the doors.

"Victor, the nightmare—I saw it so clearly. This time you were there, and you told me not to go in there anymore but I knew I had to, I had to see something in the room, and I did. This time when I saw her kneeling over my father, she was . . . oh, my God, she was holding the pistol."

He was having trouble concentrating on her words as his first waking thought had come with a rush of memory of the night, enhanced with the erotic scents clinging to their bed and skin. His effort was not helped at all by the sight of her. A thin sheet covered her nudity from the waist down, her hair fell in a tangled mess down her slim back, and his breath caught at the voluptuous sight of her rounded breasts. Dear Lord, he wanted her again! The idea that he could make love to her today, and tonight, and for the next hundred thousand days after, brought a profound lift of heart, a burst of joy—

He abruptly grasped the words. "What?"

"Don't you see? All this time I thought my father shot himself when he saw my mother like that. But he didn't. He didn't leave me like that. She shot him! And it was so strange this time." Her voice rose with urgency. "This time it was the snake woman and she shot my father!"

The blood left his head in a rush. He withdrew from the bed. He put on his breeches. She watched curiously as he went to the dressing water and splashed his face, twice, then again.

He would travel here slowly, very slowly.

"Oh, Victor." She gasped, the back of one hand to her

forehead. "They have the same awful eyes. These pale blue eyes—like ice, or the opposite, the hot blue part of a flame." She shuddered. "And now when I have the nightmare, I see the snake woman kneeling over my father, and I can see the pistol in her hand. She shot him. . . ."

He had two questions. He turned back around, surprised to find her standing behind him. She continued. "He didn't kill himself. All this time, I told myself that I forgave him, but only now do I see how much it hurt me, the idea that he shot himself and left me alone to walk into that room and see my mother. I thought he left me alone for her, but he didn't, he didn't. She killed him, too—"

"Wait. Jade. We need to talk, sweetheart. Here." He led her back to the bed. He retrieved a robe for her, his manner so serious suddenly it alarmed her, scared her more as he knelt in front of her, lifting her long hair from inside the robe.

"Jade, never once in this whole thing have you asked me, indeed, never once have you discussed, who it was who did this to your parents. Your parents' murderer. The slave woman Tara?"

"Tara?" She looked confused, but only for a moment. "You mean Jefferson's mother? What has she been saying? Dear Lord, did she lose her wits again?"

"She died, Jade."

"Oh, did she?" The reunion of love coupled with the idea that her father had not left her filled her with the most poignant sentiments, and she was having trouble concentrating on another person, but she saw that he awaited her reply. "Poor Jefferson. He loved her, you know. In the end when she wasn't drinking and all, she had become quite lucid. She was so kind then. She forgave Jefferson, my mother, everybody. My mother, you see," she thought to explain, "had separated her from Jefferson. I was only a baby then. My mother signed Jefferson's free papers and gave him to another family to raise. Tara had been hurting him, seeing and hearing these—" She waved her hand in dismissal. "These spirits. She was trying to beat the devil out of him, something dreadful like that. But when she became well, and seeing how Jefferson grew into such a fine young man, she realized it had all worked out for the best.

"You know, before we were married, before I even knew you, I used to sneak over to Congo Square on Sunday—Reverend Mother never approved!—and Tara would sit with me and describe the dancing. I loved the music, the laughter, the wild abandon, the pictures that the music put in my mind. Oh Lord, those pictures . . ."

Victor's hand spanned his forehead as if bracing for pain. He looked back into her eyes. Slowly, gently, he said, "Jade, Tara murdered your parents."

Her brows went cross with confusion. "What?"

He nodded. "As all this happened to us, to you—" He stopped, not knowing where to begin. "Jade, before I forced you to remember, when you were blind, before we were married, there was someone tormenting you—"

"Tormenting me?" The green eyes were intense, searching, confused.

"Aye. This person had you kidnapped and sent to that woman's house, and afterwards they . . . Jade, oh, sweetheart, I don't want to upset you but they hung your maid, Maydrian. Like your mother, Jade. It's how she died. You had a seizure as you came across her body. I could not tell you about it because . . . it would cause a seizure. Then someone snuck into the bedroom where you were sleeping. Mercedes opened the door as they were going to kill you, singing a sick rhyme about your parents' murder. There were numerous small incidents as well. That's when we moved to the country estate. To keep you safe."

Jade's thoughts spun over his tale, trying to make sense of it. "Maydrian died like my mother? But, my God . . . who would do such a thing? You never told me!"

"We couldn't tell you. Your seizures. Every time we tried to tell you, you suffered a seizure and lost the memory of it. It was how you protected yourself. Don't you understand—"

"I don't understand! All this time—" She stopped, trying to calm down. She bit her lower lip, anguish on her face. "This rhyme. 'Your mother is hanging'? That rhyme?"

He nodded, concern and worry in his eyes.

"I hear it in my nightmares!"

"Jade, of course, I found out who it was. I was mad with worry; we all were. Marie Saint said it was a dead woman and so, just in case, I had my agents search the recent parish deaths until we found Tara. All incidents stopped after her death. Tara, who hated your mother. Tara, who had been known to practice the slaves' religion. Tara, who was insane. She killed your parents, Jade. I wanted to tell you but you never asked—"

The hairs slowly lifted on the back of her neck. She was shaking her head slowly, then fast, as she said, "Tara did not kill my mother, Victor. I never asked you who murdered my parents because I know who did it. I saw her! I see her every time I have a nightmare. She is there every time I look into that room. She is kneeling over my father's dead body, her tears mixed with the blood covering her hands!"

His brows crossed, he jerked her up. "Who? Who do you see?"

"Juliet, my father's long-ago mistress."

"That can't be! She's dead! She died long ago."

"Yes," Jade said with feeling. "She is dead. . . ."

"Wolf Dog! Wolf Dog!"

Jade stood on the patio, calling her dog and staring off into the star-filled night. Tomorrow they were returning to the city. Everyone would be leaving but Rolez, the groundskeeper. He promised to set out food for Wolf Dog, to try to lure him inside should he come home. He promised to send word immediately when, if, he saw him. "Ain't much hope for that, though. Once the wild runs in the blood—" He had stopped, noticing the effect of his words by her expression. "You know I be trying every night . . ."

She knew Victor had postponed their leaving as long as he could. Since the day he had discovered that Tara was not her parents' murderer, he or Sebastian was with her at all times. At all times. He never let her leave the reach of his arms, which seemed to mean he rarely let her leave the bed. . . .

Even though there had not been an incident for nearly a year, he would take no chances. A dead woman had not hung Maydrian. A dead woman had not climbed over Jade's sleeping form with a raised knife. Whoever it was might well be dead now, but until they discovered who it was, he would take no chances.

They had to return to the city. Victor's three new steamboats were almost finished and he had to be there to oversee the final fitting of the new boilers. Governor Claighborne would be hosting a huge gala to celebrate the event.

"Wolf Dog! Wolf Dog!"

If only he would return!

She searched the arch of the star-filled sky. A thousand pinpoints of light shone in the black velvet above her. No breeze stirred the trees; the air was still and quiet. Crickets chirped in the darkness and the great house behind her was quiet with sleep. In the far distance she could see the shimmering starlight over the pond. . . .

She closed her eyes, trying to find comfort in the lingering warmth of his lovemaking. His sweet scent clung to her bare skin and she whispered the incantation of her heart: "Victor, I love you, I love you—"

A low howl drew her attention. . . .

Her heart pounded with sudden hope. She called out as she raced to the well-worn path. It was a narrow path through the trees leading to the pond. She could find her way along it blindfolded, of course; she knew it by heart. Her bare feet touched the cool moist dirt as she ran and the dog's name sang in the silence.

She came to the edge of the water. The starlight was so

bright, shimmering like party lights over the smooth unbroken surface. She called her dog again.

A movement caught her attention across the pond. "Wolf Dog! Wolf Dog!"

A dark shadow moved toward her from around the eastern edge of the pond. She watched, unalarmed at first. 'Twas too large for Wolf Dog. Upright like a person. "Who's there? Who is it?"

No answer came. Jade watched the ominous shadow move ever closer, her heart signaling the danger. She did not scream. She did not run. She stood at the edge of the pond as the dark shape disappeared like an apparition into the trees.

She head the hiss before she saw her.

She emerged through the trees less than twenty paces away. The snake woman. She wore tattered rags. Dirt and leaves were smeared on her skin as if she had emerged from the swampy side of the pond. A snake curled over one of her arms and another wrapped a leg. Her hair was twisted into long thin plaits, but for all of it, what Jade saw, what she stared at, were the woman's eyes.

She stopped, watching Jade's terror mount.

Too frightened to move, Jade just stared as her breaths came hard and fast.

"Who are you?" The small pained cry sounded as if from far away.

"You know me. . . . You alone know me now that she's dead." The woman's gaze narrowed, and then she laughed. "I am the shape of your madness. I am your mother's murderer."

Chills raced violently up Jade's spine as she took a step back. "You are dead?"

Viciously: "You killed me! As your father!"

"No!"

"I will torment you . . . like your mother!"

The snake woman moved toward her.

"No," Jade cried, covering her ears. "No!" She spun on her heels, running. The haunting sound of laughter chased her but she never heard the rest above the pounding roar of her blood in her ears.

"Run, little girl, run . . ."

"I am so scared. . . ."

Mercedes and Jade sat on the seat before the looking glass, and Mercedes stared at Jade's reflection as Tessie wound her long hair up. Mercedes stretched one hand out to cover Jade's hands, and squeezed them affectionately. "Everyone loves you. Just think of all the letters you have received. And I will be right at your side. Victor will be right at your side. I predict you'll have a wonderful time tonight."

Everyone was going. Governor Claighborne was hosting a huge gala to celebrate the first runs of Victor's new steamboats, the *Comet,* the *Vesuvius* and the *Enterprise*; Victor was more excited than a child on Christmas Eve. She would be seeing everyone she had never seen before but had counted as her friends and acquaintances for the first time.

She closed her eyes. The hideous image of the snake woman emerged in her mind, galvanizing her heart and pulse as she sat. Instantly she conjured the image of Victor: the thick hair that framed the fierce brows arching over the dark blue eyes, eyes filling with passion and love as he lowered his head to kiss her . . .

I love you, I love you. . . .

She had Victor's love again—the madness was a thing of the past. She would never see the snake woman again. She would be fine. . . .

"Everybody's goin' to make such a fuss over you," Tessie said. "It will be like a first reception."

Tessie's comment drew her back. "I never had a first reception," Jade said, straightening the black velvet ribbon and its precious cameo on her neck as Tessie began pinning her hair. Receptions were the parties given by parents and relatives when a girl came of age for courting. "I remember wanting one, but not wanting the Reverend

Mother to be bothered. Most all the Sisters assumed I would take the vows, anyway."

"I never had one either," Mercedes said. "Tonight will make up for it, will it not? I do hope we see some of the new waltzes!"

Jade smiled at Mercedes's reflection. A perpetual bloom rose in her cheeks, a beguiling sparkle in her soft hazel eyes. She looked lovely in the softest pale green China silk that hung off her shoulders and had a very long waist but was low in the back. Instead of flounces, it was trimmed with a matching green velvet and tinsel, which Tessie had also worked into the tight ringlets that framed her face.

Jade's dress was modest and delicate: a full skirt made of a soft, white, finished satin, covered by the palest lavender chiffon; its sleeves, waist and skirt trimmed with dark violet velvet. The sleeves hung off her bare shoulders, the dark violet contrasting sharply with her smooth white skin. She wore tiny pearl earrings. Tessie was weaving violet ribbons decorated with tiny pearls into a smooth crown.

Tessie finished her hair, smiling at a job well done.

"Tessie, you work magic." Jade smiled, feeling a flutter of excitement. She should wear the matching violet pelisse, 'twas so pretty with the dress. "Will you wear your pelisse?"

Mercedes shook her head. "Oh, no." She smiled also. "Our gowns are too pretty to hide. 'Tis still warm, too."

"I think I'll just carry mine."

She rose and stepped over to the armoire, opening the doors. She closed them and stepped to the next doors. "Oh, where did you put it, Tessie?" she said as her hand flipped quickly through the hanging dresses.

A soft hiss sounded. Jade's gaze dropped to the floor of the armoire. There it was, coiled neatly between her slippers. Her breath left her in a startled gasp. She shut the door with a start. She turned to face her friends.

She closed her eyes, catching her breath. It's just your

imagination! It's not really there! Like the snake woman at
the pond. It's all in your mind. . . .

"What's wrong, darling?" Mercedes asked.

"It is too warm for a pelisse." She forced a smile.
"We—we should be off. Victor and Sebastian will be
waiting—"

"Your slippers, Jade."

"My slippers?" She looked down at her stockinged feet.
Her slippers were in the armoire. She looked behind her at
the doors. She could not open them again if her life depended on it. "Tessie, where did you put my violet slippers?"

"They right there," Tessie said as she stepped to the
armoire and opened the door.

Jade watched with keen fascination as Tessie bent over
and, after a quick search, removed the slippers. "Here they
are."

The color drained from Jade's face. She slowly took the
slippers, then placed them on her feet. She gathered up her
ivory fan and a matching reticule, stuffing a handkerchief
and brush into it. Mercedes was already at the door, chatting merrily about how long it had been since she last
danced with Sebastian. . . .

Victor, help me now. . . .

"Jade, sweetheart," Victor whispered against her ear. "I
could not say which word describes you better: *beautiful*
or *pensive*. Sweetheart"—his hand lovingly cupped her
face—"what's wrong?"

The governor's mansion sat in the center of the American district, the Faubourg uptown, two short blocks from
their house, and yet they rode in the open-air carriage to
avoid soiling their gowns. The carriage turned down the
oak-lined lane, the two horses clipping quickly past the
massive Grecian mansions set back from the street behind
beautiful gardens.

Jade turned to meet his eyes. The love and concern

there melted the worst of her worries. "I suppose I'm a bit afraid. Seeing everyone for the first time . . ."

He smiled, and answered gently, "Have you ever noticed how little difference there is between fear and excitement?"

She glanced nervously away, thinking the difference was very acute when one saw the snake women at the pond in the middle of the night, or came across her evil pets in one's armoire. She smiled and reached a hand to his face, gently drawing him into a kiss. His lips touched hers, tenderly, chastely at first, but then as he felt the soft beckoning pliancy of her lips, the kiss deepened, changing the pace of her heart and breaths.

Victor felt the sudden stab of Sebastian's sheathed sword on his chest. "Victor. Please. Mind the lady's costume. 'Twould be an embarrassment if she arrived unclothed—"

Jade laughed as Victor leaned back with an angry grunt.

"Oh, look," Mercedes cried as the governor's mansion came into view.

Jade turned to see the colorful lanterns decorating the trees and lighting the courtyard. While she had dined at the famous mansion many times before, she had just recently viewed it, as Mercedes and she had taken a stroll to view the many sights she had missed all those years. A carefully kept lawn of ivy appeared as a black blanket in the night on either side of the tree-lined driveway, with a sprinkling here and there of white that indicated flower beds in bloom.

Victor squeezed her hand. "I'll be with you the whole time."

She nodded and smiled.

The ball was in full swing when their carriage stopped in front of the grand manor. Light poured from each window and lanterns surrounded the mansion, lighting the manor like a single star in the dark night. Music poured from the upstairs ballroom and people spilled onto the second-story balcony. Servants raced quickly to the carriage to provide assistance.

She drew a deep breath as her hand came over Victor's and she lifted her skirts as he guided her down the carriage steps. This was to be her first public appearance since she had regained her sight. Since word of the "miracle" had spread, she had spent at least four hours a week answering the numerous inquiries sent to her from friends and acquaintances, people who would all be here tonight.

The moment they stepped through the doors to the receiving line, the world became a blur of excited greetings and unfamiliar faces. She was clasping Madame Claighborne's hands, staring into the plump attractive face, taken aback by the sparkle and warmth in her kind, crinkled brown eyes. Jade had never seen her before, but she knew the woman well indeed: Victor was one of the governor's greatest supporters, and during the heady first year of their marriage, hardly a week passed when the two families weren't together socially. Madame Claighborne, Jade, and a number of colored women from prominent families had joined forces with the Reverend Mother before her death to start the Negro Women's Charity fund. Jade had always found Madame Claighborne's energies and enterprising efforts a welcome addition to the city, and she was known to chide the older Creole families for their uncharitable opinion of the good woman.

Jade felt the large flat of Victor's palm on the small of her back as he led Jade up the steps, following behind Mercedes and Sebastian. Lovely music floated down from the upper ballroom; people gathered everywhere. They had yet to even start through the receiving line. She marveled at the magnificent hand-carved doors they passed through, then the portrait gallery in the carpeted entrance hall. She knew the paintings must be of the presidents, but having never seen them, or seen pictures of them, she hardly knew which of the elderly statesmen was which. She turned to Victor, pointing her finger, when someone called out, "Jade Terese!"

Everyone looked up. Jade froze as first one, then three, and within minutes, no less than twenty unfamiliar people surrounded her exclaiming all at once.

Jade stared mutely. The voices were all familiar, but the faces might have belonged to strangers. Questions flew at her:

"Jade Terese, how did it happen?"

"What is it like to see after being blind for so long?"

"Cher, don't you know me?"

Victor held up his hand to slow the rush of sudden attention. Madame Borraem and Madame Claighborne came to Jade's rescue. "Oh, please, dear people," Helena Booraem said at Jade's side, "do give Jade some breathing room. We all mean well, but consider the strangeness of it! You know her, but goodness, she has never seen you before!"

Jade kept her eyes on her feet, trying to steady her gaze. For a moment the lovely maroon-and-blue swirls of the carpet threatened to spin out at her, but she took a deep breath and smiled shyly, wanting to be strong for him. "It is indeed strange. Why, I believe I need introductions again."

The crowd laughed, and an elderly, rather plump, gent stepped forward, his brown eyes danced merrily. "Guess who, Jade Therese!"

Jade looked at him curiously and suddenly laughed. "Monsieur Crane? Oh, my goodness!"

The crowd immediately saw the fun in this. The rules were established: as each person took a turn and stepped forward, he or she said nothing to give an identity away. Jade had to guess who each person was. Laughter erupted as she inevitably guessed wrong, and Mercedes and Helena offered her clever hints. People heard of the event upstairs. More and more people descended to watch this fun and wait their own turn with the famous lady.

Governor Claighborne and his wife beamed with pleasure as their receiving line fell apart and people rushed to greet the Noltes. The Noltes, after all, were one of the most popular couples in New Orleans. Who could remain unmoved by the romantic events and adventurous, exciting air that seemed always to surround them? Besides, everyone there knew and loved Jade; the colorful events of her recent history, events culminating in the miraculous restoration of her sight, had only increased the public's interest.

"It's going to work, Margaret," the governor whispered to his wife. She nodded, and squeezed her husband's hand affectionately. The gala had been given to celebrate the launching of the three new steamboats and what that would mean to the city's burgeoning trade, and yet the occasion would also mark one of the first times members of the Creole community would mix and mingle with their American counterparts. Over the last few years, more and more of the Creole families had started to accept the American presence. Still, it was rare for both communities to join hands for a celebration. Tonight was an exception, and due to Mayor and Madame de Bore's influence, and Jade Terese's popularity, many of the Creole families would join the Americans for music and dancing.

'Twas far too crowded for the entrance hall. Madame Claighborne clapped her hands, capturing the crowd's attention, and insisted the lively group move upstairs to the ballroom. Victor took Jade by the hand and led her up the stairs.

The ballroom was a splendid sight. Gilt-framed mirrors decorated the walls, creating an illusion that the spacious room was even larger. She was laughing and blushing at all the attention, more as the musicians set aside their instruments as the game continued. But all of Jade's laughter quieted as the next person stepped forward.

She knew who it was. She didn't know how she knew except that Mercedes had of course described Madame Pearl Williams to her numerous times, and as the plump matronly lady stood there, dressed in a lovely gown of teal silk, a small smile expectantly on her face as she waited for her recognition, Jade knew the sadness in her eyes. They had not been able to attend her son's funeral, the dear boy taken with the Reverend Mother and so many others in this year's outbreak of yellow fever, but she had sent her a letter and a book of prayers. . . .

"Madame Williams, is it you, my dear lady?"

Madame Williams nodded. The audience applauded appreciatively. Jade stepped down and clasped the woman's hands, kissing first one, then the other cheek. "How fare thee, my dear lady?"

Madame Williams felt Jade's warmth and it was so strange, she thought, as the room seemed to stop and everyone watched the tender scene, how there was a time when she would have hardly spoken to Mademoiselle Devon, upset as she was every time she spotted her sitting in the second tier, or soliciting donations for the Negro charity fund, or being kidnapped and thrown into a brothel, of all ungodly places. None of that seemed to matter now. Not when she placed it alongside the comfort she had found in the small book of prayers Jade had sent her after the funeral, or how she had cried a month later on her deceased son's birthday when Jade had remembered with a bouquet of tuberroses, the flowers of remembrance.

Jade turned to Monsieur Williams, who stood at his wife's side, and with a sparkle and a smile, she told him how all the men seemed taller and more handsome than she had imagined, and the women more beautiful. The room laughed with her and she turned around, spotting someone who could only be: "Monsieur Farragut!" Victor's banker, a shrewd, calculating man in his early fifties, a man whom Victor alternately cursed and praised, depending on the stage of their negotiations, but a man who always came through in a pinch. "Why, I believe I'd recognize that sly grin across a crowded room!"

The room laughed, more when Monsieur Farragut replied, "I believe you did just that, Madame." He bowed.

Victor and Sebastian stood alongside Governor Claighborne and two of his aides, watching Jade Terese entertain the room as she continued this game, everyone swept away by her charm. Mercedes and Helena stood alongside her, offering up clever hints with the others those few times when Jade was stumped.

"Look at her," Sebastian said in an awed whisper. "Look how beautiful she is! Here at last is the Jade Terese we know and love."

It was a special moment for Victor, watching her among their friends and acquaintances, seeing her so obviously well and happy again. His heart filled with the wealth of his gratitude and joy, and most of all, his love. They had traveled through such a long dark passage and now, finally, Jade Terese was his again, to love and cherish the long rest of their lives. . . .

Madame Claighborne finally spotted the mayor's carriage pulling up the courtyard drive. Oh dear, her husband was already upstairs. They would see it as a slight. She nervously smoothed her yellow taffeta skirts and forced a smile, mentally preparing to greet them.

Madame Claighborne was determined to demonstrate that the two communities could share in the fortune of their fine city; tonight would prove it if everything went smoothly and they could at least pretend to have a good time of it. She was well aware that behind her back Lucretia called her dowdy, plain and hopelessly provincial, dismissed her as altogether too American. She tried to forgive the mayor's wife the uncharity of her remarks, her vanity, her pretensions, all of it. She harbored no illusions about her beauty anyway, and as the eldest daughter of a Virginia reverend, she had been raised to the virtues of modesty, charity, and well, old-fashioned straightforward honesty. And while she counted as among her friends all the great men and their wives of the new republic, she would never—no never—develop the elaborate social pretensions of women like her.

Frankly, she had always been appalled at the way the mayor's wife always managed to have the rest of society jumping at her slightest whim: where to go, whom to be seen with, and even what to be seen in. It struck her as ridiculous! Practical to the end, if the truth were told, she did not care a whit what Lucretia thought of her, so long as they were able to join together for galas, fund-raisers and the community efforts that depended on them.

The good woman's smile vanished as she beheld Madame de Bore's gown, and with it went a good portion of her goodwill. It was indecent! The white silk dress's ruby—ruby, of all outrageous colors!—bodice pushed her voluptuous breasts up and out. A delicate hand went to her heart as she waited for the display Madame Lucretia's next breath would make. She would never get used to these Creole women! The way they flaunted their beauty like a virtue! Their indecent dress and shameless, flirtatious manners. Not a man here would be able to keep his eyes from the sight.

Monsieur de Bore all but vanished at his wife's side, smiling as if her immodesty was his personal creation. Madame Claighborne remembered her husband's unkind comment after a particularly frustrating incident when the mayor's wife seemed to actually prohibit her husband from joining in a state and city venture. "An idiot's grin! As if he hasn't a single thought between his ears . . ."

Lucretia's eyes filled with intense excitement. She had saved this gown for the occasion; it had been made by Paris's leading dressmaker, the man who had originally done most of the gowns for the French Napoleonic court. Besides the white silk skirt and ruby-red bodice, the flounces, the sleeves and the bodice were all trimmed in gold cord decorated with red stones. The ruby-colored silk provided the perfect contrast to her ivory skin, so that somehow the eyes were drawn to the voluptuous swell of her breasts pushing impudently through the fabric. The artful arrangement of her dark hair was lifted into a crown, wrapped many times by a long gold coil, its end sporting a snake's head with two rubies for eyes and a matching ruby necklace and earrings.

"I . . . I'm so glad you came." Madame Claighborne tried to recover as they stepped through the doors and into the nearly empty entrance hall.

Laughter from upstairs floated down as Lucretia offered a comment in French and her husband, Etienne, inquired as to the governor in French. Madame Claighborne forced a smile and begged their pardon, explaining: "I'm afraid my French is sorry indeed!" She refrained from adding the obvious: that Louisiana was now part of the United States and the proper language was English, that they had better get used to it. "Perhaps we might all converse in English?"

Lucretia only laughed at the outrageous suggestion, her hand reaching into a hidden pocket in the folds of the ruby silk overdress, and removed a beautiful fan, which she lifted to her face as she explained in French. "Madame Claighborne, I am sure your French will much improve with practice. Let me know when I might lend my assistance in your effort."

The mayor just rocked back on his heels, smiling.

Madame Claighborne was horrified at their rudeness. She began to look around for her husband, needing his consultation on just how far they should go to humor the Creole society. She forced a smile again, and pointed out that they were the last party to join the festivities. "Shall we go upstairs to the ballroom? Madame Nolte has arrived, and everyone is having fun as she tries to put names to faces. You have heard about her miraculous recovery?"

Lucretia's response was too quick for Madame Claighborne to catch, but the governor's wife understood that her guest was most eager to take a turn with Madame Nolte's game. Madame Claighborne followed behind as the mayor and his wife ascended the stairs.

Victor and Sebastian were across the room, Mercedes and Jade were clasping hands as they stepped down from the dais, surrounded by friends and well-wishers. All gazes turned to the burst of ruby and white silk into the ballroom. Whispers of excitement and awe raced through the crowd. Jade was relieved that the attention had been drawn away from her at last, and she turned to Victor. He was staring at Lucretia and her husband, Sebastian's ribald comment on the woman's dress making him chuckle.

Jade turned toward the sight. Dozens of people stood between her and the mayor's wife, and while she was tall for a woman, Jade could not see over all the men's heads. By some supernatural force an opening in the crowded room formed between the two women.

Jade beheld the sight.

Her reaction was intensely felt, and all of it physical. Her breath caught in a gasp. Color drained from her face. The hairs lifted on her neck and blood vacated her limbs, leaving her unsteady, numb, a sick rush of bile turning in her throat.

She was seeing a ghost. She was seeing the snake woman come to life again. She was seeing her mother's murderer.

She had no breath to give sound to a scream.

Lucretia moved toward her with her hands outstretched.

"Jade?" Mercedes said in a whisper, confused. " 'Tis Madame de Bore. Lucretia. Jade, darling, what—"

"Jade Terese!"

Lucretia reached out to embrace her. Jade's eyes widened more and she jerked away. "Don't touch me!"

The room fell silent. Victor was rushing through the crowd to get to her side, but it was too late. Jade was shaking her head, her eyes filled with feverish intensity, as the room started to spin. Jade's scream sounded as she stared at a blood-washed room where her mother hung upside down with her throat slit and Lucretia de Bore knelt over her dead father, blood dripping from her hands, her pale ice-blue eyes shining with an unnatural light. . . .

Chapter 17

The scandal rocked the city for days. "That poor, beautiful lady," people would begin at the market and at church, going on to lament the loss of Jade Terese, how tragic it was for her husband, a man whom everyone knew could not love his wife more. "She had seemed so gay and well just moments before!" those who were there would declare, confused by what they had witnessed. "And poor Madame de Bore. She was so startled. Imagine! She was so upset she cried as Jade Terese started screaming at her that she was a murderer, a beast woman—"

"A snake woman? Oh Lord, was that what she was calling her?" The ladies shuddered nervously, delicately, the conversation reduced to "That poor, poor young lady. Such a tragedy. I feel so for Monsieur Nolte. . . ."

His father sat silently across from Victor, offering no words because there were no words that could ease his pain. Distant clouds hung on the horizon over the river. A storm was moving in. A light wind blew the chilly autumn air, stirring the cypress leaves. Small swirls of dust and leaves rose and fell in the small garden of his father's cottage, and Victor stared without seeing.

Jade Terese, I love you. . . .

He felt so tired. So very tired. An aching numbness gripped his mind, body and soul, as if to prevent him from feeling the magnitude of his loss. To save him. As he watched the wind blow the leaves into a neat pile, he remembered his mother's funeral.

He remembered the profound finality of her death, felt

a piercing sting when the last shovel of dirt fell on the coffin. Grief had struck him so hard that he was barely aware of his father's arms coming around him, of the last tears he had ever cried falling with his father's.

He had not needed his father like that again. Until now. His gaze finally found his father's face, a mirror image of his own gravity. "She can't be left alone. Not for a minute. I don't know what I would do if it weren't for Mercedes, Sebastian and Murray. She is in such a state of distress . . ."

Her words, endlessly repeated, echoed through his mind. "You must believe me, I must make you believe me, don't you see this was her plan, to make it look like I am mad . . ."

"No reasoning or words of comfort touch the mad ideation that Madame de Bore is her parents' murderer."

Father Nolte nodded slowly. He had sat with his daughter-in-law for many hours this past week. When he wasn't at his son's house, he was fielding the endless inquiries about her. With mounting frustration, feeling inexplicably angered, he had issued a statement and left the entire matter in the hands of a subordinate. He could only thank God or nature for making his son one of the strongest men he knew. For the emotional trial of these last years would have broken many a lesser man.

"How I wish the Reverend Mother was still with us. . . ."

Victor sighed, nodding. "She could always ease the worst of Jade's—" He stopped on the word, feeling it catch in his throat with a surge of emotion.

Madness. He had lost her again. . . .

This time it looked like forever. He was finding it nearly impossible to accept. He wished his love alone had the awesome power to take back the day so long ago when a thirteen-year-old girl opened a door to behold her murdered parents. All his tenderness, gentle words and obsequiousness were no tonic for the dark shade that day drew over her precious life. The words spoken in his vision of

Elizabeth Devon came back to haunt him: "You will destroy her!"

Yes, he had destroyed her, the woman who meant more to him than life itself, the only woman he had ever loved, or would ever love. He had destroyed her.

He shook his head, scared by how desperately he wanted her still.

He said, "We will have to move."

Father Nolte nodded. Even though such a drastic thing would separate the family and nearly ruin his son's burgeoning shipbuilding enterprise, it was obviously not good for Jade to remain here, where her parents had died. Perhaps in a new location, she would gain some measure of peace.

The bell rang. Father Nolte motioned that it was time.

Victor nodded and stood up.

"I can come with you," his father said.

Their gazes locked, their mutual love and respect strong and powerfully felt. "I think I'd like that," Victor said.

The mayor and his wife had said they would receive him at three. He owed them an apology at least. He had already been received by Governor Claighborne and his wife, who gave all expressions of sympathy, compassion, and something strange and awful that he was quite unused to receiving, their pity. It was very nearly unbearable. Margaret was quite certain Jade Terese would soon recover and "be up and fine in no time!" He had barely managed to refrain from explaining that Jade did not suffer from a head cold, that one did not recover from madness very often, if ever, and that if she did ever recover, it was not likely to be for many, many years.

The mayor's house was on Bourbon Street, down four blocks past the opera house. The two men walked in silence at first through the chilly autumn air, their boots crushing the autumn leaves at their feet. They wordlessly passed a chain gang—all runaway Negroes brought from the jail, working to clean out the wood-lined gutters on both sides of the street. Neither Victor nor his father nodded acknowledgment to the white guard, his whip coiled and ready to use. The dark side of the wondrous city.

Victor was surprised to realize he was cold. The endless hot spring and summer days had obliterated the memory of winter and he wore only a shirt and vest, coatless, as if he could no longer be bothered with the details of living. Not when the foundation had been ripped from him. The bougainvillea and banana trees were scarred from a recent frost, and the normally lush landscape and fine houses looked gray and decrepit. He studied the dark clouds gathering on the horizon. Soon, by tomorrow or the next day, a storm would be upon them.

They were passing in front of the opera house and Victor caught a glimpse of the bench where a young lady dressed in white muslin once sat and had first captured his heart. Her laughter echoed through his heart, the vision of her smile, the light in her eyes, the tiny cross hanging from her neck rose in his mind. . . .

Jade, I love you. . . .

"Have you heard from Marie Saint?" his father asked suddenly.

"Yes," Victor said. "She sent a note when she heard what happened." He said nothing more and then wondered why. Perhaps it was just that the dear woman's fantastic beliefs and visions proved too much for him at this time; he could not bear even the slightest uncertainty, much less court Marie's elaborate flights of fancy.

Yet his father would not have this. "Victor . . ."

"Well"—he sighed—"the dear woman claims to be visited every night by Elizabeth Devon; she says she is visibly distressed and frightened by what has happened. Marie asked me to bring Jade to her, so she could try to determine what had happened and why."

"Oh, I see," his father said sadly.

"Obviously the last thing Jade needs is for someone to actually entertain her insane ideas and thoughts."

"I quite agree."

They rounded the corner and progressed down the

street, passing ragged children—slaves' children—playing in the street, a boy selling newspapers, an apple vendor, two statuesque Negroes on their way to the market.

The de Bore mansion came into view. It was an old-fashioned house, built at the turn of the century, and like all the finer houses in New Orleans, it was made of brick and covered in whitewashed stucco, its three stories topped by a tile roof. They turned into the garden courtyard; Victor stopped at the well. He leaned over and splashed icy cold water on his face, grimacing at the idea of seeing Lucretia again.

"I never did like the woman," he whispered to his father. His father was staring at something and hardly heard. The cistern was made of demonic gargoyles like those of the great European cathedrals. While he understood the historic symbolism of the beasts on church walls—they were believed to frighten away evil spirits—it made no sense for them to be in the mayor's courtyard.

He noticed still other oddities. The elaborate tiles of the walkway leading from the courtyard to the front steps curled in an ever tightening circle, ending in two small black tiles on an oblong shape. He tried to reason what form it took. He shifted suddenly and spotted a black drop beneath his boot. Bending over he touched it. Wax. He stood up and shook his head. "Come now. Let's be done with this."

"Aye," Victor said, and they proceeded up the stairs. They were admitted shortly by a tall Negro butler whom Victor remembered seeing on previous visits. They were told they were expected and were led into a lavish parlor. The butler withdrew.

Red velvet curtains hung over the tall windows opening out onto the courtyard. The curtains matched two sumptuously upholstered couches. A table sat between the two couches. A half dozen matching armchairs were arranged around the room to facilitate conversation. Neither man cared for the ostentatious room. It was meant to impress its visitors with its occupants' wealth, but Victor had seen it many times before and he was not thinking of it now. He was staring at the blood-red flowers that sat in a crystal vase. Abruptly he remembered the flower necklace draped over Jade's neck and decorated with tiny spiders.

In all the drama of what had happened he had forgotten that there was a very real threat to Jade, or at least there had been. His gaze lifted to the picture on the mantel. It was a landscape painting, poorly done. Dark colors drew the small clearing, lending it a hauntingly desecrated look like the very day outside. Odd subject matter, too, for a number of tree stumps had been included, and why would any landscape artist paint nature's ruin?

He turned away.

As Victor had been examining the painting, his father had been examining the intricate hand-carved legs of the armchair across from him. He rose and crossed the room for a closer look. Only to discover that the extremely clever floral arrangement carved into the legs held people in frantic orgy scenes up close. "Victor, look at this."

Victor examined this oddity and shrugged. "There is no accounting for taste in this house."

The faint scent of burning incense and the hint of voices floated down the hall. They were obviously not the only people being received today. Victor just hoped the mayor had the decency not to invite anyone else in for the meeting, and he was just about to comment this to his father when the doors opened and she was there.

She wore a starling blue gown of silk decorated with lace and ruffles, and his first unkind thought was that she wouldn't be able to pull it off much longer. She must be nearly forty-five. He had seen her dozens of times before, but he supposed he had never really looked, and as his gaze came to her face, he was struck speechless by the color of her eyes.

"Pale blue eyes, like ice, or the opposite, the hot blue part of a flame," Jade had said of her vision of the snake woman, and well before she ever saw Lucretia. A terrible coincidence, and probably the awful thing that had triggered this final episode.

The mayor; the new constable, a man named Jackson; and a Negro with a serving tray set with tea and brandy appeared as well, and all five people were exchanging how do you do's. The constable expressed surprise at Father Nolte's presence, then that he was not in robes.

The mayor was introducing him, and Jackson was extending his hand for Victor to shake. Victor never realized. He was staring at the ring on Lucretia's hand.

His heart started pounding. He still didn't notice the outstretched arm of the new constable, the man withdrawing it awkwardly, everyone staring at him, realizing something was wrong.

"Victor?" his father said.

Victor continued to stare in horror at the ring on Lucretia's finger. An aqua blue stone surrounded by tiny diamonds. Jade's mother's ring.

She wore Elizabeth Devon's ring.

"Monsieur Nolte, I understand you have come to offer an apology—"

Lucretia stopped, her eyes searching his. She had been prepared to go on, planning to assure him of how unnecessary it was, how very sorry she was, when the intensity of Victor's gaze stopped her short.

Details burst into his mind as he stood there staring at the strange awful eyes, the ring worn like a trophy: the Reverend Mother describing Juliet as blue-eyed and fair, able to pass for white, the death by an older woman's hands, her form dropped in the water, an undefinable body found downstream many days later. She could have lived! Sebastian's mother had described Lucretia's ignoble emergence into society many years later....

A hand went to Lucretia's cheek, and the mayor stepped forward with alarm. "Monsieur?"

Victor's eyes narrowed, his blood surged. "Quite the contrary," he answered the woman at last. "My purpose is altogether different. I arranged this visit to coincide with the constable's. You see, Jade is not mad, nor was she mistaken. You were once Juliet, in fact, the murderer of Elizabeth Devon. Your ring, Madame, it belongs to her, to Elizabeth Devon, and was in fact on her hand the day she was murdered."

Father Nolte gasped, his gaze darting from one face to the next, his intelligence as agile and quick as his son's. As soon as these damning words had fallen from his son's mouth, he instantly understood the urgency of this fact: a ring was not enough to force a confession.

Which was why he lied: "Two of my parishioners came forward this morning . . ."

Victor still slept in the bed. Jade rose and quietly slipped to the closet. She hurriedly pulled on her old breeches and shirt, then slipped on a pair of moccasin boots that Mercedes had given her. With an anxious glance at her husband, she fitted the plain long green cloak about her shoulders.

She slipped through the door and into the dark hall. No servant was up yet. The house was quiet. She raced down the stairs. A hand touched the latch of the front door.

"Where do you think you goin'?"

Jade swung around. Tessie stood in the parlor, the one leading to the kitchen. Curse her. Tessie was always the first person up. Tessie always woke at the slightest creak.

"You know where."

"Huh." She shook her head, her eyes serious and stern. "You know what he said. 'Twouldn't be decent for you to be seen there."

"I have to go Tessie. I have to."

She stated it as a fact, and it was. She had to go. Nothing on earth or in hell could stop her. Not even Victor's absolute prohibition.

Tessie hesitated. She knew she should go wake Victor and tell him, but the look in Jade's eyes stopped her. She knew that look; they all did.

The madness again. . . .

"Then I'm goin' with you."

She raced back and returned a moment later with her warm woolen cloak. Jade was already out the door and through the front garden. Tessie raced to catch up with her, struggling to get her hood up, shivering as her boots splashed in the flooded street. A light rain fell and it was cold. The barest glimmer of gray light cracked the far horizon over the rooftops in the direction of the river. The cold dark day did not deter anyone. A number of people, mostly all colored, but by no means all of them, emerged from nearby houses. Just across the street Monsieur and Madame Beauregard stepped out, lifting an umbrella in the sleek rain.

The rain wouldn't stop anyone.

Jade walked swiftly and with determined purpose. They reached the stables at the end of the street. They were deserted. Herman, the stable hand, had no doubt left minutes before. Jade expertly fitted her horse with a bit and reins. She leaped up.

Wordlessly, but thankful for Tessie's presence, Jade leaned over and helped Tessie up behind her. She touched Ariel's side and walked her out into the street. She turned her in the direction of Carondelet Street, picked because it opened into the square of the parish prison. She wanted to watch from behind.

"You scared?" Tessie asked.

After a moment's pause, Jade nodded. She closed her eyes briefly as Tessie's thin arms hugged her tightly. She felt terrified. Her heart pounded violently. She felt the combined effects of the sleepless night of waiting for this dawn: her limbs felt numb, her hands were clammy even as she held the reins and the small statuette. She felt as if she moved in a nightmare, a nightmare that had begun long ago and that would end at last today.

Lucretia's confession had come in bits and pieces after Father Nolte's saving lie implicating her as a voodoo practitioner. Throughout the confession, which took over three days, Lucretia never once showed any remorse. She often took pleasure in the most hideous details, pride in her clever plotting. The servants who had helped her in her evil doings had been apprehended as well. Most people felt sorry for them, as it was clear they had aided Lucretia from the unnatural fear she inspired as a voodoo queen. Still, they would be hung. . . .

The first news was that Lucretia still owned the house on Rampart that Jade's father had bought her so long ago. In blissful ignorance Jade and Maydrian must have walked by that house a hundred times. She had asked Victor to take her there, not knowing why she had to see, only that she did.

The constable's men still had been going through Lucretia's things there, and even though Victor was at her side, she felt a growing numbness as she viewed the various pieces of a nightmare created by this one woman's monstrous hatred. She saw the nun's clothing that had allowed Lucretia to slip unnoticed into her house and kill Maydrian, as well as the ruffian's clothes that made her appear to be a man when she was stalking Jade. She had found her father's small locket, stolen with the aquamarine ring when Lucretia had robbed their graves. Her mother had given her father the locket long ago and inside would be two miniatures: one of her mother and one of herself. It had taken several minutes before she found the courage necessary to open the locket. A dozen tiny pins were stuck in her mother's picture. Only two had been stuck in hers. Then Victor had opened a drawer to find the knife and an old yellow piece of paper—the banker's note . . .

She had not heard the confession herself, but Victor and Father Nolte had been there. Lucretia claimed she had never meant to kill Jade's father, but when he walked into the room and saw his wife dead, hanging, drenched in blood, he had lost his mind. Lucretia was screaming to try to make him understand that she had done it for him, that now that Elizabeth was dead he would grasp the spell Elizabeth had put him under, that Elizabeth's death was the only way to rid him of this spell. Jade's father had picked up the gun to kill Lucretia. She had lunged for him, and in the ensuing battle the gun had fired . . .

Then a thirteen-year-old girl had walked into the room.

Afterward Lucretia had set the house on fire. She had no idea how Jade managed to escape. Someone had carried her to safety. Perhaps it was a servant or a slave. Perhaps Jade had somehow managed to rise by herself. Jade did not wonder about this for long. For she knew better than most that while her life had met with this terrible tragedy, it had also created miracles and rainbows as well. . . .

Lucretia never understood the magnitude of what she had done until she met with the Reverend Mother on the levee that night. She claimed the Reverend Mother had been transformed into an avenging angel, given unnatural strength. As the older woman's hands choked the life from her lungs, she had feigned death. She said she might have even passed out then, for the next thing she knew she was in the water gasping for breath. She emerged miles downstream at that notorious smuggler's island where soon she was in the arms of a captain and aboard his ship headed for France. France, where over the years her new life took shape. . . .

It would be over soon. . . .

Hundreds of people packed the square already, more arriving every minute. Jade drew Ariel up when they were close enough to see. Her green eyes surveyed the solemn faces of the waiting people. The crowd was unnervingly quiet, though a number of people nearby began pointing her out, recognizing her despite the hood that shielded her face.

She never knew who started it. Perhaps it was Sandra, the de Galvezes' maid, or Dominic, the convent gardener, but someone stepped forward and pressed his cross into her hands. Then another and another, and suddenly lines formed. Dark hands, white hands, all hung their precious crosses over her hand, draping a small wooden statuette of Mary, gently squeezing it with warmth and sympathy. Her gaze blurred, as did Tessie's behind her, and still people stepped forward with this simple token of love and support. . . .

A wind rustled and swirled the leaves of the square into space and, gaining some supernatural force, the wind parted the clouds, revealing the glimmer of a gray dawn. Still it rained. Because their houses brought them above the crowd, Jade saw the raised scaffold, two stories high. The black-masked executioner stood by the rope. The smaller figure of a priest, Father Cobez, stood at the bottom of the steps with a Bible in hand, murmuring a prayer. The ex-mayor had left to return to Paris nearly a month ago.

The constable and his men were the only officials to witness it. No other officials would: they called it a spectacle for the lower masses. Necessary but archaic. Unchristian.

Jade didn't care. She only knew that she had to see it. With her own eyes.

Thunder rolled in the distance like a drum roll, a sound no louder than the murmured anger rising from the people as the woman was led from the small prison. The many months she had spent in jail had taken a devastating toll on her; rags covered her emaciated figure and she wore no shoes. She had aged and now looked fifty or older. Her hair clung in thick mats around her head. No expression sat on her face as a man stepped forward and swung the blindfold around her eyes. She stumbled, obviously drunk from her last night on earth.

The priest leaped forward, his voice reaching Jade and Tessie where they sat spellbound atop Ariel. Jade gasped as the woman swung her fist to knock the Bible from the poor man's hands.

"She is damned!"

"De devil be a-waitin'!"

So the shouts and epithets began. The violent swing of her fist to the Bible proved her damnation to the crowd.

She was led to the top of the scaffold.

Tessie forced herself to watch.

A murky dawn had lifted. The breeze rustled the tree-tops. The constable raised his hand and signaled the executioner. The rain suddenly pelted them as the noose was brought around her neck. For one brief moment Tessie closed her eyes, squeezing them shut against the sound of the executioner's ax against the rope which held up the trapdoor.

Thunder roared overhead.

Then she was hanging. Tears clouded Jade's vision, so she didn't see Sebastian and Victor racing up on either side of her horse, but she heard their exclamations and curses. She wiped her eyes. A collected scream sounded as sheet lightning cracked in the sky, searching for and finding the highest point to the ground, striking the body where it swung in the wind. . . .

Children screamed, women fainted, many more fell to their knees, clutching their rosary beads to their breasts. Jade herself brought the heavy handful of crosses and the small wooden Mary to her heart and closed her eyes to the sight. 'Twas over now. The nightmare had ended at last.

Samuel, the groom, was not waiting as Victor rode into the courtyard and dismounted, perspiration already pouring from his frame despite a swim minutes before. He was wet. The house seemed so quiet. All the shades were drawn against a hot noon sun burning through the clouds. The morning rain had offered only the most temporary respite from the heat. Moisture lifted from the ground in a hot mist. Clouds regrouped in the sky. With any luck, it would rain again.

Even the birds made no chatter, the oppressive weight of the heat sending them into a lethargic slumber. Lord, it was hot.

All the world had decided to nap through the worst of it. He closed the gate to let his horse wander the garden, too hot to walk him the short distance to the stables and certain he'd have to put him to a stall himself anyway. He made his way to the cistern in back, where he doused his face and neck in the tepid water.

The house was quiet. He climbed the stairs and slipped into his room. The curtains were drawn and it was dark, mercifully cooler because of it.

Jade slept on her side, a thin sheet covering her to the waist, her back to his gaze. Her dark hair was pulled back and woven into a tight braid that fell like a dark rope over the side of the bed. He had never found her sleeping in the middle of the day before, but the stifling heat combined with the last few days of celebrations: first of Tessie and Luke's marriage, and then a much longer and larger celebration of the success of his first riverboats, a celebration that over the months of planning had somehow turned into the largest social affair of the season.

The last guests had left just this morning.

A red rose lay on a small piece of paper on the nightstand. He recognized it immediately. The night before the celebration, Jade had finally managed to get to bed about midnight. He had arrived minutes afterward only to find her quite soundly asleep. He didn't have the heart to wake her, though he certainly had the desire.

He always had the desire. . . .

She had been gone when he woke up, and then people were arriving and she, Mercedes, Carl and Tessie were excited with a hundred details to attend to, all of it a whirl in his mind. Later, he was standing with a group of local bankers, discussing the season's cotton prices, and he had spotted her across the room.

How beautiful she was! Her long hair had been artfully arranged, accenting the delicate lines of her face and her thin brows lifted as she listened to her friends' chatter. His gaze lowered to her slender neck, the shoulders and curves revealed in the silk dress. Desire had struck him so hard, so forcefully, he suddenly could hardly understand the words swirling around him, and then she was there, lifting up on her tiptoes and whispering into his ear.

"What?"

"Yes," she swore passionately. "Anything . . ."

A plainly wicked grin lifted his face. He knew, of course, that every bedroom in the house would be full of women fussing over their hair, or sleeping children, and all those who had enjoyed one too many glasses of wine or champagne. "Anything, sweetheart?"

She nodded, her eyes misting with the force and passion of her love.

"Then meet me in the linen closet in five minutes."

Her eyes widened, and she looked confused. "The linen closet?"

Too late, he turned away, his attention snatched by Governor Claighborne. . . .

The linen closet . . .

Erotic images of the secret meeting wove into her dreams. . . .

Over a hundred people flowed through their doors.

The gala was a wild success. The morning rain had not put a damper on anything. But the garden was drenched and so most of the people, especially the ladies, gathered and collected inside.

The conversation had been interesting, what Jade could hear of it. Which was actually not much. Still, she nodded and laughed with the group of women who surrounded her. She was trying to remember which lady she was supposed to be friendly to—as the lady's husband was considering investing in one of Victor's new steamboats—and which was the woman Mercedes had told her was conducting an affair with Monsieur Floure, but it was nearly midnight now and after her third glass of champagne she felt a little tipsy. Really, she could hardly hear over the music and the laughter.

Distractedly, Jade searched for her husband and spotted him across the room. He looked so handsome in formal black attire! And serious as he stared back with a strange intensity, as if—

Agnes passed with a tray of battered-fried shrimp and little cheese balls, and stopped to whisper, "The bottom layer of the cake bust! Just bust like that! Chachie's in a tizzy. She says she told Mr. Sebastian ain't no one in town who can do a three-layer sugared sponge cake, but he won't listen to—"

"Tell Chachie the cake looks as if it's surrounded by a moat of cream." She returned her gaze across the room but he was gone.

"She told me that he said a man can't help but wander elsewhere to save his wife from doin' . . . well, the unpleasant things that no decent women would do—"

Jade's attention abruptly focused on this. "What unpleasant things?"

The comment elicited patient amused stares from the rest of the women. "You know . . ."

Jade had no idea. The conversation continued as she tried to imagine unpleasant things decent women didn't do that made their husbands wander. It fired up her imagination as erotic images danced dizzily through her mind, and yet none of these were things she would refuse to do.

There was nothing she wouldn't do for him! She would do anything! She would! She loved him so!

Her thoughts brought a blush to her cheeks. She looked around, as if someone might be eavesdropping, as if someone else could see the tightening in her chest and the rush of shivers up her spine.

She felt a lift of excitement. She pressed a kiss to Mercedes's cheek as she passed the artful array of half-eaten food on the table. She swiped a finger through the fallen layer cake. The finger went to her lips as she lifted the hem of her pretty rose silk gown over her slippers and practically raced up the stairs.

Bright lanterns lit the long empty hall. Voices rose from inside two of the bedrooms she passed, but no door opened. The hall remained deserted as her hand reached for the latch, pressed down and stepped into the dark room.

The delicious scent of fresh lemon and sachets filled the space. She shut the door. No light shone in this small room. She could barely make out the dark shape of his outline against the wall.

"Victor? 'Tis so dark. . . ."

He first made no reply, but she felt the probing scrutiny through the dark quiet. Then: "Madame, you of all women have experienced the curious effect darkness has on the other senses, have you not?"

Another shiver of excitement raced along her spine, and her breath caught as he took her hand and brought her to stand before him. He seemed so tall; she could hardly see his face, though she felt the heated desire of his gaze as his fingertips brushed her shoulders, reaching for and finding the back buttons of her gown. Her abdomen quickened with a spreading heat.

Her breath caught. "I compliment your resourcefulness."

His lips found her neck. "I demand more. A reward."

She whispered softly, "I am ever your servant!"

"For which, my love, I am eternally grateful."

His hands slid over her shoulders, drawing the silk straps off, sliding around to cup her breasts beneath her stays, pressing the uplifted swells even higher, so they spilled over the top in a lift of white softness. She gasped as her head fell back, offering her neck to his lips as his thumbs playfully teased the peaks to erect points. Warm firm lips kissed, and then bit, the curve of her neck, her shoulders, the lobe of her ear. Chills tingled in waves along her body.

"Kiss me. . . . Victor, please . . ."

With a husky groan he obliged, finding her pliant lips soft and parted to his demanding tongue, a welcome surrender to his plunder as he impatiently reached toward her knees, to explore beneath her gown. He expertly maneuvered through the flimsy undergarments. His caressing fingers moved between her legs, where he stroked, entered, and tested the secrets of her softer recesses, finding her shamefully open and welcoming.

She broke the kiss only to catch her breath and issue a

soft cry of pleasure. Somehow her own hands were pulling apart his shirt front, reveling in the feel of his cool skin as if it were the height of luxury and pleasure—and it was, it was. She reached to his pants, unfastening the catch even as his large hands fitted around her buttocks and he was lifting her off her feet until his lips reached the rosy tips of her bare breasts, which flushed with passion as his lips and tongue sucked them to swollen fullness.

The world became a swirling of searching lips and demanding caresses. She was lifted higher, then his hard shaft pressed against her own opening desire. Burning sensations licked through her abdomen as she wrapped her arms around his neck and pressed her hungry lips to his as she felt him slowly fill her. . . .

The sweetly erotic dream faded as she felt his lips land on the curve of her cheek and a very real voice call her up from the sweet depth of love. "Jade Terese . . ."

She opened her eyes to see the man who could land her on the very real shores of that erotic dream. Her already warm blood heated more and she slipped her arms around his neck to pull him to her. He leaned over and kissed her mouth. So tenderly, so sweetly did he kiss her, it caused a renewed spark to coil deep inside her.

He broke the kiss. "I've a present for you, sweetheart."

A smile curved her lips. She propped herself up on her elbows and glanced across the bedroom. "What is it?"

"You have to get up."

"Oh . . ." She fell back against the bed. She felt toasty warm and drugged with sleep. All she wanted was him, and nothing between them but a long lazy afternoon.

She seem to doze off again and he smiled. For a long moment he just stared. His desire rose as he watched the lush offering of her naked body. He wanted her badly, but first she had to see his present; he had worked harder to obtain this gift than he had for any other thing in his life.

His arms fit under her and he lifted her from the bed. She opened her eyes with a gasp, coming full awake. "What is it?"

"A gift. It's out on the balcony."

One of the doors was open a bit. He carefully carried her through it to the balcony overlooking the garden. "There," he said quietly, pointing as he set her to her feet. "For you, Jade Terese."

She beheld it with a gasp. Her eyes widened to encompass a magnificent spectrum of sunlit colors arching from the distant sky over the garden. A rainbow. A real rainbow, more glorious than anything she ever imagined, and she stared with awe and wonder until the rain started falling and the rainbow shimmered and faded, and yet would never disappear. Not really. For the moment would live in her heart forever.

She turned to him, her arms sliding up and around his neck as he stared down into the lovely green eyes he loved.

"I love you. . . ."

And the kiss that followed spoke sweetly and potently of this most precious gift. . . .

Avon Romantic Treasures

Unforgettable, enthralling love stories, sparkling with passion and adventure from Romance's bestselling authors

COMANCHE WIND *by Genell Dellin*
76717-1/$4.50 US/$5.50 Can

THEN CAME YOU *by Lisa Kleypas*
77013-X/$4.50 US/$5.50 Can

VIRGIN STAR *by Jennifer Horsman*
76702-3/$4.50 US/$5.50 Can

MASTER OF MOONSPELL *by Deborah Camp*
76736-8/$4.50 US/$5.50 Can

SHADOW DANCE *by Anne Stuart*
76741-4/$4.50 US/$5.50 Can

FORTUNE'S FLAME *by Judith E. French*
76865-8/$4.50 US/$5.50 Can

FASCINATION *by Stella Cameron*
77074-1/$4.50 US/$5.50 Can

ANGEL EYES *by Suzannah Davis*
76822-4/$4.50 US/$5.50 Can